HAVEN LOST

Book 5
The Guard Trilogy Extended Series
The Guards of Haven

N. L. Westaway

Original Cover Photo by Nicolas Ladino Silva
Cover designed by Beach House Press

This book is a work of fiction. Names, characters, places, and incidents either are products of the author's imagination or are used fictitiously. Any resemblance to actual persons, living or dead, events, or locales is entirely coincidental.

N. L. Westaway
Visit my website at www.NLWestaway.com
ISBN: 979-8-9850495-2-7
Printed in the United States of America

First Publication: May 2023 Beach House Press

Haven Lost

To the reader,

This novel, like the other books in succession, is not a standalone story. Book 5, *Haven Lost,* is the next in series following The Haven (Book 4), which carried readers from the original story in The Guard Trilogy, into The Guard Trilogy Extended Series, *The Guards of Haven.*
There are several more books in the series currently under development, with the expectation of at least 7 books in total for the extended series, although there is potential for more.

The Guard Trilogy
The Guard – Book 1
The Unseen – Book 2
The Believer – Book 3

The Guard Trilogy Extended Series/The Guards of Haven
The Haven – Book 4
Haven Lost — Book 5
TBD — Book 6
More to come...

This book is dedicated to my big brother Jim.

"It's the action, not the fruit of the action, that's important. You have to do the right thing. It may not be in your power, may not be in your time, that there'll be any fruit. But that doesn't mean you stop doing the right thing. You may never know what results come from your action. But if you do nothing, there will be no result.
~ Mahatma Gandhi

"In this world, it is too common for people to search for someone to lose themselves in. But I am already lost. I will look for someone to find myself in."
~ C. Joy Bell C.

Not till we are lost ... do we begin to find ourselves.
~ Henry David Thoreau

Acknowledgements

Thank you, to all who kept me grounded and my spirits up during this difficult year, and to all the readers who waited patiently for this book to be completed.

Prolog

SNOW Restaurant, December 2021, New York City, USA

During the month of December, only the front half of the restaurant was open to the public during the day, but you were still required to book a reservation months in advance for the exclusive lunch they offered. The evenings during this month, or any month for that matter, were always booked up way in advance. Depending on the size of your party, you'd need to get your reservation for the holiday season in as early as the January prior. Bookings for next December would start coming in right after the first of the year. It was also the earliest you could book for the popular season. Patrons often tried to book for next year's season during the current holiday timeframe, but Kris didn't allow it, mainly because he loved the frenzy of requests it created for the coveted festive season.

"Look, Francesca, I'll be back from First Haven before you know it—I think you can handle a few days without me," Kris said, adding another shooter glass to the display. "First stop, though, is Norway."

"Oh, I know I can—and don't call me that. You know I hate it," Frank said. He only used her formal name when he wanted to remind her he was the boss and she worked for him. She was more than capable of running this place and then some. And she didn't just work for him, she was 2nd in command, his right hand, and the one who kept things going when he was off on one of his buying sprees for the restaurant. She often knew more about what was going on at the restaurant than he did. The staff may have been enamored by his good looks and charm, but also detested working with him and were happier when he was off anywhere but here. Little attention was paid to the staff unless he was yelling at them. He paid almost as little interest to the patrons, unless he was looking for a business connection, an influential restaurant review, or he was looking to bed one of them. He never dated, and as for any friends, she was it.

The only reason she'd put up with his condescending behavior now was because she knew he hadn't always been an asshole. And well, she enjoyed working here, enjoyed the clientele, and she liked the humans she worked with. She also knew that if she didn't stick around, more than half of the staff would have bolted already.

"Go see Zach while you're there. He's still there, monitoring the Sterope location, right? Maybe the two of you could travel north together," she suggested. She hadn't fully understood why he hadn't relocated his home base to Ottawa like the others. He'd visited the city a year after they had found Thaddeus, but when asked if he would move, he'd told them he had no intentions of living in a dorm style residence with the rest of them. "You could find out the latest on you-know-who."

"Honestly, I can't blame Thaddeus for wanting to create a better race—we are superior," Kris said, examining the remaining open spots before locking the display. There were several rows with spaces for more.

"You know his cruelty…," she started to say.

"Yes—I know what he's been doing—I don't condone it." He inclined his head.

Frank glared at him.

"What—don't look at me like that." He ran a hand through his thick, dark, stylish hair. "But I, too, appreciate the finer things in life." He arrogantly ran his hand through his hair again.

"Conceit—not a good look for you," she said, smacking his elbow such that the action messed up his hair. The only thing she hated more than Kris's pompous attitude and disregard for the welfare of the humans who occupied this planet with them, was how people often misread *her* appearance.

Too often she was mistaken for a bouncer, security for the restaurant, when in fact, she was the General Manager of this luxurious three-star Michelin fine dining establishment. She knew the reason for the misguided assumptions were because of her stature and overly muscular physique as one of the Earthbound. She was tough, no doubt about it, and she wore her black hair short in a spikey pixie cut, but she was no pixie. Even though her wardrobe was high-end couture, she wore only black clothing, but never dresses or skirts. She applied dark eye makeup that showed off her amazing grey and silver flecked eyes.

Not all female Seraphim are built like her. Inanna, the Seraph she had been paired with long before Thaddeus had cast them down, was quite svelte and ethereal, fitting the stereotypical depiction humans often used to describe Angels. The two had been paired to help keep Earth's above ground temperatures balanced. Ina's area of expertise was geothermal Earth balance, and Frank's was that of physical volcanology. The respect and appreciation they felt for each other while on Pleiades had eventually turned to that of adoration, attraction, and then to love during their time on Earth. They had been together almost as long as Anael and Thanael.

"I don't understand why you need to make these trips," she said, giving the thick black leather cuff of her watch a spin. "Can't you just have them ship you what you need?" She spun the cuff a second time.

"I'll be shipping it back, but I like to see the items firsthand. My reputation and the reputation of the restaurant are my priorities. Humans are easily pleased, but you know I need to have the best—not for them, really, but for me. Plus, I need to see the salmon that I'm ordering for New Year's Eve, and you know I need to sample the juleøl."

She knew the beverage all too well. She'd indulged in Norway's Christmas beer many times over the years. Virtually every Norwegian brewery brewed the dark, rich, strong ale, from the largest mainstream breweries to the smallest microbreweries in preparation for the festive season. The kind you could get in supermarkets maxed at 4.7% alcohol, but the stronger, more authentic juleøl, you needed to go to a Vinmonopolet, *polet*, as the locals called it, meaning any place licensed to sell alcoholic beverages. It's in the bars that you are more likely to find one-off batches from local microbreweries, too.

She blew out an exasperated breath, watching Kris fix his messed hair in the reflection of the glass wall. "Okay, Kristopher," she said, using his formal name to push his buttons. "Of course. I know you need to have the best." She also knew that comparing beer in Norway was a perilous game to play, because far more important than the quality or even your own personal taste preference was the local pride. "How do you pick from the 300 Christmas beers available throughout Norway?"

Kris turned to her, taking his typical condescending posture. "I'll stick with the 190 that are Norwegian produced. Evaluate them by colour, scent, taste, and *aftertaste*. Though I'm pretty confident about what I will get—based on rankings. *Ringnes' Julebokk*—dark lager, *Færder's Færder Røkelse*—stout, and *Haandbryggeri's Fatlagret Bestefar*—traditional beer." He grinned a devilish grin. "But I still need to go taste them. Besides, I have a private tour and tasting of the Slogen beer set up at the Trollbryggeriest brewery in the beautiful and wild Norwegian Fjords," he added with more than a hint of mockery.

Frank turned away from her patronizing boss to see a well-dressed man standing just inside the main doors to the restaurant. He carried with him an ornate box, and from the way he was holding it, his glancing around and back over his shoulder, she could tell it must be of some importance. When Frank called to the hostess to attend to him, the man glanced over to where she was.

When the hostess approached him, he patted the top of the box as if indicating it was his reason for his being here and not for the well sought-after lunch menu. He shook his head sternly and wagged a finger like a schoolmaster at the hostess when she reached for the box. Then he pointed a stern finger first at himself and then over toward where she stood.

Clearly, he was not your typical UPS courier, and what he had with him was not an Amazon delivery. Not wanting to upset the man further, Frank approached and said, "Good day, sir. How may I help you?" She clasped her hands respectively behind her back.

"And you are?" the man questioned, giving Frank a snooty once-over.

"I'm the general manager. How may I be of assistance?" she asked more graciously than she was feeling, having just sparred with her boss.

"Please see that this gets to the proprietor of this establishment," he requested, his tone presenting the words more as a command.

"Absolutely," she said, "I would be most delighted to aid you in this important matter." She knew her manners better than most. She was—or had been an angel after all. What was the human saying? Something about bees and honey, meaning progress was made easier with polite requests and a pleasant attitude rather than rude demands and negativity. "Mr. Snow is otherwise occupied at the moment, but I will be sure to bring your delivery to his immediate attention." She brought her hands forward to receive what the man was presenting.

"That will do just fine," the man said, giving her a courteous bend at the waist. "Thank you sincerely—and good day to you." He turned on his heals and proceeded out the way he'd entered without so much as a wave goodbye.

"*Odd*," Frank said under her breath, returning to where Kris stood, next to the glass wall display of his collection of shot glasses, behind glass of course, for people to see but not touch.

Turning away from the display wall at her return, he said, "Ah, my cigars." Taking the box, he drew the palm of his hand across the smooth polish of the wooden box.

Frank made a face to clearly share her disgust for cigars.

"These," Kris said, removing one tube from the fancy box, "are the Rolls Royce of all cigars. A box of twenty costs $15k."

"For cigars?" She gawked at him.

"The price reflects their rarity. And they are incredibly difficult to purchase—I had to wait several years to get these. Each cigar ages for about 12 years before it is even available for purchase." He raised an arrogant eyebrow, as if the information he'd shared should mean something to her.

"Not like you don't have time on your hands," she said with a smirk.

"See this," he said, extending his hand, thumb and index fingers holding the astronomically priced cigar. "It is hand rolled in Nicaragua with aged Dominican tobacco and a very special 15-year-old Connecticut Maduro wrapper. The leaves are generously infused with Louis XIII Cognac—one of the world's most prestigious and expensive liquors." He pulled his hand back, examining the container. "Each cigar is placed inside an airtight glass tube sealed with melted plastic to ensure *His Majesty's Reserve* will always remain fresh and ready to smoke." He placed the sealed cigar in the inside breast pocket of his equally overpriced suite. "Only 75 boxes were made this year," he added, sounding more like a commercial for the disgusting things. Then he spun around to head back into the kitchen.

Luxurious or prestigious were not words Frank associated with cigars. Gross and disgusting were more accurate. She hated them, in fact, everything about them, and so did the rest of the staff. "And they stink—they make you stink," she called after him, appalled at the thought he had another box of the putrid sticks to smoke.

To add insult to injury, when she strolled back out to the luncheon area, there sitting at one of the exclusive tables was Marcus, Thaddeus's right-hand man at the Merope facility here in New York City. How his name on a reservation got past the assessment list she didn't know, but someone was getting fired.

"Francesca," he said, noticing her before she had a chance to retreat in the kitchen's direction. "What on earth are you doing here?"

"Frank," she corrected, adjusting her stance, crossing her thick arms over her muscular chest. "I work here." She wasn't afraid of him—not in the least. But she was nervous about the possibility of him seeing Kris. The Guards had stayed under the radar all these years and the last thing any of them needed was for Thaddeus to discover their existence.

"Frank… right," he countered, disdain in his voice and expression. "Who's the big man in the nice suit—clearly not your mate? You fell paired with the resplendent Inanna, if I recall."

"He's the owner," was all she gave him.

"Working for a human male? I assume you must be keeping him as a pet," he teased, though she knew he was serious. He grinned, as though amused by his own comment. When she didn't respond, he said, "Please, send over one of your servants—I mean servers. I'm starving."

Chapter 1 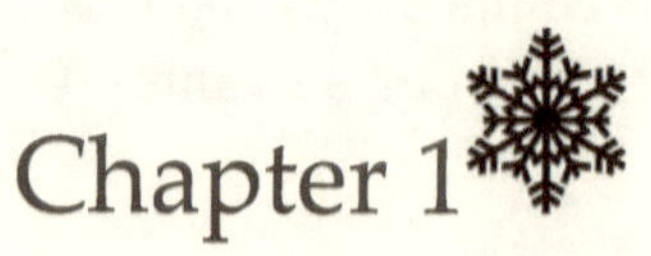

The Beach House, Saturday January 8ᵗʰ, 2022, South Florida, USA

To say this latest information that Leo and Den had shared regarding The Guards and the rest of the Earthbound had thrown me for a loop was a full-blown understatement. In fact, it had outright twisted up my poor little brain. And don't get me started on my messed up appetite.

It hadn't been so much the additional details concerning Anael's daughter for whom they'd been searching for. The real mind-warp had been more about the reality that these Earthbound Angels literally had *wings*. Then there was the part about Kris.

The details—or lack thereof, on one of their brethren, one of The Guards, Kristopher Snow, having gone missing that had prompted flashes from that horrid dream I'd had. The images of the man suspended from the ceiling—his back cut open, had revisited me over and over, further reminding me of those large pieces of what looked to be bones laying in the tray atop the rolling table. Were they the bony structures for wings?

My stomach lurched at the thought of recounting those horrific images aloud for anyone, and I pushed away the notion that my terrible dream could have anything to do with Kris and his disappearance. I'd seen that private lab firsthand. There'd been no patients, no children, and certainly no large man hanging from the ceiling. Were these dreams the result of my overactive imagination, or were they some sort of view into the past or even the future?

I'd never mentioned the details about the hanging man, nor had I shared my speculations. Instead, I'd made the conscious choice not to ponder further the possibility, shutting down the slide-flickering images and storing them elsewhere in my brain and in a space a little less shallow to the surface of my normal thoughts.

When Redmond had called Darius after our discussion with Den and Leo, he'd offered to drop off the twins back home for us. Redmond, thankfully, had clearly interpreted that my mind was still reeling after the discussion and grand reveal. In fact, the overwhelm of it all had taken me the rest of the week to fully digest the latest Angel *facts*. In turn, Redmond had told Darius that since he had to go to the studio for something, he would pick the girls up from Lily's place after. '*Two birds—one stone 'n all,*' he'd said.

Unlike me, Redmond's way of processing things had been to go over to the new facility Leo had purchased for The Guards, choosing to have it all in his face so to speak, and to assist Leo with planning the new building's layout. It was his way of creating normalcy out of the bizarre, and I loved him for that. Though, for me, this place Leo had chosen for their third Haven, or 'South Haven' as we'd begun calling it, had been the ultimate in *bizarre*.

The building was less than a mile from our home, but that wasn't the bizarre part. The bizarreness came with the description I'd read about the building on the real estate site. It stated that it was a multifamily home with a lot size of just under an acre, with 18 bedrooms, approximately 33,000 sq ft of floor space, and 40 parking spaces. When I'd questioned the strangeness of the floor plan, Redmond had clarified that the space was, in fact, broken into 9 units having 2 bedrooms, and each unit having 2 stories. He'd described the place as being *spectacular*, with the 2nd floor being lofts overlooking 20-foot tray ceilings in the living room. The upper floors had 9 ½ foot ceilings with double door balconies. Each unit had its own laundry room, private storage, and gourmet kitchen. The east side units had amazing ocean views, the west side had similar inlet views, and there was a private pool as well. It had felt somewhat less bizarre with further explanation. *Well*, right up until Redmond told me they had gutted all the lower floor living areas, opening it up into a communal living space much like the layout at the Haven in Ottawa, known now as *North* Haven. They'd also converted more than half the garage space into their *training* area, with similar workout space, weapons armory and tactical defense training areas, and a similar room setup for disguises like we'd seen in Ottawa. *"The place was still a mess,"* Redmond had added, having construction materials everywhere, but he also stated that I would need to get over there and see the new place once they were finished.

As for any of these new Angel details being shared with our friends *in the knowing*, I had originally not wanted to tell them. I had explained to Redmond that I didn't want to load them up again so soon with another otherworldly bulletin, not until I'd processed it all myself. But it wasn't something I wanted to keep from them either, so despite still digesting the various weird pieces, I'd arranged for a group video chat for the end of the week to bring them all into the new weirdness.

"Darius knew something was up when I called him and Lily earlier to come over for the group chat," Redmond said, placing his laptop on the coffee table. He was wearing a faded pair of jeans and the t-shirt the twins had gotten him for Christmas, the one that read 'Surfer Dad' with a cartoon surfboard on it.

"I suspect his concern sparked mainly because we've barely seen or spoken with them since New Year's Eve, other than the drop-off and pickup of the twins—and that had been just you." Lily had reached out to me during the week, but I had not alluded to there being anything new to report, because I hadn't wanted her to worry.

"Getting ready to update the gang, I see," Gabriel said, appearing then in the living room as Redmond powered up his laptop on the coffee table. He too wore a pair of old blue jeans, but instead of a t-shirt, he had on a grey long-sleeved thermal pullover. The weather had been cooler this past week and though he didn't feel the cold, I knew he liked to dress in accordance with the weather.

Before Redmond could respond and undoubtedly at sensing Gabriel's presence, Ryley and Hayley sock-slid from down the hall into the open space between the front foyer and living room.

"Guuuup," they squealed in unison, the two shuffling between the couches to wrap their spindly little arms around their grandfather. They wore matching overalls, though Hayley's was a hand-me-down from Ryley from last winter. They rarely dressed in identical clothes, but today they had chosen to wear the same pink t-shirts, and because of the cooler weather, they had on matching pink socks.

A knock on the front door sounded then and Redmon gave a quick, concerned glance over his shoulder my way before strolling over to answer it.

I turned to glare at Gabriel, who for most of the week had been hiding out wherever he went when he wasn't here. He gave me a guilt-ridden grin, then looked towards the front door as Redmond opened it. I refocused on the entry too, as Lily and Darius stepped into the foyer. "Come in—sit down," I said, brushing off my frustration with Gabriel.

"Hey, everyone," Lily said. Her next words halted as she spotted Gabriel. As laid-back as she was, and as many times as she had seen him, she was still shocked to see an Archangel in my home. Redirecting Lily's attention, Redmond hugged her first, then gave Darius their typical bro-hug with a manly smack on the back. The twins were on her next, encircling her in a mess of tiny arms. When Lily reached me, I gave her a soft hug and a gentle squeeze.

I knew better than to hug Darius, not unless I needed a spinal alignment, so instead I played as though I was going to give him a one-two punch in the gut. He took his usual guarded posture with my play-fighting, hands up, pleading as though he was fearful of getting hurt. "Mercy," he said, faking cowardice before pulling me in for a hug despite my efforts. Lucky for me the embrace was brief, because the girls were on him then like a jungle-gym.

Darius let out a grizzly bear growl, scooping them into his massive arms. The girls shrieked with mock fear in response to him dipping them upside down, bursting into giggles as they were righted again. "Agaaaaaaaaain," they pleaded, enjoying the playfulness of their personal giant. Down they went again, bellowing another squeal of joy. Then Darius set them both down in a *whoosh*, releasing them to their now unsteady feet, all equally breathless, the twins gasping for air. Steadying themselves, they each took up one of Darius's massive hands and then led him to the nearest couch.

Before the twins could get settled in beside Darius and Lily, Gabriel said, "It's a lovely, cool day. How about you two come with me—help me hunt for white seashells? I have a special project I'm working on, and I need all the help I can get." He gave an eager glance back and forth to each of them, then over my way.

"Uhmm, okay," Hayley said, reluctant, glancing then at Lily. "You'll still be here, right—when we get back?"

"Of course," Lily said, giving Hayley a rib-tickle.

"You too—right?" Ryley said, addressing Darius.

Darius crossed his arms over his hefty chest and leaned against the back of the couch. "What's in it for me?" he asked, forcing down a grin.

Ryley's eyebrows pinched, and she lifted an index finger to her mouth, tapping it on her pursed lips. Her sister leaned over then, whispering something into her ear. Ryley gave a pleased smile, turning and nodding to her sister. Their faces lit up over whatever had been shared. "Well...," Ryley began, directing her attention back to Darius, "... there's a half-full bag of pretzels in that tip-top cupboard we can't reach. If yer still here—we'll share them with you."

"Deal," Darius shot out, unfolding his arms, extending both his hands to the girls in offer of handshakes.

Each of the girls took a hand and shook on it. "Deal," Hayley added, sharing a smug grin, as though she'd come up with the best trade ever.

"We'll take the dogs with us," Gabriel said then, refocusing the girls back on the shell hunt. "Go get on your warm pullovers," he added, turning, and smiling at me again.

I smiled back this time. He'd get a *pass* for his not being around this week in trade for his suggestion of taking the twins out while we updated the rest of the gang on the happenings.

We'd already had a talk with the twins about the new angels and how they were setting up a second home up the way from us. They'd cared little about any of the details. Their only comments had really been about how fun it must be to have wings. And I had to agree with them.

Hoodies now on when the two returned from their rooms, Ryley came over and stood right in front of me, her head cranked back, looking up. Those same shaped eyes as mine—though hazel, not grey, stared up at me from a worried face. She was evidently sensing something from me. Something, possibly on how my neutral expression was not balanced with my inner turmoil, I was sure, and I gave her my best reassuring smile. Her sister scooped up her hand then, tugging her towards the patio door where their grandfather now stood with Summer and Snow.

The dogs *"chuffed"*, and Gabriel opened the patio door for them to exit. Ryley shoved her feet into her sneakers, then took a quick glance back at me before following her sister and the dogs through. Gabriel gave me a thumbs-up before hurrying out after his shell-hunting grand-cherubs.

I let out a weighted sigh and turned back to my husband and friends seated on the couches. "Update time," I said, moving to take the open spot on the couch next to Redmond.

He had set up the video chat such that we could see the others displayed Brady Bunch style in four respective screens spread over our 60-inch TV. Luc and Dunya were in the upper left-hand corner next to Derek's screen, while Mac, Olivia, and Alison jammed together in the lower left-hand corner, with Vicki to the right on her own screen.

Belated Happy New Year's greetings were exchanged by all, with the faces of Darius and Lily popping in and out of view of the laptop camera for their salutations.

"Where are the girls?" Dunya asked out of the gate. "We haven't seen them in ages."

"Gabriel took them to the beach," I said, pushing up the sleeves of my sweatshirt. The reality of it being that the girls would never have been able to hold their tongues about the new angels.

"This must be serious if you had the girls leave—is everything okay?" Olivia asked, worry showing on her brow.

I tried my reassuring smile on them and said, "We have some interesting news to share—but first I want to hear how all of your New Year's celebrations went." I smiled again, hopeful none of them would push for our details first.

"Seriously?" Darius questioned, out of sight of the camera on the adjacent couch.

"Yes," I said, flashing him a stiff closed-lipped smile before looking back at the screen. "Tell us what you've all been up to since New Year's *first*—our news can wait." I glanced at Darius again, and he gave me a suspicious side-eye.

"Was in bed by 9 p.m. on New Year's Eve. And this past week, nothing much here. Normal stuff, boring—and I like it that way," Vicki said, going first with her update. "Eric is out snowplowing the drive. *Normalcy.*" She grinned and leaned back in her office chair.

"I watched the new year come in across the world on the TV in my den while I rearranged the space to start the new year off fresh," Derek said. "The rest of the week I spent tinkering with my new computer setup." He had his face turned towards what I presumed was one of the numerous monitors set up on his desk. "I don't like being bored— you know me." There was the sound of fingers clacking on a keyboard.

"We stayed in while the boys went out for get-togethers with their friends. Normalcy is about 50/50 here," Mac said with a snort of laughter. "Right now, the boys are out with their dad—they went to the outdoor rink at the park. They're getting a little hockey exercise while I'm over here at Olivia's playing with plant growth— communing with nature. A little house plant magic." She did a couple of side twists and bends in her chair as though she'd just been talking about finishing her own workout. "Don't get me wrong, I get outside too—alone. It's cold right now, but I like the peacefulness of my walks," she added.

"How are Monica and Fred?" I asked, missing the normalcy of Mac's parents.

"Slowing down—I'm sorry to say, but they won't admit it." Mac puffed out an exasperated breath.

"I wouldn't want anyone witnessing me slow down, either," Redmond said. "Would be hard to admit—when your brain still thinks you're young. My parents are slowing down too—but don't tell Pop that." He bowed his head and shook it slowly several times. "I leave that up to my mom." He gave a sympathetic grin. "Hey—where's Mr. Mike?" Redmond directed at Olivia.

"At the grocery store," Olivia said cheerfully. "Getting supplies to make dinner for me and the girls. They're coming over tomorrow for family dinner night." Olivia blew out her own exasperated breath. "Hard to get both here now, with Rachel having so many long shifts at the hospital. But she's loving it—and loves being able to keep an eye on her old mum at work, too. Plus, it's her first week not living at home—she's renting a house with two other nurse friends."

I laughed at that. "I'm not surprised—as a kid, she never liked to be away from you for too long."

"It's good that someone is keeping an eye on you," Alison said, wagging a finger at Olivia.

"Where are *your* men, Alison?" I asked.

"Ken is probably outside helping our son shovel the drive. Though Kevin could manage it himself, I'm sure. We had a big dump of snow last night, Lynn, as you might have figured."

"Ya, I'm grasping that from the snow removal comments," I laughed out. "Were you back at work this week?" I asked my question for Alison.

"Next Monday," Alison said. "Had this week off—it was great. As for New Year's, we went down to Parliament Hill for the fireworks. It was pretty amazing, except for the part where we had to fight traffic after, to get out of the downtown area with ten thousand others doing the same."

"Nice on the week off—boooo on the traffic crap," I countered, enjoying the bits and pieces of their normalcy.

Alison gave a little bounce in her seat. "Oh, almost forgot. I followed up with Carlie."

A shiver ran down the length of my spine. "And?"

"Carlie mentioned Lane had contacted her. I had given Carlie the heads-up to expect her call," Alison said.

"Right," I said, reminded that Max and Julian's daughter Lane had offered to watch over Taylor.

"Carlie said she'll be setting up a second visit for Lane to further check out the facility. The first one was just a quick intro and first floor walk-through. They've concocted the ruse that Lane's a student doing a paper for this type of facility. Setting the stage as though she thinks that Carlie's boss is a hero for working there—to get on his good side."

"Smart," Olivia cut in. "The guy running that facility was a piece of work. I got bad vibes off him, and he's definitely not the kind of person who should oversee people with special needs."

"I second that—he was an asshole," I said, recalling the salesman style bluster he gave us regarding the care they provided. "The guy gave me all the *wrong* feels, too."

"Didn't help that Carlie seemed so uneasy when he was around," Alison said, fidgeting in her seat.

"It was clear that Taylor didn't like the guy either. There's more going on there," I said, another shiver running up my spine. "Keep me posted on how things go for Lane's second visit."

"You got it," Alison said, giving me the peace sign.

"Luc—what say ye?" Redmond asked, shifting everyone's attention.

"I'm happy to say things are status quo—pretty normal here," Luc said, turning to look at Dunya.

"All is well," Dunya added, planting a sweet kiss on Luc's cheek.

"Aaawwww," came from all of us on the chat.

Luc's face flushed.

With a chuckle, Redmond said, "I've got a few gigs coming up at the studio over the next couple of months that I'll need you on."

"You got it—happy to help, as you know. Need to keep my fingers nimble," Luc replied, cracking his knuckles, and wiggling his fingers. His time now consisted of enjoying his life with Dunya and frequent visits with his sister and her kids ever since they'd moved up to the Orlando area, and the occasional gig to jam with bands Redmond and Lily were working with.

"Dunya, you can come hang with me and the twins, if you want," I said with a wink.

"I'd love that," she said.

"Uhm," Derek said then, his tone impatient, facing back to the monitor that had his video feed. "Ya—these updates are all great and everything—but Lynn, yer killing me here. You called this meeting—what's the news?" He cut a quick study of another monitor, then back to facing us.

"Yer killing me too," Darius said, arms crossed again, his patience running thin also, it seemed.

"Yes, right," I said. "Olivia, Mac, do either of you know an oncology nurse named Nic—*Nicolas* North?" I asked, before transitioning into the heavy stuff. Olivia, along with Mac, supported the neonatal and expectant mothers program at the hospital where Nic worked.

Olivia stole a glance over her shoulder as if checking to see if they were alone. "Yes—why?"

"He's one of The Guards...," I began.

"Oh man, that explains a lot," Mac interrupted. "Have you met him?"

"No," I said, shaking my head once. "Not yet. Why—what?"

Olivia leaned into the computer screen. "Well, to see him, you'd think he'd walked straight out of a romance novel. Tall, dark, and handsome—way over 6 feet, *built*. Looks sort of Native Indian—*Polynesian*, maybe? He has long, thick, shiny black hair down to his waist—keeps it pulled back in a low man-bun. And those eyes of his are, well, dreamy, brown with caramel flecks." Olivia paused, then said, "The female staff—and some of the male staff too, act all love-struck around him." She paused again, this time to look over her shoulder the other way. "I'll admit—if I were single, and 10—well, 20 years younger, I'd be swooning too." She let out a giggle. "It's nothing he does on purpose—it's just him, he has a way, it's a calming thing."

"He's in the right department. Everyone in oncology—staff and patients, could use all the *skills* he has to offer," Mac added.

Olivia nodded. "He and Rachel get on quite well. It's funny though. I pointed out how handsome he was, but she basically sluffed off my comment. Said, '*Ya, the nurses are all gaga over him—I get it, he checks all the boxes*'. I was shocked. Then she said, '*I just think he's a cool person—I've learned a lot on the job from him, too*'. It had me thinking about how often that happens to women—unwanted attention just for their looks. Wait till I tell her what he is," she squeaked out. "Oh, crap—can't tell her—can I?" She leaned back from the screen, mortification showing on her face.

"Probably not a good idea," Mac said, "with her not being part of things, the gathering—in the knowing, etc. The guy *is* hot, though." She gave a couple eyebrow raises.

"Would it really be all that bad if she knew—was *in the knowing?*" Olivia asked. "Katherine has shown no interest in my new *talents*, but Rachel is always asking me about them. Do you think I could bring her in?"

"Eric knows," Vicki interjected. "He wasn't part of the gathering, either."

"True," I said, considering the idea. "Let me ask Gabriel—or maybe I should ask Leo. Not sure it's our secret to tell."

Cutting in again, Vicki said, "Though I think sometimes he'd rather not know. Sometimes I think *I'd* rather not know. Life would be much simpler, not knowing." She nodded in agreement with her own statement.

Glancing at Redmond, I took in a long draw of air and held it. I knew now was the time to get the latest info out. "Speaking of knowing… there's something else." Blowing out my held breath, I tossed it out there, "Wings." Before anyone could respond, I headed into the long explanation of what had happened that morning after New Years when Hayden had arrived.

"It makes sense," Luc said, speaking out first. "Considering all the research and references I'd found on Seraphim—about them flying. In the Book of Isaiah, the term *Seraphim* is used to describe a being with six wings that flies around the Throne of God. And in another text, it referred to them as *flying elements of the sun,* and those had twelve wings."

"I always figured the references to flying angels were exaggerations from what people thought were Angel sightings—or old biblical stories, and not actual real wings," Darius said, giving his head a swift shake.

"Do these halflings have wings, too?" Dunya asked.

"Yup, they do, and more the reason for their searching for Anael's daughter," I stated. "Sometime around age 20 their wings emerge—fully developed. Obviously, the major problem being that the halflings rarely know they have wings…."

"Until when—they burst out of their backs?" Derek interjected.

I nodded, my mouth twisting in a grimace. "And only a few have been known to survive." I huffed out a breath. "They don't know why the twentieth year is so key. They look just like human 20-year-olds, though if they *can* make it into adulthood, they are healthier, super fit, and are just as stunning in appearance as these other Earthbound."

"Before their wings come out—they are strong, but are even stronger after, if they survive it," Redmond added.

"Survive?" Alison questioned, pressing her lips tight together as if not wanting to know more despite her question.

"I had asked the same thing," Redmond responded. "The ones who survive the complete development of their wings will have full function, but they would have no knowledge of how to use them. Someone would have to teach them."

"What about those who don't know they are halflings?" Mac asked, worried like the others, like Redmond and I had been when learning about this.

Redmond rubbed his jaw. "Finding those who weren't raised with a Seraph parent, the sudden appearance of wings and the pain that accompanies the first release…." He paused. "… Leo said it can be devastating to the body and mind."

"Though the greatest challenge Leo told us is helping them to accept what they are," I said, finishing for Redmond.

"So, do you think that's why Taylor said the word *wings* to you, Lynn?" Alison questioned.

"I considered it—yer probably bang on. It's gotta be what he was trying to tell me."

"Hey, did you find out if that woman from the Mall is one of them—Earthbound?" Alison asked, full of questions. It was understandable considering the details I'd just dropped on them.

"What woman?" Derek asked, his curiosity perking up. He gave a rakish grin, coupled with an exaggerated wink.

I cracked up at his hopeful expression, welcoming the comic relief. "Well, her name is Julianna—*Jules* Leo called her for short, and she was gorgeous," I said, before launching into another short recap of events, along with Leo's opinion of her relocation.

"I agree with Leo's take. It might be good for her to be in Ottawa—since she knows what The Guards have been tackling," Derek said, approving.

"Leo explained she knows *of* me—my existence, just not who I am exactly, or that I've been involved with any of their business. She wouldn't have known that was me at the mall that day either, but Leo said he would bring her up to speed." I grinned, hopeful. I was curious to formally meet her.

"Apparently she's familiar with the Taygeta facility in Manau City, Brazil—that's another of Thaddeus's labs," Redmond clarified.

"I'd love to meet her," Derek said. "It's only ever been these guy-angels. Would be nice to meet a female one—and not a nasty one like Mac and Olivia encountered at the Celaeno building." He made a face like he'd eaten something rotten.

"I guess you'll just have to come up and visit the Ottawa crew again for that to happen," Alison suggested, turning a knowing smile to Mac and Olivia.

We all knew it had been *ages* since Derek had a girlfriend.

"I'm sure she would love to meet you too, Derek. But keep in mind, she has a son," Redmond said in his fatherly tone.

"I take it he's one of these halflings," Alison redirected.

"Yes," I said. "His name is Mason. He plans to attend the University of Ottawa for Food and Nutrition Sciences. It's why Jules took the job offer of teaching Environmental Geoscience at Ottawa U. She goes by Professor Julianna Forest. Both courses are part of the same Science department. They'd just arrived from Brazil that day we saw her. She was shopping for winter clothes for both of them."

"Talk about climate change," Derek said.

"I take it, he's... okay?" Alison asked, showing her motherly concern.

"From what Leo told us, he is. Though he's mute." Redmond said, placing his fingers at the front of his neck. "He had some kind of genetic abnormality during the fetal development of his airway. Called it, HP?"

"Hypersensitivity pneumonitis—it's a rare immune system disorder affecting the lungs," Olivia said, jumping in to clarify.

"Leo said the condition was comparable to something called BFL—Bird Fancier's Lung," I added, "and has something to do with exposure to avian proteins found in bird poop and feathers of certain birds."

"That's it—right—no more angel weirdness? Vicki questioned, her words riding the heels of my last.

"Well… no." I said, stunned by her first comments on the news.

"No—meaning *no more*?" she asked, irritated.

"No, meaning I have one more thing," I tried to explain, still shocked by her abruptness.

"Oh-my-gawd—there's more," Vicki spewed, throwing her hands up in the air, further annoyed.

An uncomfortable silence fell over the group following Vicki's outburst.

I surveyed the others present in our living room, pulling in a cleansing breath to harness the building frustration I was feeling over Vicki's impatience. Releasing the breath, I said, "The main reason they revealed their wings wasn't so much about Anael and the fact that they are searching for her daughter…." I took another long draw of air. "Remember how I told you that The Guards had relocated to Ottawa when they realized Thaddeus was there… all but Kris?"

"He's the one who's still in New York City—owns a fancy restaurant, if I recall," Alison said. "I remember making note of it in my current celestial journal. I love New York City." She grinned big, her cheeks bunching, the corners of her eyes crinkling.

"Ya, Spook, that's correct." I grinned back at her, grateful for her spark of joy in such a trying moment. "Kris has been keeping tabs on the Merope lab—and he keeps his own place in the city. As for the others, their main lodging is in Ottawa, however, they still travel to keep tabs on the other five lab locations."

"But I'm guessing he has no interest in dealing with the rebellious Earthbound—only watching the lab in New York, and that being the extent of his involvement?" Darius surmised, as though he were upset at the lack of the Angel's heroism. He wasn't far off if that was what he was thinking.

"From what Den and Leo explained, Kris can be self-centered—arrogant," I said. "Has to have the absolute best of everything, especially in his restaurant. Does lots of traveling around the world for what he considers *the best*."

"He's not a complete asshole," Redmond tossed out. "They also said he was an amazing cook. Julian and Max have gotten some incredible recipes from him, and that he has always been good to their daughter—so not all bad."

"Okay, so?" Vicki cut in, as though to hurry us along.

I paused again, adjusting my perspective, considering how all of this must feel for her—for all of them. Nonetheless, Vicki's exasperation over my trying to share information was riding my last nerve. Pulling in a breath and beginning again, I said, "None of them have heard from him since they were all called up North for their discussion with Thanael and Anael. Kris never arrived."

"Are you saying he's missing?" Mac asked, worriedly chewing the corner of her thumbnail.

"Can't Gabriel and the others find him?" Vicki challenged, flouting all the other info I'd shared, including the whole *wing* thing.

"I wish," I responded, frustrated also at whatever Angel code they lived by. It meant they couldn't help their own powerless brethren. "They can't be involved. Their quest stopped with us. *'They're not permitted to help,'* Gabriel told me—when I'd suggested they try."

"So, they *can* interact with the Earthbound—but *can't* help them?" Olivia questioned, concern swelling in her voice.

"Sadly, no. The Earthbound are pretty much on their own." I sighed, then added, "And get this, since The Guards were created on Earth—not on Pleiades, they are considered *Forsaken* in the host of Angels. Neither human nor Angel, yet both in a way." I frowned. I was still trying to process the prejudice. "Gabriel said that's the label given when an Angel chooses to leave their divine existence behind for good. Or with The Guards, those who were not created in the celestial realm—that includes halflings." An unexpected chill tickled along my bare forearms, and I pulled my sweatshirt sleeves back down to my wrists. "The worst of it, despite their superior strength and greater size to the others—the cast down Earthbound, The Guards having been created on Earth versus in the stars, they are *also* vulnerable to injury and aging like the Earthbound."

"Harsh," Derek said, "Bad deal." He ran the palm of his hand down his face as though to wipe away his adverse feelings on the topic.

He and my other friends already knew the full deal on Thaddeus and the Earthbound, about how The Guards were created and why, and about Purah and the Stewards, along with the other Seraphim who remained amongst the stars of Pleiades, but this was still a great deal of *you've got to be kidding me* to process. "The fear—and even worse deal," I said, letting out another held breath, "is that Leo believes that Thaddeus might have Kris—have him held somewhere."

There was a collective gasp from everyone over the last part of my not so great news, well, not from Vicki. Instead, she said, "That's it— right? Please tell me that's all of it." Her words felt more like a demand than a question.

I focused on Redmond first, because I hadn't yet shared this tidbit with him, and I knew he wouldn't like what I was about to say. I peered at Darius and Lily next, mainly because they were right here. Then I brought my attention to the others on the TV screen, and said, "I need to go to that lab in New York City."

Chapter 2 

Jana drove the 30 minutes from Seydisfjordur to Egilsstadir, then turned off the main road and on to the long snow-covered driveway up to her father's house. She had not kept up the snow removal of the drive after her father's passing two years ago, instead she'd taken to driving his truck during the winter months. The 1983 Land Rover Defender was great for the trips to and from town. '*It was the best and most reliable land rover model*', he'd always told her, and now, it was one of those sought-after models car collectors looked for. It had also been the vehicle her father had taught her to drive on, and driving it now gave her the welcomed comfort she needed in the painful wake of missing him.

As she rolled to a stop near the end of the drive, her cellphone vibrated in the center console. She snatched it up, answering it as she exited the truck. The frosty January wind whipped her pale blonde hair around her face. "Hey, Geir," she said, already knowing who it was.

"Are you at the house?" he asked. Geir Sigurdsson had been a veterinary intern training with her father when Jana and he first met. They'd hit it off and had remained friends to this day. In fact, he'd taken over her father's practice when he'd retired.

"Just arrived." She'd been going out to the place once a week when her father was alive and had continued venturing out after his passing, now only every two weeks.

"When are you going to sell that place—you could use the money? The bakari barely makes enough to keep the lights on," he said, referring to the Icelandic baked goods shop Jana owned.

"It brings in enough." She let out an exhausted sigh and unlocked the front door.

"You'd have more than enough if you just sold that old place—you don't need to be paying the utilities for a house you don't even live in."

"I know—but I'm just… not ready." She couldn't bring herself to sell it, not yet anyway. She had maintained her father's modest home and the small barn on the property for the past two years, though the idea of selling it visited her more often these days. It basically sat unlived in, nothing other than old memories and a few boxes of her father's personal items and clothing remained.

"Okay," he said, "Let me know when you're heading back into town."

"I'll text you before I leave," she said before hanging up, smiling over his concern. Geir hadn't only taken over her father's practice, he'd also taken over her father's habit of checking on her when she drove anywhere outside of town.

Once inside, she went through her usual routine of strolling down the short hall, checking each room, and talking aloud as though speaking to her father as she went. "All seems well," Jana said. When she reached the kitchen and last room on her walkthrough, she set her cellphone on the counter and continued to the next task of walking around the perimeter of the house, with a quick stop at the outbuilding at the back of the property. Before going back out into the cold, Jana pulled on a pair of her father's winter gloves, the ones he'd always left hanging by the back door in the kitchen. Then she exited out to the back property.

She paused in her steps, noticing there were large footprints in the snow leading from the back step away to what appeared to be a large pile of snow. As she traversed the distance to the mound, the fresh snow crunched under her boots.

Stopping in front of the pile, she scanned the area in search of more footprints but found only the ones that had led her here and those she'd just made. The snow heap shook then, forcing a startled breath from Jana, coupled it with a curse. Mustering her wits, she leaned towards the end closest to her, spying what appeared to be the tops of dark-coloured shoes peeking out from under the snow. The snow pile quaked again, revealing more of what hid under it. It was no snow pile.

It was a *man*—a giant of a man, resting on his side against the cold, snowy ground. Around him was wrapped what looked like a long white blanket, exposing only small sections of dark clothing. The nearer end of the blanket wrapped around his bent legs while the far end was folded over, concealing the man's head. She leaned in again to get a better look.

The man shuddered, startling and sending Jana tripping backward over her own feet to land ass-first in the snow. "Helvíti!" she cried from her cold spot on the ground, then added a few English *Hells* for good measure. When movement continued from beneath the covering, she sat stunned, watching as the top layer of snow sluffed off to display more of the blanket. Jana shifted up off the cold snow to her feet, then cautiously stepped up within reach of the unconscious giant. "What the… hell?" she said, wide-eyed.

What had sheltered the man hadn't been a blanket at all. The covering was in fact two lengths of densely layered white grey-tipped feathers, *wings*. Fascinated, Jana removed one of her gloves and bent forward. She reached out to touch a section of the downy white feathers, but then thought twice about it. Drawing back her hand, she patted the pocket of her bomber jacket. Her cellphone, she quickly realized was back in the house on the kitchen counter. Turning away from the man, she ran back up the path to the house.

So much for a simple survey of what she had assumed was a simple pile of snow, she thought as she pushed through the back door to the kitchen. A second later, she was rushing back down the path again, cellphone to her ear. She'd hit the speed dial for Geir before going back outside.

"They're gone," Jana breathed out, coming to a halt before the still prone man on the ground, the cellphone still ringing in her ear.

The ringing cut off, replaced by Geir's voice. "You're traveling home now?"

Before answering, she took a quick scan of the area around where the man lay. "Uhm," she said, baffled. The wings she'd seen wrapped around the man were now gone, disappeared, though the man remained in the same position as when she'd left him only moments ago. "No—sorry, I… need your help."

"What happened—are you okay?" Geir questioned. A chair screeching across a floor sounded in the background.

There is an enormous man passed out behind my father's house, she should have said, but all she could get out was, "Nothing happened—I'm fine." But she wasn't fine. "I aaahh… just need you to come over. I'll explain when you get here." She wasn't sure why she hesitated in telling him everything right then.

"Can it wait? I have one last patient."

"Just come when you can," she said, hanging up and sliding the cellphone into her coat pocket. Had she really seen wings? Or had it been a trick of the snow, she wondered as she pulled her glove back on. Then she took a tentative step towards the upper part of the man's body.

He wore only a suit and dress shoes, she noted. No overcoat or winter boots. Without the covering to obscure his face, she could see he had his chin tucked in towards his chest, the angle revealing his deep brown, almost black hair. "Hah-low," she said, using a local Icelandic greeting before chancing another pace forward. She should be scared, but she wasn't. And she knew she should probably call the police. But she wouldn't do that, not yet.

A deep "groan" escaped the stranger, but Jana stayed where she was. At least he was still breathing. The man's head lilted back then from its tucked position, shedding light on his face… his magnificently beautiful face, all hard lines, square-jawed and shadowed cheekbones.

"Hello," she tried again, this time in English. "Are you okay?" she asked, leaning in, tilting her head to better observe his face. Could he be injured?

Another "groan" left the stranger's full lips, followed by a grimace of what Jana could only assume was pain. Clearly, he wasn't okay, and what she should have been questioning was what the hell was this guy doing out here in the middle of nowhere on her father's property? Or, for that matter, why the hell wasn't she calling the police or an ambulance? The man's eyes opened then. Dark navy-blue, albeit glassy eyes, gazed up at her. He gave her a weak smile before his thickly lashed eyelids shut again. Without hesitation, she knelt in front of him, reaching out and placing a bare hand on his upper arm.

Wet? The sleeve of his suit jacket was soaking wet. Sliding her hand down the sleeve, she found it partially frozen, the fabric crunching under her touch. She then drew a shaky hand across the front of his jacket. It too was soaked. Leaning down towards his legs, she repeated the fabric check only to find that the man's suit pants were also drenched and crunchy. He couldn't have been out here very long, she surmised, especially with wet clothing. Iceland's temperatures can reach extremes and unprotected from the harsh winter elements, human tissue could freeze at around -0.5C. She stood then, glancing over to the outbuilding, shifting her gaze slowly across the property which was fenced in on all sides. Turning to face the house, she stared past it to the end of the driveway, frowning.

She had seen no one on the drive in. Had he arrived shortly after she had, while she'd been inside the house? "Where did you come from… and how did you find your way to my father's home?" she asked, turning back, and staring down at the unconscious stranger. "You're not dead—but you're going to be if I don't get you inside." She shot a glance back at the small barn at the side of the property.

The barn was closer than the house and if she was going to have to drag him to shelter, it was going to be her best option. Circling around to behind the motionless man, she bent and then rolled him as gently as she could onto his back. She was met with a weedy "moan" and another grimacing facial contortion.

"Sorry," she said, then took hold of him under his armpits. "Okay, here we go," she announced. Using all the strength she could muster, she leaned back and heaved, but her hope of sliding him over the snow the few yards to the barn was short-lived. The reality of it slammed to a halt when he didn't even budge, not even a smidge. To make matters worse, she'd ended up on her ass again, her jeans dampening further on their way to icing over, just like the man's clothing.

He was too big and heavy for her to move alone, but she didn't know when Geir would arrive. What she did know was that if it hadn't already, hypothermia was going to be setting in soon. "What am I supposed to do?" she said, tilting her face up to the cloudless sky as if asking the universe. She eyed the barn again, an idea forming on how to move him.

Scrambling to her feet and brushing the snow off her ass, she hustled it over to the barn. Cranking open the double doors, she blew out a breath, spotting what she hoped was still in there. "Yes—thank you," she exclaimed, racing inside.

It took her no time to hook up the compact tractor her father had in the barn for lifting livestock. It was a simple and quick one-person operation that used loader arms or hay forks along with strong zinc plated hooks for durability. Thankfully, it started up right away despite sitting for several years. The universe had listened, she thought as she drove the thing up to where the man lay.

Hopping off the tractor, she lowered the heavy-duty PVC sling alongside the man's body. Swiftly, yet at the man's unfortunate discomfort, Jana slid the crossed straps and support pad under his body. Then she attached the C-hooks to the loader arms. She remembered her father saying, *"The width of the sling helps to ensure there are no pressure points, allowing large animals to remain in the sling comfortably."* Despite hearing several *groans*, she hoped it would do the same for this large man, so off they went.

Once in the barn, she lowered him down near a stack of livestock blankets. "Better than nothing," she said, covering him with several of the light-weight cotton stable blankets. She stared down at the man now buried under the old blankets. "Who are you—how did you get here?" she questioned aloud. Geir's truck horn sounded in the distance then, pulling her attention away from her musings and announcing his arrival up the drive. Jana hurried out of the barn and back up to the house.

In the backdoor and through the kitchen again she hustled to where Geir was steadily knocking on the front door. "Come in," she said, pulling the door open wide. "Follow me." She turned, leading back the way she had just come.

"Hello, to you too," Geir called after her as he trailed her through the kitchen and out the backdoor. "What—where are we going?"

Jana said nothing as she marched through the snow, into the barn, and back over to the stack of blankets. She pointed a gloved hand at the overlapping pile of old stable blankets on the ground.

"What—you need my help with old horse blankets?" He frowned, his expression one of confusion.

The pile of blankets moved suddenly, followed by a shallow "moan" from what was hidden beneath.

"What the...?" Geir shouted, taking several steps back from the pile.

"I found him outside," Jana said, leaning down and pulling back several of the blankets.

Geir stared down at the man, apparently lost for words. Then he said, "Outside—is he drunk? Why haven't you called the police?"

"I don't think so—didn't smell any alcohol on him." She draped the blankets back over him.

"Did you call the police?" he barked, shoving his hands into his coat pockets. He took an anxious stride sideways, moving to stand next to her.

"I think he might be injured," Jana said in response to his police comment. "I could have sworn…."

"Sworn what?"

"I can't figure out how he got here—why he was laying out there on the ground." She paused, staring down at the blankets. "We need to get him inside."

"He is inside." Geir extended his arms, waving them back and forth. Then he drew his bare hands to his face, cupping them and blowing warm breath into them. He rubbed them together, repeating the blowing and rubbing several times.

"Inside the house—where it's warm," Jana said, clearly needing to state the obvious.

"Are you out of your mind? Call the police, Jana," Geir insisted, jabbing his hands into his coat pockets again.

"No." Jana stared back down at the pile.

"No?" Geir questioned, glancing around the small barn area.

"No—he's not some... some derelict, or drunk tourist or whatever—he's wearing a suit," she said with a huff. "I don't believe he's a threat—but I do believe he needs our help."

Geir turned to look at her, then hesitantly bent to pass a hand in front of the man's parted lips. "He's still breathing," he noted.

"For now. We need to get him into the house—he's soaking wet, and he'll freeze to death out here." She pulled back some of the blankets again.

"Why is he wet?"

"How should I know?" She flipped the last of the coverings off him, and a faint steam rose from his now exposed, well-dressed body.

"Are you sure we should move him?" He surveyed the practically empty barn again.

"I moved him in here," she said, piling the last of the blankets back on the stack.

"Fine. Let's see if we can rouse him," Geir said, moving closer. "Sir—can you hear me?" he said near the man's ear, repeating the question in Icelandic for good measure.

When a low *groan* escaped the man's gaping mouth, Geir knelt and said, "Here, help me." Then they moved swiftly together, repositioning the barely conscious stranger, rolling him from his back to resting him on his side. The man stirred then, making a wobbly attempt to maneuver himself over further and on to his hands and knees. Geir and Jana assisted him, easing him back to settle on his heals.

"We need to keep him from falling back down, from passing out again—till we can get him inside," Geir said, shifting himself under the man's left side. Jana did the same under his right. "One, two, three," Geir said, and the two of them raised the man up to an unsteady standing position. Then they walked together, leading him out of the small barn and towards the house.

Jana had been an athlete in her youth, and even though Geir's tall wiry frame was *not* built for heavy lifting, the two of them managed to get the guy over the snowy ground and into the house. It was not an easy feat, considering the man's heft and poor awareness.

Once in the house, they sloppily guided him into the living room. "Need to get these wet clothes off," Geir said, shifting to the front, bracing himself then to take the full brunt of the man's weight. "Quickly, remove his suit jacket." Jana did as he instructed, then together they rested him down on the long sofa. He was so tall, his feet extended past the far end of it.

"Get his shirt and tie off, while I grab some of Dad's clothes for him to wear," Jana said, rushing off to the back bedroom. Her dad had been a large man with an athletic build even into his 60s, so she was confident she could find something that would fit.

She returned carrying a stack of clothes and a wool blanket, only to stop short in the opening to the living room just as Geir yanked off the man's dress pants to reveal navy blue boxers. She quickly lifted her gaze to Geir.

"His pants are soaked," Geir said, when he noticed her. "The guy is seriously built," he added, nodding, giving Jana a wicked smile followed by a couple of eyebrow raises.

She returned her attention to the almost naked man lying on her father's sofa. She couldn't help but stare, his body was… *amazing*. Built was an understatement. He was… he was spectacular, she thought as she allowed herself to take in the full beauty of him, her gaze traveling up and down the length of his muscular body.

"His boxers are wet too," she heard Geir say. Not taking her eyes off the man, Jana handed over the stack of items. "I'm going to remove his boxers," Geir stated then, stepping forward and blocking her view.

Her attention transferred to Geir. "Boxers—right—got it," she fumbled out, turning away, fixing her gaze now on the navy suit draped over the back of the old armchair next to the sofa. She hadn't thought to grab underwear to go with the sweatshirt and track pants she'd pulled from her father's wardrobe box. Her goal had been to retrieve items that would fit, that would keep him warm. It wasn't cold in the house, even so, it made sense not to dress him in dry clothes over wet boxers. She stepped up to the wet suit on the old chair.

"That's an expensive suit," Geir commented from behind her. She could hear the shuffling of clothes being pulled on. "It's a Brioni."

Jana turned back towards the sofa. "What's Briono?" she asked, noting that Geir had the man fully dressed now in her father's tracksuit.

"Brioni," he corrected, "Brioni Vanquish II Suits are the ones you sometimes see James Bond wearing in the movies." Geir placed the man's dress shoes on the floor next to the sofa, then dropped the wet socks over them.

Geir had hung his winter coat on the upper corner of the sofa, she noticed, so she did the same with hers at the end near the armchair. Turning back, she began going through the pockets of the man's suit pants. "No wallet, no cellphone," she said. "Nothing to indicate who he is or even where he came from." She placed the pants back over the chair, then patted the front pockets of the suit jacket. Finding nothing, she fanned open the jacket, searching the inner pockets. In the left breast pocket, she retrieved a small glass tube and a paper wrapper. The wrapper was soaked through like his clothes.

Leaving the suit jacket on the chair, Jana took the two items with her into the kitchen. She tossed the glass tube into the garbage bin but left the wrapper on the counter to dry out. She stared at the coffee maker and considered if she should make some. It was already getting dark out and it could be a long night. "I need to tell you something — but you're going to think I'm crazy," she announced from the kitchen.

"After this — I already think you are crazy, so go ahead," Geir said, strolling in then.

"I saw the footsteps… found the pile of snow… when I realized it was a person — and I could have sworn I saw — that he… well, that he had… wings." She paused when he said nothing and only gaped at her. "Or he was wrapped in wings — that's what I saw. But they were gone when I came back from retrieving my phone from the house." Crazy beans now spilled, she stared back at him.

He inclined his head. "You must have been mistaken, obviously. Too many sleepless nights worrying about the bakery." He placed his hands on her shoulders. "Not surprising with that restaurant next door offering to buy you out for the space."

She made a tight smile, nodding in agreement, and he dropped his hands from her shoulders. "You're probably right," she realized. She hadn't been sleeping. Coupled with the shock of finding a strange man passed out on the property, imaginary wings wouldn't have been far off the exhaustion course. Craziness aside, right now, she was grateful she'd kept the utilities functioning in the house. She hadn't liked the idea of the house going cold, though she knew she wouldn't be able to keep up with the expense of heating it much longer. She was hopeful she could keep it until Spring.

"Well, from what I could see through my fumbling of undressing and redressing the man, he doesn't appear to have any injuries. He has a couple of interesting tattoos on his back. It's strange…," he said, then paused.

"What is it?"

He rubbed a hand across his jaw. "I knew someone who had similar tattoos." He paused again as though lost in memory. "But I haven't seen him since college," he clarified, then he turned and went back to the living room.

Jana followed, watching him as he shook out the folded wool blanket and laid it over the man. She smiled approvingly at the kind gesture. Her stomach grumbled then, and she peered back through the living room's opening to the kitchen, wondering what food, if any, remained. She hadn't said it yet, but she planned to stay here and monitor the sleeping giant.

Chapter 3 

The Beach House, January 8th, South Florida

"Why do you need to go to New York City?" Olivia questioned, leaning into the screen again.

"She doesn't," Redmond said, firmer than I would have expected. "It's the last place she needs to go."

"Says you," I pushed back, crossing my arms over my chest.

"Says Leo—and Den," Redmond threw back. "Tell everyone why." He leaned away from me, resting his back on the arm of the couch. "Go ahead."

"Holy crap—not more," Vicki said, tossing in her two cents. "Ladies and gentlemen—I think I've had enough *news* for one day—for a while, in fact. If you need my talents of translation for something—I'm here. If not, I need to get back to the regularly scheduled programming of my normal life. Sorry all—Happy New Year," she added before waving and logging off the screen.

It was abrupt, but I couldn't blame her for the quick exit. I wondered then if I should have told them the latest, included them in all this again. I should have asked if they wanted to be part of it versus me just throwing it all out there. But I hadn't asked them to do anything, hadn't asked them to take on this latest problem to solve. My four girlfriends, along with Luc, Darius, Derek, and Redmond, had participated in something that had changed our lives, changed the world around us and it had been epic. But the exhilarating feeling that had accompanied such a profound event as the gathering and all the things leading up to it, had dissipated and grown distant as our lives settled back into normalcy. Things for me had shifted dramatically with the knowledge that Gabriel, an Archangel, was my birthfather, but despite the exhilaration of the experience, the excitement too had leveled out for me as well. Now, with the presentation of these new celestials, that feeling, the thrill, had resurfaced for me. There was no obligation for any of them to be involved, but I couldn't *not* tell them.

"I'll go with you," Alison said, beaming with enthusiasm.

"She's not going," Redmond stated, his tone a tad too caveman for my liking.

"Why not?" Alison asked, her enthusiasm bubble deflating.

Redmond gave nothing in response, only glared at me.

"Dammit," I cursed under my breath despite all eyes waiting on me. I tightened and twisted my lips, deciding where to start with this next bit of info. I had hoped to avoid sharing this potential hiccup in my plans. I uncrossed my arms.

"Okay, I'll tell them," Redmond began before I could compose my words. Then he turned to the TV screen and said, "Leo also informed us of what Kris was doing prior to his disappearance." He cut a side glance my way, then focused forward again. "Leo spoke with the general manager of Kris's restaurant, Frank...."

"Francesca—she's one of the Earthbound," I said, providing clarity, but Redmond gave me a scolding look for interrupting him.

Turning back to the others, he said, "And apparently, Kris had full intentions of meeting the others up North, but Frank said Kris would be traveling to Norway first to order the salmon for his restaurant and the Christmas beer supply. He made it to Norway—she'd spoken to him while he was at one of the vendors. But when Leo realized that Kris had not returned to his home in New York after, they set out to retrace his steps." Redmond leaned back against the couch cushion. "Leo stated that two of The Guards, Marq and Zach, met up in Norway to speak with the vendors Kris was to meet with, and they confirmed that he had made all his scheduled stops, but found no trace of him after."

"So, what does this have to do with Lynn and me going to New York City?" Alison asked, her enthusiasm stalled.

I squeezed my lips shut when Redmond shot me another scolding look. Then he said, "Frank also told Leo that Marcus—one of Thaddeus's top collaborators—was at Kris's restaurant. He recognized Frank and questioned who it was she was working for." Redmond went back to leaning against the arm of the couch and frowning at me.

"Leo also said there was nothing indicating that *Thaddeus* was in New York City," I added.

"I agree with Redmond—you don't need to go," Darius said. "Don't forget that Seraph—Purah, said one of Thaddeus's guys had already spotted you in New York—saw you speaking to that Watcher Angel."

"That happened three years ago," I said, in defense, crossing my arms again.

"Purah said someone had been watching you since the gathering. Knew of your abilities to sense Archangels and Fallen," Darius stated. "I'm sure they suspect you can sense those Watchers too, as well."

"Look—no one—I mean none of these Earthbound have ever been near me. Trust me, I'd know. I'm pretty confident that if they thought my talents were useful to them—they'd have come around by now," I said, uncrossing my arms and sitting forward on the couch. "Now, had they seen me talking to Leo or one of the other Earthbound, that would have certainly stirred up suspicion at the capacity of my abilities—but they haven't seen me with them."

"I know they can't find you—sense you, like Gabriel and the others can," Redmond said, his words softening. "But you could still be on their radar even as a curiosity." He took hold of my hand closest to him. "This Thaddeus seems desperate enough, malicious enough, to act on anything that would justify or perpetuate fulfilling his sick venture."

"The last thing we need is for one of his guys to spot you snooping around his buildings—labs, or whatever," Darius added.

"I got in and out of the Ottawa building with none the wiser."

"We were lucky," Redmond said.

Before I could protest, the heads on screen and present were all nodding in agreement.

"Okay-okay," I said in less agreement, choosing to drop the hot topic. "I will think on it further. I respect your concerns," I finished, mostly for the sake of peace in our little assembly.

Gabriel and the girls came through the patio door then, saving me from any further dispute with the others. "Come say hi to everyone," I called to the girls, grateful for the lifesaver.

The cheerful dispositions of my little angels and one big Archangel after their shell hunting on the beach had spared me, and there had been no further discussion on the subject after the call ended, not even with Redmond after Darius and Lily had left. Though I suspected he was holding back a lecture on the topic until after I got the girls tucked in their beds.

As I approached Ryley's bedroom I overheard through the crack in the door, her and Hayley talking, using that twin language they sometimes still spoke in.

"What are you two chatting about?" I asked, pushing open the bedroom door.

They were both sitting on Ryley's bed already in their yellow and white floral flannel pjs their Nana and Poppy had gotten them for Christmas. Their innocent cherub faces blazed with surprise up at me, then they focused on each other.

"Who is the angel in the back room—the hanging one?" Hayley asked. Ryley pinched the back of Hayley's arm. "Ouch!" Hayley cried, swatting her sister's hand, then rubbed the ouchy she'd made.

"Hey now—stop that," I said, shutting the door behind me. "What's going on? What are you talking about—what angel?" I asked, worried they may have overheard more than they should have. But I'd told no one about that angel, the one from my dream I'd seen hanging in that small back room in the lab. "Was this something you saw on TV?"

"No," Hayley said, glancing to her sister. "It was in my dream." She fiddled with the soft hem of her pajama top.

"What dream?" I asked, coming to sit on the bed next to them. I took Hayley's hands in mine.

Ryley followed by putting both of hers on top of mine. "She had a bad dream about an angel being hurt," Ryley said. "They cut off his wings. I had the same dream."

Okay whoa. *What the hell?* I wanted to scream, but I kept my composure as best as I could under the circumstances. Swallowing hard, I then said, "I have bad dreams too sometimes, and it helps to talk about them." I'd not shared all the details of mine with anyone, so I was feeling a bit hypocritical. I had intended to tell Redmond, but there never seemed to be a good time to share the horrific details. "Can you tell me—do you remember more of your dreams?"

"It was cold… and it smelled like that stuff you put on our cuts. Rubby-cohal," Hayley said.

"Do you mean rubbing alcohol?" I said, confident that's what she was trying for.

Hayley nodded.

"I was in a small room, and I could hear people talking," Ryley said then, continuing further with the particulars of the co-dream they had shared.

"*Don't tell Da,*" Hayley said in a whispered plea.

"Why?" I asked. Could they have seen the worry on their father's face, the worry on Leo and Den's faces, on my face, I wondered? "It's possible you dreamt about this because of all the new angels around and them having wings," I said, though my gut told me that hadn't been it. The dream they described was too much like my own, minus the little boy on the metal slab and the sick kids I'd seen. But the man, the *angel*, suspended from the ceiling and the white bones Ryley recalled, the ones they had both thought were *sticks* on a tray, had been scarily like my dream. "You girls aren't afraid of Leo and the others, are you?" I asked, knowing it was a stretch.

"Noooo," they both said.

"It feels… *good* when they are around," Ryley said, patting the top of my hands with hers.

"Okay great." I smiled in relief, debating on how much more I should tell them about these new angels, but knowing they felt unreserved empathy for all living things, I said, "One of their friends is missing."

"We know," Hayley said, surprising me with her response.

"How do you know?" I asked, switching to holding one of each of their hands in mine.

Hayley reached her now free hand over to hold Ryley's free one, completing the circle of handholding. Then they both shrugged. "We just do," Hayley said, smiling, glancing down at our clasped hands.

I knew how hard it was to explain my *feelings* relating to otherworldly things, and I could only imagine it would be even more difficult for them to articulate what they felt. They also sensed things differently than I did. They had other detecting abilities I didn't, and theirs were ever-changing and evolving. "Have you sensed anyone—other than Den and Leo and the others?"

They answered with head shakes.

"And no other children or adults like that little boy from your class—the one like Mum?" I asked, eager for the answer yet trying to keep the worry from my face.

They shook their heads again.

"Promise me, if you ever feel anything strange or new that you can't explain or maybe don't understand, or if you have another bad dream—you'll come tell me, okay?" I gave their hands a little squeeze for emphasis.

"We will," Hayley said, before the two of them leaned into me for a three-way hug.

"You girls ready for bed?" came Redmond's voice from Hayley's room. Summer and Snow came into the room then through the open bathroom door that joined the twins' bedrooms.

"Almost," Hayley squealed, jumping up and racing to the bathroom.

"Need to brush our teeth," Ryley added, in pursuit of her sister.

Redmond popped his head in around the door opening from the bathroom into the bedroom, spying me still sitting on Rylie's bed.

Summer had plopped down next to the bed at my feet, while Snow had followed the girls back into the bathroom.

"Everything okay?" he asked, his brows pinching.

I ran my hand over Summer's soft furry head and down her back. "Yup—all good, just some girl talk," I said, giving him a little impassive grin.

"Girl-talk, Da," Ryley spouted as she returned to her room. She gave Summer a hug, then crawled into her bed.

"Girl-talk," Hayley confirmed, calling from her adjoining bedroom.

"Okay-alright, I get it," he said, standing in the bathroom viewable from both bedrooms, hands up in surrender.

"Night, Mum," Hayley called out.

"Good niiight," I called back as Redmond disappeared into Hayley's room. Howls of laughter from both followed.

"Night-night, Mum," Ryley said in a sleepy voice, her eyes fluttering closed as I tucked her in.

"*Night-night*," I whispered, placing a gentle kiss on her forehead.

Shuddering awake from the nightmare and what should have been the oblivion of sleep, I turned my head to see the clock on my nightstand glowing 12:12 a.m.. Gruesome images swirled in my mind along with the unanswered questions that still lingered from my dream... *An elderly couple... being consoled next to an autopsy table... a body of what looks like a small child covered by a sheet atop it. A deep voice repeated the same words over and over.* "He was very week. We explained the treatments might not work—that they may put a strain on his little body. The risks were high, but it was his only chance." *The smell of antiseptic had shifted to the sour stench of sweat... that room, in the back of the lab like before....* This time there had been no medical staff, but I had known what would be there, hovering above the ground... *the figure hung in the same manner... the same tools were on the tray beside him on the rolling cart... and like before, his face was obscured in the darkness of the small room,* but I knew it was the same man... the same angel. I squeezed my eyes shut hoping to push away the memories, though one question remained. "*Is it you, Kris?*" I whispered into the night.

* * *

Somehow, I'd fallen back to sleep, devoid of any horrible images or dreams of any kind, that I could remember anyway. Redmond had said nothing about my wanting to go to New York after we'd tucked the girls in and still hadn't brought it up when we'd retired to bed, either. I had been grateful for that. And now, between the dream the girls had told me about, how I wasn't to tell their father, and the dream I had last night, my brain was in conflict about what I should and shouldn't tell him.

"Where are the girls?" Redmond asked as he poured his morning coffee. Based on his clothing, a grubby old t-shirt and worn cargo pants, he was up and ready to do yard work.

"Out back with the dogs," I said, running the charms on my necklace back and forth.

"How did you sleep?" he asked, leaning against the kitchen counter.

"About that…," I said, or I attempted to say, but Redmond cut me off.

"Darius is on his way over—asked him to help me with trimming the palm trees in the back. Then we're going over to the South Haven to help out there." He walked past where I stood next to the island and headed for the door to the downstairs.

"Can you ask Leo and Den to come over?" I asked, catching him before he descended the stairs.

He paused in the open doorway. "Why?"

I ran the charms to the left on my necklace. "I wanted to speak to them about Olivia's ask of bringing Rachel into the knowing. And…"

"And?" he asked, as though eager to get started on his outside chores.

"And, I… had a dream—a bad one. I need to tell them about it," I said, rushing out the last part.

He left the door ajar and walked back over to where I stood. "Tell me about the dream," he said, brushing the stray hairs that had escaped my ponytail back from my face. "Are you okay?"

I ran the charms to the right. "Can I tell you about it when they get here? I'm okay—just not feeling up to recapping it twice."

"Sure. I'll call them right now." Redmond snatched up his phone from the counter, kissed my cheek, then turned and went back through the open door to the lower level.

Redmond may have been eager to get outside to do his yardwork, but Leo and Den had been twice as eager to hear what I had to say, as they were at the front door within 15 minutes of Redmond's call to them, and just shy of Darius's arrival. To my amazement, it had been less daunting having to describe my dreams to them and their eager faces as they sat in my living room than I had originally expected.

"You never mentioned that part before," Redmond said with concern.

"I know—I didn't understand its relevance at the time. But with the *wing* thing—and dreaming about it a second time… I mean—what if the angel from my dreams is Kris? I should have said something—but the images were just so horrible. If I had said something sooner—maybe I could of…." I said, then paused.

"Could have what—prevented him from going missing?" Leo, finished for me.

"Maybe." I shrugged.

Den tilted his head. "We should have told you about our wings sooner perhaps—then you would have felt more comfortable sharing those parts of your first dream," Den suggested.

"I don't even want to say this out loud—but what if… what if Thaddeus has him?" Redmond asked, the pain of the idea reflected in his expression. "What if he finds out who he is—what he is? You have worked so hard to keep yourselves hidden from Thaddeus and his followers all this time."

"I hope you're not still considering going to New York City," Darius said then, glancing around at the others.

I stared down at my sock feet. "No. But now I need to go to the Norway location."

"What? No!" Redmond roared, shifting closer to me in his seat.

I stared up at him. "What if Kris is there—I'm the only one who could sense him?"

"*If* he's there," Leo said, drawing in an audible breath through his nose.

"We need to get into that lab. I need to find him," I directed at Leo.

Redmond stood then, staring down at me. "Then I'm going too."

"No—I need you to stay here with the girls," I said, cranking my neck to look up at him.

"Gabriel can watch them—they would love that," Redmond said, returning to sit beside me again. He kept his hands on his knees as though he were going to suddenly stand again.

"Please—I need *you* here." I placed a hand over his. "I'll explain later," I said, pleading. I would tell him about the bad dreams the girls had had, what they had been *feeling*, and how they somehow knew Kris was missing. He'd understand then why I wanted him here, needed him to stay here with them.

In the wake of my appeal to Redmond, Leo said, "Zach is still staking out the Sterope building in Norway as usual, watching to see if Thaddeus makes an appearance.

"I'll go with Lynn," Darius said, bolting up from his spot on the couch. "Staying here in *Guardian* mode—while she's halfway around the world, would just put me over the edge, anyway."

Leo studied Darius then did the same to me, then focused back on Darius. "I think I have the perfect cover for you both and the perfect disguises."

Chapter 4 

Over stale pasta and thawed, then reheated spaghetti sauce she'd found in the freezer, Jana had successfully convinced Geir that someone had to watch over this guy and that someone was *her*.

"I don't suppose your father has a gun stashed somewhere in the house—something you can use for protection, just in case?" Geir asked.

"I recall something," Jana said, leaving the table and heading to one of the back rooms. Returning, she said, "How about this?"

"Don't tell me all you have is a vintage Daisy Red Ryder BB-gun?" Geir said, amused, slapping a hand on his thigh.

"And a bottle of Copperhead BBs," she said, holding up the plastic bottle.

"Do you even know how to load one of those?" he countered.

"Are you really asking me that?" She cranked the pump lever, then smirked.

"Fine—at least load it up before I go. And promise me you'll call if he comes too, okay?"

"Yes—yes," she agreed. "And I'll call the authorities in the morning." At least to find out who the poor guy was, she thought to herself. "Now help me clean up these dishes before you go."

Jana waved from the front doorway as Geir backed out of the drive. Then she shut the door and leaned back against it. *"He might be right—maybe I am crazy,"* she muttered to herself. Before going back into the kitchen to finish drying the dishes, she took a quick pass by the living room to check on the slumbering giant. His breathing was heavy, as if in a deep sleep, and it had been over an hour since she had heard any uncomfortable *groans* from him.

Dishes dried and put away now, Jana went to her father's room to retrieve another blanket. This one was for her to use since she'd opted to sit by his side through the night. The last thing she wanted was for him to wake and wonder where the hell he was. She felt it would be a better comfort for both if she were there to ease any disorientation he may experience. Settling into the other armchair near the end of the sofa where his head lay, she unfolded the blanket and wrapped it over her lower body. She'd already swapped the bright overhead lights for the lamp on the side table next to her chair and had prepared herself for the long night with a hot cup of coffee. To keep her company, she'd selected a thick book on Icelandic wildlife from the bookshelf.

Jana bolted awake, knocking the barely read book off her lap to the floor. Glancing around, she swiftly recalled where she was, then bent forward to retrieve the book. Reaching for the book, she turned a glace to the sofa only to see the big, beautiful dark-blue eyes of the stranger staring back at her. "Oh-my-gosh!" she yelped, dropping the book to the floor again. "Sorry—I didn't know you were… awake."

He continued to stare at her wordlessly. During the night he must have shifted to laying on his side.

Evidently, she'd dozed off. "You must be wondering… a lot, actually," she said. She retrieved the book again, not sure what to say or explain first. He would have lots of questions, but so did she.

"Where am I?" he rasped out, his voice deep and gravelly.

Jana set the book on the side table, then turned slightly towards him. "You're safe. You're in my home—well, my father's home, actually."

With languid eyes, he searched her face as though for recognition, then his eyes traveled around the room, his body not moving.

"What's your name?" Jana asked.

His wary eyes returned to focus on her. "Who are you?" he said in response.

Before she could answer, he shifted, pushing himself up to a seated position, the blanket draping off one shoulder. She watched as he extended his long arms out in front of him, turning them right and left before glancing down and running his hands over the front of the sweatshirt he was wearing. Then he stared down at his bare feet.

"Are these my clothes?" he asked then, scowling.

"Yours were wet," Jana said, pointing to the armchair at the other end of the sofa.

"What?" he said, his glance shifting in the direction to where she pointed.

"Kristjana," she said, answering his previous question. She gave him a kind smile when he gazed back her way.

"What?" he questioned, swaying a little in his seat. He took another survey around the room, then his attention settled back on her.

"My name—you asked who I was. I'm Kristjana—Kristjana Stephansson," she explained. Wow, this guy wasn't quite all there, she realized. Still, she wasn't getting any risk of threat from him. "And those are my father's clothes you're wearing." She smiled again.

"Pleased to meet you, *Kris*," he responded, his focus on her wavering, eyes heavy lidded.

"Jana," she corrected, giving him the correct shortening of her given name.

He scrutinized the chair with his clothes, then glanced back at her. He opened his mouth to say something, but then his head tilted back, his eyes rolling to the whites as his body slumped to the side.

"Oh—shit!" Jana cried, leaping from her seat, reaching out to keep him from falling off the sofa. She settled his limp upper-body down to the sofa.

"Thank you, *Jana*," he mumbled, correcting his misstep before his eyes fluttered shut.

"Sir," Jana said, giving his shoulders a gentle shake. "Sir—can you hear me?" She leaned in, ear hovering near his mouth. "Breathing." She gave a sigh of relief but knew that if he had sustained a head injury, it was probably better to wake him. Concussions could be deadly if overlooked, and the only thing worse than having an unconscious stranger on your sofa would be having a dead one. "Sir," she said again, louder this time. She observed as his broad chest rose and fell with each slumbering breath. She stood then, unsure what to do. "Dammit." She hated the helplessness she was feeling. What was she thinking, letting Geir leave her here with this man, this stranger? She didn't have any medical experience. She leaned over and checked his breathing again, finding it strong and steady. He hadn't appeared to be in any pain when he'd come to, and now he seemed to be resting comfortably, she considered, trying to convince herself that he would be fine.

She checked the time on her cellphone, but it was still too early to call Geir. When she'd searched the online news last night, she'd not found any mention of someone gone missing. She'd thought to call the police as well to see if they had any reports of a missing person, but quickly realized that would have prompted all sorts of questions back at her.

Taking her phone with her to the kitchen, she then snatched up the now dry cigar label she'd left on the counter. Opening a browser on her phone, she searched for the brand name *His Majesty's Reserve* shown on the label. "Oh my," she gasped out. "This wrapper is from a cigar worth seven hundred and fifty American dollars." That's over a hundred thousand Icelandic Krona, she estimated. The website stated they were extremely hard to get. "Only for the rich."

Most public places in Iceland prohibited smoking. She didn't even know anyone who smoked cigarettes, let alone anyone who would or could pay such a dear price for a cigar. "Who are you?" she asked, staring through the kitchen's entrance to the unconscious man in the living room. She focused back on the label in her hand. Then instead of tossing it in the trash, she folded it in half and tucked it into the slot at the back of her cellphone case. Still unsure what to do next, she went with filling a large glass with water to bring back to the living room, in case he woke again. He'd be thirsty for sure and possibly hungry; however, she wasn't going to feed the poor guy any of the expired food she'd found in the cupboard.

Taking the glass of water with her, she strode back to the living room and set it down on the side table. Then she leaned in once again to check his breathing. *"Still alive,"* she said under her breath, stepping back and settling into the armchair again.

For the next hour she continued with reading the book she'd started from last night, flipping through the colourful pages of birds and animals, periodically checking to see that he was still breathing. At 5 a.m. she checked the online news on her phone for any updates regarding missing persons but still found nothing. As she went to set the phone on the side table, it rang in her hand. "Hi," she answered, before it could ring a second time and wake the man.

"Still alive, I see," Geir replied, his sarcasm emptying into her ear.

"Yes—both of us," she responded. "He woke up actually…."

"What—you promised you'd call," Geir interrupted.

"… Then he passed out again," she said, finishing her statement.

"Oh." There was a long pause, then Geir asked, "Did you call the police?"

"Not yet—but I checked several times online to see if there were any missing persons reported. I tried to wake him too—I was worried he might have a head injury based on how out of it he was during the few moments he was awake. He gave no sign he was in pain, and he's been sound asleep, mostly."

"Maybe you should get him to a hospital. I'll come back over."

"Uhhmm." She stared over at the sleeping man. "I'll call Doc Jonsson." Doctor Jonsson was an old friend of her father's and since he'd been retired for several years now, he wouldn't need to report anything to the authorities. He also wouldn't ask a long list of intrusive questions either.

"Okay. But I think you should call the police—let them take it from here."

"I'll keep you posted," she said, ignoring the police option, and hung up. She set down her phone in exchange for the book. Before diving back in, she took a last look at the man.

Jana sucked in a breath at seeing that his eyes were open again. "Hi," she said on the exhale.

He blinked but said nothing.

"Jana," she said, tapping her hand on her chest. "Do you remember me?"

He blinked slowly several more times.

"Are you in any pain?" she asked, frowning. "I can call a doctor if you need." She moved forward to the edge of her chair, readying herself should he need any assistance. "Do you need help to sit up?"

He shifted then as he'd done prior, maneuvering, and attempting a sitting position again.

"Let me help you," she said, standing, stepping forward to aid him back against the sofa.

"Thank you, Jana," he said then, stabilizing himself. He glanced over at his clothes still resting on the chair.

"They're still not dry." She sat down again. "Not exactly the type of garments you toss in the dryer." She grinned anxiously when he looked at her.

"I am fine. Quite comfortable in this." He peered down at the clothes he was wearing. Focusing back on her, he said, "How did I get here… to your father's home?"

"I found you out back… on the ground… you were passed out," she said, feeling suddenly uncomfortable in the comfy chair, remembering how she'd first used the cattle lift to move him. "I had a friend help me get you inside."

"Jana," he said, then paused as though searching for his words. "I find myself in need of your… facilities."

"Facilities?" she questioned, shrugging.

"May I use your bathroom?" he said then.

"Yes—of course," she said, embarrassed at not understanding him the first time. "Down the hall to the left." When he moved to get up off the sofa, she stood. "Do you need any help?"

"I think I can manage," he said with a little chuckle before pushing up to stand.

"Oh-my-god. I didn't mean—I was only. Grrr," she grumbled out.

He gave her a playful smile, then shuffled off down the hall.

Jana sat down, mortified, covering her face with her hands. Her mortification still hoverer as she watched him returned up the hall, strolling now on steadier legs.

Instead of returning to the sofa, he went to the chair that held his clothing. "You say these are mine," he said, more as a question than a statement as he lifted the suit jacket.

"Yes," she said, remaining where she was.

He turned to look at her. "Did you change my clothes?"

"No-no—Geir did that," she blurted, embarrassment flooding her as she noticed he was holding the navy-blue boxer. "I only provided the outfit you're wearing."

"Well, I don't recognize the suit—nor these." He tossed the boxers back on the chair. "I don't recognize this house or recall how I got here," he added, his voice growing with frustration. He ran both his hands through his hair. "In fact, I didn't recognize my face in the mirror just now." He dropped his arms and stared at her.

"You don't know who you are?" She grimaced. She hadn't expected that.

"Not a clue." He flailed his arm out in disbelief, then swayed unexpectedly.

Jana jumped up, rushing over to steady him. "Let's get you back on the sofa," she said, leading him over.

Settled again, he said, "Jana… tell me again how it was that you found me."

She sat back in her chair and turned to him. "Well, I was doing my usual review of the property," she began, moving on to explain the series of events that eventually led him from the backyard to him being swapped out of his suit and waking up here this morning. "You couldn't have been out there long. If you had, with wet clothing and no overcoat, you'd have been well on your way into hyperthermia." She felt a flush at the memory of him in only his boxers. She handed him the glass of cold water, though she was tempted to take a swig of it herself. "How are you feeling?"

He took the glass. He sipped first then chugged it down. Gasping, he said, "Other than some minor aches and pains, and this delightful layer of amnesia, I'd say I feel quite well, considering."

"Do you have any memories? Maybe where you live? Friends, family?" she asked. "Geir said that your suit is expensive—and you had the remnants of an extremely pricy cigar in the breast pocket of the suit jacket."

"Cigar?" His face scrunched as though disgusted. "I find that even more confusing."

"That makes two of us," Jana said. "I can't think of any reason for you to be out this far—away from town, or how you found this house. You can't even see it from the main road."

"Where am I exactly?" He leaned forward, elbows resting on his knees, hands still holding the empty glass.

Was this guy telling the truth, she wondered? It all just seemed a bit farfetched. "Egilsstadir," she said, giving the name of the area the house was in.

"Eglis-what?" He frowned.

"Egilsstadir. It's about 30 min from Seydisfjordur."

He tilted his head, giving her nothing but a stunned expression in response.

"Do you feel up to moving—getting out of here? I'd like to get you into town, bring you to my place—have the doctor look at you."

"I guess," he said, leaning back and shrugging.

"Let me grab a few more clothes for you before we leave. You're going to need some socks and boots. Do you know your shoe size?"

"Sixteen—wide," he tossed out. "Okay—not sure how I know that." The stunned expression returned to his handsome face.

"Lucky for you, my father had big feet, too."

Jana outfitted the lucky stranger with a pair of wool socks, work boots, and a warm winter coat she had previously packed away in her father's bedroom. After locking up the house, the two of them climbed into her father's truck.

Before backing out the drive, Jana made a quick call to Doc Jonsson, explaining that she had a friend who had been staying at her father's place, who was feeling under the weather, and that she was bringing him in to town now, and asked if he could stop over to give him a quick exam. She'd played down the actual events, stating that she'd found him unconscious, no apparent injuries, but that he'd been having some fairly serious brain fog. Fortunately for them the doc had said *yes* to meeting them at her apartment.

On the way, her new acquaintance sat in the passenger's seat glancing out the window at the not-much-to-see countryside the drive had to offer. It was mainly open terrain surrounded by mountains between the house and the small town where she lived. Occasionally, he glanced over at her with an unreadable smile coupled with the alternating expression of confusion and frustration. His still damp, unfamiliar suit was in a plastic garbage bag at his feet, while on his lap, he had a cardboard box packed with more unfamiliar clothing Jana had scrounged up for him.

She looked his way to see a hopeful smile on his face this time. He patted the side of the box. "Thank you for these—for your help."

"Of course," she said, refocusing on the road.

"We're going to your home, yes?"

"My apartment—it's above the bakery I own." She shot him another quick glance. He nodded before she turned back to the road.

"Uhhmm," he said, pulling her attention back. "What state are we in?"

"State?" Jana questioned, glancing back and forth between him and the road ahead. "Do you mean *region*? We're in Austurland—the Eastern Region."

His expression went far beyond that of confusion then, bordering on bewilderment and perhaps even a bit of frenzy.

"You do know you're in Iceland at least, right?" She pointed at the Route 93 road sign stating they still had another 10 kilometers before they reached Seydisfjordur.

"Iceland," he muttered, turning to stare out the passenger side window again.

They rode the rest of the way in silence.

Jana knew she probably should have called Geir, but she realized then that it was more urgent she have a doctor look at the man versus trying to explain to Geir why she still hadn't called the police. "This is it," she announced, pulling in behind the two story building. The left side of the building held her bakery and her small apartment above. The right side included a full-service restaurant with the owner's office above.

Jana waved out the window of the truck, on seeing Doc Jonsson waiting by the backdoor that led up to her apartment. "Góðan daginn," she said in greeting as she exited the truck, then switched from Icelandic to English, "Thank you for meeting us." She knew the doctor spoke both languages fluently, having to deal with the American tourists that frequented the town over the years. "Doctor Jonsson, this is my friend… *Kisur*," she said, faltering for a name and pulling something from the wilderness book she'd just read.

"Like the bird?" Doc Jonsson questioned.

Jana's *friend* glanced at her then shrugged and smiled at the doctor.

"Yes—it's just a nickname I call him by," she laughed out. Kisur was the slang word used for Kittiwakes, birds that apparently nested on the cliffs here, and considering she'd thought the man had wings, it was the best she could do under pressure. Flustered, she unlocked and pulled open the door to the stairwell leading to her apartment.

"Okay, Kisur, let us get upstairs and have a look at you," Doc Jonsson said, extending a hand for us to go first.

His patient nodded and proceeded up the stairs.

In the small living room in Jana's apartment, the doctor had his patient take off his coat and sit on the sofa for the examination. "Have you been having any headaches or nausea?" he asked, removing a stethoscope from the little black bag he had brought with him.

"No," the accommodating patient said.

Putting the ends of the apparatus in his ears, the doctor said, "Breathe in and out for me." He listened, checking breath and heart sounds. Removing the stethoscope from his ears, he then swapped it out for a special penlight and began checking Kisur's eyes and then inner ears. "Any dizziness or ringing in the ears?"

"No," he said again.

"Sleepiness or excess fatigue?" The doctor palpated under the patient's jaw and along his neck.

When the patient gave Jana a sideways look, she answered, "He slept quite a bit in the last twenty-four hours."

"Did you find any vomit near where you found him unconscious?"

"No," she said, responding for him this time. "His main issue has been the memory problems."

"Okay, other than the memory loss and foggy brain, you don't have any other symptoms of a concussion," the doctor stated, gently tilting his patient's head forward and checking behind his ears. "And no battle's signs either."

"Battle signs?" Jana questioned.

"It is a much more serious condition. Shows up as a bruise indicating a fracture at the bottom on the scull. Sometimes showing up as bruising around the eyes too—which you have neither. You see this kind of fracture from a serious fall or car accident, often in sports-related injuries or even whiplash." He put his penlight back in the bag. "I can't say what's causing the amnesia. You seem to be in exceptional health, minus the brain haze. You may have hit your head when you passed out—or passed out because of hitting your head. Either way, I don't see any urgent concerns. But Jana, monitor him, watch for any clear fluid draining from the ears or nose—it's indicative of brain trauma."

"Will do," she said, glancing from doctor to patient.

"Loss of memory like this normally passes in a day or two, but you should get yourself formally assessed at the hospital if things persist or you experience any of the symptoms I asked about," he advised his patient. "The hospital is better equipped to check for things like brain damage or infection."

"I'll watch him and take him to the hospital over in the next town in the morning if things don't get better." She smiled appreciatively at the doctor. "Thank you for coming over—aaaand before I needed to open the bakery," she said as the doctor headed for the apartment entrance.

Glancing back, he said, "Oh, can you save me a nice slice of your Skúffukaka? I'll circle round after my morning walk." He turned then to face the patient on the sofa. "I love a piece of her chocolate cake with my coffee. If you haven't—you should try it." He winked and grabbed up his coat from the hooks on the wall near the doorway, then he went off down the stairs that led out the back entrance.

"Scuff cake?" Kisur, the birdman, questioned.

"Skúffukaka she corrected with a teasing smile. It's a traditional Icelandic chocolate cake with a toasted coconut frosting—and it's one of my best sellers." She checked the time on her phone. "Will you be okay while I take a quick shower? I need to get ready and open the bakery."

"Yes, I'll be fine," he said, scanning the tiny apartment.

"You must be hungry—help yourself to whatever food is in the fridge," she said before hurrying off up the hall and shutting the bathroom door.

In the shower she tried desperately not to think about the gorgeous man in her apartment. Out of the shower and now dressed, she secured her still damp hair up in a clip. As she left her bedroom, her cellphone rang. It was Geir. "Hey, I'll call you later. I have to go down and open the bakery," she said, slipping her feet into the sneakers she wore for work.

"Where is he? Did you leave him at your father's house?"

"No."

"Wait—is he at your place?" Geir's voice rose with concern.

Jana grabbed up her keys. "Yes, I had to get him into town to see Doc Jonsson."

"Where is he now?"

"Having a shower. Look—I must get going," she said, taking the interior stairs that led down to the office inside the bakery. "I'll call you later." She hung up, then gazed back up the stairs to where a beautiful man was naked and showering in her apartment. Refocusing, she turned away and preceded through the office to the bakery.

As the Sunday opening rush dissipated, the bell over the door jingled again. Jana spied a remarkably gorgeous, freshly groomed gentleman enter through the front door of the shop. He wore a pair of faded blue jeans, and a familiar navy coloured sweater over a matching turtleneck in the same shade, all of which flattered the deep-blue of his stunning eyes. Walking over to meet the man, Jana smiled admiringly and then said, "That colour looks great on you—but you're going to need something other than my father's old-man clothes."

Chapter 5 

The Hotel Norge by Scandic, Monday AM, January 10th, Bergen, Norway

I'd finally been able to persuade Redmond to let me do the trip to Norway without him. He had asked, *"Why couldn't Gabriel just check things out? What about one of the other Archangels?"* I'd told him he already knew why Gabriel couldn't get involved—not directly, and it was the same for the others. He'd questioned why Gabriel couldn't at least be there with me—watching out in case something happened, and I'd reminded him that Gabriel couldn't intervene, even if he wanted to. For whatever reason, he was allowed to protect my family—his family, but he was barred from getting involved in the other angel business. I didn't know all the rules, but like with going into the lab in Ottawa, Gabriel wasn't able to be there either, I'd reminded Redmond. He had promptly reminded me back with, *"But I was there."* I told him that I would rather Gabriel remain there with him and the girls since I wouldn't be around to sense any unwanted visitors. It had been a no-win discussion until I told him what the twins had said about their bad dreams. It was then that he'd given me his reluctant blessing to go without him.

The twins had known something was up too, their awareness was getting sharper. When they'd question my leaving, Gabriel had done his best to distract them with the idea of getting some new school stuff. But Redmond's acceptance came mainly because Darius was going to be there, and he was like a fire alarm for any immediate danger regarding my wellbeing. Before I'd boarded the plane, to further ease him, I'd given Redmond one last thought on the situation, telling him that as far as we knew, Thaddeus had no clue who I was, only that I existed. And that if he did, the sicko would have already sent someone to find me. Leo had also promised to keep Redmond posted every step of the way, to let him know when we had completed our task, and this seemed to have provided him with the further security he had needed.

Within 24 hours of me telling Leo all about my dreams, he had me on a flight to Norway with my Guardian in tow. And less than 9 hours after that, 2 p.m. Florida time, 11 p.m. Norway time, we'd checked into the hotel Leo had booked for us.

The Hotel Norge by Scandic was one of Bergen's most prominent hotels and was just under 20 minutes from the airport. Zach had been waiting for us at the airport and had driven us to the hotel, which had given me enough time to put on the short dark wig and dark glasses, along with a long overcoat for the first part of my disguise. We'd traveled under our regular names and passports, simply because we didn't require visas to go to Norway and with what we were about to do, no one would be tracking our real names. However, once at the hotel, I'd checked in under the false identity Leo had created for me. Thus, creating a trail linked to this fictional woman, in case anyone from the facility we were visiting had researched the name.

Leo had provided us the fake IDs we would need, ones Marq had designed for us. The name he had chosen for Darius was one that was overly common and easily forgotten. Mine, on the other hand, *Brina Hagen*, the last name he'd chosen purposely lent focus on several of the wealthiest families in Norway. Leo had not stated that this Brina person I was playing, was actually related to these wealthy people, although it had been implied during his call when he'd set up the meeting with the person in charge of the facility. He'd used an untraceable number, of course, and he'd stated that *Ms. Hagen* would be in the area and had requested a schedule time to speak to someone about her son and his future treatment needs. Leo had informed the person that I, *Brina*, was from a very prestigious family, a cousin whose child needed their services. Money talks, or a wealthy last name, it seems, because Leo had gotten us the appointment which would get me in the door, and if all went as planned, I'd be granted a tour of the facility.

Even though Zach had a residence in Norway, Leo had the three of us staying together in an extra-large luxury suite on one of the upper floors to provide us the most room, and which also gave the impression of wealth while providing security. The hotel had a spa with a pool and various meeting rooms, all of which wouldn't be needed. There were several places to eat, from a simple cup of coffee to their award-winning culinary meals, but all I had cared about was if I could get room service or not. And I could. Darius had received our food at the door, while I'd hid in the bedroom section of the suite. I'd ordered a traditional Lapskaus stew, made with chicken, onions, potatoes, carrots, and celery, hoping it would provide me the sustenance I needed, which it did. And as I'd eaten, I had also been comforted by its familiarity to something similar my mother used to make. After eating and before making an attempt to sleep, I'd called to Redmond to check on how he and the twins were doing. He had assured me they seemed fine, that they had even helped him with making pizza for dinner, though they were full of questions about where I had gone and when I'd be back. He had been sweet on the phone, exchanging *I love yous* with me, but I'd known he still worried about my being here without him.

Sleep having evaded me the night prior, I had hoped to get some shuteye before I had to be up and ready to go. But no such luck. I'd been up and down the entire night partially because of the excitement I'd been feeling about the trip and the sense of purpose it gave me, but also because of the whole time change thing. Our meeting was scheduled for 10 a.m., which for me was 4 a.m. Florida time. Plus, it didn't help that Norway in winter experiences a period called *polar nights,* where the sun doesn't rise above the horizon, suffering 24 hours of dark. I'd read in the hotel's *Places to See* brochure that some areas of Norway there was no sun at all in December and early January, no daylight, only a twilight around noon with the moon and snow creating the effect. Talk about messing with your body-clock. And despite the sleep deprivation, right now I needed to get my act together, and that *act* included the disguise Leo had provided.

We'd gone over the plan with Leo and rehearsed the story I was to go by via satellite phone on the long plane ride here. And though the costume he'd provided was excellent, it was Zach who brilliantly helped me get into it. He'd suggested I try channeling *Virginia Hall*, who he informed me was an American spy in the 1940s, and part of the CIA from 1951 to 1966, also known as 'The Limping Lady', having lost part of her leg in a hunting accident. I'd never heard of the woman, but I incorporated a slight limp to go along with the other disfiguring prosthetics that were part of my ruse. As part of the disguise, I wore the same shoulder length mousey brown wig, fashionable but plain, and huge high-end stylish sunglasses. Zack had placed a fake scar on my face that stretched from my right eyebrow across my right eyelid, which I had to keep closed, and down across my nose to my left cheek ending with disfiguring the corner of my mouth. I also had on one dark brown contact lens in my open eye. For my wardrobe, Leo had picked for me to wear an haute couture yet plain long dark-grey shift dress, long chic black boots, and a long designer brand overcoat to hide my body, aiding in it being nondescript. In addition to the facial scar, Zach had also supplied me with long leather gloves to cover my *scarred* hands until the opportunity to expose them was provided.

Functioning as my bodyguards and almost a matching set, Zach the second largest of The Guards, with his light blond brush-cut style hair and my big Guardian Darius echoing him with short cut strawberry blond hair, dressed in expensive dark suits and matrix style sunglasses. Both wore old-school coil earpieces to give the facility onlookers a false impression for the form of communication they were using, but in reality they had high-tech hidden earpieces in their other ears. All three of us had them, such that we could communicate, if need be, and so Leo could listen in.

Darius sat in the back with me as Zach drove us to the Sterope building in the same expensive black sedan he'd picked us up from the airport in, one he'd procured from a local contact. The plan was that Zach would wait by the car, since he could sense any danger to do with fire or explosives both natural and manmade, while Darius would go in with me since he could sense when I personally might be in potential danger. Either way, we had full communication with our sophisticated earpieces.

Through the main entrance, Darius announced my arrival to the receptionist providing our IDs and the address of where we were staying. Then he returned to standing at my back or *at my six* like Zach had instructed him. Darius pretended to check his fake earpiece while actually testing the real one. "Roger that," he said in response to Zach's, *"Can you hear me?"*

As I stood waiting in front of the reception desk, something, a feeling sharper than static electricity, ran the back length of both my arms. I swiveled my head to the left and then to the right, where I spotted a statuesque, strikingly handsome yet militant looking man, *Earthbound*, approaching the desk.

He had dark-red hair cut in a tight brush cut, with eyebrows that matched. His eyes were green, unnaturally so, and to the world it would appear he was wearing contacts, but to me, I knew the brilliant green of his eyes was all natural—or supernatural as it were. He dressed in a dark green almost black suit over a deep green dress shirt and tie, all of which were clearly well made, yet he wore it more like a uniform than for fashion. Other than his face and neck, his hands, the nails cut short and buffed, were the only other skin that was exposed. I found the differences between the female Earthbound Mac had described from the Ottawa location and this massive male shockingly in contrast, but I did my best to keep my facial expression neutral.

"Mrs. Hagen," he said in acknowledgment. "I am Kendrick." He gave a head-tilt and the slightest chin-nod in place of a hello, reminiscent of something I'd seen in an old black and white movie involving *Nazis*, the imagery making me nauseous and giving me the creeps.

Stowing my sense of disgust, I responded with a firm, "Ms. Hagen," correcting him.

He sucked in a sharp breath through widened nostrils, obviously offended at being spoken to this way, and from such a trivial human such as me. Clearly checking himself, he forced the smallest of smiles and then said, "Of course. *Ms.* Hegen. Please follow me." Then he turned stiffly on his heals to lead the way.

I followed without a word, Darius tight behind me, though I slowed the procession down some because of my *limp*. Interestingly, we weren't required to leave our cellphones at the desk, as had been the case previously at the Ottawa location. But it wouldn't have mattered since neither of us were carrying cellphones to hand over. It was just another way to avoid being tracked, since Zach wasn't sure of what surveillance methods they were using at this location.

"You're in," came Zach's voice in my earpiece.

I caught up with the big redhead when he stopped at a door in the long hall. Upon opening the door, he led me into a sparsely decorated office with two guest chairs opposite a desk and a larger chair. The desk itself was bare except for a fancy multi-button phone attached to a landline. There were no other items in the room, no art, no plants, and no windows, the feeling of it more like an interrogation space and less like a client meeting room.

"Please wait outside," I said to Darius, my instructions to him part of our plan. I needed to be alone to show that what I was going to say required the utmost privacy.

Darius did as I instructed, the both of us receiving the confirmation *"check"* from Zach. Darius nodded at me, then closed the door, leaving me alone with the sternly mannered Earthbound.

I took the chair closest to the door. "Let's not dilly-dally with pleasantries—I'm here for one reason, my son," I said, before Kendrick could sit down. I could do stern too.

"I notice you don't have a Norwegian accent," Kendrick said, curious, ignoring my insistence.

Surprised by the comment, I pushed up my sunglasses, giving myself more time on how to respond. "I was raised in Canada. Only later did I join my relatives here...," I said, only to be cut off when Kendrick raised his big hand to stop me.

Lowering his hand, he picked up the handset for the phone, then hit a button and began speaking in what I assume must be Norwegian. Done with whatever he had urgently needed to speak with someone about, he hung up, though his eyes remained centered on the phone.

I opened my mouth to speak, only to be shut down by his raised hand again, his eyes still on the phone.

The phone rang then, and he answered it. "Okay," he said in response to whatever the other person had said. Then he lowered the handset to its cradle.

"What was that about?" I asked, attempting to gain back control of this meeting. Despite the electrical current like sensation running the length of my arms, I couldn't appear weak.

"I was just checking on your accommodation," he said, passing the fingertips of his right hand over his right eyebrow. "Confirmation as to where you are staying while you are here." He jutted out his chin.

That statement wasn't a shock, though I hadn't expected he would check while I was sitting there.

"I assumed that would have been taken care of the minute we checked into the hotel," Zach stated, sharing my feelings on the comment. *"Take control back,"* Zach guided then.

"Look it," I said, using my best bitch tone. "Obviously, you know now that I am not staying with family." I paused long enough for him to grasp my words, but not long enough for him to respond. "The fact is—I'm not a cousin, and though my father loved my mother, his *wife*— on the other hand—did not. To the outside world, I am a distant cousin, but I am my father's daughter to our inner circle."

"Ms. Hagen," he began, but this time I cut him off.

"Kendrick—is it?" I said, dominating the conversation, sitting forward in my chair. "I told you I was here for my son, when in fact I am here for *both* my sons."

Kendrick ran his fingers across his brow again, evidently trying to keep his cool, the action clearly a nervous tell.

As the massive Seraph stared back at me, I held his attention by removing my gloves. Free of them and the burn marks Zach had cleverly affixed to the backs of my hands now exposed, I slowly reached into my overly expensive Burka handbag. With his silent interest now fixed on me, I retrieved two photos, handing the first across the desk to him.

He stared at my hands and then at the photo. The one I had given him showed two young boys standing near a swimming pool, arms wrapped around each other. Twins. One healthy and one disfigured similarly to Taylor.

"Story time," came Zach's voice in my ear again.

As Kendrick gawked at the photo, I explained that their birth-father was a cruel man and was no longer in their lives. Then I removed my large sunglasses to push home his cruelty. "As you can understand—I don't get out much," I said, the tragic scar on my face glaringly visible now that my dark glasses were off. "The details of my life are very much a secret. Their father was never seen again after the… *unpleasant* incident." I straightened in my chair and replaced my glasses. "It was soon after that I learned I was pregnant. It was later, after my mother's passing, that my family brought me to Norway. I was provided a private physician for the delivery and for the care of my sons—mainly the one, although my other healthier son suffers from asthma." Kendrick frowned at the photo. When he didn't interrupt, I went on. "They are home tutored and are inseparable. They are 10 years old now, though my one son becomes weaker with each passing day. I feel strongly if I don't do something to help him—I could lose them both. So, what I want from you is to see your facility. I need to make sure this is the right place for them." I leaned back in my chair.

"Verily, they are in need of our services," Kendrick said then, his voice softening ever so slightly.

Leaning forward again, I said, "If my family knew I was here—they would be furious. They think I'm at an appointment with a plastic surgeon. I'm beyond help myself, but if I returned to them with a promising solution—a treatment for my sons, they couldn't refuse me the option to bring them here."

"Unfortunately, we do not give tours of our facilities without proper justification and approval," Kendrick said, drawing a single finger across his eyebrow. "But before you depart, I can provide you with a list of the various conditions and treatments we facilitate here at this location."

"Oh really?" I challenged, then slid the second photo across the desk to him, this one the back view of both boys.

Kendrick stared at the photo, his eyes bulging, although he was swift to compose himself and his expression. "They have… matching… *birthmarks,*" he said, evidently recognizing the snowflake markings.

I grinned, triumphant. "Yes, they've been there since birth—oddly beautiful, in my opinion."

"Yes." Kendrick continued to glare at the photos.

I reached forward to take the photo evidence back.

"May I keep them—for their files?" he asked, glancing between the two photos.

"I'm afraid I must refuse," I said, leaning forward, snatching both from his hands. "These are the only photos I keep of them. Other than the ones from their birth, those I keep in my private quarters." I tucked the photos back in my bag. "As far as the world knows, I only have one son—and my family wishes to keep it that way. To them, reputation is everything. Perfect bloodlines, as it were."

"Let me see what I can do," he said, abruptly getting up from his chair. "Excuse me while I check on something."

My stomach grumbled as he passed where I sat.

Halting, he said, "Are you in need of something to eat?"

"No, thank you—the tour is all I need," I said, surprised he had heard that.

When the office door closed, I said, "Darius, keep an eye on him."

"Well done, Lynn," Zach praised through my earpiece.

The exhilaration I was feeling was through the roof, but the sharp sensations at this Earthbound's presence had me wanting to crawl out of my skin.

"He's on a cellphone," came Darius's response into my ear. *"I can't hear what he is saying, but he seems excited, animated even in his communications."*

"The photos definitely sparked his interest," I confirmed. Leo had Marq create the fake photos of the fictitious boys using the same graphic software he'd used for the fake IDs. Marq was quite the artist.

"He's off the call—looks like he's trying to rein in his composure. He's coming back this way," Darius informed us.

Opening the door, Kendrick announced, "I have secured approval for a tour."

"Jackpot," Zach's voice cheered into my ear.

I stood, replacing the long gloves over my scared hands. Saying nothing, I pushed my oversized sunglasses further up on my nose and then limped towards the open door.

"You'll need to leave your cellphones at the front desk," Kendrick informed us.

Ah, and there it was. "We don't carry them—too easily tracked," I explained. "I like my privacy."

With a nod, Kendrick then led us to the left and away from the way we'd come in through the lobby and main entrance.

Unlike the Ottawa location, this building was only one story, and as we traversed the long hallway, we were shown how this floor was divided up into a huge lab filled with various complicated looking medical equipment, a short row of cubical offices, and one substantial main treatment room with several hospital style beds and a single surgical space just off the treatment area.

"We don't have any patients staying with us, as there are only day treatments being done at the moment," Kendrick said, waving a hand over to where a young girl was having her blood drawn. I couldn't tell if she was a halfling or not, though I could see by the pallor of her skin and frailness of body that she was not well.

On the far side of the treatment area, as we were directed to another hallway which appeared to lead back to the front lobby, I noticed something odd… an elevator. I slowed my limping pace.

"What's wrong?" Darius asked from behind me.

"Elevator," I murmured. With the building being only one story, I made a quick survey of the elevator as we passed it. The only option being a down arrow, I assumed it must descend to another one of those lower private labs we'd found beneath the greenhouse at the Ottawa location. Stopping, I focused back the other way down the hall, where I saw a set of double doors at the far end. *"There's more to this building,"* I said in a lowered voice. Something hadn't been right about the dimensions of this place and the areas we'd been shown.

"Leo tried to get floor plans—but that was a no-go," Zach stated.

Then, to my disbelief, when I peered back up the hall towards where Kendrick had gone, I spied a large white-winged butterfly landing atop a framed photo of some Norwegian landscape. *"Butterfly,"* I whispered, pointing at it as I continued with limping forward. The butterfly was like the white ones I'd seen back home in the yard, though this one had dark grey along the outer edges and was almost identical to the ones I'd witnessed in the Celaeno building's greenhouse. "Do you have a greenhouse?" I asked as we reached the front desk.

Neither the receptionist nor Kendrick responded to my question. It wasn't until we passed the desk into the lobby space that Kendrick turned and said, "No—why?" He stared down at me as if aiming to intimidate.

"No reason," I said, shrugging and giving a cool smile. I kept my composure despite the tiny hairs on my arms prickling due to my proximity to him. This sensation was linked solely to him, as I had sensed no other Seraphim on the premises during our brief tour.

"When can we expect the boys?" Kendrick asked then, blocking the way to the exit. He had a binder in his hands of what I presumed was the list of treatments he had offered while in the *interrogation* room.

In a display of irritation, I hiked my purse up on my shoulder. "As I explained earlier, it will take some convincing of my family to allow me to bring them here," I stated, my voice low in keeping with the *secrecy* of things.

Kendrick glanced over to the reception desk, then back at me and asked, "May I have your contact information then—for our records? To make ready for your sons?"

It was a poor attempt to gain my favor, and I tightened my lips to show further annoyance. "I have *your* name. Someone will contact you if I am able to secure consent."

In a last attempt at currying my favor, he said, "Please, perhaps the names of the boys? To secure a place for their treatment." That's when he handed over the binder. "My—our staff will be most eager to meet them, I'm sure." He gave a stiff tilt of his head to one side, the action refreshing my previous nausea.

"He's a persistent one—I'll give him that," came Zach's voice, mirroring my precise feelings. *"Time to get out of there."*

This suck-up was not interested in helping *my sons*. He was merely thrilled at the opportunity to please his boss, Thaddeus. I took the binder but gave no answer as I navigated myself around his enormous body and limped towards the exit, Darius still at my back. A security guard started forward in our direction, but Darius put up a hand as though to say, *don't come any closer*. The guard stopped in his tracks, allowing me to be escorted out of the building by Darius, *my* personal security. Without turning back, we continued to our waiting car and Zach.

We returned to the hotel and immediately finished packing our bags. And just in case someone had followed us back to the hotel, Darius and Zach left with the car and most of the luggage while I stayed to get into my next disguise.

For this one, I donned a long red wig along with a lengthy forest-green wool cloak over my own clothing of dark jeans, and a black tunic. The cloak had an attached scarf that I used to cover the lower part of my face, though I had left my hands uncovered and the sleeves of my tunic pushed up, revealing *no* scares. The disguise covered me enough that I wouldn't be identifiable as myself, though the outfit was meant to be noticed and showing in contrast to that of my Brina disguise.

Dragging my small rolling carry-on with me, I left the suite and proceeded down the elevator to the next floor. Then I used the stairs for the rest of the way down, then proceeded out the front. Prior to leaving the suite, I'd called down to have the concierge arrange a car to take me to the airport, and as I pushed through the main doors, I saw that it was waiting for me out front.

I was to meet up with Darius back in the charter area for private flights, while Zach disposed of our other disguises and took care of the car we'd used. The plan had been simply for me to convey if I had detected Kris, to indicate if he was being held at that location. If I had, then Leo and the others would devise a plan to extract him. But I hadn't found Kris, and I had detected no other Earthbound. It was clear in the dialog on the call Zach had made to Leo, that they were disappointed we hadn't located Kris. I'd had mixed feelings about finding him. Not that I didn't want to find him, it was more about what condition we might find him in. I cringed, recalling again the images from my dreams.

As the car pulled into the airport, I swiftly took off my wig and stuffed it into my carry-on bag. Then I sent Redmond a quick text message with a simple, *Coming home.*

Frankly, despite the disappointment of not sensing Kris, I was feeling very Mata Hari-esque and enjoying it. Darius was grinning proudly at me when I settled myself into the seat next to him on the plane. He was obviously pleased I was again in his safe hands, and we were on our way to safer pastures, so to speak. Before I could say anything to him, he handed me a clear plastic tote full of airport snacks. I took the snacks and smiled back at him, and not because of the food. I was hungry, yes, but that wasn't it. The truth being that this had been a stealthy caper we'd just pulled off, and as a result, I was riding a pretty spectacular high.

Chapter 6 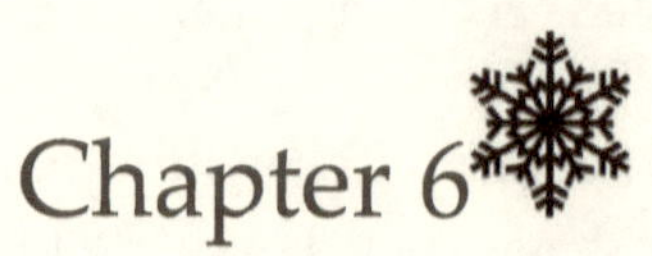

Merope Building, Tuesday AM, January 11th, New York City

Thaddeus had designed and built each of his buildings equipped with both a medical treatment area and a morgue. He had an on-call coroner for each, and who he compensated well for their discretion and silence, which was especially beneficial for when treatments didn't go as planned. Thaddeus also found it beneficial not having to transport bodies to other medical facility not controlled by his staff.

Thaddeus drew back the top part of the sheet to reveal just the face of his latest casualty. "There is nothing more tragic than the loss of a child," Thaddeus stated, placing his right hand over his heart. *The genuine tragedy is mine for not being able to extend my testing on this abomination. Consoling families, or grandparents in this case, over the loss of their progeny is an element of the overall deception I detest the most. But a necessary evil required to justifying a means to an end.*

"We just had such high hopes your treatments would help him," the old woman said, glancing down at the greying face of her grandson.

"We had the same hopes," Thaddeus said. "But he was already so weak by the time you brought him to us, I'm afraid." *I would have had more time for my testing had you brought him sooner. Idiots.*

The old couple nodded, as Thaddeus covered the exposed face of the boy.

"Please know that our kind and compassionate staff are here for you, to aid you with any or all the service arrangements or preparations. There are many practical details to decide upon, but more importantly are your emotional needs. No two people are alike nor any two families, and we understand how vital it is to address your loved one's wishes, their choice of preparation." *What a lie. You humans are all the same. Weak.* "While honoring your loved one is our highest priority, we also want to help you through this difficult time. We are affiliated with a wide range of resources that are provided to you as part of our services." *This is the only part of this time-consuming process I agree with—handing you off to someone else.*

"That is much appreciated," the old man said. "You and your team have been so great—and we know you did your very best to help our grandson."

"In *personally* reviewing your paperwork, I found your grandson wished to be laid to rest next to his mother. This is a beautiful wish." *I wish this were over already.*

"Yes. Our daughter chose cremation and internment at our family's plot back home, and her son asked for the same."

"I will call down for you to have preparations addressed with the utmost care and responsiveness, such that you may bring your grandson home to his mother without delay." *Cremation all the way—burn them all, I say.* Thaddeus hit a silent call button on the wall.

Within moments, one of the facility's female care staff joined them.

Thaddeus shifted then, positioning himself on the opposite side of the autopsy table from the old couple. He knew better than to remain at their side, since part of human grief often involved the need for physical contact in the form of a handshake, or even worse, a hug.

"Please allow me to escort you both to a quiet gentler space for our conversation on the next steps," the staffer offered, further allowing Thaddeus to step back, literally, and figuratively.

"God bless," the old woman said as the staffer guided them out of the morgue.

Thaddeus forced a sympathetic smile. *"Ha—right. You have no idea,"* Thaddeus said under his breath, followed by a guffaw. "Now, back to business." Thaddeus picked up the handset from the phone on the desk next to the autopsy slab and dialed an extension. This phone, like the others in the facility, were for internal communication only with no outside access. "Marcus, make the arrangements," Thaddeus said into the phone.

"What size dog do we need?" Marcus asked in response.

"A forty pounder," he said. "Thirty-five will do, if you can't get the first." Thaddeus twisted the phone cord around his index finger.

"I'll send someone to the local shelter. And we'll use the same cremation center as the last time."

"Wonderful," Thaddeus said. It was always so much better when cremation was the choice, because it meant he could keep the body, well, the bones, the spine and scapula to be precise, since those were the pieces that most interested him post-mortem. His staff would then provide the family with a sealed container of their choosing for the interment, but instead of the deceased, they were given the ashes of an unwanted canine. This allowed for Thaddeus to have the bones of this halfling sent to his private lab in Ottawa. He had read in one of the many serial killer novels he owned, how one clever killer kept parts of his victim's as trophies, such that he could revisit them and relive the thrill of his time with them. Thaddeus had done the same with the bones of his victims with keeping them in cabinet drawers, locked away only for his viewing and enjoyment. "I need to reassign this task of speaking with the families to someone else. I find it draining to maintain the façade," he added.

"You know, it's the personal touch that gets us such wonderful reviews and feedback and keeps any suspicious naysayers away— which allows you to keep doing what you so love to do."

"True. Though I wish I could find the answers I seek. These small humans no longer provide me with what I require. I need to find older specimens, those who have come of age." Thaddeus uncoiled the phone cord from around his finger, watching as the blood and circulation returned.

"I have another matter that we need to discuss," Marcus said.

"Later," Thaddeus said, hanging up by returning the handset to the phone cradle.

In his private quarters, Thaddeus hunted through the fridge and cupboards for something to feed his growing hunger. Nothing interested him and he longed for the personal chef on speed-dial and all the other creature comforts of his Celaeno residence. This location was not as well equipped, and he found it too confining with being half the size of his home-base in Ottawa. The tiny condo served his basic needs for the short time periods spent in it, but he needed to get back to Ottawa, plus he missed Brutus. "Attendant, call Amahle," he said, shutting the fridge after searching its confines a second time.

"I have an update from the Sterope facility in Norway," Amahle said upon answering.

"That can wait—how is Brutus?" Thaddeus redirected.

"He is doing wonderfully—he just had his morning meal and is now on his stand in your wardrobe watching the world go by."

"How is his colour?" Thaddeus opened the snack pantry next to the fridge.

"He is his fabulous amethyst purple colour, as always."

"Is that music I hear in the background?" He shut the pantry door, then pulled a random bag from the Harry & David Premium Gourmet snack gift box that had been left for him on the counter.

"Why, yes, it is. I've procured a copy of a live recording of his favorite music for him to listen to, since I will be in meetings most of the morning."

"Nicely done," Thaddeus said, opening the sesame sticks snack package. Praise was not something he gave often, practically never, but for his Brutus he would grant Amahle this. "What is the update?" Thaddeus went and sat on his massive bed, then laid back.

"Kendrick says he is still waiting to hear from that woman regarding her sons."

"That's not an update." Thaddeus sniffed the contents of the bag. Scrunching his nose, he set the bag on the bedside table.

"Kendrick noted the secrecy aspect of her visit as most important, as was the militant way her bodyguard had functioned. He respected her for that."

"Respect for humans is a waste of time." Thaddeus checked the time on his vintage Patek Philippe pocket watch. "This call is a waste of my time. I'll speak to him myself," he said, then hung up.

"Attendant, call Kendrick.

"Sir!" Kendrick answered.

"Tell me you have secured my new patients."

"Not yet, sir."

Thaddeus let out an impatient breath.

"But I took it upon myself to personally contact the family. I've spoken with several of their representatives, however they all stated they did not know the person I was inquiring about. When I suggested she may be a distant cousin, the consensus was that they had many of those. Clearly, the woman had been accurate regarding the secrecy around her existence and her sons," Kendrick confirmed.

"Yes." Thaddeus brought his hands to the sides of his head and massaged his temples.

"It was clear from the photos that those two were halflings."

"Obviously, the woman is not Seraphim."

"No, in fact, she was hideous, both in character and appearance."

"And the father?" Thaddeus massaged his forehead, the stress over this conversation building.

"She never mentioned his name—only stated they are not in contact. I'm guessing he doesn't know of the offspring."

"Why did you not get more information? Her contact information. More details on the father," he spat out.

"I tried, sir. There was no swaying her. Well, not with her bodyguards waiting on her."

"You had her alone, did you not?" Thaddeus questioned.

"Yes, but...."

"Wait, didn't you report the woman toured the facility with a single bodyguard?"

"Yes, she did. She had one with her and one waiting by the car. The one with her was big, but the one who stood by the car was massive, larger than me even."

"Kendrick... do what you have to—to find that woman. I want those boys." Twins. One sickly, one not. An ideal opportunity for more experiments. He'd never tested on twins before, twin halflings, that was.

"Attendant, text Marcus," he said, in replace of hanging up. "Message that I need to see him immediately."

Marcus was at his door within minutes of his text, and with Thaddeus's favorite treat in hand.

"Mini icebox cakes from Magnolia Bakery," Marcus said, crossing the threshold into the efficient condo.

"Perfect timing," Thaddeus praised, his second accolade for the day. "You stated you had something to discuss." He placed the box in the fridge to eat and enjoy in private later.

"Ms. Westlake," Marcus said, standing at ease just inside the tiny kitchen space.

"What about her?"

"Do you recall my telling you about seeing her?"

"Refresh my memory." Thaddeus leaned a hip against the counter.

"When I saw her three years ago." Marcus clasped his hands behind his back.

"Ah, yes-yes, something about how you believe her to be one of these descendants," Thaddeus said, annoyed, loosely crossing his arms over his chest.

"Correct. The lesser angels had spoken of them—the ones who were part of that *balancing act* the Archangels initiated."

"You know I don't care for rumors—nor do I care what the other castes of celestials partake in." Thaddeus didn't believe in any angelic hierarchy, but he knew the Archangels were considered the favorites. Thaddeus still considered himself above them all.

"I saw her around the time you sent me to this location. It had been a fortuitous stroke of luck my seeing The Watcher appear. Obviously, I hadn't—couldn't sense him, nor could he sense me."

"None of them can sense us," Thaddeus said, uncrossing his arms, adding a flippant hand gesture to push home his disinterest.

"Yes, but she hadn't seemed shocked by his appearance—perhaps she had encountered others like him. She's supposed to have the power to sense The Fallen and Archangels—I was told."

"And Watchers now too? Please," he said dismissively, turning and pulling open the fridge door again. He was starving. "How did you know she was the same woman they spoke of—one of these *balance* descendants?" He retrieved a container of the expensive bottled water he liked from the top shelf and set it next to the gift basket.

"I'd glimpsed her once before."

"What—how?" He turned back to face Marcus.

"The lesser angels had been keeping tabs on them all during that first year after the gathering, although their interest in them swayed to other matters, causing them to lose track of their whereabouts."

"You said you saw her—where?"

"At a hospital—in Ottawa. She was visiting some old woman. I was on one of my scavenging hunts searching for halflings, right before those blasted Stewards trapped us down here. Later, when I saw her here in the city—I recognized her instantly. It was then the Watcher appeared."

"Are you trying to tell me you believe she is the same woman who was in my Ottawa building—in my private lab—posing as a city worker?" Thaddeus crossed his arms again.

"I never forget a face." Marcus raised his eyebrows.

Thaddeus turned back to the water on the counter and grabbed it up, tearing the black wrapping from the top.

"What about her abilities?" Marcus asked.

"Yes, for The Fallen and Archangels—I have no use for any of those worthless beings." Thaddeus popped the cork from the fancy water bottle.

"Don't you think it's possible she can sense our kind too—Seraphim? And maybe why she was in your building?" Marcus suggested.

Thaddeus glanced over his shoulder at Marcus before pouring the pricy water into a champaign glass. "I'll remind you again—none can sense us. Not even those egocentric Archangels."

"I never thought to inquire about her name—I didn't much care at the time, but now," Marcus said.

"I have it," Thaddeus stated, facing Marcus, and leaning back against the counter.

"You know her name?" Marcus dropped his hands from behind his back.

"I've had Lyndon doing some digging for me. He found several women with the same *surname* living in Canada. Based on the approximate age, there were only two women who fit. So far, he has only found records up to 2006 for the one, and the other it seems, has several homes scattered across this globe. I have him checking all of them." Thaddeus took a generous sip of the water.

"You're sure she's one of these two?"

"Sure—no, but the others on his list don't meet the age criteria." Thaddeus took another sip.

"The one may have left the country if there are no other records for her." Marcus rubbed the back of his neck.

"Lyndon swears he saw the same woman—or sister of, visiting the group home. I instructed him to call—speak with the facility's manager. To see if that fool recalled the woman's first name for verification."

"Any luck?"

"No. But he informed Lyndon that the woman who had called about visiting the group home had asked to meet with Taylor specifically." Thaddeus filled the flute glass with water again.

"Maybe she knows about him—us—and the other Earthbound?"

"How could she?" Thaddeus shook his head.

"Why him then, if she doesn't know?" Marcus spread his arms out in question, then let them drop down at his sides.

Ignoring Marcus's question, Thaddeus said, "Lyndon has his minions watching the homes and workplaces of the other two women who were there at the group home." Thaddeus sipped, then examined his stemware he was holding.

"For what purpose?"

"To watch for this Ms. Westlake, of course," Thaddeus said, looking past the glass to Marcus.

"Sounds like a long shot." Marcus let out a heavy breath.

Thaddeus examined the water in his glass like one would a fine wine. "I had him call the Ottawa sewer service number—from the paperwork left with Amahle, as well. It was the same number on the tag hung near the pipe they supposedly repaired."

"What did he find out?" Marcus asked.

"Attendant, call Lyndon." Thaddeus held up the index finger of his free hand, then took another sip of the cool water.

"Yes," Lyndon answered.

"Sewer workers," Thaddeus said impatiently.

"Right. I inquired about the employees who worked that emergency job. The person on the other end said something along the lines of, '*Like I told the others, they no longer work here*'. When I asked if I could get their names? He said he couldn't give out any personal information. Said they were part of a group who played the lotto weekly, that he'd had several calls—people '*coming out of the woodwork*', because of the money. Apparently, the crew won last month—quit their jobs."

"Thank you for nothing, Lyndon," Thaddeus said, before ending the call.

"It's too great a coincidence that the woman I saw here in the city three years ago, looks so similar to that female city worker from the video—minus the glasses and short dark hair, *and* resembles the woman from the group home—as per Lyndon." Marcus rocked on his heels, as though anxious.

Thaddeus tilted back the champagne glass, finishing the remaining water.

"What if she's figured out what we've been doing?"

"And what—she some sort of covert… *spy*?" Thaddeus said, cynicism oozing with each word. For 20 years, he and his followers have been searching out the offspring of their kind. Pretending to focus on genetic testing for childhood diseases, for cures, but he'd been testing *on* them—not for them. "No one knows what truly goes on at my facilities—I'm sure of it." He set the glass on the counter next to the bottle.

"I don't know what to make of it—it's curious indeed. But what's even more intriguing are these men." Marcus cracked his knuckles.

"Men—what nonsense are you talking about now? And you know I hate when you do that," he said, frowning disapprovingly, looking down at his own hands.

"The other city workers with her—from the video footage."

"What about them?" Thaddeus assessed his hands, focusing on his nails.

"Both were very tall—one was huge in fact, and they just happened to need to come to *your* building—into *your* lab, to fix a gas leak? Then by chance they win the lotto and are gone." Marcus gave his head a tilt, coupled with a single eyebrow raise.

Thaddeus said nothing, only narrowed his eyes. He despised being made to look like a fool.

"Speaking of huge," Marcus redirected. "You won't believe who I spotted a few weeks ago at that fancy restaurant." Marcus smirked.

"What restaurant?" Thaddeus's hunger surged.

"*Snow*. It's right near the bakery on the Upper West Side—where I got you those cakes you like so much." Marcus pointed at the fridge.

Thaddeus gave some consideration to the fridge's contents, then rubbed his stomach. "You know I don't enjoy guessing games—whom did you see?" He licked his lips, imagining how delectable those cakes were going to taste.

"A certain female."

It was Thaddeus's belief that they had all been equal on Pleiades, but here on earth, females—human or Angel, were utterly inferior. He had two females of his kind join his rebellion, Amahle who now headed up the Ottawa location, and... *Ariadne*. She had rebelled further, deserting their modest faction the minute they'd been cast down. "Who?" Thaddeus asked, focusing back on his second in command.

"Francesca," Marcus announced. "She works there—for a human, no less."

Chapter 7 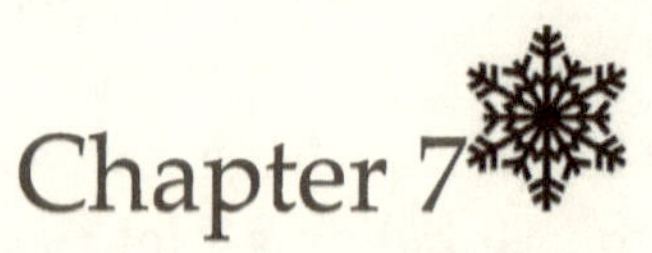

What we'd accomplished had been risky I had to admit—dangerous even, but not nearly as perilous as it would be telling my friends what we'd done. Maybe I could just give them the highlights I supposed, as the video chat whirled to life on the screen. Then, when everyone's faces appeared on the big TV, I said, "Update."

Vicki blew out an audible, clearly exasperated breath, right out of the gate.

Despite Vicki's lack of enthusiasm, when none of the others said anything in response, I went on. "So, Kris has still not been seen at his restaurant in New York City, or in the lab's vicinity there, nor was he at the lab building in Norway."

"What are the chances he is still in Norway, somewhere?" Derek asked, glancing away from the screen, clacking away on his keyboard.

"Uncertain, at this point," I said, cutting a glance Darius's way.

"Wait, how do you know he wasn't in the Norway lab?" Vicki asked, suspicious, crossing her arms.

My heart pounded in my chest. "I went there—with Darius—we met up with Zach," I blurted out, the feeling much like ripping off the first of many securely stuck band-aids, knowing similar pain was imminent. And as mouths gaped, I continued with the discomfort of outlining our caper.

Freaked out comments came from everyone regarding our boldness and the potential peril we'd put ourselves in.

I couldn't blame them, but I also couldn't let them in on how thrilling it had been. "I felt safe every step of the way—especially having both Darius and Zach there," I expressed. And to be honest, it had been an amazing rush. Though I wouldn't tell them that.

"Why do you keep putting yourself at such a risk like that?" Vicki demanded. "First the lab in Ottawa and now this escapade in Norway. I get that you're preternatural sensing and all—but these guys, from what we've learned, are superhuman and super *dangerous*." Vicki uncrossed her arms and put her hands to her head, rubbing the sides. "It's too much—all of it. My acceptance—the leap I made with us all having these gifts—powers, whatever, and the gathering, was one thing—and don't get me wrong I've made a good living with my abilities, but this—The Guards of Haven thing—the Thaddeus thing, it's just too much for me." She lowered her hands to her lap. "I'm getting too old for this," she said, slumping, finishing her tirade.

There was another one of those long awkward silences following Vicki's rant.

Then Darius spoke up. "I had mixed feelings, the conflict being Lynn's proximity to danger coupled with the exhilaration I'd felt with going undercover. Understand that I was there with Lynn the whole time. And she was amazing!" Darius focused over on Redmond. "And we've—Redmond and I, have been helping Den with some of the renovations at South Haven. And I've also been learning more about self-defense and protecting others." He smiled thoughtfully at me then. "I'm happy they are around—helps take some of the burden off me with my *need* to protect Lynn."

"I like having them close by, too," Redmond agreed. "By the way, I talked to Leo about you, Olivia. Asked if it was okay for you to tell Rachel everything." He smiled proudly this time, focusing in on Olivia, Mac, and Alison's screen. "He said to go ahead, then also let Nic know—when she knows."

"Fantastic—that will be a weight off my shoulders. It's been killing me keeping it from her," Olivia said, breathing out a sigh of relief. "I just need to find the right time and place to blow her mind."

"You didn't tell me you were going to do that," I said to Redmond, feeling a little left out.

"Didn't know I had to ask." He gave me a tight discerning smile and raised his eyebrows.

"You don't, I just…."

"Why would you want her to know—why get her involved?" Vicki questioned, directing her inquiry at Olivia.

Before Olivia could respond, Derek said, "I've been trying to figure out where Kris could be based on flight patterns and the tracking app on his cellphone. Leo had Marq provide me with the exact locations Kris went to, along with cell tower reports. Marq's first love may be art, but his specialty is definitely surveillance and security, internet and structure security, including biometrics."

"He designed our fake IDs and the photos I used for my pretend sons. He put in our security system here at the house, too," I added.

Luc nodded, then said, "How would cellphone reports help find him?"

"Cellphone *pings*," Derek said. "It's the act of determining the estimated current location of a cellphone. You can accomplish this via GPS data or by using cell tower triangulation. Obtaining a cellphone ping is a valuable technique often used for a variety of emergency situations, but tracking a switched off phone is difficult because when it's off, it will stop communicating with nearby mobile towers, and can only be traced through its last location when it was last on. But I don't believe he's still in Norway."

"Why is that?" Alison asked. "I'm keeping track of all of this, by the way." She waved her notepad and gave a big, jovial grin.

"Thank you, Alison," I said, grateful someone was keeping track.

In answer to her question, Derek said, "Marq has been teaching me how to use this electronic surveillance tool, a cell-site simulator, which mimics a cellphone tower. It can force mobile phones and other devices to connect to it instead of a legitimate one."

"And why do we want that?" I asked, not fully grasping the concept.

"Because, in doing so, a phone reveals information about itself and its user. See where I'm going with this?"

"Yup," I said, following now.

"How does it work?" Redmond asked, leaning forward in his seat.

Derek typed something on his keyboard. "With regular cell towers, phones periodically and automatically broadcast their presence to the nearest one to them. That's how the phone carrier's network provides service in that location. This happens even when the phone is not being used to make or receive a call." Derek paused, and I gave him a thumbs up before he went on. "The key thing is that when a phone communicates with a cell tower, it reveals a unique ID associated with the SIM card in the phone. This cell-site simulator masquerades as a cell tower to get a phone to ping it, and in doing so, you can get the phone's ID number. It can't function like a regular tower because it doesn't process calls and messages when it's communicating, but once you find or capture the ID number, you just release the phone and tell it to find a different tower. No one is the wiser. And since we already know the ID number of Kris's phone, we can program that number into the device to search for him."

"Were you able to discover anything?" Luc asked.

"Marq was able to get a historical log of all the cell towers Kris's phone had pinged, tracking where he'd been."

"What do they do now?" Alison questioned, jotting more notes down.

"Can they do anything?" I tossed out.

"Obviously, I hadn't known about your adventure in Norway when I'd spoken to Marq. But he told me that Zach and he were going to use it from a vehicle, drive around the different neighborhoods where Kris had appointments. If they can identify Kris's phone as active, they can narrow his location to a specific area or a building by measuring the phone's signal strength as it connects."

"Then what?" Darius asked then.

"Once you narrow down a location, you can switch to a hand-held option, which offers even more precision." Derek typed again on his keyboard. "They know it's a long shot."

"And if they can't find his phone?" Mac asked, her turn for a question.

"Kris's last cellphone ping was at the port near the salmon distributor he visited. And if we are now assuming Kris *did* leave Norway, he may have taken off from that port area of the last ping." Derek stopped to check something on his own cellphone. "Marq has another devise called a *dirtbox* or DRT box—Digital Receiver Technology, which can be used from an airplane or from the air...," Derek stated, flapping his arms. "... to intercept data, hopefully from Kris's phone."

"Is there a reason they haven't filed a missing person's report in the area he was last seen?" Olivia questioned, frowning.

"As much as they want to find him, the last thing Leo and the others need is unwanted attention on any of them," Redmond explained. "Over the years, if they got injured, Nic was the one who readily patched them up. They never go to hospitals because of their *unique* anatomy and fast cellular regeneration. Too much attention—too many questions."

"Is it possible he's just gone off grid?" Luc suggested. "Time away?"

"Not likely," Redmond said. "He told the general manager at his restaurant he was going to meet the others up at First Haven. They thought little about it when he didn't show. But when he never returned to New York City, that's when they realized something was wrong." Redmond leaned back into the couch.

"Leo said he always put his business first and the role of The Guards second," I added.

"More like dead last—from what they told us," Redmond clarified. "And he wouldn't have just abandoned the restaurant—it's his baby."

"This may be another longshot, but Mac—any chance you could do some kind of locator spell?" I proposed, lost for any other ideas.

"Olivia and I already talked about me doing a spell. I've been working on something that might work—I didn't want to mention it until I felt more confident. But it would work better if I had something I could track—something of his, a personal item." Mac stole a peek at Olivia to her right, then at Alison to her left.

"Let me reach out to Leo—see if he has anything of Kris's you can use," Redmond offered. "I'll have him contact you directly if he finds something."

Mac nodded, then grinned knowingly at Olivia.

"That's all of it—all I have," I said. "Anyone else have anything more? Derek?"

"That's it from me—I'll keep working with Marq, though." More keyboard clacking followed Derek's comment.

"I have everything recorded and up to date," Alison said. "So, if there are no other details from your caper Lynn—Darius, I'm going to work with Mac and Olivia now—record all the upcoming spell details."

"Sounds good," I said. "Oh Alison, let me know if you hear anything from Carlie."

"Rodger that," Alison said, closing off their video feed.

Chapter 8 

After the Norway gig, I'd utilized the rest of the week to dedicate time to my abilities, even reaching out to the universe in hopes of fresh ideas. Regrettably, I'd come up with nothing fruitful to aid in the search for Kris. And by the end of that following weekend, my endeavors had been further quashed when Leo had informed us that they too had found no new leads aimed at locating Kris. Zach and Marq had checked the areas around where he'd been seen, and all the hospitals and police stations throughout Norway. Leo had returned to Ottawa, and he and Nic had done the same, using the *dirtbox* tool Derek had told us about, searching Ottawa in case he'd travelled there for any reason, and New York City in case Kris *had* returned to the city and somehow could not reach out.

In reflect of the miserable outcomes, I'd opted for switching gears and putting my focus on people and things closer to home, and using the few weeks left in January as a cooling down period for me *not* to think about the Earthbound and their difficulties.

Redmond and I talked at length about my going to Norway, about the risks I'd taken, but mainly about how I'd made the decision to go without talking it over with him first. We'd also spoken on how I had felt about him going to Leo about Olivia's ask for Rachel to be in the knowing. Compared to the autonomous decision I'd made, his actions had been minor, and it had given me insight into what he had felt about my thoughtless actions. I was guilty; I knew it. It was through our dialog that we'd both realized we'd been functioning in parallel but had forgotten how to talk to one another. I needed to be reminded that we were a team, and that the celestial happenings were not mine alone to navigate. And I had to remind myself that what I did had an impact and if I wasn't careful, it might end up having a *negative* impact. We'd made a promise to talk things out like we used to. Regarding the twins, we agreed to talk with them more regularly about all our angelic ties and not taking their connections for granted. We have come to realize they were not smaller versions of me and were, in fact, developing their own unique skills. A return to communication needed to be a big part of all our lives, with the twins individually and as a family.

Our talks with them had gone well, and we had stressed the importance of communication, so they truly understood they could tell us anything—either of us. The goal had been safety, for them to feel comfortable to tell us everything, not just the pieces they chose to share. The only way for us to keep them safe was for them to be honest with us, both of us. I told them, going forward, I would *not* keep things like their dreams, or anything otherworldly in nature from their father. With the hard talks accomplished, we'd spent more time on walks on the beach as a family, sitting out on the deck with blankets around the firepit, and open conversation around the dinner table.

We had needed more walking on the beach just the two of us as well, time on the deck with a bottle of wine and the firelight, and sneaking away to reconnect, replenishing our friendship, our partnership, and our love for each other. There was also a mutual consensus that I needed a healthier pursuit, one that didn't involve trying to solve the mystery of the missing angel. So, as part of my reconnecting with my personal path, I'd tossed my resume into the employment-hat for a volunteering gig at the local hospital. This past Friday I'd gotten a call to come in for an interview, to speak with the director in charge. And that interview was today.

Since Redmond was at the studio with Lily working on a deadline this morning, it had fallen to me to figure out how to get both the girls to school on time at the far end of the island *and* get me to the hospital for my interview off-island at the opposite end of town. If only I were a twin, I pondered as I packed the girls' lunches.

"I'll take those," Gabriel said, appearing next to me at the kitchen island. "Is everyone ready for the morning drive to school?"

"Not exactly," I said. "I have my interview this morning and I'm going to be late."

"How can I help?" He grabbed up the packed lunches and followed me to the front door.

"Giiiirls!" I called down the hall. "Let's get a move on it." I turned to face Gabriel and grabbed back the lunches. "Any chance you can learn to drive in the next 5 minutes?"

He grimaced. He'd never taken it upon himself to learn to drive. "You know I love to be on the drive but…," he began, when a knock on the front door interrupted him.

Den stood in view of the front door window, smiling and waving.

"Good morning," I said, opening the door. A quick view of the driveway showed me he hadn't appeared out of thin air. His kind couldn't, but consequently his SUV it seemed, was blocking my way out of the driveway.

"What are you doing here?" Gabriel asked over my shoulder.

I wondered the same thing. It wasn't like him to just show up unannounced, well, except for that *first* time.

"I brought this over for Redmond," he said, handing me a metal box.

I stared at the dark grey metal container, then focused back on Den, confused. "What is it?"

"It's a safe, to keep things in—passports, paperwork, valuables— and it's fireproof." He grinned confidently as if that helped to make more sense.

"Redmond saw the one I have—asked if I could get him one."

"Okay," I said. Safe was good. I set it on the entry table near the front door. "Thank you—I'll make sure he gets it. Sorry I can't visit right now, but I need to get the girls to school early, then get across town for my interview."

"Interview?" Den leaned his shoulder against the doorjamb as though not sensing the urgency.

"Ya—for a volunteering job at the hospital." I hitched up my purse on my shoulder. I hated purses. "Giiiiiiirls—let's go!"

"Hi, Den," Ryley said, casually entering the foyer.

"Haaaaaaaydeeeeen," Hayley squealed, arriving on the heels of her sister. Summer and Snow lumbered behind her.

"Hello, ladies," he said in response, exchanging high-fives with both. "I can take the girls to school for you, if you'd like."

"Yes-yes-please," Hayley said, clapping her hands.

"Excellent," Ryley added.

Turning to both, I said, "Are you girls okay if Den and Gabriel take you to school this morning?" It was an ideal solution. "It gives me more time to get to the hospital without having to rush."

"Fly?" Ryley asked, swinging her backpack over her shoulder.

"Yes!" Hayley agreed, struggling to fix her knapsack onto her back.

As part of our discussion with the girls, Redmond and I had made it crystal clear for them to be extra careful concerning the new secrets about the wings, and how they would be seeing more of our new friends around. They'd been thrilled about having more airborne buddies and were always up for a ride, but obviously this wasn't the time.

"No sillies, in my SUV." Den gave them both a little jokey shove. "Or not—I can just go," he added, playing it as though leaving offended.

"No-no!" Hayley pleaded, grabbing his hand to pull him back.

"I call shotgun. Meet you in the truck," Gabriel said, before disappearing.

"Okay—lets go then," Den said, spinning Hayley towards the front door.

"Lunches," I said, reminding them and handing off their lunch bags. "Behave for Gup and Den, okay?"

"We will," they said in unison as they headed out the door.

"I'll be there to pick you up after school." I mouthed a *thank you* to Den before he followed after the twins.

"Good luck," he called back as I shut the door.

In the driveway, Den found Gabriel already buckled up in the front seat of his SUV.

"I want to ride in the front seat," Hayley whined, tugging on the door handle.

"Sorry, Hayley. You have to sit in the back," Den said, opening the passenger side door for her to sit behind Gabriel.

"It's that I'm too small—isn't it?" she said, a pout already forming on her little face.

"Hey," came Ryley's voice from the other side of the car through the open passenger door. Ryley placed her backpack on the floor in front of her seat. "Don't you want to sit with me?" she asked, buckling herself in.

Den took Hayley's backpack so that she could climb into the other booster seat next to her sister. He handed back her bag before closing the door. He circled around to the driver's side to get in, then said, "Neither of you are big enough nor old enough to sit upfront."

"I'll be 9 in May," Hayley disputed, dropping her bag to the floor.

Den buckled his seatbelt. "You have to be at least 13 years old to sit in the front. Until then, you both need to use booster seats and sit in the back. Besides—if your mom saw you or found out, I'd never be able to drive you to school again. Is that what you want?" He turned to look at both in the back seat. Ryley was bigger than Hayley by at least 4 inches and had about 15lbs on her, but even so, she wasn't allowed in the front seat either.

"No," Hayley said in a quiet voice. She clicked her seat buckle, then crossed her arms over her tiny chest and continued her pouting.

"Plus, I called dibs on the front seat anyway," Gabriel said, shifting to look over the back of his seat at her. He grinned at her, but she didn't smile back, didn't even look at him. When Gabriel turned forward again, Den put the SUV in reverse and slowly backed out the drive.

"What grade are you guys in now?" Den asked as he turned off their street and onto the main road.

"Third," Ryley answered.

"How are you doing in school?" he asked, checking in the rearview mirror to see if Hayley was still pouting. She was.

"I'm mostly Bs and a few As," Ryley shared. When her sister didn't respond, she said, "Hayley's all As—oh, and one C."

"What did you get a C in, Hayley?" Gabriel asked, surprise ringing in his voice.

"Don't tell!" Hayley said to her sister in protest.

"PE," Ryley tattled.

"Stop, Ryley!" Hayley cried.

"You got a C in gym class?" Den questioned. "How could that be—you're speedy-fast and agile? You always catch me when we play tag."

"She's the smallest kid in our class," Hayley shared despite her sister's protest.

"Oh, so it's not about coordination, it's about size." Den spied in the review mirror again to see that Hayley had her index finger up to her mouth, shushing her sister. "Why would you want to be the same size as everyone else—that's boring?"

"She's a fantastic surfer, too," Gabriel said, putting his hand through to the back seat, palm facing up. Hayley smacked it. "Yaaa," he said in response to her giving him a low-five.

Den took another quick glimpse in the mirror. Hayley was smiling now. Shifting the focus, he asked, "What other classes are you taking in school?"

"Math, reading and writing," Ryley said.

"What kind of math?" he asked.

"Decimals, fractions, and multiplication. And how to measure stuff," she said.

"Like following the instructions for a recipe?" Gabriel asked, leaning his head back to look at Ryley.

"Ya—but I already knew how to do that from Da," she explained.

"What about your reading and writing classes?" Den asked.

Hayley answered this time. "We read chapter books and learn how to find information in dictionaries and other reference books in the library."

"And Writing?" he inquired, keeping the dialog going.

"We do short essays and stories with beginning, middle and end," Ryley said, taking her turn.

"We have a writing assignment," Hayley added. "Have to pick a family experience—something enjoyable or an important moment."

"Did you pick it yet?" Gabriel inquired.

"Not yet," Hayley said. "But we have to tell Mr. McCray our topic today."

"Let me know if you need any help," Gabriel offered.

Den glanced at Gabriel and smiled. "No other subjects?"

"Science," Hayley said, clearly enjoying the conversation now. "And Social Studies. Computers, too."

"Science—like what?" Den was loving the back and forth with his little passengers.

"Experiments," Hayley tossed out. "The solar system, the sun and the moon. Social studies is just maps and stuff. The names of the states and capitals for each."

"You learned how to locate places in your neighborhood, too, don't forget," Gabriel reminded.

"Oh ya," Hayley said with a little giggle.

"Computers is mostly typing on a keyboard and basic programs," Ryley said. "It's too easy."

"Did you have any homework?" Gabriel asked, turning slightly in his seat to face them.

"Nope. We usually get ours done in class," she responded.

"We still have the writing assignment," Hayley noted. "But it's not due until Monday."

"No language studies?" Den peeked at them in the review mirror.

"Next year," Ryley said, sounding disinterested, playing with the button on her door that lowered and raised the window.

"I speak fluent French—if you ever want to learn," Den told them.

Whispers followed his offer, along with a giggle from Ryley. When he checked in the review mirror again, he saw Hayley had her little fist clenched and held out in threat to her sister.

"We're here," Gabriel announced, pointing for Den to pull into the school lane.

Den merged in along with the other few early-birds dropping off kids. Then, when it was their turn, he stopped and put the SUV in park.

Both he and Gabriel exited the vehicle. Den opened the door for Ryley, then observed the other parents. Mothers and a few of the fathers were gawking at him and Gabriel, he observed.

When Gabriel noticed Den surveying the others, he said, "It happens every time."

"What?"

"The staring," he said. "I just ignore it." He smirked at Den.

"Hi, Mr. McCray," Ryley said, pulling Den's attention from the onlookers and over to their approaching teacher.

"Hey gang. Gabriel," the cheerful teacher said, nodding at Gabriel as he came to a stop near the SUV. "Hello," he directed at Den, extending his hand in greeting. "I don't think we've met. I'm Gavin—Mr. McCray, the girls' teacher."

"Pleased to meet you. I'm Den—Hayden," he said, shaking the man's hand, before refocusing his attention on the girls. "Later, Sport," Den said, extending his fist to Ryley.

"Later," she replied, switching her lunch bag to her other hand, giving Den a fist bump explosion with her free one. Then she moved over to give Gabriel a hug. "Later, Gup."

"Later, Ry," Gabriel said, tucking the stray hairs from her ponytail behind her ear. She smiled sweetly up at him, then turned to head off.

Hayley took her turn then to hug her grandfather. "Bye, Gup," she said, struggling to lift her knapsack to one shoulder while holding her lunch bag.

"Bye, Surfer-Girl," Gabriel said, pulling the stray strap of her pack up to the other shoulder.

"Thank you," Hayley said, turning to Den, tipping her head back to look up at him.

Den knelt to meet her eye to eye. "Anytime, my little butterfly," he said, adjusting the shoulder straps further on her too-big knapsack. She leaned in and gave him a kiss on the cheek, then turned and followed after her sister to the entrance. Den watched to see her glance back quickly, giving him a big joy filled smile before going through the main doors.

"Looks like someone has a little crush," teacher Gavin said, regaining Den's attention.

Shifting his focus, Den gave the teacher a thorough once over, finding that despite the cooler weather, the teacher was wearing flip-flops. He found the man's casual attire intriguing and refreshing. He'd never cared for the stuffy formal environments of his earlier education and much preferred the college days he'd experienced from this decade. "Crush?" Den questioned.

Gavin gave a chin-raise in the direction the girls had gone. "Hayley," he said with a teasing grin.

"Oh, we're buds. It's a name thing, Hayley—Hayden," he said with a shrug.

"Okay," Gavin said with a smirk. "I haven't seen you here for drop off before."

"No—it's my first time," Den shared. "Lynn has some interview this morning, so I offered to drop off the girls for her."

"I don't like to drive," Gabriel clarified. "Den is an old friend of mine from…." Gabriel hesitated, unprepared for this situation.

"Amsterdam," Den said, helping his fellow angel out. Fascinated by the teacher, Den had almost forgotten Gabriel was still there. "I recently moved here from Canada, and now I live here." He smiled innocently, relaxing back against the front corner panel of the SUV.

"What brings you here to our small town?"

Mr. Flip-flops was very curious, Den mused. "We purchased a place on the island to use as a home base for… my business." He cut a glance to Gabriel noting the Archangel's eyebrows were raised. Amused, Den looked back at Gavin.

"We?" Gavin frowned slightly.

Why so bothered by that? Den pondered. "An investment with my business partners," he said, watching the positive shift in Gavin's expression at his response.

"What sort of business?"

Den looked Gabriel's way again, noting the Archangel's eyes were bulging a bit. Focusing back on Gavin, he said, "I work as a bodyguard for high-end folks—celebrities, diplomatic escort. And as you can imagine, I travel a lot. Needed a place where I could escape the big cities when I'm between assignments."

"They bought that multi-residential three story sand-coloured building that's been up for sale since the pandemic," Gabriel said with a questioning grin, glancing back and forth between Gavin and Den.

"I think I know the place. I've passed it on the way to Redmond and Lynn's house." Gavin nodded at Gabriel. "You need that entire building?"

"We should probably get going—we're blocking the drop-off." Gabriel waved a hand at the vehicles attempting to maneuver around them.

"Right—sorry to keep you," Gavin said then.

"It's not just for me—it's for my… *partners* too, who travel. It's a place to train—workout, to get away and relax, really," Den explained, pushing himself off the SUV. "I wasn't keen on the office building thing, and this way we can have a place to work from, or crash. You know?" Den grinned quizzically at the teacher.

"I do," Gavin said, smiling playfully, extending his hand this time in farewell. "I do indeed. And I look forward to seeing you around."

Chapter 9 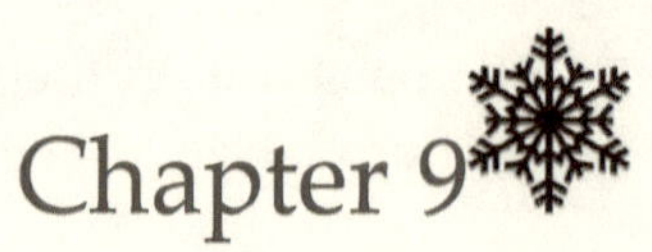

Lane had been waiting for the right opportunity to revisit the group home, so when Carlie called letting her know that the facility manager would be out for the entire day, she didn't hesitate.

"We should set you up as a volunteer," Carlie suggested, greeting Lane at the front door. "That way, you wouldn't need to wait for a chance like today."

"That's an excellent idea." Lane said, tapping her snowy shoes on the edge of the front steps. Then she passed through the entrance into the group home's foyer.

"Here," Carlie said, "give me your coat." She opened the door to a small hall closet that had obviously been part of the original layout of the mansion-style home.

Lane handed off her black bomber jacket, then rearranged the strap of her purse across her chest to be hands free.

"You cut your hair since last time," Carlie said, "Suits you."

"Oh ya—thanks," Lane said, grinning, tucking a section of her black wavy bobbed hair behind her ear.

"That reminds me, I need to get this mop cut." She adjusted her ponytail. "We'll set you up with an ID card and security fob to allow you to come and go." Carlie shut the closet door. "Follow me," she said, leading them away from the front entrance.

"I'd still prefer to be here when you are, if that's okay." Lane noted how the facility appeared more like a house from the outside, reminded now that she was inside of something more institutional, like that of a hospital setting.

"Not a problem. I can send you my schedule. Just text me when you're dropping over, and I can put your name on the schedule as volunteering. I can let you know the temperature of things before you get here, too." Carlie rolled her eyes.

"Thank you in advance for that," Lane said, taking a quick glimpse back at the entrance.

"You never know what mood the boss man is going to be in—best to be as prepared as possible. I reaffirmed to him how impressed you were by his choice to work in this industry and that you thought it was an honorable job." Carlie laughed. "He ate it up—so I'm sure you'll be welcome anytime."

"My fathers' friends didn't much care for your boss," Lane said with a knowing chuckle.

"No one likes him."

"Is it just staff and patients here today—no visitors?" Lane shifted her purse around to rest against her lower back.

"Yes. We call them residents though—not patients."

"Right—sorry." Lane grimaced.

"No worries—you'll get the hang of things. I'll teach you the ins and outs." Carlie gave her a kind smile. "Oh, you may see Lyndon around," she added.

"Lyndon?" Lane peered back up the hall. She knew that name, knew he was one of Thaddeus's guys, and that he had been here the same day Lynn and the others had visited Taylor. "Is he another staff member?"

"Not exactly… I think he works directly for the organization that funds this place. He doesn't do anything—nothing I can see, just lurks around watching. Mostly the outside. His presence makes my boss exceptionally nervous, so we kind of like having him around." Carlie grinned teasingly back at Lane. "He's harmless." She grinned again, then stopped in the hall at a small desk with a laptop on it.

"Okay," Lane said as Carlie stepped in behind the desk.

Carlie leaned over and typed something on the keyboard. "Need to take your photo for the ID badge. *Smile,*" she said, clicking several more keys on the laptop.

Lane smiled at the small camera affixed to the computer's monitor.

Carlie turned and unlocked the door that was behind the desk. "This is the office where we keep everything that needs to be secured, like medications, resident files, all our office supplies and paperwork." She stepped inside out of view. "Here you go," she said, returning, handing Lane a lanyard with her new volunteer photo pass and fob attached. "Let me give you the full tour and details this time."

Lane draped the lanyard over her head, letting it hang down from her neck. Then she followed Carlie back up the hall they had just come down.

"This location has nine children," Carlie began. "Most of whom have been here 10-plus years with no plans to leave anytime soon." She gave Lane a sorrowful look. "There's a living room here." Carlie pointed at the large open space. "The kitchen—is like what you might find in a regular home. It's back there at the far end." She pointed back down the hall to where the desk and office were.

Lane made mental notes on everything as Carlie informed her of each of the spaces and rooms in the facility, surveying each area as they passed through, memorizing the layout for future visits. "How many people work here?" she asked then.

"We have a high staff-to-resident ratio to make sure each one receives hands-on supervision. There are six full-time and six part-time." Carlie stopped at a set of stairs. "There are two sets of stairs. These, and the ones on the west side of the building next to the garage. We have an elevator there as well. It has a dual-entrance—one from the garage for transferring residents to the van for transport and one from inside for taking them up to the rooms on the second floor."

"That's smart," Lane said, nodding.

"It wasn't part of the original home, but it sure comes in handy. Staff use the stairs mostly—it's faster." Carlie proceeded up the stairs.

Lane stared down at her pass labeled *volunteer*. "What are the different roles?" she asked when they reached the top.

"There's the coordinator—my boss whom you met already." She rolled her eyes again, making Lane laugh. "He's here most days. We have a systems manager and two supervisors. And there are part-time and full-time residential counsellors, like me."

"You mentioned last time I was here that you have clinical responsibilities."

"Yes. All our residential counsellors follow behaviour support plans provided by a clinical behaviour specialist."

Lane nodded again. "Do any of you live here on the property?"

"No. We do shifts. At nighttime, one of us is here while the residents are asleep—we alternate. Daytime, we supervise and do meals and activities with them. And we take care of the medical records, other paperwork, as well as the laundry and cleaning."

"You had the office door locked, I noticed. What other kinds of security measures do you need to take?"

"Resident rooms are *always* unlocked. But we keep the doors to the outside locked all the time and bolted at night. Mostly we don't want people coming in without being on the schedule—or strangers wandering about. They set up cameras," Carlie added, "but they don't work. I think the boss hates being on camera, so they are mostly for show." She smirked.

"How does it work with visitors, then?"

"They get visitors but more often staff bring them to their families. They are allowed to have phone calls and video chats with family and friends, too. Most come from loving families or have personal caregivers who play a crucial role in supporting them. Although the families come to us for help as well. Compassion fatigue is a real thing for full-time caregivers. And sometimes what they need most is a break," Carlie said, stopping at an open door to one of the bedrooms.

Lane looked inside to see a female staff member braiding the hair of a teen girl. The girl waved one of her prosthetic hands their way. Lane noticed that along with the artificial lower arms, the girl had prosthetics on both her legs from the thigh down.

"Hi, you two," Carlie said, waving back at the girl and her caregiver before moving turning and further down the hall. "My coworker is getting her ready to be picked up by her aunt. The aunt took over the care of that sweet girl when her parents died in a car crash. The aunt needed a break."

"I can understand that," Lane said, taking a quick peek back through the open door. "Everyone needs a break from responsibility every once in a while."

"Those friends of your fathers, Alison and the ladies who came to visit Taylor, were the first visitors he'd had in years."

"Has he had any since?" Keeping tabs on Taylor was Lane's real reason for being there, but she understood keeping up the facade that Carlie and she had devised for her to be there, they had to give the appearance she was a volunteer now.

"Nope," Carlie said. "But my boss tried talking to him after their visit." She paused at the entrance to a large room, one that had exercise and physio equipment in it. "This room is for working with the residents for mobility and strength," she said, then looked both ways up the hall, then at Lane.

"How did that talk with Taylor go?" Lane pressed her lips tight together.

"Taylor always freaks out around him, and the boss can't handle it. So, he questioned me too—asked if I knew why they wanted to see just him, and not any of the other residents. I suggested it was probably because he's the only one here who doesn't have any family." She focused back up the hall again. "Alison works in social services, so it was a plausible explanation, I figured."

"Did he buy it?" Lane asked. She knew Carlie was aware of the story about Taylor, most of it, but Carlie was encouraged by the idea of him having more visitors. She'd welcomed the idea Alison had proposed with having Lane visit with him.

"I'm guessing so—never mentioned it again." Carlie shrugged.

"Would it be a good time for me to see Taylor?" Lane clasped her hands together, hopeful.

"Definitely. He's in the playroom near the office." Carlie waved a hand, motioning for Lane to follow her. "We'll take the far stairs."

At the bottom of the stairs, Lane spotted the elevator Carlie had mentioned. "Is there a basement?" she asked, seeing the up *and* down buttons next to the elevator door.

"Yes, but staff don't go down there. You need a special security key to make the elevator go down. The laundry is on the main floor near the kitchen, and anything utilities related, access for that is from the garage only. I had to bring a repair guy down there when the water heater stopped working last year, though all the service equipment—electrical, furnace, etc. are together in the same small room."

"Cut off from the rest of the basement." Lane shot the elevator door a cold stare. "*Interesting*," she said under her breath.

"Here we are," Carlie said, breaching the entrance to the playroom.

"I was told this was Taylor's favorite place—and I can see why," Lane said, entering the large room.

The view outback through the expansive windows was magical with their frosted edges and the falling snow landing on the trees and bushes. There were several bird feeders in view placed around the yard, showing lots of activity. The playroom's interior had round tables placed in each corner, though only one person was in the room.

Taylor sat in his wheelchair, facing the magnificent view out the window. Carlie crossed the room, then knelt to one side of the wheelchair. "Hi Taylor," she said in a soft voice. "You have a visitor."

He smiled jovially up at Carlie, then turned his head to look Lane's way.

Carlie moved past him to sit in the chair on the other side, leaving the chair closest for her.

"Hi Taylor. I'm Lane," she said, centering on his sweet face and bright green eyes, overlooking his obvious disfigurement. "I'm a friend of Lynn's." She paused to see if he would understand her words.

He smiled, his eyes twinkling.

Lane took the chair next to him. "Lynn said she really enjoyed spending time with you."

"He was very receptive to Lynn and her friends. It was a very calm visit until you-know-who came in." Carlie scowled.

Lane nodded knowingly. "Would it be okay if I visited with you for a bit?" she asked Taylor.

Taylor gave Lane an even bigger grin, his cheeks scrunching up his eyes.

"He lives in a world that most don't understand—most don't try even, but we do." Carlie reached into a bag hanging off the back of his wheelchair.

"The Etch A Sketch," Lane acknowledged. "I was told about this—his way of communicating."

Carlie smiled at Lane, then placed the toy on the small tabletop attached to the front of Taylor's wheelchair. "It's a helpful tool."

Taylor's enthusiasm was immediate as he placed both his hands on its edges.

"Do you want to talk to me?" Lane asked, as she slid her cellphone from her handbag.

He grinned jovially at her again, then refocused on the toy and began turning the white knobs. The stylus moved across the gray screen, a shape forming as he twisted and turned the controls.

"When he's done, he'll clap his hands and rock," Carlie explained. "He shakes it up right after—but he'll show you first." Carlie gave a knowing chuckle.

"Amazing," Lane said, leaning in, watching as the image became clearer. She snapped a quick photo of what appeared to be another floor plan. She'd known about the other one he'd drawn for the ladies.

"Carlie," a woman called from the entrance of the playroom, grabbing her attention, and waving her to come over.

Carlie glanced back at Lane. "I told Alison earlier that I'd give her all the details after your visit."

Lane pushed up from her chair to stand. "I can do that—you have a lot to take care of here," she said, looking over at the other staff member waiting.

"I'll text you my shifts for next month. Let me know what works for you." Carlie looked down at Taylor. "It feels good knowing that the others want to keep a close eye on him. He's a special little guy. I'd miss him, but I would rather he find a better home—a proper home." Carlie gave her a mournful smile.

"Or at least get rid of the guy running this place. Make it a little less clinical and a little more, homie."

"I second that," Carlie said, smirking. "Thank you for coming—I hope you don't find being here too overwhelming." She put her hand out for a handshake.

Lane took Carlie's hand, then pulled her in for a hug. She hugged Lane back. "You are amazing—the residents are so lucky to have you and your staff," Lane said before releasing her.

Carlie gave Lane a much brighter smile this time. "Feel free to look around."

"Right—thank you," Lane said, running her thumb under the length of the lanyard.

"You've got your badge and your fob to get back in if you go outside too," she said, before turning and rushing off.

Taylor clapped his notice of completion pulling Lane's interest back to him.

"Thank you, Taylor," Lane said, as he shook away his creation. "Would it be okay if we chatted again sometime?"

He set down the toy on the tabletop and then clapped again as if in agreement.

She caressed Taylor's tiny hands. "Wonderful—I promise to visit you again soon." Motion outside the window caught her eye, pulling her attention away.

Lane moved closer to the window to see out to the yard better. Leaning in, she noticed there were footsteps in the snow that led up to the window from the right, then away to the far left side and out of view. "Someone was out there," she said, her breath fogging part of the window. She glanced back to the doorway, but Carlie and the other staff member were gone. She peered over at Taylor, but he seemed to be back in his own world, gazing out into the yard again.

Returning to the table, she said, "Taylor, did you see someone outside?" Taylor's eyes shifted to her, but then he returned to gazing out to the snowy landscape. The scene out the window was mesmerizing, but it was clear by the fresh footprints that someone had been watching them.

Lane checked the time on her cellphone to see she still had time before her meeting with her professor. "Solo tour," she said to herself, as she left the playroom.

She wandered back through the areas on the main floor, and as she strolled the halls, she observed several other caregivers attending to residents, none of whom had time for anything more than a quick hello and exchange of names.

Lane paused in the living space near the front door. Glancing down at her security pass, she lifted and examined the small blue fob attached. *"I'm free to come and go… and outside I will go,"* she murmured, moving then for the front door. She retrieved her coat from the hall closet, shrugged it on, and then she swiped her fob over the security pad next to the door to exit.

Outside on the front step, Lane zipped her bomber jacket up to her chin, then she descended the steps and went to the right of the home. Traversing the grounds around the side of the building, she searched for an opening to the backyard only to find her way blocked by a 6 foot fence and a lofty snowcapped hedge. She turned and circled back the way she'd come, navigating to the left this time where she was met with the same fence and hedge, though this part of the fence had a gate. She pushed on the gate, but it appeared to be locked. Then she noticed the gate had a security pad, like the one at the front door. Retrieving her lanyard from inside her coat, she then waved the fob part over the black pad. The gate lock gave an audible click and clunk, and Lane pushed again.

The snowy ground gave some resistance as she shoved the gate open, but she managed to move it back most of the way. Once in the yard, she noticed that there were no footprints leading to the inside of the gate. It wasn't until she reached the far edge of the hedge at the side of the house that she spotted the footprints she'd seen from the window, the ones that had led this direction out of view. She viewed the way back to the gate, seeing only her own footprints in the snow. The ones in front of her had stopped abruptly. "How…?" she questioned, breath wafting from her gapping mouth. A sudden crunching on the snow behind her shifted her awareness, and she stared back at the gate. In its opening stood a massive man.

"Oh, hi," she said, startled. Gathering herself, she turned fully to face him. The man wore a long faded black trench coat open in the front, grey jeans, and a black shirt. He had his enormous body in a three-quarter stance, but even in that position, she could see he was scowling at her. Despite his stern expression, Lane found him quite attractive, although his shoulder-length black hair needed to have a brush run through it. "You must be Lyndon," she said.

The man's scowl changed to one of shock.

"Carlie mentioned you hang—work here." Lane forced a smile.

The man tilted his chin up and to the side slightly, glaring down his nose at her.

"I'm Lane," she said, extending her hand and taking several quick steps in his direction.

The man stepped back as though to avoid Lane's approaching contact.

Lane halted in her snowy steps. "Sorry," she said, pulling her hand back.

"I am Lyndon." He dropped his stare to the ground, his dark glossy hair falling forward and hiding his face. Then he adjusted his coat, straightening the collar and running his large hands down the front as though to smooth out its disheveled appearance.

The bottom of his trench coat was damp, and salt stained, Lane noticed. "You watch over the group home, yes?" Lane took a tentative step forward. The man's head shot up, and it was then that she saw the full view of his face. The side he had kept from her showed burn scars, although the structure of his features appeared not to be damaged. Lane smiled despite her shock, knowing that most people he encountered would more than likely look away. "I'm volunteering here," she said, holding the badge end of her lanyard out for him to see.

There was more to this guy. She knew it. Leo had made her aware of the events that had occurred when Lynn and the others had visited, how Lynn had sensed something, someone there or in the vicinity. It was the other part of why Lane was here. When he didn't respond, she asked, "How long have you worked here?"

"I...," he began. Then, as if suddenly remembering his scars, he bowed his head and covered the damaged side of his face with one of his big hands. "... have to go."

"Please don't," Lane requested, taking several gutsy strides forward to stand within reach of him.

As if surprised by her boldness, Lyndon took another step back.

"It's my first day. I'm writing a paper for school about wonderful facilities like this one, and it would be great to learn about your perspective on working here." Taking a more passive stance, she put both her hands in her coat pockets.

He said nothing in response, only dropped his hand from his face.

Lane smiled again. She knew she was pushing her luck with this one, but if she could somehow win his trust, there was no telling what she might learn from him. She'd known all about the Earthbound since she was very young. Leo and the others weren't just her fathers' employers, they were her family. She felt confident that the enormous man standing in front of her was one of the Earthbound she'd been told about, and more than likely he was the 'something' Lynn had sensed.

"Another time perhaps," Lyndon said. He turned then swiftly disappearing to the left out of view.

Lane rushed forward through the opening of the gate but when she stared in the direction he had gone, instead of seeing him dashing away, she saw there were several strides of footprints... and then nothing. The prints in the snow just stopped. "Definitely Earthbound," she breathed out.

Chapter 10 

Jana's Bakari, Monday AM, February 14ᵗʰ, Seydisfjordur, Iceland

Over a month had passed in a whirlwind since that first day Jana's handsome stranger came into her life. She had done as Doc Jonsson had instructed, and since Iceland has a state-centered, publicly funded universal healthcare system that covered the entire population, she'd taken Kisur to the nearest hospital in East Iceland that following morning. The doctors there had done a thorough examination along with an MRI of his brain matter, only to confirm that other than the amnesia he was experiencing, there didn't appear to be anything wrong with him. Following the hospital visit, to Geir's delight, Jana had contacted the local police. But there had been no one matching his description reported as missing in this area, nor in all of Iceland. The police had even checked with Interpol, where they had come up empty again. The authorities had assured her they would make contact should anything related come across the channels.

Further to the lack of findings, Jana had gone as far as contacting each of the fourteen embassies in Iceland. She'd gotten the same response from each of them; how tourist visiting Iceland didn't have to carry passports with them, but it was sensible to keep some form of ID on you. Stating that they deal with a significant and increasing number of lost passports each year and recommended that people write their next of kin details into the back of their passports. When she'd clarified the person she was trying to help was suffering from amnesia, the response they had given her was, *"In an emergency—unconsciousness, serious bleeding, difficulty breathing—do not spend time trying to contact a doctor. Dial 1-1-2 and ask for an ambulance."* And considering the doctors had said he was basically fine, that information had been useless. The only good thing they had told her was that since he had no name—no ID, and no known country of citizenship, he couldn't be extradited out of the country. Geir hadn't been happy when she'd told him she had agreed to take guardianship for the memory-lost visitor, signing legal documents stating she would be responsible for him until such time that either his memory was restored, or his identity was discovered.

In the brief time Kisur had been with her, he had embraced the small-town living and had grown fond of the colorful Norwegian style buildings. Her hometown was on a fjord, which gave it a wonderful natural harbor surrounded by snowcapped mountains, waterfalls, and beautiful sea views. Kisur spoke often of the town's landscape and how it was part of why he adored it here. He'd loved hearing about its history as well. Jana had told him about the town settlement in the Seyðisfjörður area having started in 1848, settled by Norwegian fishermen, and how it still had less than 700 people living here. The wildlife had intrigued him too, and she had taken him to the Skalanes nature reserve where you could see reindeers wander the area, and seals and porpoises frequenting the shores. He'd also gotten used to the nickname *Kisur*, she'd given him and had been amused to see the actual Kittiwakes birds nesting on the cliffs.

On that first visit he'd taken down to the bakery, he'd asked if he could *'help out'*, and unbeknownst to both of them, he was a natural in the kitchen and had been a godsend ever since. He seemed to have a vast knowledge of cutting techniques and chef knives, and Jana had found him more and more intriguing each day that passed. Geir had come to like him and had appreciated how helpful he was at the bakery, though he hadn't loved the fact Jana had allowed this stranger to stay with her, sharing her apartment.

Jana had set him up in her spare bedroom with a simple double mattress and linens that he barely fit on, and she had gotten him some more modern pieces of clothing as well. He'd promised to pay her back for the purchases and her kindness once he figured out who he was. When Geir had expressed his concerns over all she was doing for someone she didn't even know, Jana had explained that there weren't many options and that his proximity had worked well with his support in the bakery. Geir had reluctantly accepted the idea, although he stressed he would be keeping a close eye on this guy. It made his acceptance easier when he'd witnessed how much Kisur enjoyed working in the back kitchen, and how he seemed to get the most pleasure from being out front serving the patrons.

Today being what the American tourists called *Valentine's Day*, which isn't traditionally celebrated in Iceland, it meant it would be a good day in the bakery. And since this Sunday was the Icelandic celebration of Konudagur, *Women's Day*, Jana had already prepared plenty of festive treats and special baked goods for both days, which included single grain sourdough bread, Rye bread, Vegan and regular Cinnamon rolls, Vanilla donuts, Croissants, Chocolate filled or filled with Ham and Parmesan, and an assortment of Cookies and Scones. Jana took pride in her recipes and didn't use any junk in the baking of them. She didn't care about anything other than using first-class organic ingredients because it gave everything a much better taste.

Jana spent most of her morning filling orders, prepping for the special breakfast she would be doing on Sunday, while Kisur tended to the visiting Americans' Valentine's Day needs. He'd recalled what Valentine's Day *was*, but not whether he'd ever celebrated it before since he had no memory of a wife, girlfriend, spouse, or partner of any sort. Jana had felt a pang of guilt at her joy at hearing this affirmation, though it wasn't as if his memory could be trusted, and he could very well have a wife and kids somewhere. She found it frustrating how he could remember some things but drew a complete blank on others. But she could only imagine how maddening it must be for him and did her best to keep those thoughts of frustration to herself, those along with the attraction and growing affection she was beginning to feel for this stranger.

"Is it like this each year?" Kisur asked, pushing through the swinging door to the kitchen in the rear of the bakery.

"Busy you mean?" Jana responded.

"No—the tourists—and their ridiculous questions," he said, transferring the fresh baked goods from the cooling trays to the display ones he was refilling for out front.

Jana snickered. "I say it at least a hundred times a year that tourists coming here should read the, *what you should know before you travel blogs.*"

"What should they know? And what's a blog?" He frowned, then began transferring the now cool Kleinur, twisted donuts. He was wearing one of the bakery's long-sleeved logo shirts in forest-green and a pair of dark blue loose-fit jeans. She'd ordered several of the XXL size shirts for him, but he could have really used the XXXL since the sleeves were too short on him and he had to wear them pushed up on his forearms.

Jana smiled appreciatively as she watched him work. They'd discovered he had a sweet tooth, the Kleinur fried donuts being one of his favorites at the shop. "For one, Icelandic weather is very unpredictable. Thermals or wool underwear are a necessity no matter the season. But guaranteed, someone shows up here thinking regular jeans will do. And in winter, you'll have limited daylight, so they need to plan well!" She brushed her hands on her apron and studied her attire. She wore a matching light-blue logo shirt to Kisur's but in its place of jeans, she wore her chef pants, the standard in kitchens with the tiny black and white check, under a long waist level wraparound apron.

"What else?" he asked.

He was stalling, Jana guessed, watching him break one of the fluffy light-on-the-inside-crispy-on-the-outside donuts in half and take a bite. When she saw him lick his lips, she felt a flush of heat run up her neck to her face and quickly focused back on the rye bread she'd been rolling out. "Uhmm… you can use credit cards almost anywhere. There's no McDonald's or Starbucks—so the recommendation is *try something new.*" She peered up to see him pop the remaining half of the donut in his mouth and grin rebelliously at her. "And don't buy bottled water. Icelandic water is some of the best water you can find in the world."

At her last comment, Kisur grabbed a drinking glass from the drying rack and filled it with water at the sink. Then he said, "You told me it is so clean that in most cases it's safe to drink from the rivers and waterfalls." He took a big gulp, then emptied the glass before gasping in satisfaction. Then he came to stand next to her. "When we went to the nature reserve, you suggested we bring water bottles and fill them up along the way."

"You are an excellent student," she praised, running a hand down his bare forearm. Geir came through the swinging door to the kitchen then and spied Jana before she could pull her hand back from Kisur's arm.

"Gefa undir fótinn," Geir said, smirking, eyebrows raised.

"Geir!" Jana shouted, moving away from Kisur. "Ég kem alveg af fjöllum. "

"What?" Kisur questioned, pulling their attention. "*You're totally giving under the foot?*" he translated, giving them an expression of uncertainty.

Jana glowered at Geir.

Geir roared out a laugh, then covered his mouth guiltily.

Jana gave him a swat with her flour covered hand, leaving obvious handprints on his tan sweater. "Ignore him," she said.

Kisur's skills in the kitchen had been a surprise, but his language skills were even more amazing. He couldn't remember who he was, but he could speak several languages. They'd discovered this talent while he'd been speaking with customers, with responses to them in Mandarin Chinese, Hindi, Spanish, French, Arabic and even some Icelandic, coming effortlessly from him.

"And what was that about *coming completely from the mountains?*" Kisur asked, interpreting Jana's part of the conversation.

"I told him, *'I have no idea what he's talking about'*, but I'll explain that later," she directed at Kisur.

Kisur shrugged. "Is there a Men's Day to go with the Women's Day?" he asked, scooping up the display trays now filled with pastries.

"Yes—Bóndadagur," Geir answered, brushing the flour off the front of his sweater, "You missed it. It was back in November. But every day should be Men's Day," he added.

Jana swatted him again. "What are you doing here?" Jana said to Geir then in replace of a hello.

Kisur chuckled, pushing backward through the swinging door, trays of goodies in both arms.

"You like him," Geir said when the door swung closed.

"Please stop," Jana said, moving the bread pans she'd filled into the large oven.

"Admit it." He stepped up close enough to run a finger through the flour on the counter, but not near enough to get anything on his clothes.

Jana rolled her eyes. "What do you want?"

"Besides one of your Konudagur treats," he said, snatching one of her vegan cinnamon rolls from the cooling trays.

"Seriously?" She slapped his hand when he went to grab another.

"Okay-okay—I had an idea?" He sniffed the roll, then took a generous bite.

"About?" she asked, donning oven mitts. Then she slid out the last of the chocolate sheet cakes, the Skúffukaka, the one Doc Jonsson liked so much, the cake everyone loved so much, from the other large oven and set it on an open cooling tray.

"Tattoo database," Geir said, pulling a section off the roll before shoving it into his mouth.

Jana blew out a breath and shook her head, then pulled off the oven mitts and rested them on the counter, waiting.

"Hear me out." He held up his free hand in appeal, then took another bite of his cinnamon roll.

Jana put her hands on her hips, then studied the kitchen. "I don't have time for this—but please—go on."

"I don't know why I didn't think of this sooner—but you know how livestock and even domestic pets are often marked with tattoos to identify them—should they get lost or stollen?" Geir went to the sink and washed his hands.

"Yes." Jana shrugged, confused, shaking her head again.

"Well, we have a database that we keep all the tattoo markings with owners recorded—should we need it."

"Geir," Jana began, taking a second glance around the kitchen.

"The police have something similar."

She frowned, still perplexed at where he was going with all this.

"Kisur's tattoos—remember?" he said. "Maybe we can find out who he is by his tattoos."

Jana's mouth dropped open then she closed it, tightening her lips. She wanted to know who he was, but she couldn't admit she was afraid to find out who he was. Afraid to lose him. "I'll ask him if he's willing to do that." She began tidying her workspace.

"Why wouldn't he?" Geir asked, leaning a hip against the edge of the sink counter. "You've seen them, haven't you?"

She nodded. She'd told Kisur about his tattoos, even taken a photo of them for him to see them better. But he once again had no recollection of ever having or getting them, or what they meant. She stared at Geir then, examining his face.

"What—do I have cinnamon on my face?" he asked, running a hand over the skin near his mouth.

"No." She stared longer, and Geir rubbed his fingers over his lips. "How often do you shave?"

"Ha—you're asking me about my grooming habits?" He passed his hand across his jaw then. "Every day—why?"

Jana continued to stare at Geir's face. "How much would you say grows in a month?"

"About half an inch per month for most guys. But seriously, why?"

She glanced at the swinging door, then back at him. "I bought Kisur some toiletries, deodorant, mild scented shampoo, and some razors and cream to shave with. But I don't think he's ever used the shave stuff—and he never shows any stubble on his face."

Geir gave a puzzled look back at her, then said, "Well—not sure about that, but his body is completely hairless. You must have noticed."

"How could I know that?" Jana put her hands on her hips again and gave a tight press of her lips.

"I guess you wouldn't if you haven't seen him naked." Geir gave her a sly smile. "But I have." He followed his roguish smile with a couple of eyebrow raises.

Flustered by his comments, Jana busied herself with retying the strings of her apron, then she said, "Okay, I'll ask him later about the tattoos—but right now I have customers to serve." She moved from behind the huge counter, heading for the door to the front of the bakery.

"I understand," Geir said. "I'll let myself out the back way."

Jana turned and waved at him before pushing through the door.

In the small cafe area, Jana spotted Kisur serving a few regulars their coffee and croissants. The woman at the table dropped her spoon and Kisur knelt to retrieve it. The front door to the bakery opened then, allowing a potent smell of tobacco to waft in.

Kisur swiveled his head towards the stench to where a short chubby man stood just inside the open door. The man called out something, in what Jana thought sounded like a Russian accent, to an equally chubby woman—probably his wife, who stood at the order counter, and more than likely his request for food. Kisur, clearly as annoyed as Jana, glimpsed her way, then turned his head to address the man from his kneeling position. "Smoking in restaurants, bars, public transport, and public buildings is prohibited. Anyone caught smoking will be asked to leave the premises and may be fined." The man stared back at Kisur, oblivious to his error. Before the man could say anything, Kisur repeated his declaration in whatever the man's primary language was. In response, the man arrogantly plucked the stinky brown stalk from his mouth and waved it about like a statement, then pointed the cigar at Kisur. Slowly and stealthily, Kisur stood from his lowered position, his massive body extending up, up, up, giving the man the vantage point and realization of just who he was dealing with. The man nodded feverishly, then said something as though excusing himself while he backed up to wait outside the bakery.

Without missing a beat, Kisur turned back to the seated customers and pulled a clean spoon from his server's apron, setting it down next to the woman's coffee cup. "Enjoy," he said to them. Then he turned away and headed toward the swinging door to the kitchen. He gazed at Jana as he passed her at the counter, his expression grim.

Jana followed him into the kitchen. "Are you okay?"

"I don't know. The smell it…," he said, sitting down on a stack of crates.

"I know it was gross. Like I mentioned, some people—tourists, just don't know any better," she said, watching him as he stared down at the floor.

"No… not the smell—I mean yes—it was nasty, but the smell… it felt like… a *memory*." He gazed up at her then.

"Did you remember something?"

"Not really… it's hard to explain… but something about it was familiar." He went back to staring down at the ground.

"Do you think you may know the man?"

"No," he laughed out. "But that smell—I… don't know." He shook his head from side to side, then pushed up from the crates. He went to take a step forward but swayed instead. When he threw out his arm, Jana grabbed it.

"Are you sure you're okay?" she asked, helping to steady him against the counter.

"Yes-yes," he said, shifting to take another step, but then he swayed again.

"No—you're not." Jana put his bulky arm around her shoulders, then led him through the office and to the stairs to her apartment. "You, my friend, are going to go lay down upstairs. The rush is over—I can finish up here," she assured him. She maneuvered his arm from around her shoulders, securing his grip on the railing that ran up the stairs.

"Are you sure?" he asked, glancing back at her, placing a foot on the first step.

She grinned confidently up at him. "I'm used to doing it alone, anyway."

He nodded and then proceeded warily up the stairs.

Jana watched him until he made it to the top and disappeared through the opening of the stairwell to her apartment. Then she dashed back through the office into the bakery and to the remaining waiting customers.

After handing off the last customer order and closing up, Jana ascended the stairs to her apartment, where she found Kisur slumped and asleep on the small sofa in her tiny living room. She kicked off her sneakers, then collapsed into the armchair next to the sofa. *"What a morning,"* she said under her breath, resting her head back and closing her eyes.

"Did I miss anything?" she heard Kisur ask then, though she kept her eyes shut.

"Nothing other than silly tourists asking silly questions," she said, opening her eyes then, tilting her head to look at him. "Could it hurt them to learn a few basic words or phrases like, *yes, no, please* or *thank you?* I don't expect them to know the odder sayings." She noticed he had shifted from slumped to upright. "Are you feeling better?"

"Much," he said, smiling. "What odd sayings?"

"Well, for example, like for this past month. Icelanders don't say, 'I can't believe that just happened!' We say, *'Það eru margar undur í höfuðkúpu'.*

"There are many wonders in a cow's head," Kisur translated, snorting.

She raised her head from resting on the chair. "Or the fact that you are a master in the kitchen. Icelanders wouldn't say, 'that was a surprise', we would say *'Það er rúsínan í pylsuendanum'.*

"That's a raisin at the end of the hot dog?" he translated again, laughing even harder.

She laughed with him. He was beautiful when he smiled and even more spectacular when he laughed. "Speaking of kitchen talents, are you hungry?" She knew she was. She'd only had half a chocolate croissant the whole morning. "Would you like to get pizza at the Skaftfell Bistro?"

"Sure," Kisur said, patting his flat belly.

"I need to change first," she said, glancing at her work clothes. "And let's get it to go? I've had enough of dealing with people for one day."

Kisur hadn't remembered ever having pizza, but he liked it. "The town may be small, but it is vibrant," Kisur said in appreciation as they walked the route back to the apartment. He still wore her father's coat, but she enjoyed seeing him in it.

"January is the coldest month of the year, and we have limited daylight—a mere four hours. Some find it harsh. But we have everything we need here too," Jana said, adding to the sentiment. Then she pointed to a shop sign on the building next to hers that read *Apótek*.

"Pharmacy," Kisur said, translating. Pizza takeout dinner in hand, he followed her as she proceeded up the steps and into the shop.

"I wanted to pick something up for you—a supplement that might improve your memory issue." She turned down an aisle with rows of shelves containing various sized containers on each of them. She grabbed what she'd been looking for, then held up the white plastic bottle for him to see.

"MSM," he said, taking the bottle from her to read the label.

"Methylsulfonylmethane," Jana said. "Doc Jonsson said it was helpful for the different types of *memory* we have. Sensory register like with our five senses, along with short-term and long-term memory. Patients with Alzheimer's disease are recorded as having a positive response to it and likewise for people suffering from a foggy brain." She gazed at him, examining his magnificent features as he read the back of the bottle.

"Sounds good," he said, looking up from reading. He grinned at her seductively, holding her stare.

She gazed up into those sparkling navy-blue eyes of his, lost in their depth as if hypnotized. Jana's body warmed as Kisur stepped closer, his gaze fixed on her, only the pizza box between.

"Can I help you find anything?" someone said then, pulling Jana's attention from the thrall of Kisur's handsome face. To her left stood the young shop clerk. "Did you find what you were looking for?" he asked.

"We're good—thank you," she said, stepping back to give the clerk room to pass between them. "Let's go," she said, taking the bottle from him without looking up at his face. "Pizza's getting cold," she added, proceeding up to the checkout counter.

Once back in the apartment, while Kisur took the pizza to the kitchen, Jana went off to her bedroom without a word. When she returned, she found Kisur had plated the pizza and had set the plates and paper napkins on the coffee table, along with two large glasses of water. Without looking at his face, she sat down on the couch next to him.

She had brought a small wooden box with her from her bedroom. "I don't know why I kept this, but I guess I thought it might be a clue to who you were." She opened the box and pulled out the cigar wrapper that she'd originally kept in her cellphone case. Handing it to him, she said, "Maybe you smoked cigars?"

"I can't imagine I would—but maybe." He flipped the wrapper over, the water stain showing on the backside.

"I did a little research on the brand," she admitted, eyes fixated on his hands.

He flipped the small bit of paper back over to the show the label. "What did you find out?"

"Well… it's an ultra-premium cigar *fit for a king*—they say. And at $1000 a pop, it certainly was." Jana studied him then, thinking that he could be a king, or a prince, or… someone far too sophisticated for her.

Kisur let out a long, drawn-out whistle. "Sounds almost too intimidating to smoke. If I did, I hope it was worth it," he chuckled out.

Jana grinned. "Between that and the very expensive suit you were wearing when I found you, it could indicate that you are—or find yourself in the company of extremely wealthy people."

He smirked. "Doesn't feel familiar—can't picture myself as rich." He huffed a laugh and handed her back the wrapper.

Taking it, she placed it back in the wooden box, then said, "I realize I had forgotten to mention this, but with the fact that you were wet—when I found you, I'd contacted the port office to see if any of the ships were missing a passenger. The port authority contacted the only ship, the Norröna, which had been in the area. It had been in port on the 14th and 15th of December, but those dates didn't correspond to when I'd discovered you. I checked all the places to stay in town that were open this time of year, but no one recalled anyone fitting your description." She paused, glancing down at the box, reluctant to say her next words, then she said, "Someone must be missing you." She hoped it wasn't a girlfriend or wife, but still she knew if it were her, she would be a complete wreck had he gone missing from her life.

"What did Geir say to you when he came in?" he asked, shifting the conversation.

"What do you mean?" She closed the box and set it on the coffee table next to the plates, then looked back at him.

"I know the words, but not the expression," he clarified. "Geir said, *'you're totally giving under the foot'*."

Heat rose again on Jana's neck, tickling the edges of her face. "Oh that—it's nothing—just a stupid saying. He was just teasing me." She bit her lip and regarded the box on the coffee table, hoping that was enough of an explanation for him.

"What does it mean?" he asked, her answer obviously insufficient.

"It means…." She gave him a quick glance, then returned to gazing at the box. "*You're totally flirting*."

There was a long silence. Then, as though to lift her apparent disquiet, he asked, "What's with the box?"

She blew out a breath, relieved he wasn't going to make a thing out of what Geir had said. "It's a memory box—my father's. It's nothing priceless or anything." She studied him.

He just nodded. She wasn't sure if he was waiting for more or choosing not to ask more, then he said, "You mentioned he passed away a few years ago… I think you said you were thirty-one at the time." He reached for her hand.

His hand was warm and comparable in size to her father's, though the fingers and the palm of his were smooth unlike her father's, whose hands had always been rough from his working outside. "Yes," she said, staring at his hand resting over hers. "He was sixty-five—and still working. He was a large animal vet, but you already knew that. Geir has his practice now," she reminded, still staring at his hand. "A horse struck him… in the head, while he was examining it. He'd been trying to keep the farmer's grandson away from the horse when it happened." She let go of the breath she'd been holding. Her father's death had stolen her breath and had crushed her heart.

"Will you tell me more about him?" He took up her hand in his. "I have no recollection of family myself, as you know."

"Well," she began, glancing up to look him in the face. As though to comfort her, he ran his thumb over the back of her hand and then he gave her the subtlest of smiles. "He was an Olympic speed skater," she continued. "In the 1988 winter Olympics in Calgary—that's in Canada. Do you know what the Olympics are?" She grinned quizzically at him then.

"Yes—I do, actually. World sports competition," he said, releasing her hand. "It confuses me what I can and can't recall." He turned in his seat to face her, resting his elbow on the back of the sofa, leaning the side of his head against his fisted hand. "Did he skate for Iceland?"

She felt the harsh absence of his warm hand immediately. "What a struggle it must be not knowing what you know or don't know," she said, boldly shifting to face him, pulling her knee up for more comfort. "And—no, he skated for Norway. He's originally from there—moved here with his parents. My grandparents were farmers in Egilsstadir. My father was thirty-five when he came out of retirement to fill a spot on the team. A young speed skater had tested positive for steroids."

"How did he do?" He mirrored her, pulling his knee up, it tapping against hers.

"There were no medals that year for speed skating." She shrugged.

"Maybe he should have skated for Iceland." He smiled playfully.

She laughed then. "Iceland has never won a medal at a winter Olympics."

"Oh well—never say never," he said, hopeful. "You haven't mentioned your mother."

Jana sighed, then reached for the memory box. Setting it on the sofa between them, she opened it and retrieved a photo. "My mother was an American figure skater. That's where they met." She handed him the photo of her parents. "My mother—Joy, and my father married shortly after the games, and she returned to Iceland with him. I was born a year later."

"Does she still live in Iceland?" he asked, smiling down at the photo.

"No, she took off a few weeks after my first birthday," Jana said. "My father explained to me she had grown board and restless living in such a remote place and having been only twenty years old when they'd married, she had wanted more excitement in her life. He was an introvert—she was an extrovert." Kisur handed her back the photo.

Jana stared at it for several heartbeats, then said. "When I was old enough, during those early years, I noticed that the photos of my father and mother together began to dwindle. By the time I was sixteen years old, the photos had gone down to just this one, which he'd kept on the mantle next to a photo of my mother and me from the day I was born." Jana handed him the photo from her birth. "When I turned twenty, my father gave me this box of photos and mementos."

He took the photo from her but didn't look at it. Instead, he placed it back in the box and closed the lid. Then he took both her hands in his and stared directly into her eyes.

Jana swallowed hard. "What?" she questioned, heart pounding, uncertainty flooding her brain. "Did you remember something?"

"No." He shook his head once. "But those memories… those keepsakes, Jana. They are priceless."

Chapter 11 

Last week I'd gotten some updates from my girlfriends in Ottawa. The first being an interesting report from Alison on Lane's visits to the group home.

Lane had made several visits back to spend time with Taylor, and some other residents mainly to keep suspicions down, working with them doing cognitive and mobility activities that helped those with developmental disabilities. And since Leo had a photographic memory for anything relating to buildings, Lane had provided him a photo of a floor plan for his review, one that Taylor had drawn. She had also outlined for Alison, her meeting Lyndon, mentioning his face and the burn scars, though she'd not seen him since that first encounter. It had been Derek who had read about Thaddeus testing the influence of sulfur on Lyndon and how it had burned half of his face. And we'd known about Lyndon from Purah, how he was one of Thaddeus's guys, that he had been the other Seraph who had been cast down with Thaddeus, from her home star, Celaeno, and that Lyndon was also the one who monitored the group home.

The next update had been from Olivia, stating that she'd finally brought Rachel in on things, explaining also that Rachel's acceptance of now being part of *the knowing* had been easier than she had expected.

She'd also shared the information with Rachel about the Earthbound and nurse Nic, adding that Rachel felt this last bit of the puzzle made more sense now considering she had considered her fellow nurse to be 'out of this world'.

Mac's update had been short, stating she hadn't had any luck so far with the locator spells but would keep working on it.

And Vicki, her updates had been focused on future travels with Eric.

Other than the initial otherworldly updates, I had experienced nothing supernatural, not since my meeting with that Earthbound, Kendrick, in Norway, not unless you count the familiar, yet curious sensation of my being watched. It was much like what I had felt while at my job in the hospital in Miami, a similar sensation as when I had sensed Gabriel. That, and I could have sworn I'd caught movement out of the corner of her eye too, a flash of long blonde curly hair, though it only seemed to happen at my new volunteer job at the hospital and only around the Maternity ward.

The hospital had offered me the volunteer gig on the spot, though it wasn't the position I had hoped for. They were impressed with my work in the NICU at the Miami hospital and my recommendations, but since it had been over 10 years since I'd worked in a hospital, what they offered me, what they needed right now, was an additional volunteer who would be responsible for tracking the location and status of medical equipment. In simple terms, it meant my job would be to locate abandoned wheelchairs and move them to more accessible areas used by the porters. I'd been hesitant to accept the job and less than thrilled at the idea of being a wheelchair monitor until they informed me they had tracking software for the task.

The hospital's wheelchairs were equipped with special tags that emit a signal based on Bluetooth Low Energy technology at a pre-set interval transmitting information about the exact location in real-time, received by the base stations placed around the hospital. During orientation, I'd been told the lack of availability of wheelchairs had a direct impact on patient care, and in some cases it could be critical. Every second a medical staff member spends searching for an open wheelchair takes time away from the patient experience and can negatively impact the patient's health outcome, not to mention the impact on operational continuity. The entire hospital workflow relies on getting patients where they need to be quickly and efficiently. The absence of adequate tracking can create delays that impact processes and efficiency of a hospital.

I'd known from my previous work that wheelchairs were a standard feature in any hospital, but it wasn't until they had integrated me into the process these past two weeks that I fully understood the impact they had on nearly every aspect of the hospital. Now I was proud to cover this task and would be doing so from 10 a.m. until 1 p.m. on Tuesday, Wednesday, and Friday mornings, working for Floor Services with the Escort/Courier Services as part of the 500 dedicated volunteers for the 330 bed hospital.

Redmond's time out of the house these previous two weeks had been split between him helping refurbish the South Haven location and time with Luc at the music studio. Dunya hadn't come down as she'd been feeling under the weather, which was just as well, as my mornings were now taken with my new job. When I'd called to check on her, it was obvious by the coughing and nose blowing that she had a full-on cold. I'd told her that most of my mornings were busy from the hospital gig anyway and reminded her of the invite for her and Luc to come down again this year for the off island Easter egg hunt in April with the twins. My mention of the upcoming event had made her feel better about not making it this time, plus, it was best she rest and recover.

Last night, Redmond and the twins had made 4 dozen chocolate cupcakes and this morning they'd helped their father decorate the tops with white icing and tiny red candy hearts in preparation for Valentine Friendship Day at their school today. Their teacher, Mr. McCray, was a big supporter of equality and inclusivity and had advocated at the school for renaming the day. Love is love, is love, so why not make it about friendship, we had all agreed.

On my volunteering days like today, Redmond took the lead with getting the girls ready for school, making lunches, *and* filling my travel mug with coffee for my drive to the hospital. Before leaving, I had packed up two dozen of the cupcakes into a large plastic container to give to the nurses in the maternity ward and NICU. In addition, I had grabbed two more cupcakes, one for me to eat on the way to the hospital, and one to bribe the parking attendant into letting me have a spot closer to the building's entrance.

"Happy Valentine's Day, Vinnie," I said, pulling up to the attendant's window to get my paper printout. "Brought you a little something to make your day." I handed off the chocolate bribe wrapped in parchment paper. Vinnie, *Vincenza,* was a retired army sergeant who worked the early-morning shift and ran the hospital parking area during this time like she was guarding a military post.

"You're going to have to walk the expanse like the rest of your garrison," Vinnie said with a wink, handing me the printout with the special green sticker on it. The green sticker meant I could park in the first three rows, which was nine rows closer than where I was normally expected to park.

"Thank you—have a great day," I said, placing the parking pass in view through my car's front window before driving on.

Friday mornings in the Emergency Room at the hospital were the slowest I'd been told, Monday being the busiest, but this was only my second Monday working, so I had little experience yet to go on. It had surprised me to hear that the number one and the most common ER visits were because of headaches, the second being foreign objects in the body, followed by back pain, cuts and contusions, upper respiratory infections, broken bones and sprains, and last being toothaches of all things. And I was further surprised to hear that they had a dentist on call at the hospital.

On my way to the East Annex, where I readily started my wheelchair hunt, I made my preliminary stop at the entrance to the Maternity Ward and NICU. I'd be back this way again on the wheelchair roundup, but I wanted to drop off the Valentine's Day treats first. I'd introduced myself to the nursing staff in both wards on my first week when I'd realized I would be frequenting these zones. I'd been pleased to hear that the person in charge of both areas had also seen my resume and was impressed by my past work, and that over time I could eventually work my way back to a similar role to what I'd had at the Miami hospital. And I was cool with that.

"Good morning and happy V-D," I said to the two familiar nurses behind the main desk. "Love and friendship," I added, chuckling, lifting the lid of the plastic container to reveal the delicious cupcakes.

"V-D? Nice, Lynn—not," nurse Tina, the younger of the two, said with a laugh.

"Spread the love," I said. "These are for the entire crew."

"You shouldn't have—but I'm glad you did," Kim, the other nurse, said, taking the container and stashing it under the overhang of the half-moon shaped desk.

"My hubby made them—so they're actually delicious. Be grateful I didn't make them." I checked my watch. "How are your tiny charges doing today?" They'd had several newborns in their care last week.

"Getting stronger each day, I'm happy to say," Tina shared.

I'd found out that first day on the job when I'd gotten the tour that they all knew about my background with working in the NICU. During the short time I've gotten to know this revolving crew, we'd exchanged several stories of our time in the NICU. "That's the best answer," I gave her in response, aware that 'stronger' meant a lot in this realm. "Enjoy, ladies. I'll see you again on my walkthrough." I waved and traveled back towards the starting segment of my hunt, which was the Behavioral Health Center.

My coworkers had informed me the center had a program to help people in distress to develop skills to deal with life's difficulties more positively. It was also explained to me that this hospital was a Designated Baker Act Receiving Facility, meaning doctors and mental health professionals, along with judges and law enforcement, could commit a person at this location for up to 72 hours if they displayed certain behaviors such as hallucinations, suicidal thoughts, depression and hopelessness, substance use, or even someone unable to care for themselves, like declining to take care of basic needs like sleep, eating, personal cleanliness or taking medications. The purpose was to grant time to perform a mental health evaluation and to de-escalate any crisis. A person could also choose to participate in a voluntary Baker Act, but they must be willing and able to consent to treatment. This happened more than I'd realized, mainly because mental health aid was becoming more accessible and more mainstream with the negative stigma of mental health issues being shifted. Though I hadn't witnessed any one being brought in yet.

At the base station, I swiped my access card to log into the system, then checked the map for any rogue wheelchairs. I had access to almost every area of the hospital, but the Behavior Health Center had special security to enter, so staff left chairs at the entrance hall on my side of the doorway to make it easier for pickup. They kept a select few in their ward, but any used for transport needed to be retrieved and brought back to the main entrance and the emergency area. This morning there was only one wheelchair dot indicated on the map waiting for me.

As I approached, the sliding security doors to the center's entrance swished open to release three people. Two were doctors I'd already met. The third was a short red-haired woman in a dark grey suit, and possibly another doctor I hadn't seen before.

"Lynn—wonderful to see you!" the first doctor said, noticing me. This one always seemed oddly chipper, considering the ward he worked in. "This is Dr. Stone. She is our new on-call psychologist—so you might see her around." He swept a hand towards her as though he were working the display on a game show. "Doctor, this is Lynn, one of our valuable volunteers here." He swept his other hand my way as though the two of us were to meet in the middle.

Behind the extravagant introduction of the first doctor, I spied the second doctor with his hand over his mouth, holding back a laugh. When he rolled his eyes, I tightened my lips and turned my attention back to the new doctor. "Welcome. Pleased to meet you," I said, giving her a warm grin.

The new doctor stepped forward and extended a hand in greeting. "Thank you. I won't be officially on staff until September, but I look forward to working with you." She smiled mischievously back through tight lips as though she and I were in on the same joke, the joke being the over-the-top greeting performance of her colleague.

I shook her hand, giving her a wider playful smile this time. "I'm fairly knew here too, but I've gotten pretty good navigating the floors and hallways with this job, so feel free to ask me for directions."

"Thank you again—nothing worse than getting lost on the job," she laughed out. She had a genuine laugh, and I liked her right away.

"Let me show you the way out," the doctor said then, pulling our attention. He extended his arm, this time in the direction of the way out.

"Bye—Lynn," Dr. Stone said with a quick wave before heading the way of the doctor's extended hand.

"See you soon," I said, moving on toward the abandoned wheelchair.

As the morning flowed, I moved through my tracking task, checking stations throughout the hospital for discarded wheelchairs. Time passed swiftly as I repeated the circuit for the fourth and final time before the close of my shift. My last pass was by the entrance to the maternity ward, but I already knew from the station map that they didn't have any extra wheelchairs that needed transferring. I also knew I was starving.

"Any of those cupcakes left?" I asked, leaning over the top of the main desk to where the container had been stashed.

"You're funny," nurse Kim said, retrieving the plastic container from the far side of the desk.

"Ah, it was worth a try." I tapped the lid of the now empty container. "My shift is basically over—can I go in?" I asked, tilting my head once in the direction of the doors to the maternity area.

"Sure, the babies seem to quiet down when you're around," Kim said, passing her ID card over the security pad. "You've got a gift."

"Tell that to my daughters," I said with a chuckle.

She pulled open the door. "Tina—the baby whisperer is here," Kim announced, grinning ruefully at me as I passed through the opening.

"Hey, Lynn," Tina greeted, as she tucked the end of a flannel blanket under a baby wearing a blue beanie. All at once, the cries and protests of the three rows of new babies all lowered to a soft cooing. "I'm going to take advantage of you being here—to run and grab something from the vending machine."

"The brave cannot survive on chocolate cupcakes alone," I said as she scooted by me and through the door.

I joke when I speak of my daughters as babies because they too, like the babies in the maternity ward in Miami, calmed at my presence. It wasn't until later that I'd learned it wasn't just me that had lulled them, it had been the combination of both mine and Gabriel's ethereal presence that had done it. And it was why I knew I wasn't truly alone now with these babies.

I stepped back away from the bassinets, my back almost touching the wall. Then I closed my eyes and focused on my breathing to increase my awareness of the present moment. Taking in some deep breaths in and out, I repeated a mantra silently to myself. *I am open to all that releases me.* I repeated it a second time, then a third, and a fourth time. Then I opened my eyes.

Before me stood a statuesque woman with waist length blonde ringlet hair, wearing an elegant white linen pantsuit, the blazer part of it worn over what appeared to be a basic white round-neck t-shirt. "You pulled me from behind my veil," she stated, hands clasped behind her back.

"I knew I wasn't alone." I stared up into her lovely face, examining her flawless skin, her mesmerizing dark green eyes, and her furrowed brow.

"You are powerful." She unclasped her hands and took a step closer, staring back at my face and examining me in the same manner.

"I know you're an angel, but who are you exactly?" I questioned, leaning back against the wall to give more distance between us.

"I am Archangel Diniel." She lifted a hand, and I thought she was going to touch my face, but then she lowered it back to her side.

"The protector of infants," I said, remembering the name and role from what Gabriel had told me about the other Archangels. I peeked past her and scanned the rows of babies behind her.

"Correct." She tilted her head to one side. "You are knowledgeable as well." She blinked, then shifted her head to center again.

"What… are you doing here?" I blew out in a breath. "I know it's a maternity ward and yer all about the babies—but why are you *here-here*?" I pointed and gestured several times at the area around us.

"I've known about you and what you can do—your gifts, but I was hoping to witness them myself." She did the head-tilt thing again. "You did not disappoint."

Okay, this was weird. "You're here to see me? Do you need me for something?" I shrugged.

Realigning her head, she said, "No… Angels need nothing from humans."

Okay, this was weirder than weird. "Right. Great—well, my shift is over."

She said nothing, only continued to gaze at me as though she were observing a piece of art in a gallery.

I nodded, eager for this encounter to be over. "Alright then. Later—I guess." I turned to exit the room, then peered over my shoulder to find she was gone.

Through the front door of the house, I rushed in searching for my husband. I knew he was home because I saw his truck in the carport. "Heeey—where are you?"

No response.

I dropped my purse on the front table, then went to our bedroom. Through the bedroom opening to the ensuite bathroom, I spotted Redmond. "Yer not going to believe who I saw—met, today," I announced, then paused when I realized he was bandaging up a long scrape from his knee down his shin.

"Hey," he said, glancing up between wraps of gauze around his shin.

"Need any help?" I asked, kneeling to get a better look at the injury. "Looks like road rash." Then I noticed several smaller scrapes and discolouration. "You got all these cuts and abrasions from helping renovate at South Haven?"

"We're almost done," he said, taping off the end of the gauze strip. "So, I've been spending time with Ben. Learning some self-defense techniques," he added, as though brushing off the visible wounds was acceptable.

I'd seen a few extra scrapes over the past few weeks and now I knew why. "Okay," I said, standing, not sure what else to say.

Redmond stood. "Ben was only here for a short time. Between his teaching at the university in Ottawa—and his surveying of Maia, the Tokyo Japan facility, I was lucky to steal time with him."

I knew Ben was a professor of Human Kinetics at Ottawa U. "Busy guy." I gave him my whatever face and stomped out of the bathroom.

"You'll have to meet him next time," I heard Redmond call, as I reemerged into the bedroom. My stomach growled. Further exasperated yet in need of sustenance, I spun around and ventured back to where my personal chef had been patching up his boo-boos. I found him in our walk-in closet. "What the hell is that?" I screamed, seeing my mild-mannered husband holding a handgun.

"I was just putting it away," Redmond said, in defense of my upset. "I keep it in the safe Den brought over."

"To keep things safe," I remembered Den saying. "And?"

Redmond held the gun out for me to see as though doing so would make it less terrifying. "I was going to tell you about it—seriously." He put the gun into the case, then tucked the metal safe in behind his hanging suit jackets. "I want to be able to protect you and the girls. I've been learning how to use other weapons too, not just learning self-defense." He rested his hands gently on the tops of my shoulders. "Who did you see today?" he asked, attempting to change the subject.

I brushed off one of his hands and turned away to exit the closet. "I'll tell you later. Where are the girls?"

"At Lily's. Darius and she thought we could use some alone time since it's Valentine's Day," Redmond said, following me back through the bedroom and out into the living room.

From where I had stopped in the living room, I discovered Redmond had the dining table set for a dinner for two. A glass vase sat between the place settings, filled with huge half-blooming white roses. My favorites. My mood softening, I said, "I understand… you want to take care of us." I took a breath and turned to look at him. "But it scares me having a gun in the house."

Redmond put his big, warm hands over the sides of my shoulders this time. "That's more because you haven't held one, used it—practiced with it. It's an unknown and you hate things that are unknown." He rubbed the sides of my shoulders.

"You're right." He was right. I hated when he was right. "Well, if it's going to be in our home, then I think I should learn how to shoot, too."

Chapter 12 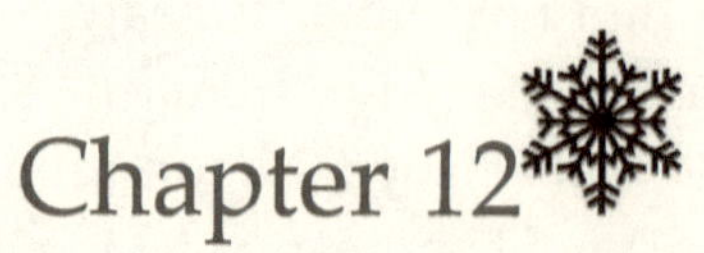

Thaddeus rode the private elevator from his condo down to the personal lab under the building's greenhouse. He had Brutus in one hand, and in the other, he grasped the handle of a silver rectangular medical case. "Wait until you see what I have here, my colourful friend," he said, when the elevator door slid aside. He opened the way into the lab by dangling the special key fob over the security pad. Then he set Brutus's bowl atop a lone filing cabinet isolated away from the other wall of cabinets.

This single column of drawers was for his unique keepsakes. Next to it was a narrow table with only a desk lamp and a box of surgical gloves on it. It was there that he set the case down flat on its side, the handle facing forward. Flipping the switch on the desk lamp, its sharp light illuminated the metallic casing of the container. In unison, Thaddeus released the two latches on either side of the handle. The contents shone bright white against the dull grey of the container's lining. "Hello, my beauties," Thaddeus gushed, clasping his hands under his chin. "Don't be jealous, Brutus. This is just a little Valentine's Day gift to me," he said, cutting a quick glimpse at his purple beauty. "You know you are stunning in your own ways."

Turning to the cabinet, he pulled open a drawer, the second one from the bottom. Then he grabbed for a pair of rubber gloves from the open box next to the lamp. As though handling a priceless artifact, he gingerly reached into the case and retrieved the first of three items.

This first item was essentially thirty-three items interlocked with each other. He'd had them all laced together. "Look at this specimen, Brutus. This at the top—this is the atlas," Thaddeus said, pointing out the first vertebra. Then he went on, naming the major segments. "These sections here are the cervical, thoracic, and lumbar vertebrae, and all the way down here is the sacrum and coccyx." He held out the spinal column for Brutus to see before placing the linked vertebrae onto the soft cushion that lined the drawer. He repeated the transfer with the next two items, a pair of scapulae or shoulder blades, all of which were bleached an unnatural white. "You can get a plastic version of skeletal bones from any medical supply company," Thaddeus said. "But these lovelies, these uniquely deformed beauties, are from another of those creatures I've told you about." These he'd taken from the remains of that last little sick boy he'd tested on. He'd had them stripped of any soft tissue, muscles, tendons, ligaments, and nerves, and the protective membrane, the dura mater, and the spinal cord removed. Then he'd gotten them bleached to their now gleaming perfection.

Thaddeus stared adoringly at his trophies in the drawer. "That makes seven sets," he said, before rolling the drawer shut. "So much for lucky number seven." He turned and paused, facing the open area of the lab, then walked directly over to his desk. "I wish I had something to celebrate with," he uttered, glancing back at Brutus. "One of my favorite icebox cakes from that bakery in New York would surely top off my day." He considered then that The Scone Witch bakery here in Ottawa, two streets over, might have something festive considering the day, and the bakery was only a 15-minute walk away. "On the topic of restaurants," he said, shifting his focus back to his desk. "Attendant, call Marcus." Thaddeus had demanded Marcus get eyes on that female, Francesca, the one who now called herself *Frank* for some idiotic reason, and he had wanted more information on that boss of hers, the restaurant owner.

"Yes," Marcus answered, his tone full of annoyance.

"Update—on that female," Thaddeus barked. "What is she doing there—and why is she doing it?"

"Managing the place, it seems."

"Why would a Seraph be working for a human?" Thaddeus turned and sat on the edge of the desk.

"I've had Zuriel watching the restaurant, but he reports there's been no sign of the boss-man—not since I'd seen him there," Marcus explained, voice resonating with boredom.

"What have you discovered about him?" Thaddeus crossed his arms over his chest.

"I'm no further along finding out anything about him."

"Nothing?"

"Nothing other than what I told you. Like the mention of him in articles about the restaurant—how it was the most sought-after place for a romantic dinner and lavish celebration." Delight threaded Marcus's voice now.

"This… is absolutely… maddening," Thaddeus said, drawing out the words. Much like he was, this restauranter too was a recluse, it seemed. "These humans disgust me with their need to express this emotion of love for each other." He'd loved no one other than Brutus. He glanced over and smiled lovingly at his faithful companion. *I am superior to these humans.* His pleasure came from more nefarious endeavors. Though he'd not had a halfling to experiment on, of late, not since that old couple had surrendered their weakling of a grandchild to his facility in New York City. The boy's scrawny body had expired too soon, following the procedures and tests he'd inflicted upon him. The boy's demise had rendered what little remained as useless, leaving him nothing other than the trophies he'd claimed for his collection. Thaddeus gazed affectionately at the cabinet of bones again. For 20 years, he'd been searching for offspring of their kind. He longed to create a domination of powerful offspring to rule over these feeble humans. To date, he had been unsuccessful in producing what he considered a *pure* progeny, where both genetic contributors were celestials, having to settle with mere testing on these abominations, these halflings, instead. "Keep looking—I'm curious why one of ours would lower herself to work for a human. He must hold something over her—a threat of some sort." Thaddeus dropped his arms and stood facing the desk. "In the meantime, direct your focus on these other men—the ones who accompanied that woman into my building."

"Who do you think they are?"

"I'm not sure. But somebody hired these men—this woman, to investigate us—me, it would seem." Thaddeus placed both his hands on the top of the desk, leaning in to examine the pin mat on the wall over his desk.

"Could it be the other Earthbound—Thanael and Anael, maybe? Or perhaps one of the others?" Marcus questioned, a touch of curiosity ringing in his words.

"It is possible…." These men were big like Seraphim, one was massive even, but they weren't any of the angels he had cast down. He knew all of them. "… but they have all lain low over the years—not concerning themselves with my doings, only their own survival." Thaddeus straightened, still gazing at the mat. "Some quite well, though what could they possibly gain from violating my building?"

"I concur. Their time is better spent keeping their own identities hidden. When I spoke with Amahle, she expressed the same sentiment about them avoiding any unwanted attention."

Thaddeus ran a hand across his jaw. "I will more than likely *hate* your answer to my next question, but… what news do you have regarding that defiant Seraph—the other female?"

"Ariadne—not a word. No one has seen her," Marcus gave him.

"Stay on it—all of it!" Thaddeus roared, ending the call.

He refocused back upon another of his collections, the display of pinned Lepidoptera butterflies he kept above his desk. Butterflies had always fascinated him, especially these in the Pierinae family, which were named for their white wings and black marginal markings, whose similar makeup reflected that of his own white with black edged wings.

Thaddeus blew out an infuriated breath, then focused down at the file folder on his desk. He flipped it open and began perusing through the pages and photos captured from the video footage he had reviewed. He had taken it upon himself to analyze all the recordings from the Ottawa facility logged in the past few months. There had been very few people come and go over the time, parents of sick kids, delivery people, staff, and very limited visitors of any sort. In fact, the only other people who had come into the building besides those city workers, had been the two women who had requested a tour of his state-of-the-art facility. Amahle had informed him they were the ones from the hospital. "*Another good contact,*" she had reminded him.

Thaddeus wasn't interested in new contacts, what interested him about these guests, was when he'd showed the front desk footage of them to Lyndon, he had indicated that the one with the short blonde hair, was also one of the women he'd seen visiting the group home. Although, the brunette with her in the footage was different from the third woman he'd seen at the group home. Lyndon had never seen this person before. "Attendant, Call Lyndon," Thaddeus said then. There was a click sound of connection, but before Lyndon could say anything, he said, "I need you to come here."

"I have something…," Lyndon tried to say.

"Get over here!" Thaddeus demanded, cutting the call short.

It took Lyndon 30 minutes, 20 minutes longer than Thaddeus would have liked, to arrive at the door of his personal lab. "You look… different?" Thaddeus scrutinized.

Lyndon peered down at himself.

"Are you wearing new clothes?" Thaddeus questioned, waving a hand up and down Lyndon's torso. "Your hair—it's… *clean.*" He scowled and squinted at Lyndon.

Lyndon said nothing, only ran his palm down the front of his open overcoat.

"Wait, don't tell me—you, of all Seraphim, have a date for this ridiculous human day of *love.*" Thaddeus made a gaging noise. He didn't know what the Seraph did, when he was not doing his bidding, nor did he care, as long as Lyndon did what he was told. "The homes of this Westlake woman—tell me."

"I went to each of the locations, checked the houses, even spoke with the neighbors. Some were quite talkative."

"What did they say?" Thaddeus asked, already impatient, slowly circling Lyndon.

"Her maiden name is Brown—it's one of the most common surnames here in North America."

Thaddeus rolled his eyes.

"And she's married to a British guy—his last name is Westlake." Lyndon surveyed the lab, his expression dreary.

It was no secret to Thaddeus that Lyndon hated anything that resembled a hospital. "No other family, no children?" "

"The neighbors stated she and her husband did a lot of traveling. He's one of those *doctors without borders* physicians. She also works with the program." Lyndon nodded like that extra bit of info was worth something to Thaddeus.

"I need to know *which* of these women was in my building, and at the group home. Can you tell me that?" Thaddeus questioned, even more infuriated with Lyndon now.

"The neighbors said the couple are out of the country. Could still be her, though. You said she was a college of the woman from the hospital. Fits, sort of."

"I don't need your assumptions. What I need now is for you to investigate—what I consider another long shot, see if this *other* Westlake person—the other one lacking any current records, find out if she has any relatives here in Ottawa." Thaddeus couldn't understand why he had to handhold this idiot, why couldn't he have already done this search? "How about you try to be more proactive with these tasks, Lyndon," Thaddeus recommended. "You're dismissed."

Lyndon stood in the shadows outside the group home, watching through the window to the playroom at the staff and volunteers interacting and playing games with the residence. He'd checked the schedule earlier to see if there were volunteers slated for today and when he had seen Lane's name on the roster, he'd gone and cleaned himself up, showering and dressing in the new clothes he'd purchased. He had planned to watch Lane, hopefully even talk to her, but he'd been called away. Thaddeus had mocked him, and he'd felt foolish for his attempt to improve his appearance. And now, as he watched Lane through the window, he realized he completely lost his any courage for even a simple *hello*.

Chapter 13 

The Group Home, Wednesday March 16th, Ottawa, Canada

Fear and self-loathing had kept Lyndon from visiting with those in the group home this past month, and it also kept him from what little joy he allowed himself these days.

His most cherished activity had always been spending time with Taylor. He had been assigned to watch him and the group home from the day Thaddeus had abandoned him here. Unlike most, Taylor never flinched or turned away from looking at Lyndon's horrid appearance, his behavior was quite the opposite. Taylor, in his unique way, conveyed empathy towards Lyndon, and the two of them shared a mutual understanding of what accompanied their individual challenges. Taylor was an 8-year-old, practically non-verbal autistic, with congenital limb defects, who seemed to exist in his own world, and he was Lyndon's only friend. He suspected Taylor understood more and could communicate better than he let on, but that secret was safe with him. "I apologize for being away so long—I promise to do better," Lyndon said, settling down in the chair next to Taylor. "I've missed you."

Taylor smiled sweetly up at him, reaching to touch a hand to Lyndon's face. "*Angel*," he said in a tiny voice.

"Hello, Angel," Lyndon said in response to the sweet boy. "Would you like me to read to you today?"

Taylor clapped, his face beaming, smile stretching.

"I'll take that as a *yes*," Lyndon laughed out, soaking up the boy's excitement. "What will it be today?" He presented one of their favorites, a well-read hardcover classic he'd acquired when he'd first begone his time with Taylor.

"Hi, what are you two fellas doing?"

Lyndon stood up abruptly from his chair, clutching the old worn-out book, and staring into the face of another angel. As Lane's beautiful smile radiated back at him, he was momentarily dumbstruck. He hadn't checked the roster this time to see which volunteers would be here. He'd been afraid, yet hopeful she would be here today.

"I'm sorry—did I interrupt?" she asked, her bright smile changing to that of concern.

"Yes—I mean, no. We were just picking a story to read." Lyndon did his best not to gawk at Lane, but this was the first time he'd been this close to her. She was so close that he could smell her. It was a clean scent, a combination of mild soap with a hint of vanilla, and so like her, fresh and sweet.

"Please sit—I didn't mean to startle you," she said, her generous smile returning. "What do you have there?" She pointed at the weathered tome in his hands. When he sat again, she took the chair next to him and placed her black bomber jacket and small black leather purse over the corner of the chair-back.

"It's an anthology of Hans Christian Andersen's stories—he was a Danish author," he explained, turning the book to show her the cover.

"I'm familiar with his fairy tales," she said, still smiling as she admired the book. "The Little Mermaid is my favorite—but then I've always loved the ocean."

As she gazed at the book, he gazed at her. She wore a black cable-knit sweater, black jeans, and grey hiking boots. "Did you know he wrote 156 stories—translated into 125 languages?" Lyndon shared, enthusiastic about the works *and* her proximity to him.

She glanced up at him. "I did not," Lane said, eyeing the book again.

"He wrote mainly for children, but his stories present lessons… of virtue and resilience—in the face of adversity. They have inspired plays, ballets, and films." Lyndon shot a look at Taylor, who was watching them both.

Lane pulled the book closer, glancing at him, clearly amused. Shifting her eyes down again, she flipped to the first story, and then read, "*The Snow Queen.*"

"Ah, yes—The Snow Queen," Lyndon acknowledged. "It's a story about the strength and endurance of childhood friendship."

Lane flipped ahead several pages. "The Emperor's New Clothes," she read out.

Taylor clapped then, letting out a squeal of delight.

"That's a good one, I take it," Lane guessed, turning her attention to Taylor.

"It's a humorous one," Lyndon said, allowing his own joyful laughter to escape. "It's about an emperor who accidentally goes out in public in only his underwear."

Lane laughed along with them, turning more pages in the thick book.

"The moral is that it is best to trust oneself and be honest," Lyndon added. "The irony of the story is that the reader knows from the beginning that the weavers of the clothing are dishonest, and it allows the reader to see how deception plays throughout the rest of the story. Without honesty, people often end up looking very foolish."

Lane nodded her understanding. "Okay, what abooout… this one, The Ugly Duckling?"

When she peered up at him, he turned to look at Taylor and said, "That's one of our favorites." Keeping his eyes on Taylor, he said, "It's the journey of an awkward little bird…." He passed the palm of his hand across Taylor's upper back. "… trudging bravely through hecklers and hunters… and through cruel seasons." He turned his face to Lane. "An unforgettable survival story, where the ugly duckling blooms into a graceful swan."

Lane grinned thoughtfully. "What lesson is presented here?" she asked in reflection of what he'd said at the beginning.

"It is a reminder of the patience often necessary to uncover true happiness." This story meant a lot to him since he identified so strongly with the ugly part.

"I think we should read this one." She gave him a warm smile and turned the book so that the words faced him.

Lane was lovely, and it took all his strength not to reach out and touch the soft porcelain smooth skin of her face. "Another day." He pulled the book closer. "Today we will read *your* favorite." He turned the pages back to The Little Mermaid. "Ready?" he asked, lifting the book so Taylor could see what he'd picked.

Taylor clapped his agreement.

"Alright then," Lyndon said, stealing a quick peek at Lane before beginning to read aloud. "*Far out in the ocean, where the water is as blue as the prettiest cornflower....*" He stole another glimpse at Lane, then continued to read. He read through the entire story, changing his voice to match each character, all the while Taylor *oohed* and *awed* his responses. "*... But when we see a naughty or a wicked child, we shed tears of sorrow, and for every tear a day is added to our time of trial.*" He closed the book and gazed up at Lane.

She was wiping away a tear. "Uhm... that's quite different from the story I'm familiar with," she said. "I've never heard that version— it's not the happy-ever-after Disney adaptation I watched as a kid. I like it much better—but wow, it really got me in here." She pointed at the center of her chest. "Choked me up."

"It did for me too the first time I read it," Lyndon shared. He lifted his hand to take hers, but then thought better of it and placed it back on the book.

"Thank you—for reading that to us," she said, setting her hand on the edge of the book, extending her fingers to graze the side of his.

Lyndon pulled his hand away, startled by the touch. Taylor had been the only one he allowed to touch him now, and that had only ever been his face.

"Gosh—I'm sorry," she said in response to his abrupt withdrawal.

"No-no... I just wasn't expecting... it's fine, truly," Lyndon fumbled out, surprised, and exhilarated by the contact. He reached for her hand, but she had hid both under the table in her lap.

She drew in an audible breath through her nose. "Where do you live?" she asked, blowing out the breath.

"Here." Lyndon stared at her.

"Here?" Her eyebrows raised.

"Yes."

"You mean you have a room here?" She pointed up.

"No—not exactly. I have my space in the lower level," he said, pointing down.

"In the basement?"

"Yes." When the workers who had renovated the mansion to accommodate the special needs residence, he had them adjust the lower level to meet both the needs of the facility, and those of his own as well.

"Will you show me your living space?" Lane asked, bringing her hand back up to the table.

"Another time, perhaps," he offered, finding it a struggle to refuse her. He had taken care with his grooming and his attire in case she showed, as he had wanted to appear different to her somehow. Softer maybe. Not so severe. He'd even combed his hair back away from his face since she'd not seem bothered by his scars. Even with his clothing, he had wanted to appear less… *harsh*, maybe. And he'd worn new blue jeans and a new long-sleeved grey thermal pullover in hopes it might soften his surface, even if his exterior was still a little rough. And she wouldn't be seeing him in that horrible old filthy trench coat ever again. But he hadn't been prepared to show her his accommodations. No one had seen his private space. He cringed, remembering he had left the towel from his shower draped over the back of a chair.

"Sure, another time," Lane said with a nod.

His cellphone vibrated then, and he retrieved it from his pants pocket. Thaddeus. "Will you excuse me for a moment—I need to take this call." He pushed up from his chair and crossed briskly to the far side of the playroom. He glanced over at Lane to see her engaged in a playful exchange with Taylor. "Yes," he said, answering the call.

"Did you find the information I asked for—if the woman had any relatives local?" Thaddeus asked, his voice filled with disdain.

Lyndon stole a glance Lane's way again. "The woman came from a large family, but only she and the oldest brother are left." He crossed his arm over his chest, tucking his free hand into his armpit under the bent arm holding the cellphone. "Records show the brother lives in the country a few hours outside of Ottawa."

"Go check him out. And if it's a dead end — I'll need you to call that woman who had booked the Celaeno building tour. Use the hospital contact number she gave Amahle."

"I already talked to her." Lyndon took another glimpse at Lane, then he turned away, listening as Thaddeus snarled malice comments into his ear.

"No — you idiot. Not to talk to her about the visit to the building — ask about her visit to the group home — who the other women were with her, namely this Ms. Westlake." Thaddeus's mood was reminiscent of a grizzly bear who'd been woken before his hibernation was done. He hung up before Lyndon could respond.

With a "*Huff,*" Lyndon returned his phone to his pocket and turned back around.

Lane stood right in front of him. "Hi," she said, when he just stared at her. The clean scent of her traveling through his olfactory senses.

"Hi," Lyndon managed, unsure of what else to say. She already had her coat back on, he noticed.

"I... have to get to the university," she said, adjusting her purse crosswise over the front of her coat.

"I have to leave as well," he said, though what he wanted was to spend more time with her. Unfortunately, Thaddeus wouldn't get off his case until he found some useful information to aid his obsession with this Westlake woman. "May I drop you at the university?"

"You drive?" her eyebrows pinched.

What an odd question, Lyndon thought. "Yes — of course." It would be a quick detour before he had to make the long drive out-of-town. "Shall we?" he asked, pulling his truck keys from his other pocket.

"Uhm, sure," Lane agreed, sliding what looked like one of those transit passes back into her purse.

"Let me say goodbye to Taylor first," Lyndon said, crossing back to the table where he sat. He was gazing out the window again, lost in his thoughts. "I'll see you later, my friend." He patted Taylor's shoulders and kissed the top of his head. Then he grabbed up his new trench coat from the adjacent chair and turned back to Lane. "Ready?"

"Did you go to university?" Lane asked as they pulled onto the highway.

"Yes—no, I mean yes, I did studies, but it was a while ago," Lyndon fumbled out.

"Where—here in Ottawa?" she asked, gazing intently out the passenger side window as they sped along.

"No." He didn't know how he could explain he had attended the University of Al-Karaouine the oldest and first university on Earth, established in 859 AD, in Fez, Morocco.

"What did you study?"

"Religious studies," he said, truthfully, pulling off the highway onto the ramp that led to the front of the main campus. He hadn't been a formal student back then, but he'd spent hours being entertained by various lectures on religion.

"Here's good," Lane said, pointing at a building entrance labeled *The Biosciences Complex*. "Thank you so much. I hope to see you again soon." She unlatched her seatbelt and smiled at him briefly before reaching for the lever and opening the door.

"It was my pleasure. And I look forward to more time with you as well." Boldly, he reached out and touched her hand.

When she glanced back, he gave her a genuine smile, despite the burn scar pulling tight at the corner of his lip. He didn't need to hide his face from her. "Bye, Lyndon," she said, her eyes crinkling as her smile widened.

"Goodbye." Lyndon watched as she got out and shut the door. He waited as she crossed the sidewalk that led to a long set of stone stairs. As he pulled away, he observed her through the review mirror as she climbed the steps. Then he made a U-turn near the end of the building to go back to the highway. He took one last glimpse at Lane and spotted her at the top of the stairs, speaking to some woman. As he rolled by, he recognized it wasn't just *some* woman, it was one of the original Earthbound. *Julianna*.

Lyndon cut an immediate right into a student parking area and directly into an open spot near the entrance. From where he parked, he could see Lane still speaking with Julianna. When their exchange ended, Lane descended the stairs and proceeded towards the entrance of another building, the campus library, and he got out of the truck to follow her. Lyndon pursued Lane, passing through the library's entrance. When she paused to pull something from her purse, he moved to stand in front of her and said, "How do you know her?"

"What?" Lane asked, looking up from retrieving whatever it was from her purse.

"I saw you talking to Julianna." Lyndon stated, blowing his breath out through his nose.

"Were you following me?" She pointed at him, and he noticed she was holding a laminated ID card in her outstretched hand.

"Answer the question," he said, sternly.

"For your information—not that it's any of your business—I'm doing my master's degree in environmental engineering with Professor Forest," she defended, glaring back at him.

"What are you talking about?" Lyndon glowered back at her.

"Professor Forest—the person I was talking to—she teaches Environmental Geoscience."

Lyndon knew that already. He knew all about her, but he hadn't known she was now a teacher here. Last he'd heard she was in Brazil.

"How do *you* know the Professor?" Lane countered.

Lyndon didn't answer. Instead, he said, "I thought you were doing schooling in social work."

Lane blew out what sounded like an aggravated breath. He had undoubtedly angered her, but he was furious first. Visibly annoyed, she said, "I'm not sure why I have to explain myself to you." She put her other hand on her hip.

Lyndon said nothing. *Was she stalling*, he wondered?

"Carlie lied for me—okay? I needed the volunteering piece to complete my graduate studies. She said I could do it there," Lane explained, dropping her hand from her hip, her voice less irritated.

Okay, he felt like the idiot Thaddeus had labeled him as, but now he deserved it. He'd confronted her like he'd caught her stealing from him. "I've been a fool—I'm so sorry for my disrespectful behavior," he said in a softer voice. He dropped his gaze from her face to stare at the floor. He was so ashamed. They had a lovely morning and now he'd gone and ruined it. "I have difficulty trusting people." He raised his hand, running the tips of his fingers over the scar where it met the edge of his jaw, keeping eyes downcast. "Lane, please forgive me."

Lane touched his arm then, lowering his hand from his face. When he gazed up at her, she said, "Besides, I like it there."

"I like it there, too," he responded.

"Do we need to talk about this?" Lane questioned, her voice gentle now.

Lyndon sighed. "I would talk with you for hours—if I could… but regrettably, I have a chore I must attend to."

Chapter 14 

A month had passed since Redmond had agreed with me about my learning to shoot, although during that time he had redirected me to focus on learning some self-defense instead.

On my first visit to the South Haven location, Redmond had taken me on an extensive tour of the place. Den had provided him with biometric driven security access designed by Marq, which allowed him entry in through the ground floor parking area using just his thumbprint. They had converted the 40 spot parking area, using half the garage space as the *training* area, for workouts, weapons and tactical defense training, along with a few other useful rooms. Initially, the grand home had 18 bedrooms broken into nine units on two floors, but the suites had been redesigned, and all the lower level areas, gutted to open up into a common living space and gourmet kitchen like what I'd seen at North Haven. It had been Max and Julian who had given instructions on setting up the kitchen area as Max had overseen the build-out for several posh restaurants and Julian had been a designer of industrial kitchens back in the day. The upper floor still had a loft style hall that overlooked the 20-foot tray ceilings into the new shared area, but the construction material that had been everywhere was no longer an issue. The. Place. Was. Amazing.

During these past few weeks, I'd spent most of my free mornings in the training area with either Den or with Ben, when he had time for visits. Ben is the one who trained the others to fight. He's a master of martial arts and he's been training me on those that require no strenuous force. These only require touch and pressure point combat and reverse weight influence. Ben can sense strength and weakness in any living thing, including me, obviously, so he provided me with a nutrition plan to help enhance my endurance and strength. He's a big advocate of meditation as well, so I've added more of that to my daily regimen, too.

I hadn't seen Gabriel during this time, though I had called for him several times, hoping to get more clarity on why Archangel Diniel was hanging out at my job. But he'd not come when I called. I'd tried again this morning, reaching out for him, but got nothing. Eventually, I told Redmond about the visit I'd had with her in the hospital's nursery, and like me, he'd found her behavior odd, but unlike me he had brushed off the visit as typical considering the numerous visitors I had in the past. I understood that Diniel watched over babies, but what reason did she have for being at that hospital, my hospital? The unknown of it continued to plague me.

After I'd tried to reach Gabriel this morning, I'd received a text from Den informing me that this morning's instruction would be hand-to-hand training, being he's the expert in this specialty, but he was also going to be late. And since I didn't have to go to the hospital today, and I had my own biometric access to get in, he'd told me to go ahead over for the usual time, anyway. He also mentioned Marq was visiting today, and that meant I would finally get to meet him. So far, the only ones I'd met in person were Leo, Den, Ben, and Zach. Nic I hadn't met yet, nor Kris, for obvious reasons. I'd heard lots about Nic from Olivia and Mac, but Marq, the only real mention of him had been through Derek and how he had been working with him on locating our missing angel. All Den had shared with me was, *"Marq is an interesting fellow,"* and that he'd borrowed his last name from some Dutch painter. Marquis Malouel was an enigma to me, so I wasn't sure what to expect.

There was no sign of rain this morning, so I rode my bicycle over to South Haven and entered through the garage entry using my thumbprint as usual. While I waited for Den, I tied back my hair into a ponytail and dropped my bag near the end of the mat. Then I did a little warmup routine and stretching, knowing that the physical requirements needed for his training would be much more strenuous than Ben's pressure point combat.

"I didn't know you were coming here today," said an unfamiliar resonant baritone voice from behind me.

Turning over, I sat up from my floor-stretching on the training mat to see a towering dark-skinned male approaching from the far side of the room. His features were a magnificent combination of what is considered African and Asian origin, but his hair was like Purah's, though his presented in long white twisted lengths similar to dreadlocks that reached past his chest. "Hey," I managed to get out. He wore loose faded jeans and a baggy white t-shirt that appeared to be splattered with different colours of dried paint, and he was barefoot. I tried not to gawk, but he was stunning in all that contrast. "I'm Lynn," I said, stupidly. Obviously, he knew who I was.

"Oh, I know," he said with a deep howl of laughter. Then he proceeded to do a cartwheel across the mat, followed by a back handspring and then a back flip with a twist that had him landing on the mat several strides in front of me. He ended his acrobatics with a simple front roll that brought him up right next to me. "I'm Marquis—but everyone calls me Marq," he said, followed by a wide, brilliantly white smile and another robust laugh.

"That was excellent!" I tossed back, impressed by his skills. "No one told me you were a gymnast." I tightened my ponytail, reminded of my younger days of doing gymnastics.

"I'm not—I just like the tumbling." He grinned and sat cross-legged, holding his ankles and full of enthusiasm, reminding me of how kindergarteners looked right before story-time. "I'm so grateful to meet you, finally. You're smaller than I pictured—and your hair is longer too." He reached over and ran his hand down the length of my ponytail. "I like it." He grinned again. His hair may have been white like Purah's, but his expressive eyes were not the same, his were whisky coloured, yet equally breathtaking.

"I love your hair. How long did it take to grow it like that?" I asked, impulsively.

He wrapped his hand around a grouping of tendrils, bringing them forward and examining them up-close. "As I'm sure you know, we're all fast healers but slow with ageing—as is our hair growth," he said, letting the grouping fall back over his massive shoulder. "So it took me an extremely long time—I'm tempted to buzz it off, though."

"What—no!" I blurted. "It's fabulous at that length."

He laughed again, the deep tone sounding almost operatic. Then he asked, "Do you visit here often?"

"I've been coming here once a week to learn some self-defense tricks. Found out Valentines' Day that my lovely husband had been over here learning to fight and shoot." I smirked. "Hey—thanks for putting in our security system at the house." He'd come over while I had been in Norway, and I hadn't had the opportunity until now to thank him.

Marq put his palms together at his chest and bent forward. "It was my pleasure."

"Marquiiiiis!" boomed Den's voice as he entered the training space. He was already in his workout clothes, loose-fitted black martial arts pants and a black t-shirt with the neck band cut out.

"Haaaaaydeeeeeeen," Marq bellowed back, rolling stealthily onto his feet and into a fighting stance. "Did you just come from updating Frank?"

"Yup—she's holding down the fort—or restaurant, as it were. Said they had a full house last month for Valentine's—but are closed today for a private St. Patrick's day party."

The two circled each other as though they were about to engage in a wrestling match. Den was the strongest and the biggest of them all, so Marq would have quite the challenge in a full-contact fight.

"Speaking of Valentine's Day," I said, interrupting, attempting to draw them out of their fighting mode. "Did either of you do anything for Valentine's Day?" When they both looked my way, I did a few eyebrow-raises. "Any special someone in your life?" I added, directing the question at Marq.

They both straightened from their fighting postures.

Den shrugged and then looked at Marq.

"Honestly," Marq said. "We rarely have someone in our lives… mainly because of the pain of loss and the difficulty with commitment."

I hadn't thought of how complicated it would be to be in a serious relationship, or even just date. "It must get lonely," I said, wishing I hadn't mentioned it at all.

"I'm not sure which is worse—the loneliness or losing someone," Den said.

"Hey—you still got me, brother," Marq joked, slapping the male on the back of the head before returning to his fighting stance.

Den gave Marq a menacing grin, then grabbed him before I could even register the move, bringing the enormous male down to the mat in one fail swoop of long white hair, landing with a loud *smack*.

"Alright you two—is that anyway for Angels to behave?" I yelled, getting up on my feet. "Yer worse than the twins," I added, putting my hands on my hips.

Den released Marq, and he spun out of his reach and into a series of back handsprings. "Showoff," Den said with a roar, faking as though he was going to attack again. Turning to me, he said, "On the topic of updates, have you seen much of Gabriel?"

"Huh! I see *you* more than I see him these days." I tightened my ponytail again in case he was going to pull that attack stuff with me. "When he's around, Gabriel involves himself in family time with the girls, etc."

"And your friends—do they see their… ancestral protectors much?" Marq asked, coming to stand next to me. "I'm referring to the Archangels who have watched over them and their ancestors since the time of The Fallen."

I nodded, I knew who he meant. "I don't think they see them much anymore."

"The impression I get from Gabriel is that they have washed their hands of things and were pretty much just standing back and watching events unfold now," Den said, relaying the same impression I had gotten.

"Their true involvement ended at the gathering, though they have allowed themselves to become accustomed to and more familiar with this generation of Charges," Marq said, also adding to what I had already assumed. "It is not their place any more to guard your friends—but that's not to say they wouldn't step in to protect them if something otherworldly were to threaten their wellbeing or *safety*."

"I agree," I said with a nod, grabbing up my bag from the edge of the mat. "About Gabriel—or Archangels, rather. I met an interesting somebody a few weeks ago."

"Who?" Den asked.

"Diniel," I said. A cellphone text chime coming from my bag followed my reveal. Then, as though he'd been eavesdropping, Gabriel appeared right as I retrieved my phone.

"What about Diniel?" Gabriel asked.

Ignoring him, I checked the text on my phone. It was from my brother James, and it read,

Are you guys doing anything for St Paddy's Day?

I'd sent the girls to school in matching green t-shirts. They were part Irish, after all. Part from my birthmother and part from Redmond's mother. I had sent her photos of the girls first thing this morning in their green attire.

I typed back,

No, but the girls are. I'll send you photos. How are the dogs?

He responded with,

Something spooked them earlier. Had to take them for a run through the woods. But they're good now. It was weird.

I hated he was out there all alone in the middle of nowhere, and I wrote,

I wish you didn't live in such a remote place.

But I already knew what he'd say,

I know, but I enjoy the peace and quiet. Except with the dogs, they're barking, need to let them out.

That cracked me up.

Okay, talk later. love you.

He wrote a quick,

Love you, too.

I attached and sent the photos of the girls in their St. Paddy's Day green to James. "Ooohhh—how I adore normalcy," I tossed out, sliding my phone back into my bag, still ignoring Gabriel. Even though I was surrounded by angels and learning to fight from two of them, this past month had actually been great. I had even told Redmond this morning that things were beginning to feel *normal* again.

"Lyyyynn," Marq called, waving a hand for me to come over to what was now the security and surveillance system space in the massive training area.

I continued to ignore Gabriel but allowed him to follow me to where Marq sat in front of several large computer screens. "What are you working on?" I asked, curious to hear what they had been doing to find Kris. Though I hadn't felt comfortable asking Redmond if he had heard anything.

On one screen was a digital map of all the regions of the world spread out flat for viewing all at once. "This shows where all the Earthbound are currently located—the ones we know of, and the halflings—where they were found or currently live," Marq said. Then he clicked something on the screen, and it changed to show a series of dotted lines in an assortment of colours that began from an area near the North Pole, to reaching out across the different locations. "This view shows the migration from when the first were sent down a hundred and twenty years ago, to where each resides now."

"That's pretty cool," I said, noting that some had traveled extensively while others had stayed closer to their starting places.

"Derek helped me with creating the program. I'm a pro with surveillance programs, but not with creating something like this from scratch," Marq admitted.

"What about the others—Thaddeus and his crew? Are they on this map, too?" Where the Earthbound were located was interesting, but I was more concerned about where my adversaries were situated.

"No, I wasn't able to track their movements—not like they would report in to let me know their activities. But I do have a list of which of Thaddeus's labs they work out of," Marq shared. "Some have changed locations, and we only know that because we have eyes on each of the buildings. I keep the names in a spreadsheet." He pointed to the adjacent screen, which displayed a list of names, roles, and locations organized under statuses of original and current.

"I recognize some names," I said, indicating Thaddeus and Lyndon. It showed them as being at the Ottawa location, of course. "I know of Marcus, but not this *Zuriel.*" They were showing as being in New York City now, with their original location as Brazil. "Kendrick, I know as well, but again, not this *Addison.*" Both showed as being in Norway, where I'd met Kendrick. I had sensed no other Earthbound at the facility, but that's not to say he wasn't in Norway. Both Zuriel and Addison had the role of *Tracker* next to their names, as did Lyndon. "Does Tracker mean they work in the same location but separate from buildings?" I asked for more clarity.

"Yes—in a way," Marq said. "Those labeled as Manager, run the facilities, and those with Tracker roles tend to run errands—do the grunt work, we'll say."

I noticed there had been a few switch ups in locations. "I recognize Amahle's name." She showed as being in Ottawa as well, though her original location had been New York City, along with an *Ariadne* who was also a Tracker, but her current location showed as *Missing.* "What happened to Ariadne?"

"Of the fourteen in Thaddeus's group that were cast down by the Stewards, two were female," Marq shared. "But we only know the whereabouts of the one now, Amahle. The other, Ariadne, who—if you saw her, you might consider a twin to the other, as she is identical yet opposite in appearance to Amahle. The difference being that Ariadne is what humans would call albino. Their roles on the Pleiades star Merope were associated with moonrise and sunrise—a balance, taking care of the ocean's tides."

"Wow, they would be an interesting pair to see together." I noticed Marq eyeing Gabriel. "What?"

"We have her marked still as a Tracker—but she's a killer." He paused as though to give me time to digest this tidbit. I'm sure my face showed shock but when I said nothing, Marq added, "She worked alongside Amahle and Thaddeus early on, but it seems the unwanted attention she got because of her unique appearance, was more than she could bear. She became unhinged and took off on her own."

"And you don't know where she is?" I frowned and chewed the corner of my lip.

"No one has seen her—she's a ghost," Den said, his face giving nothing away.

The tiny hairs on the back of my neck and along my arms tingled. "Not creepy at all." I shook my head, then refocused on the spreadsheet again. I knew none of the name shown under Italy, Japan, or Amsterdam, and for Brazil there were no names at all as replacements. "Who runs the Manau City location in Brazil now?"

"No one, currently—no Earthbound, I mean," Marq stated. "Before Nic moved to Ottawa, he had kept tabs on that location. Jules had been living in Brazil conducting research, and it was she who had informed us that Marcus and Zuriel were no longer there. Kris had found them in NYC—he normally watches that location, and we also realized Amahle had also relocated—to the Ottawa location. We are not sure why the switches were made, but we believe it has something to do with Ariadne's disappearance."

"Maybe Thaddeus thought that if Amahle was with him in Ottawa, he would know better—sooner, if Ariadne returned." I shrugged. "Jules moved to Ottawa too—but because of her son Mason, Leo told me."

"Correct," Marq said, tracing a finger along the migration line shown for Jules. "Having her in Ottawa is very convenient for us—she can recognize the original Earthbound—being one of them, and Thaddeus and his followers as well, since they were all together for a millennium."

"I guess you guys are at a slight disadvantage since you've only ever been on Earth." I stared at the seven green dotted migration lines marked for their movements. They and the original Earthbound had started out together on Earth, not in the stars, and had not spent the same span of time with them as Jules.

"Photos help," he said. "We try to keep those up to date best we can." He brought up a series of photos. "We have our photos and history in here as well." He clicked through a series of headshots.

I recognized Leo, Den, Zack, and Ben right away, and of course Marq's photo now as well. I even knew Nic's photo but only because Olivia had described him. The last photo, however, the one titled, Kristopher Snow, was the only one that threw me. I'd never known what he looked like, hadn't even guessed at it. Now I knew he had thick dark brown hair and magnificent navy-blue coloured eyes. My stomach flipped. Not because of his appearance, he was handsome no doubt about it, but the stomach flips were about what I couldn't see. *"Where are you?"* I muttered, touching his photo. Was he the angel from my dreams, in the twin's nightmares? The sound of my cellphone text chime drew me from my musings. I pulled it from my bag to see that it was from Olivia.

It read,

We need to talk to ASAP!

"Hey, Nic says he needs to speak with us, Lynn—right now," Den called to us, holding up his cellphone.

I turned to look at Gabriel, but he was gone. I may have spoken too soon, I realized. "So much for *normalcy*," I grumbled out.

Chapter 15 

Redmond had come over right away when I'd texted him, showing up just as we were getting ready for a video meeting with the others in Ottawa. Marq had us set up in the common area on the sectional couch. He and Den were to my left, Redmond on my right, in front of the 80 inch TV screen. Marq hit a key on his wireless keyboard and Olivia and Mac, along with Nic between them, appeared on screen in a single video feed. Based on the background, they were in Mac's house situated at the kitchen island.

"Hello, I'm Den, and this is Marq," Den said in introduction, extending a hand to point at Marq.

"Good to meet you both," Mac said with a hand-wave.

"Hi, all," Olivia said, her eyes wide. Olivia gave me a knowing grin despite the nervous look that accompanied it. "Hey, Lynnie,"

"Hey, Liv," I said, before turning my attention to Nic. He was still wearing his hospital scrubs. Okay yup—he was hot. He appeared Native Indian with a hint of Polynesian, but something about his appearance gave way to sultry tales of Arabian Nights. "Hi Nic—nice to finally meet you." I gave him my best calm smile. I wasn't sure what this was all about, but right now I was feeling a combination of uneasiness and excitement.

"Ladies, good to see you," Redmond said. "Nic—good to meet you."

Nic nodded and gave us a gorgeous smile back. "It's great to see you both, finally."

"So, what's going on?" I questioned, addressing no one in particular. I wanted to get this show on the road, or whatever.

"Nic, you have something important to tell us?" Den asked.

Nic cleared his throat. "Yes—well, Olivia informed me she received a call this morning, from someone asking about the woman who had accompanied her on the group home visit." He glanced at Olivia then back at the screen.

"I take it they didn't mean Alison," Redmond said, putting a hand over mine.

Olivia leaned forward. "The guy tried to explain that his reason for calling was that there was no first name for Ms. Westlake on the document sign-in sheet, nor a contact number for her. I told him you were a visiting colleague." She leaned back and focused on Nic.

Nic gave Olivia's hand a quick pat. "But then he asked how he could reach her or where he could find her?" Nic added.

Olivia continued to appear distressed. "I told him I couldn't give out personal information or even where you had been visiting from."

"You handled that well," Den said, "if they call back or if anyone asks about *Ms. Westlake*, stick with the same dialog."

Olivia nodded, her distressed expression lessoning.

Redmond squeezed my hand, then focused my way.

"I'm good—we're good," I said, acknowledging his concerns while still flouting the implication of what this could mean. So, someone was interested in knowing more about me. If they could find the information themselves, they wouldn't have felt the need to call.

"Leo and I are still watching the Celaeno building," Nic said. "However, we received a call too."

"From whom?" Redmond asked, shifting forward on the couch as though he were going to stand.

"Was it the same person?" I questioned, squeezing Redmond's hand back.

"No way to know," Nic said. "I didn't recognize the voice, but the man asked about the utility workers from that sewer job at the Celaeno building."

"Has to be one of Thaddeus's people," Redmond said, taking my hand in both of his now.

"The number used for the fake utility services goes to the North Haven cell switch, which Leo or I can answer from our cellphones." Nic lifted his cellphone in view of the screen. "I told the caller that the employees he was asking about—no longer work for the city—that a group of them won the lotto and had all quit."

"Was this today also?" I asked, wondering if someone from the facility was on a calling spree. The sewer job and the group home visit should not have appeared related.

"No," Nic said.

"When?" Redmond demanded, squeezing my hand harder.

"January?" Nic responded, his tone remorseful.

"What—why didn't you tell us sooner?" Okay, I was pissed off now, knowing they'd kept this from me, from us. Both Redmond and I were there with Leo for sewer gig, so they were asking about all of us.

"We didn't want to worry you," Nic said, giving me a thoughtful smile.

"Who else knows about this call?" I turned in my seat to look at Marq and then Den. I gave each of them a scrutinizing glare.

"We knew—not in January—today," Mac shared. "We found out when we told Nic about Olivia's call." She glanced at Olivia. "I already told Alison about both calls—for her records."

"What about Vicki?" I asked.

Olivia turned her gaze on Mac.

"I'm not sure she'd care," Mac said with a shrug. "None of this involves her, really.

"I texted Derek—just waiting for him to join the call," Marq said, typing something on his wireless keyboard. Obviously, he and Den had known more than Redmond and me if he'd already reached out to Derek. I was not comfortable being the last to know.

"I'll update Darius and Luc," Redmond offered, the squeeze on my hand lessoning as he got his phone from his back pocket.

"Also, Leo spoke with Lane, yesterday," Nic added.

"And?" I asked, letting go of Redmond's hand so he could text the guys.

"The photo of the floor plan Taylor drew, it's the lower level of the group home." Nic typed something on the keyboard at their end, then pointed at what I assumed was another monitor. "I'm just showing Mac and Olivia the photo."

"Why do you think he would draw that?" Mac asked.

"He'd drawn the floor plan of the Celaeno building—and clearly he wanted us to know about the private lab," I reminded. "Perhaps he wanted us to know about the lower level. Maybe we need to get in there, too." Was I the only one seeing the connection?

"Well, that's the kicker," Nic said. "She ran into Lyndon at the group home yesterday. And this time they had an actual conversation—a lengthy one if you can believe it."

"Why was he there—I mean, I know he watches over the place, but I got the impression he just lurks around."

"He was reading stories to Taylor." Nic raised his eyebrows.

"Really? That seems so… *out of character*, I want to say." This was not the type of behavior I'd come to expect from Thaddeus's people.

"Exactly. Unexpected—I agree. What's even more surprising is that Lane said they had a really enjoyable time together with Taylor. Up until she realized he was following her."

"He what?" Had anyone anticipated any of this? "Seriously?" I questioned.

"Well—sort of," Nic said, tilting his head side to side. Then he said, "He gave her a ride to the university. She was going there to meet her professor—who just happens to be *Jules*. He must have recognized her—seen them talking, and since he knows who and what Jules is— he confronted Lane at the library, asking how she knew her."

"Oh-my-gawd—what did she say?" Olivia spewed out, dumfounded, I'm sure, as we all were. I know I was.

"Lane said she was caught off guard, but she pushed back with the truth. She really was there to see her professor and told him about her graduate program," Nic explained. "Of course, she didn't let on that she knew more."

"How did he handle it?" Redmond asked, chiming in.

"He bought it—it was the truth, even if it was only part of it." Nic said. "Lane said he apologized profusely after. Something about how he *has a hard time trusting people*. Said he hoped to see her again soon."

"Wowsers—way to go, Lane!" I cheered, giving a little hand-clap.

"She also said she wished she had your spidey sense, Lynn, so she could know if he was around. But she also expressed that she believes that he's a good guy." Nic chuckled.

"*Good guy*?" I questioned, glancing again at Marq and Den. Was I missing something here?

"Maybe he's stuck, has no choice but to work for Thaddeus. He did burn the guy's face, don't forget," Mac reminded.

"Perhaps its necessity and not loyalty that keeps him linked to Thaddeus," Olivia said in agreement, nodding at Mac.

"Oh, I almost forgot—the floor plan connection," Nic cut in. "Lane said Lyndon told her he *lives* in the lower level of the group home."

"I think my brain just exploded," I said, giving my head a spin. "So, what—Taylor drew this guy's basement apartment? Why?"

"Lane said that Taylor seemed to like Lyndon—adore him even— like they were good friends," Nic added. He smiled as though he liked the idea.

"Olivia, Mac, have either of you seen anything strange at work or around your homes?" Redmond asked, leaning forward with his elbows on his knees.

"Do you think someone has been watching our homes, our workplaces?" Olivia asked, her expression returning to worry.

Mac waved a black notebook. "I've been working on protection spells for all our homes—I already did mine, Olivia's and Alison's," she said, flipping open the notebook. "No entry without permission."

I'm pretty sure my mouth had been hanging open, but Mac's comment about *permission* changed the course of my thoughts. "That makes me think of the whole Vampire thing—where if you invite one into your home they can come and go as they please—until you revoke their access," I tossed out. "But by then it's usually too late, you're already under their thrall." I surveyed the others for some kind of understanding. Instead, I got several eye rolls.

Even Mac rolled her eyes. Ignoring my comments, she said, "I've cast a series of protection spells around our properties. The numbers five, seven, and nine are usually associated with protection, so I cast *five* spells, using *seven* herbs, and *nine* knots in the thread of one of the spells." She went on to read a list of items and process needed for each from her the notebook. "One; Black and white protection powder. Ground pepper and sea salt blended and sprinkled around the perimeter of your home. Two; A red charm bag with salt, rosemary, and ashes from a fireplace, tied off with nine knots and hidden near the front door. Three; Sigils. Use a scented wax cube with five protective sigils carved into it, then melted in an oil burner. Four; A threshold protection. Grind St. John's Wort, fennel seeds, and chamomile into a fine powder, then pour in a line under a doormat outside the front door. And Five; Compass Sentinels. Cut cinnamon sticks of four equal lengths, placing them at the compass points around your property." Mac paused from reading. "It's a lot but I can totally feel the protection around my place," Mac said. "I had Alison write it all down—she likes to keep track of everything, as you know." Mac gave a resolute smile and closed her notebook.

"I can feel it at mine too," Olivia said. "Doing them all creates a deeper safeguard. Plus, we have the house alarm, a well-lit yard and, of course, Bella, our dog. She's old, but she still barks loud." She grinned as though proud of herself.

"Well done—very proactive," I said, giving them the thumbs up. That was the best I could do, considering I was feeling slightly *out of the loop* once again.

"Is there anything we can do here, for our house—just in case?" Redmond asked.

I turned to look at him. Did he really ask that? "I don't think we need…," I started to say, but the worried look he gave me back, shut me up. I turned back to the screen.

Mac had flipped open her notebook again and was turning pages. "Here—a shielding and protection charm," she read out, tapping the page she'd stopped at. "I'll text it to you, but you'll need bullet casings, shed claws or clippings, a shard of seashell, a drop of blood… and a dash of pepper." She glanced up briefly. "Place them into a small pouch and bind them with your intentions. Then place the pouch above the entry's doorframe. Do it for all your entryways," Mac instructed. Then, using her cellphone, she snapped a photo of the page. "Sent."

Redmond's phone gave a *bing* then at the arrival of Mac's text. "Got it," he confirmed. "Thanks."

"Shortcut!" I called out when Derek's face appeared then on the screen.

"Hey, y'all—everyone up to speed now on the happenings?" Derek asked in greeting, waving both his hands at everyone.

"Seems so," I said, glancing around and scrutinizing our attendees.

"I've sent updates to Darius and Luc," Redmond confirmed. "I'll circle back with them later."

I didn't hear any *we* in Redmond's comment, I mused. I tightened my lips and chewed the inside of my cheek to hold back any negative remarks.

"We're good too," Nic said, nodding at Olivia and Mac and then at the screen.

"Hey, Nic—nice to see you," Derek said, giving a respectful nod and grin.

"We've only exchanged emails and text messages," Nic clarified. He grinned too in the same manner.

I was not grinning. Not. Even. Close.

"How goes the deciphering?" Marq asked Derek then.

Derek shifted some papers on his desk, then typed on his keyboard. "I've gotten through another section from Thaddeus's notes. It's again about more experiments on other Earthbound and halflings. Testing the effects of sulfur and other elements on them. Weird experiments—horrific ones, even on his own followers. The testing is like what he did to that Lyndon guy's face. I'd consider it torture more than testing." Derek paused from scrutinizing his papers and peered up at the screen. "You told us you were fast healers, but apparently not-so-much with these various sulfur compounds, based on the results of these experiments. I sent you all some of this before, however, I'm still working on resolving the rest of the notes."

"Didn't Luc suggest something about that?" Redmond questioned. "That maybe this sulfur sensitivity was unique to the Earthbound, because of the whole *brimstone* thing?" he reminded. "What are your thoughts on that?"

"Brimstone—burning stone," Derek said. "Fire and brimstone and divine punishment and purification, Luc told us, if I recall correctly."

"The fate of the unfaithful." Marq added.

Derek nodded. "For those of you who don't know already, Brimstone is an ancient term synonymous with sulfur. It evokes the acrid odor of sulfur dioxide given off by lightning strikes," he informed us.

"And lightning was understood as divine punishment by many ancient religions," Marq said, continuing to add a taste of his own knowledge. "The association of sulfur with divine retribution is common in the religious texts."

"I can see how it might be linked to the angels—to you guys," I stated. I didn't really expect a response and resumed chewing on my cheek.

"The notes mention other minerals as well, that Thaddeus tested on your kind," Derek said. "I wonder if there is a safe way to test your vulnerability to some of these compounds." Derek paused and turned to look at another of his monitors. "It's ironic though, the same elements he used to test with, are the same as those found in healing hot springs."

I knew nothing about hot springs. Only that my girlfriends had been, several times in fact, and I had not. "Like what?" I asked, needing to feel part of the conversation.

"Well, liiiike...." Derek typed on his keyboard. "... *Calcium* for one—it boosts blood circulation and increases oxygen flow. *Potassium*. It promotes skin health and helps remove toxins from the body. *Magnesium* is used to clear acne and blemishes and keep skin glowing, and *Sodium*, it helps regulate the lymphatic system and reduce pain and inflammation in joints."

"Thaddeus used all those in his experiments?" Olivia asked, eyebrows raised.

"Yes, and the results...," Derek tried to say, but Olivia cut him off.

"Don't tell me. Please—don't tell me," she said, clearly not wanting to hear about the damage they caused.

"Right—sorry," Derek apologized. "And *Sulphur*, it treats respiratory problems and dermatitis." He gave a sorrowful smile.

"Speaking of hot springs—we should plan a day trip to the Nordik Spa," Mac suggested, seemingly in need of shifting the topic of pain and torture to that of health and healing.

"You and the twins should come up in May, Lynn—girls trip," Olivia proposed, grinning cheerily, obviously onboard with Mac's idea of less suffering and more soothing. "You pick the dates—and I'll arrange it."

"And, Hekla," Derek said, cutting in, evidently having more to say on his research.

"What?" I questioned, my attention pulled from a spa-day visit with my friends, back to whatever it was he wanted to tell us.

"It's the name of a volcano in Iceland…," Derek said, like we were following along. His head oscillated back and forth as if waiting for one of our groups to catch on. When we all just stared back, he added, "… that for many years, was believed to be the gate to *hell*."

I shook my head once and glowered, then gazed around at the others. Redmond shrugged. Marq shook his head several times. Den made a face and shook his head, too.

"Would Kris have any reason to go there?" Derek asked then.

"To hell?" I shot out, deepening my frown.

"No—Iceland," Derek clarified, rolling his eyes as if we were all idiots.

"No idea," Den responded. "It wasn't on his agenda—why do you ask?" Den leaned forward in his seat.

Derek typed again. "It was one of several options I researched." He turned the other monitor on his desk to face us. "For possible trajectories for Kris's travels." The screen displayed a map showing Kris's last known location and a variety of lines for routes to different destinations. "And, well, Iceland… it is full of it."

"Full of what?" Den questioned.

Derek shifted the monitor back in place so we could see his face again. Then he said, "Sulphur."

Chapter 16 

With the workday over, Mac, Olivia *and* Nic had agreed to meet at North Haven to review Mac's locator spells. Mac's husband and boys were fending for themselves for dinner, as was Olivia's husband, who was quite content to eat in front of the TV watching the hockey game.

The three had all left work at the same time, but when Mac and Olivia arrived at North Haven, they found Nic had already changed out of his scrubs and into baggy jeans and a black long-sleeved t-shirt. He wore no socks, which they found amusing.

"Sorry for the bare feet," Nic said when he noticed them checking out his exposed toes. "All my socks are in the laundry."

"I guess angels have to do laundry too," Mac tossed back, totally not offended by his nude feet.

"Actually, I do their laundry," Max said, appearing from down the hall with a basket of what looked like whites from the laundry.

Julian followed behind him. "We haven't formally met," he said, bowing and giving a flamboyant, almost magician like hand-spin gesture of greeting. "I'm Julian."

"And I am Max." He handed Nic the basket. "Pleased to make your acquaintance. May I take your jackets?"

"This is Olivia, and Mac. And these are the masters of the house." Nic handed off their coats to Max.

"Hardly, but we do keep the place running and these big boys fed," Max said with a jovial laugh. He pressed a spot on the wall near the entry, opening a spring-loaded door to an opening set into the wall, then stowed the jackets in the small closet. "It's my husband who does the feeding, actually."

"Speaking of food—are any of you hungry?" Julian asked. "I was about to fix some spaghetti carbonara." He opened a kitchen cupboard to retrieve some cooking items.

"Oh-my-gosh—yes," Olivia blurted. "That would be wonderful."

"It's my favorite," Nic said, giving his obviously flat stomach a rub.

"I'm in," Mac said, pulling out one of the eight barstools lined up at the kitchen island. Then she hooked the strap of her enormous purse over the back before sitting. "Have you heard from Marq?"

"About the whole sulfur-Iceland thing Derek mentioned?" Nic questioned, setting the basket on the counter.

Mac nodded. "Ya—I wasn't clear on the whole thing." She adjusted herself in her seat.

"Me either," Olivia followed up, taking the stool next to Mac.

"I believe Marq was going to meet with Derek to go over the other routes they had calculated," Nic said, rifling through the laundry and pulling out a pair of socks. He moved the basket to the far end of the island, then pulled out another of the barstools to sit and put on the socks.

"What are you three getting up to this evening?" Max asked, sounding as though he were interrogating a bunch of teenagers.

Mac blew out a breath, her long bangs raising up off her forehead. "Testing magic spells," she said, lifting her hands, gathering up her long chestnut hair into one hand.

"That's right—you're the witch," Julian said, filling a deep pot with water. When it hit the right level, he set it atop the stove, tossed in some salt and turned on the heat.

"I prefer kitchen-witch or sorceress—either or," Mac said, giving them a toothy grin. With her free hand, she reached and unzipped her purse, pulling a simple black hair-tie from its confines. Then, with both hands, she assembled her hair into a loose bun. She gave another bright smile.

"Your home is exquisitely decorated," Olivia said, glancing back at the open space and long living room, noticing the pool tables and bar and the huge multi-seat sectional in one of the two sitting areas. "Yet it still feels comfy-cozy for such a large open space."

"That's all Max and Julian's doing," Nic shared. "I'm lucky if I can get my clothes to match." He chuckled. "That's why I prefer wearing scrubs."

Olivia laughed too. "I wish we could wear scrubs at work."

"Oh, the plight of management," Mac said, patting Olivia's back. "I think I'd get bored wearing the same thing day in and day out."

"Here-here," Julian said, pushing up the sleeves of his light-blue pullover sweater, readying himself for the meal prep.

"I let Julian pick out my clothes—he knows what I like, and has better taste," Nic said with a chuckle.

Julian nodded and winked at Nic.

Max set out the fresh pasta, eggs, parmesan, and bacon he'd taken from the fridge out onto the prep area of the island next to Julian.

"Thank you," Julian said, stealing a kiss from his husband before wrapping a navy coloured apron around his waist.

"Of course," Max said, before turning to face us. "I have chores to do—but I'll be back to join you all for dinner." Then he picked up the laundry basket from where Nic had set it and headed off back the way he'd come earlier.

"Will Leo be joining us?" Julian asked, opening a package of pasta.

Olivia and Mac both looked at Nic.

"No—sorry, he won't be," Nic said. "Since you got that call yesterday, Olivia, he's been doing surveillance on the Celaeno facility. Watching to see if Thaddeus or Lyndon—or any of the others come or go from the building. We are fairly sure Thaddeus is there—we just haven't seen him lately."

"His loss—but I totally understand why he's absent," Julian expressed.

"So, Mac, tell us about how your magic—these spells work." Nic requested, leaning an elbow on the counter to face the ladies.

"I'm dying to know too," Julian said. He cracked several eggs into a medium-sized bowl, then whisked in parmesan until well combined.

"Well, the type of magic I do, works according to several principles," Mac said, launching into her explanation. "All living things have a life force energy with specific vibrations, and I need to tap into and then direct the energy—or power, inherent in the plants, while doing the same with my own personal power. The herbs I use, the differences between their energies, are very subtle. Some of it is love energy, some courage, and so on. My part is to focus my intentions on a positive goal."

"Intentions?" Julian questioned. Next to the pot of heating water, he had a large skillet on medium heat, cooking the bacon.

"Yes—it's one of the basic rules of magic." Mac said, watching Julian as he flipped the bacon in the pan to cook the other side.

"Your intention needs to be a positive one that does no harm." Olivia explained.

"What else?" Julian asked, transferring the crispy and ready bacon slices to a paper towel-lined plate for draining.

"Grounding and centering come first." Mac licked her lips.

The water in the pot bubbled, and Julian tossed in the pasta. "The fresh pasta takes no time. About eight minutes," he said, glancing up to see their starving faces.

They all watched as Julian added the minced garlic to the skillet with the reserved bacon fat, cooking it until fragrant. The pasta was almost ready.

Mac grinned, hopeful. "When casting a spell, I take a deep breath in…." Mac said, closing her eyes and drawing in the scent of bacon and garlic. "… and visualize all my negative emotions and stress draining away." She opened her eyes to see Julian tossing in the cooked pasta, folding it until fully coated with bacon fat. "There is more to it, but that's the gist," Mac finished, breathing in more of the delicious aroma.

"Then there's the law of three," Olivia stated, adding to Mac's account. She'd helped Mac with various spells.

"Right. This has to do with the energy you send out, and how it will return in kind—times three," Mac said. "You know the saying, *'what goes around comes around'*? That's why you don't do harmful or negative spells."

"And respect yourself and others," Olivia said, nodding at Mac.

Mac smiled thoughtfully at her. She couldn't do full magic per se, but Olivia knew all the Wiccan Redes. "Affirmative magic is about harming none. This is a fundamental rule," Mac confirmed.

"What spells are you going to try?" Julian asked, smiling, undoubtedly intrigued.

"I'm going to try another attempt at a locator spell—to find Kris." Mac blew out a breath as though the idea was daunting.

Julian's curious smile dropped at the mention of Kris's name. "Another attempt?" he questioned, his eyebrows pinching. He removed the skillet from the heat before pouring in the egg-and-cheese mixture, then he stirred it vigorously until creamy. Taking a quick glimpse at them, he said, "The trick is to be mindful—you don't want to scramble the eggs. Add some of the pasta water—a few tablespoons at a time—this loosens the sauce." His struggle to stay focused on the food was clear to them all, due to the mention of the one who was missing. Julian seasoned the mix generously with salt and pepper, then broke up the bacon into bite-sized pieces and stirred them in. "Who's ready?" he asked, quickly dicing some parsley as though securing his control on the here and now.

"Is that a trick question?" Mac answered with levity, any remaining thoughts on her spell-work leaving her mind.

"Me," Olivia said, giving Julian a sweet smile and raising her hand.

"I most definitely am," Nic said, before pushing up from his stool to circle around to the far side of the island. He retrieved a stack of white bowls from the cupboard near the wall-ovens and set them on the counter next to Julian. He ran a comforting hand back and forth across Julian's shoulders.

"Please—if you will, put out the placemats," Julian said, giving Nic's cheek a soft pat.

"Right," Nic said, bending down and pulling a pile from under the counter. Then he set one out for each of them.

"Voilà," Julian said, transferring the mixture into the individual bowls. He then drizzled the pasta with olive oil and a mixture of sea salt, parmesan, and the parsley he had diced. "Bon appétit," he added, handing off the first bowl to Mac.

Next was Olivia and then Nic. "A lesson in patience," Julian said, filling his own bowl.

"That smells amazing," Max announced, reentering the kitchen. "You've done it again." He kissed the cook.

Over a fabulous meal prepared by one of the masters of the house, and shared with the available occupants, they focused back on the different attempts Mac had made with her locator spells.

"What was your first try at locating Kris?" Nic asked, filling his bowl with a second serving of pasta.

"I've already tried using a pendulum," Mac said, stabbing a piece of bacon in her bowl with her fork.

Olivia swirled her pasta onto her fork using a spoon. "What did you use for that?" she asked.

Mac chewed the piece of bacon she'd liberated from her bowl, then said, "I have a sterling silver chain attached to an amethyst stone. The silver is a superior energy conductor, and the amethyst is a strong spiritual crystal."

"Why amethyst?" Julian asked, still standing, bending over to eat his serving of pasta on the island. One of the wall ovens chimed, and he went over with oven mitts to retrieve from it, what we already knew from the smell was a loaf of sourdough bread. He set the warm bread on a cutting board on the counter within reach of everyone.

"It can open the crown chakra for clear thought, connecting to higher guides—helping to embrace open thinking," Mac clarified. "It's perfect for finding the answers hidden deep in your unconscious, and often used in the finding of lost things. But it's limited to answering yes or no questions." She made a frowny face.

"Not great," Olivia said, sympathetic to the challenge.

"Nope," Mac confirmed. "After that, I tried to cast a Beacon Spell. This kind of spell employs local spirits around your home to act as a beacon for the lost person—so they can find their way back."

"And how do you manage something like that?" Nic asked. "I actually thought you said *bacon* at first." He grinned playfully, then tore a piece of bread from the hot loaf.

Mac responded with a head-shake and an eye-roll, then said, "I used the tall tree outback at my place—the taller the better. I worked a meditation while placing my hands on the trunk of the tree. Explaining to the tree what the situation was and asking for it to help by acting as a beacon."

"And?" Nic said between bites of bread.

Mac gave a *huff* of disappointment. "You're supposed to feel something in your gut. If it's a bad feeling, you move on to another tree. If it's an agreeable feeling, you've found the right one," she explained. "I felt nothing, but I thanked the tree for its help, anyway. I could always try another tree, but so far, neither of these spells produced any workable results."

"What other options are there?" Max asked. He'd sat at the counter on the stool on the other side of Nic and had been silent for most of the meal.

Mac leaned forward over the counter to see Max better. "I'd thought of trying Journeying. It's a shamanic method of meditation that allows you to visit the spirit world and interact with nature spirits—those who can offer valuable information, but it can be tricky. And for a lost person, I'd need to journey to the *Middle World*, the shadow side of the physical world—the invisible aspect of the mundane… and it's not without risk." Mac sat back.

Olivia gawked at her. "Yikes," she said.

"Ya, I put that option aside." Mac scooped up the last of her pasta. "This was a delicious meal," she directed at Julian.

"Delectable. Thank you so much," Olivia said. "Lynn will be so jealous when I tell her," she added with a giggle. "

"Now you see why it's my favorite," Nic said, running another piece of the crusty bread through the creamy sauce.

"Okay. Now what?" Max inquired, resting his fork in his now empty bowl.

Mac grabbed up her empty bowl, along with Olivia's and Max's, bringing them all to the sink, and then she ran the water to rinse them.

"Let me do that," Julian insisted, finishing the cleaning up for Mac.

"Thank you," Mac said. "The guys are so lucky to have you both."

"I second that," Olivia said as Mac returned to her seat.

"I'm the lucky one," Max said, blowing a kiss to Julian.

Mac lifted her huge purse from hanging on the corner of the stool-back. "I guess it's time to use our imaginations," she began, resting the bag on the counter.

All their faces focused her way.

"The success of a spell is based on these elements." She raised her hand in a fist, then extended her index finger. "*Purpose*—obviously, with a sequence—a clear beginning and end," she said as the first item. Extending and adding her middle finger for the second, she said, "*Sacred Space*—this can be anywhere, but it needs to be a clean, pleasant, and happy environment. And you bless the space by calling on the goddess to assist you. *Supplies*," she added with her ring finger. "I use herbs, candles, fabric, and ribbons of different colours." Lowering her hand, she pulled from her purse a white marble mortar and pestle and her chopstick wand that she still used, though it had some colours and symbols etched into it now and a black ribbon tied around the handle end. "Timing plays a role in all forms of magic. Days of the week, seasons of the year, and phases of the moon. Last, the most important is creativity and imagination. How you use these supplies is up to the caster's imagination. As long as the items required are present, you can create your own spells if needed." She pulled her cellphone from her purse and clicked on an app, then said, "It's a full moon, and since it's Friday, the planetary influence is Venus. "

They all stared at her with blank faces, even Olivia.

Mac cackled. "We are going to use pink and aqua green candles, and the herbs that are also associated with Venus. Got it?"

Mac received all nods.

While Julian gathered up the remaining dishes, Mac set up for the spell-making at her end of the long island counter.

She set her mortar and pestle along with her wand to one side of the placemat. Then she placed the coloured candles, pink and aqua green, out in front at the top edge of the mat. Digging into her purse again, she produced a small black notebook. "I need to write out the incantation—the spoken part of the spell." She cracked open the book and flipped to a blank page. "*Intention*," she said, then wrote out what the spell needed to accomplish. "*Grounding and centering*." Mac took several moments with her eyes closed, murmuring soothing words of affirmation to herself. Opening her eyes, she said, "Nic, I'm going to need something of Kris's."

"I'll check to see what—if anything, he left in his room," he said, dashing off up the line of inner doors that lead to the individual suites.

"I think he left a toothbrush," Max called after him.

Nic returned with a toothbrush. "Here," he said, handing the barely used item to Mac.

"It will have to do," she said, setting it down on the placemat. "We have everything we need now." Then she pulled out a large plastic pill box divided into several rows and columns, each with individual labels affixed to the lids of the compartments. "I have… elder, foxglove, iris, orris root, periwinkle, thyme, and…." She paused and flipped open a lid. "Crap, I don't have any catnip left. I used to grow it, but it attracts the neighborhood cats." She blew out a frustrated breath.

"Is there a substitute you can use?" Olivia asked, disappointment stealing her excitement.

"*Valerian.*" Mac snapped the lid shut and slummed in her chair.

"I have some valerian root tea—would that work?" Julian offered. "I use it as an herbal sleep aid."

"Ever since Kris went missing, Julian's sleep had been horrible, Max said, caressing Julian's hand.

He and Max may live amongst The Guards, but they were just as helpless as everyone else, Mac realized. "Yes—perfect!" Mac said, straightening in her chair again.

The incantation took about 20 minutes to perform. Although, unfortunately, the spell they had created had not been *perfect*. Not even close. In fact, it stunk, *literally*, like the reek of rotten eggs.

"Heaven help us," Nic said, covering his nose and mouth with both hands.

Olivia and Mac both gagged and moved away from the kitchen island.

Max held a dishtowel over the lower part of his face. "Heaven can't help with that," he said through the cloth.

Following several expletives, Julian retrieved some lemon scented spray from the cupboard under the sink and doused the entire open space.

Mac grumbled. "I don't understand why this didn't work." She returned to the island and slumped back into her chair. "How are we ever going to find him?"

Julian reached across the counter and put a hand over Mac's hand. "You put too much pressure on yourself. The others are working on solutions as well. It's not all on you — we'll find him," he said to Mac, giving the top of her hand a gentle squeeze and caress.

Nic leaned in. "Maybe you can try something easier… like tracking *me* for instance," he suggested, giving Mac a supportive smile.

Chapter 17 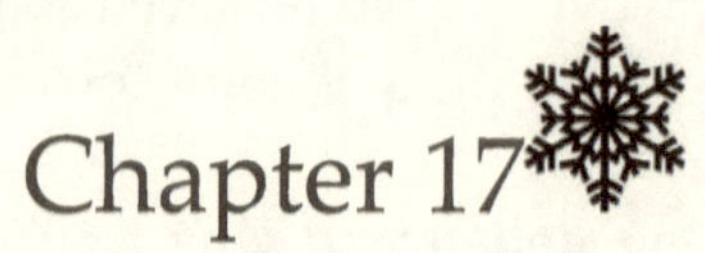

Jana's apartment, May 8th, Mother's Day, Seydisfjordur, Iceland

"*Cryptomnesia…,*" Kisur read out quietly from the dictionary website on Jana's laptop. "*… the phenomenon of not recognizing the return of an old memory as a product of memory, but instead regarding it as a new or original thought or idea.*"

"What are you reading?" Jana asked, passing by the small living room where he sat, heading into the equally tiny kitchen.

Kisur closed the page. "Nothing—really," he said. "Was looking up Mother's Day."

"And what did you find?" She left the kitchen and snagged her sneakers from the landing at the top of the stairwell.

"What you'd expect. That it's a celebration honoring mothers, as well as motherhood and maternal bonds. And the influence of mothers in society."

"It is celebrated on different days in many parts of the world," Jana said. "Here, we celebrate the achievements and efforts of mothers—and mother figures. And thankfully, people give gifts and sweets, so it will be another great day in the bakery—a busy one too." She sat in the chair next to the sofa to put on her sneakers.

"We sold out of chocolate Éclair cakes at Easter, so I made sure we had plenty for today," Kisur said. The icebox cake with layers of graham cracker, pudding, and chocolate was one of the two new items, along with panettone, that he had created and added to the list of treats sold at the bakery. He had been grappling with the surfacing of memories and he wasn't sure if he'd made them before or perhaps had only eaten them. He had wrestled with a lot of imaginings and memories over the past 4 months he'd been here, though he hadn't shared his struggles with Jana.

"I wasn't surprised. Easter is always a wonderful time for tourists to visit Iceland. It's the start of Spring, birds flock here for nesting, there are migrating whales for watching, and the Northern lights are still dancing at night."

"And mountains of chocolate appeared in the stores," he laughed out.

"Don't forget the páskaegg."

"The Easter eggs—right," he agreed.

"The foundation of Easter may be a religious holiday, but for most Icelanders, it's the long weekend from Thursday to Easter Monday we enjoy. Part of why we'd sold out of so much then was because I always close the bakery on the Sunday and Monday."

"It was great we could get together with Geir and his friend Jón, for the traditional meal of roasted leg of lamb," Kisur said with a grin.

"Thank you again for cooking, by the way. If it's not a baked good, I'm not attempting it." She snickered.

"It was enjoyable for me to cook for everyone."

"I forgot to ask you where you found that recipe? It was exquisite."

"I just searched traditional Icelandic roasted lamb," he lied. He had looked nothing up, he'd made it from scratch. Hadn't known then, nor now, how to explain his ability to do that. It was easier to just play as though he had a knack with cooking, and baking too, it seemed. It was like his creating the desserts, the how and what they each needed just sort of came to him. He set the laptop on the small coffee table before getting up and going into the kitchen. He filled a glass with water from the tap.

"Ready?" Jana asked, done with tying her shoes.

"As ready as I can be," he said before chugging back the water with his morning memory supplements.

As they descended the stairs to the bakery, they joked about being baker warriors and their impending hectic day.

"Sold out again!" Jana exclaimed, flopping onto the sofa, and kicking off her shoes. "What a day—I seriously could not have done it without your help."

"It feels good," Kisur said from the tiny kitchen, filling a glass with water again. "I enjoy being productive—useful." He tossed back three more of the MSM capsules, chasing them down with the water.

"Are those the memory supplements?"

"Yes." He finished the last of the water.

"Didn't you already take those this morning?"

"I did. But I've started taking the serving twice a day now." Within several seconds of swallowing the last of the water he swayed on his feet, his sight clouding over.

"Are you alright?" Jana asked, getting up from the sofa.

"I...," he said, wobbling again. He leaned against the counter. Every muscle and ligament in his body weakened, even those holding his eyes in his head sensing them roll back. His vision abandoned him as he lost all command of his body. He felt Jana's arms go around him as the weight of his body brought them both to the floor.

"Kisur—Kisur," her panicked voice sounded. "Can you hear me?"

He could hear her, but it was difficult with the ringing in his ears. Even so, his mouth wasn't working, and he was unable to answer her terrified words. His heart and lungs continued to function, as did all his senses. This crisis was not unfamiliar, and it had been happening more frequently. And he always remained fully conscious, though in a state of paralysis. He had hoped upping his supplements might help keep these collapsing events at bay. Though this was the first time Jana was here to witnessed one. They had never come on this fast before, and he'd always been able to isolate himself until the ailment passed.

"Kisur," he heard Jana call again. He sensed the pressure of her hand against his neck, checking for a pulse, he assumed. Then he felt the soft brush of her hair on his cheek as though she were leaning down to check his breathing. He drew in her scent, then exhaled a breath to show he was still able. The muscles of his face and eyes always returned first, and he forced open his eyelids. "I'm fine," he said, now that he could move his lips and tongue. His head rested on Jana's lap, he realized, now able to turn his neck. Gazing up at her, he said, "Are you okay?"

"Am I okay?" she laughed out, though tears ran down her cheeks. One dropped to land in a warm splash on his forehead, and she wiped it away. "You're the one who collapsed—I thought you...." She whipped away the tears still traveling down her face. "It doesn't matter what I thought—are *you* okay? Can you sit up—are you hurt—what happened?"

"I believe so," he said, muscle tension and further sensation returning to his arms and legs. Slowly, he shifted himself up off Jana's lap to a sitting position, shifting to rest against the fridge. The coolness of the door against his back soothed the aches that always accompanied these episodes.

Jana pulled her knees to her chest as she leaned against the cabinet doors below the sink. Worry and relief battled for control over her facial expression. "You really gave me a scare." She swiped away a stray tear.

"I'm sorry you had to see that—I had hoped to avoid further episodes by taking more of those pills." He brought one knee in and then pushed himself up off the floor.

"More episodes—this has happened before?" She followed him up off the floor, staring up at him.

He gripped the edge of the counter to steady himself, glancing at her worried face.

Panic won over her expression, then swiftly morphed into anger. "How could you not tell me?"

"I didn't tell you—because I didn't want to worry you."

"Too late. Please, come rest on the sofa," she said, motioning for them to go to the living room. She walked beside him as though ready to catch him should he collapse again. "Lay down," she said with authority, moving the small pillow from the chair to the end of the sofa.

She rested him down on the tiny sofa, his head on the pillow, his feet hanging off the far end. Then instead of sitting in the small armchair, Jana pushed the coffee table to one side and lowered herself down to the floor. She placed an arm on the sofa cushion next to his, leaning her body against the sofa to face him.

"How long?" she asked, annoyed, yanking free the hair elastic that had held her hair back.

"How long, what?" He knew what she meant, but he didn't want to tell her it had been happening since Valentine's Day, almost the whole time he'd been staying with her. She had been so kind to him, allowing him to stay here, not knowing who he was or anything about him. He would be forever grateful no matter the outcome of this memory journey of his. She'd provided him up with clothes to wear, a warm bed to sleep, and a job working with her in the bakery. He often found himself thinking, *who does that for a stranger*? Since he had no recollection of friends or family, maybe it was what some people did, the generous and kind people in this world. He had the notion it was not that common. And he'd learned from some of his own foggy memories that *he* had definitely not been one of those kind people. But he wanted to be.

She gave him an intense expression that screamed, *don't mess with me.*

"Tell me more about the Rainbow street," he asked, hoping to shift the attention off himself and his weakness, and on to something more joyful. He had grown to care about both Geir and Jana, her in ways he wasn't ready to share because he already felt vulnerable enough not knowing what had happened to him, how he got here. What he felt for Jana went beyond the gratitude he felt. It was… something he'd never felt… a longing for connection, for purpose. Like there was a reason she was in his life, and he just hadn't figured it out yet. Like his past, she was a mystery… but like when trying to find your way in a dream, his heart seemed to know the way to her.

"You are going to have to tell me, eventually."

He smiled, amused. "Geir told me it's a sign of support for the local LGBTQ community. That the church where the street ends, was originally located in another spot near here."

"They moved it back in 1920 to its current spot." She paused, then said, "And… Geir told you that your tattoos weren't in the police database too, didn't he?"

"Yes." Geir had told him, but he'd not brought it up with Jana. He had figured she'd hear it from him too, so no need to dwell on the bad news. Although he hadn't considered it bad, it was just another topic he hadn't wanted to discuss with Jana. "Tell me about the Rainbow street," he requested again, a plea much like that of a child wanting another bedtime story. Not that he couldn't recall any bedtime stories, telling them or being told.

Jana crossed her feet at the ankles, allowing her body to rest heavily against the sofa's edge. "On a sunny day in the summer of 2016, one of the most beautiful community projects began." She smiled, thoughtful. "The residents and employees of the town got together and painted the paved part of the street in the colours of the rainbow. They didn't know it at the time, but they had created what would be one of the most visited landmarks in East Iceland. Regnbogastræti—*Rainbow Street*. Each year, visitors and pedestrians get the opportunity to grab a paintbrush and help paint the colourful street, but visitors come to see it all year round. It ends at the Blue Church, as you mentioned. The church is only open from June to August, but it has a concert series that takes place during that time, and it is one of the main musical cultural events with musical performers from all over the country."

"June is Pride month."

"How do you know that? Did Geir tell you about that, too?"

"No…," he said, focusing on bringing in the recollection. "There are two faces that come to my mind—memories, I'm guessing. Of two… women…." He lifted his head and ran a hand through his hair, then bent his arm to tuck it beneath the pillow.

"Two women?" Jana asked, the sound of hesitancy ringing in her voice.

He didn't turn to look at her. Instead, he tried to pull in the details he had recalled. "They were very high in contrast," he began. "The one was no doubt the tougher of the two…." He paused. "… But that was just her physique. The images of her in my mind showed she had short black spikey hair… she was well-dressed—wearing black clothing.

Dark eye makeup encircled grey opalescent eyes. She was striking, really." He paused again, conjuring images of the other. He smiled pensively. "Hmf. The other was slender and delicate, and she dressed in soft pale feminine colours. Her hair...." He gazed at Jana. "It was pale blonde—like yours, though hers reached her waist. I don't recall any names other than *Frank*—which obviously doesn't seem to align." He chuckled and searched for more memories. "And I remember shot glasses, a wall of them—of all things, being part of the same memories." He chuckled again, this time at how convoluted his recollections could be. Shifting onto his side to face Jana, he brought his arm over to rest next to hers on the sofa cushion.

"Could Frank be your name?"

"I don't recall anyone calling me that."

She didn't look at him. "Maybe... maybe one of these women is someone... special in your life." She pulled up one knee to her chest, wrapping an arm around it, then stared at the empty armchair next to the sofa as though lost in her own thought and memories.

"I get the feeling they are important to me—friends maybe, but there is no romantic attachment in my memories... I think *they* were a couple—and why they came to mind when we spoke of LGBTQ."

She continued to stare at the chair.

"Jana," he said, attempting to pull her awareness back to him.

"Hm?" she muttered, turning finally to look at him.

"I've come to like my life here," he shared. They had become close and there had been a spark, an attraction between them. He'd been hesitant to act on it despite the affection he felt for her. How could they move forward, how could he, with not knowing who he was? Without knowing who might be in his life? He could have a girlfriend, a wife, children even.

She gave him an adoring smile. "I like you being here."

He looked away. He didn't want to see her reaction when he spoke his next words. "What do you think will happen if I never find out who I am?" He'd had glimpses of who he was from his old life. It was more like flashes of how he behaved. At least he believed it was his previous life. However, he hadn't been pleased with what he remembered, who he was or how he had spoken to others he believed to be part of that life. Four months had passed since Jana had found him on her father's property. Four months he'd spent in his new life, with her. He focused back on her.

She said nothing, just gazed back at him, a sorrowful expression crossing her lovely face.

"Have you ever heard of Cryptomnesia?"

She frowned, as though perplexed.

"It's something I looked up this morning." He'd performed many searches on many things these past few months, but none of the searches had been on finding out about his life. He hadn't wanted to know if anyone was searching for him, maybe in the beginning when he was originally disoriented, but now, things about this life here, they felt *right*. He felt happy. He didn't want to find out where he had come from.

"Sounds like something from a Superman movie—wait, no, that's kryptonite."

"I've heard the term super-man, but I didn't know it was a movie."

"You don't remember who Superman is?"

He shook his head, then gave her an encouraging grin.

"He's a superhero in comic books. There are Superman books, movies, and television shows—and video games. He's from the planet Krypton, his real name is Kal-El—well, the Kents named him Clark— they found him as a baby. He has superhuman abilities—and he wears a red and blue costume and a cape—works for the Daily Planet," she rambled out.

The corner of his mouth tipped up in an amused smile. He thought hard, drawing in what he could from his scrambled, barely-there, memory banks. He knew what movies were and television, although there was no movie theater in the town, and Jana didn't have a TV. She preferred reading or outdoor activities. He liked outdoor activities but didn't care for reading books. He did like watching Jana read, though. It made her uncomfortable, *self-conscious* she'd told him, so he'd asked for her to tell him about the book she was reading. She read a lot. They had gone out to her father's home to exchange the ones she had already read from here at the apartment, for several she'd wanted to read from the bookshelf in her father's living room. She'd taken him outside to the barn that same day, out to where she had found him. He hadn't been able to remember anything, other than he had recalled the sensation of being wet, not in the backyard but in some open body of water. Jana had explained there were no forms of water within walking distance of her father's place, especially not in that frigid temperature. "I don't recall this superman." He shrugged.

"Lois Lane, General Zod, his archenemy Lex Luthor—none of that ringing any bells?"

He loved her enthusiasm when explaining things to him. Sometimes he knew or remembered what she was trying to describe, other times, like now, he was at a loss. "Nope."

"Never mind. What about this crypto-thingy?"

"Cryptomnesia."

"Yes—what is it?" She waved her hand, gesturing for him to go on.

"It's the phenomenon of regarding an old memory as a new idea. Crypto from the Greek words krýptein meaning to *hide* and mnêsis meaning *memory*—also used in the word *hypermnesia* which is used for *enhancement* of memory—it typically happens under abnormal conditions like trauma, hypnosis, or narcosis."

"Okay, you've lost me. Why are you asking me about this hidden memory thing?"

"Because I think I've been experiencing it."

"What do you mean?"

He tucked an arm under the pillow where he rested his head, leaning the other next to Jana's. "I can't tell if the things I know—or my ideas, are truly mine or old memories of things I've been told. I read about *Memory Bias*, where the tendency is to selectively recall memories that related to your current emotional state. I don't know if I'm remembering something because it's congruent with my own memory or with something someone said had happened."

"I don't think that's the case," she said. "Do you remember what the doctors told you about Amnesia—how it isn't just the loss of memories? It includes the loss of information—facts, and experiences. They said then that your recent memories were lost, and it's why you can't remember how you got here. But your ingrained memories might have been spared and could come back."

"I can recall lots of things—but not *how* I know them."

"The loss of memory hasn't affected your intelligence—your general knowledge. You can understand written and spoken words from quite a few languages, I might add. And you can remember new things—like everything I taught you about the town—about Iceland."

"You know… I don't recall any memories of having… a mother. Isn't that awful?" He observed Jana's hand next to his on the sofa.

"Sometimes I wish I could forget mine."

"I know your mother left… has she ever reached out to you?" He went to touch her hand, but she moved her arm to push up from the floor.

"I'll be right back," she said, leaving the living room.

He sat up on the sofa. "Jana," he called, annoyed with himself for bringing up her mother. She never talked about her. All her stories she'd shared with him had been about her father.

When she returned to the living room then, he said, "I'm sorry— it's none of my business." Then he noted she carried the memory box her father had given her.

"No—it's alright," she said, sitting next to him on the sofa, hands wrapped around the box. "It was ten years after she left, when my father was contacted by a friend of my mother's. He had been told she had died—and been named next of kin." She stared down at the box in her lap.

"Oh, Jana—I am soooo sorry." He wanted to hug her, but she continued, having more to tell him.

"He was told she ran in the fast lane with the wrong people, drinking and doing drugs—had overdosed at a weekend getaway." She glanced up at him briefly, then returned to focusing on the box.

He said nothing, giving her the space to get it all out.

She drew in a long breath. "It was required that he go to New York City to take care of the paperwork and retrieve something that she had left for him." She tapped the lid of the box. "It was this box—it's not really my father's—it's her memory box. It was filled with photos of her skating and articles about her career." She paused, then said,

"Funny, my mother had kept the same two photos that my father had." She opened the box. "The one of her with me, and one of her and my father from the Olympics." She retrieved the two photos, holding them up for him to see again. She'd shown him these when they'd first been at her father's house, but he had not looked at the one with her and her mother. He took time to review both, understanding now that she had no memories of *her* mother, either. Other than the blonde hair and similar build, he had noted that the resemblances between them were few. Jana had her father's light coloured sparkling eyes and his trusting smile.

"When he returned from New York, is when he gave me the box. At the time, he had only shared that she had passed away. It wasn't until I was in my twenties that he told me more about what happened to my mother." She placed the photos back in the box and closed the lid before setting it over on the coffee table. "When I was a child, I fantasized she was off on a grand adventure, or performing for royalty. It was much easier than thinking your mother had abandoned you." She stared at her hands in her lap.

He reached and took up one of her hands, and she looked up at him. He clasped her hand between both of his, resting them on his knee.

"It's fine, really. I understand how life goes. I hadn't known her, so the loss—her death, had little impact to my world. It was just sad how she wasted her life. Losing my father was the hardest thing I've ever had to face."

He tightened his grasp on her hand, feeling the grief as though it were his own.

She placed her other hand over his and smiled thoughtfully up at him. "He also told me about a woman he met in New York." She let out a little laugh. "I'd wondered why he had been so chipper upon his return, considering his reason for traveling there." She patted the top of his hand.

"He'd met someone." He smiled knowingly back.

"He said it wasn't meant to be anything other than a few stolen moments, and that it had been nice to feel wanted again." She gazed down at their entwined hands. "It had shifted his mind and heart," she said, tilting her head to gaze up at him. "I've never been to New York City. I've never been anywhere in the U.S..

"Magnolia Bakery on the Upper West Side has some amazing icebox cakes."

Her eyebrows kicked up, and she tilted her head, then she glanced over her shoulder at the coffee table. "Wait—what?" she said, pulling free from his hands. She turned and grabbed her cellphone from off the coffee table, then typed something on the screen. She held up the phone, turning it his way. "How did you know about this bakery?"

On the screen was a website with a photo of a bakery storefront. He took the phone from her and stared at the image. "I… I don't know."

Chapter 18 

Leo and the others had spent the past 2 months performing the same extensive search method Zach and Marq had done. Nic and Leo had traversed and examined every main, side, and back roads on the Ottawa GPS and had repeated a similar approach in Brazil, from the Taygeta building in Manaus City. Ben and Den had navigated the same way through Tokyo and Amsterdam, extending their searches from the Maia and Alcyon facilities respectively, to the outer reaches of each city. Marq and Zach had done the same with Electra, the Rome location, as they had for Norway and New York. They had even returned and completed an additional search in both locations, extending the search zone out as had been done with all the facility locations. What remained of their exploration options was to contact all the hospitals and police stations throughout.

Derek continued to work on Thaddeus's notes, and Marq and he combined efforts on the viable options for where Kris could have travelled to. It was a slim chance he would have gone to Iceland considering the threat of sulfur exposure, however, he wouldn't have known about the testing Thaddeus had done, none of them had.

There had been no sightings of Thaddeus during the search timeframe and Lane had not seen Lyndon since their last confrontation at the University library. Redmond and I had a lengthy discussion about leaving the searching to them, and about me *not* being involved. But I had really wanted to talk with Lane about what had happened with Lyndon, to get a clearer take on this 'good guy', but our schedules hadn't allowed us an opportunity for a private chat.

Mac and Olivia had told me about the location spells Mac had tried and all about their stinky spell they'd performed at North Haven. Mac had said she was going to keep researching for more options when she had time between family and work obligations. Olivia had gleefully added the details about how they'd shared an amazing meal with Nic, Julian, and Max.

Those of us here had all done the *no entry* spell Mac had given us for our homes. There had been no other calls to Olivia or Nic, no suspicious happenings, no one lurking near homes or work that they could tell, but then again, there had been no sign of Kris, either.

I made sure that Den and the others, including my girlfriends in Ottawa and my lovely husband, kept me in the loop, even if all they had was a brief update. I hadn't enjoyed being left out, and I wasn't going to tolerate the discomfort of it again. We have all been searching for Kris, but I'd been willing to put my safety, my life, on the line to help. There was no way for us to know if he was injured, unconscious, or if Thaddeus actually held him captive. And there was nothing indicating Thaddeus, nor his followers, were privy to the existence of The Guards of Haven. But if he had Kris, he would surely know now he was not human. None of us had the stomach to broach the subject that Kris might be lost for good or possibly that he may be dead.

I'd asked Gabriel privately if he would in some way know if Kris had passed on. His answer had been that, *"death was not his area of expertise"*. He'd suggested I reach out to Zaqiel, being that he was also the Horseman *Death*. I was aware Zaqiel sometimes visited with the twins since they were also descendants of his through my birthmother's side. Although I'd not felt his presence in quite some time. In reality, I wasn't sure I had the guts to ask him. I didn't want to hear Kris was dead, and I didn't want to be the one to share it with Leo and the others. Despite the dreams I'd had and the nightmares the girls had had, a big part of me believed the hanging angel was *not* Kris. Part of it was because I hadn't gotten a clear read on who this angel was. And regarding Thaddeus not being seen, I wasn't sure if I was relieved or unnerved by the fact. Either way, seen or unseen, even if I hadn't wanted to admit it out loud, it appeared all evidence showed it was *me* he had turned his interests on.

On the evenings when Den dropped over with updates, he had taken the twins flying, circling around the area from the South Haven down the island near their school and back home. He tried not to do it late in the evening as it made for a challenging time getting them to sleep after. It was a wonderful treat for them, although I think Den secretly did it because it was a treat for him, a peaceful few moments and distraction from dwelling on how helpless he truly felt regarding their failure to locate Kris. It was good to see him smile and laugh with the girls. I had no new ideas to help their cause, nor words of wisdom to aid the burden they carried. The weight of it was heavy on all of us.

I'd been reluctant to mention how *uncomplicated* the last two months of my life had been. My volunteer work had been both stress-free and angel-free. I had kept up with my training at the South Haven, though I hadn't felt ready for shooting practice just yet. Redmond had been happily occupied with preparing the girls for school on my volunteering days, with learning more about self-defense and weapons, and with time at the music studio with Lily. He'd even spent time on virtual calls with Derek, working together to restore a 1995 Fender Yngwie Malmsteen signature double-neck Stratocaster 12/6m, whatever, that Derek had purchased. I knew it was a yellow double-neck guitar, and that was about it, but if working on it made Redmond happy, I was all for it.

Easter had come and gone, and we had a wonderful visit then with Luc and Dunya. Luc still played guitar occasionally for the band at the Non-denominational Christian church he attended, though he and Dunya were spending more time in Orlando these days with his sister and her family, as well as with Dunya's daughter and fiancé who lived nearby. And Dunya has been joyfully immersed in helping Aleah with wedding plans. When her daughter had gotten engaged, Dunya had a visit from Shamsiel, and he'd shared that Aleah had not inherited Dunya's gift like she had from Mitra, but it was possible a future daughter of Aleah's might still. I've not seen or felt Shamsiel for a long time, not since the twins were born. Darius is one of his descendants, but he never mentions if he sees him or not, and I don't ask.

Darius had gotten busier with his fitness clients at his gym and had spent extra time training with Redmond at the South Haven. He and Lily had come over for Easter, of course, and we'd all taken part in the off island Easter Egg Hunt event. Gabriel had been there too. However, he hadn't had anything more to say on my Archangel visitor at the hospital. His answer to my inquiries was always that she'd merely been curious. *Right.*

Leo had kept his promise to keep me informed, though he hadn't asked me to go on any more searches or help by using my senses. Redmond had obviously spoken with him about my not getting involved. As a compromise, I'd suggested that if I couldn't help the Earthbound, then I could at least make *belated* birthday plans with my girlfriends in Ottawa. It had been their plan initially, so it had worked in my favor as the ideal negotiating tool.

My birthday had passed by uneventfully on the 3rd of May and just how I liked it. I was full of gratitude for being alive and enjoyed the gift of another birthday with my family. My brother James always sends me homemade birthday cards and this year's was a comical one with a photo of him and his dogs wearing birthday hats.

Mother's Day had been this past Sunday on the 8th, and the twins having their birthdays this week, we'd combined all three events together extended to today, May 10th, the girls' birthday. We had kept them home from school yesterday, Monday, being that today was a PD Day, a professional development day for the teachers, so the kids were off, making it an extra-long weekend. With the merging of celebrations, it also meant we had a full house.

Redmond's parents hadn't been able to make it for Easter, but luckily, they were able to visit now. It had been wonderful having his mom with us for Mother's Day, since my mother wasn't with us anymore. Mother's Day was always bittersweet with the battle of conflicting emotions, so I made a point of making space for the loss of my mother while celebrating the gain of my own motherhood. And it was extra special being able to have both her and Poppy here to celebrate Ryley and Hayley's birthdays with us.

It was no secret that I was adopted. Not having known my birthmother, I had often wondered as I was growing up if she thought of me on *my* birthday, it being not just the day of my birth but also the day she had to give me up. Today, it had me wondering about the Earthbound, *Anael*. She may have created The Guards of Haven, who were almost like sons to her and Thanael, but it was she who had chosen to give up her biological child, her daughter. Having daughters of my own, I couldn't imagine giving them up, or even missing their birthdays.

The plan for the twins' birthday this year had been marked *Party with the Rays* on the calendar ever since the two of them had gone on that school field trip to the Florida Oceanographic Society. It was an interactive visit that makes use of the Coastal Center property and the 'Conservation Ambassador' animals to teach children about marine biology and the environment. They were designed to address 'Next Generation Sunshine State Standards for Science', their teacher Gavin, had told us. Ryley had talked about wanting to become a marine biologist ever since, and Hayley had said she wasn't sure what she wanted to be, but she was sure it would involve animals. They had enjoyed it so much, we had signed them up for summer camp there right away. They offer a fun and educational marine science-themed summer camp, and they each selected differed programs to do. Ryley had picked *Classy Creatures* and Hayley had chosen *Island Explorers*, which were both full-day camps. They had been thrilled to show Nana and Poppy the Live Fish Cam, which is part of the feeding program we tuned into every Sunday. They'd told their grandparents all about the Gamefish Lagoon with its 750,000 gallon saltwater aquarium, how it's home to over twenty different fish species, including stingrays and nurse sharks, and 4 non-releasable sea turtles. But today's trip would be our first time going there with the twins.

They had begged to do the birthday party the facility offered, but when we'd reviewed the party offerings, we'd found the options a bit juvenile for what the girls were hoping for. Instead, we'd chosen to book a private tour. Luckily, the facility allowed you to book them on

Closed Days, being that they were only open Wednesday through Sunday. What had additionally turned us off the party option, had been that we had to provide our own food and decorations. The girls had agreed with the private tour instead but had asked that we eat at their favorite taco place on the island after. They hadn't wanted a typical party with their friends this year either and they were thrilled when we told them their grandparents would be here and that Lily and Darius would be coming too.

Today's weather report said we were going to have an average around 75 degrees, so I'd instructed the girls to put on shorts and long-sleeved t-shirts, along with ankle socks and sneakers. They could always push up their sleeves if they got too warm, but most indoor places here had the air-conditioning cranked. I'd put on a pair of shorts and a long-sleeved t-shirt as well, though Redmond had opted for shorts and a regular t-shirt, this one being an Ohana Surf Shop tee he had gotten from a surf event the store had put on.

While Redmond's parents were outback with Summer and Snow, Redmond was on the couch in the living room playing the acoustic guitar he kept in there, doing what he always did when waiting for us girls to get ready.

When I came out from the ensuite bathroom, I found Hayley in front of the floor-length mirror in my bedroom.

"We match," she giggled out when she recognized we were both wearing navy-blue shorts and white long-sleeved t-shirts, although her shirt had a sunflower on it and mine was plain.

"Whatcha doing?" I asked, grabbing my watch from the bedside table.

"I'm not tall enough to see my whole body in the bathroom mirror." She turned side to side, checking out her outfit. She was still growing slower than Ryley, but it didn't seem to bother her other than limitations like this.

"Bathroom mirrors aren't great for getting the full view for anyone—that's why I have this long mirror. Has nothing to do with tall enough," I reassured her.

"Can you do ponytails for us today?" she asked. The light over the mirror crackled and flared, then went out. Hayley let out a shriek and said, "Did you see her?"

Another scream echoed from down the hall, and I heard Redmond's heavy footfalls as he went from the living room to the girls' bedrooms.

"Redmond!" I called out through the bedroom door.

"On it!" he yelled back. "Her bedroom light blew, is all."

I turned back to Hayley. "What—who?" I asked, coming to stand behind her at the mirror.

"Ryley—was in the mirror—I saw her on her bed in her room!" Hayley rushed out, wide-eyed. Shock filled her face. She reached a hand to the mirror, then quickly pulled it back as though afraid to touch it.

I knelt and turned her to face me. "Okay, slow down. Tell me again what you saw."

"When the light sparkled, I saw her. Ryley. In the mirror. In her room—she was scared," she said, rushing out the last part.

It was daylight out, but other than the loud crackle and the spark of light, I wasn't sure what had frightened them. Though, I knew better than to brush this off, considering the twins' ever-expanding abilities.

"All good?" Redmond asked then from the doorway. He had Ryley over his shoulder. She was giggling, so I knew she was fine. "Are you ready to *Party with the Rays*?"

I stared back at the mirror. Only Hayley and I were in the reflection. *"I don't know what happened,"* I whispered to her. "But I'll get yer father to fix the lights, okay?" I added in a louder voice for Redmond to hear.

She nodded. *"Do you believe me?"* she asked in a soft voice.

"Of course, I do." I took both her hands in mind and kissed the backs of them. "Ready for the rays?"

She nodded again and gave a sunny grin. "Ponytails," she reminded.

I addressed the need for ponytails, even giving myself one, before we exited the house. Darius and Lily had arrived moments earlier, as they had arranged to have Redmond's parents ride with them to the aquarium, since it made little sense to take three cars.

We arrived at the Florida Oceanographic Society 15 minutes prior to our private tour, which was to start at 10 a.m.. The person who had helped us book the tour said it would take approximately 2 hours. As a bonus, our tour included a free, one-year Family Membership which allowed unlimited visits, plus other membership benefits I hadn't yet read about.

Our tour guide, who was waiting for us at the front desk check-in, introduced himself as the *Director of Education for the FOS* and announced that we would start our journey with a presentation on and a feeding of the Cownose and Southern stingrays.

Thankfully, the first presentation was more of a hands-on interaction than a lecture.

"We learned about all this on the field trip," Hayley said to me in a whisper, waiting for her turn to feed the rays. Next was the presentation about Florida's water quality issues and algae blooms, and Hayley said the same thing, but then again she got to feed the fish in the 750,000 gallon aquarium.

What I had found most interesting though, was that a brightly yellow striped fish, Hayley told me, was a *Porkfish*, seemed to follow her as she strolled along the walkway of the lagoon. She ran ahead, and it raced after her, and when I called her to come back, it made a sharp turn and followed her. "Did you notice the fish following you?" I asked her, pointing at it.

"Ya, I've seen him before—last time I was here." She waved at the fish, and it made a tight circle as if acknowledging her. "C'mon let's go!" she said, addressing the fish. She raced up the walkway again, the fish zooming along next to her in the water.

"What's going on?" Redmond asked, stepping up next to me.

"I think our daughter can talk to fish," I said, straight-faced.

"Seriously?"

I turned to face him. "Seriously—watch the yellow fish." I pointed at Hayley at the far end of the walkway, leaning over to talk to the fish. "Hayley—can you come here for a second?" I called to her.

Instead of running this time, she skipped her way back up the walkway.

Redmond watched as the fish kept pace with her. "Well—look at that," he said as Hayley reached us.

"Is it sea turtle time?" I asked, pretending that was what I'd wanted her for.

"Sea turtles!" Ryley announced as she passed by, gripping the hands of both Lily and Darius. Darius was bent over, trying to hold her hand as she pulled them along. "Nana—Poppy!" she called, turning back.

Redmond's parents were doing their best to keep up. They both showed signs of exhaustion already as they attempted to hustle past us.

"Slow your roll," Redmond called to Ryley. Then he grabbed up my hand. "I think we need to see if she can talk to turtles, too." He winked at me.

During the turtle presentation, it wasn't so much the Director of Education who did the talking, it was both Ryley and Hayley who shared their knowledge, reciting what they had learned the last time they'd been here.

"You see that green sea turtle there, that's Turtwig—or Turt, and that one over there is Hank," Hayley informed us. "They call them sub-adults because the people who take care of them don't know if they are boys or girls yet."

"Iliana!" Ryley called out to the lagoon. A huge turtle surfaced near where she stood along the railing.

"Iliana—or Lily, weighs almost three hundred pounds," our tour guide added, eyebrows raised as he observed the interactions of our daughters and his turtles.

"She's a big one!" our Lily exclaimed.

"She's a *He*," Ryley corrected with a giggle, smiling over at our *little* Lily.

"Anna Belle, our adult green sea turtle, is also male. We call him Abe now." The guide smiled at the twins.

"He doesn't mind if you call him Anna Bell," Hayley said then, peering over the rail next to her sister.

The tour operator nodded and grinned at the rest of us, though he seemed flabbergasted by the exchanges the twins were having with the wildlife. "And we end our tour with a short nature-trail walk back through the mangroves and hammocks," he said then, regarding the twins, removing his brimmed hat to scratch his head.

I can't say how intelligent turtles or fish are, but Redmond and I have both witnessed some exceptional moments between our two dogs and our daughters. I had a powerful sense that the twins, even as babies, had some unique form of communication with Summer and Snow. But after what I'd witnessed today, I was more than certain of it. Summer and Snow are fiercely loyal and protective of them. As babies, the twins would make cooing noises in their cribs and the dogs would go check on them. When they were beginning to talk, they had certain hand gestures that they did, and the dogs would follow their directions, commands we'd never taught them. And the hand gestures didn't work for me or Redmond. Even now, they use subtle facial expressions mixed with words. The girls had always had their own twin language, but this was something altogether different. When we'd moved to the beach house, the girls had gotten their own rooms, and the way the dogs had responded to the split and to them individually and collectively, the connections between the four could not be ignored.

Could they communicate with all animals? I wondered as they hopped and skipped along the nature path. "Who's hungry?" I tossed out then as we reached the end of our tour. I knew I was.

I received a unanimous, "Meee!" from all. Even a few of the volunteers passing by at the entrance said it. They smiled and waved at the girls as we went through the gate. Evidently, everyone was hungry.

At the taco place, while the girls took their favorite spots on the barstools at the bar-top, they were greeted with Happy Birthdays from all the staff. Redmond's parents were on the first two stools, followed by Hayley and Ryley, bookend by Darius and Lily, with Redmond and me at the far end. We all loved the place and the food, and it was especially enjoyable sitting up at the long counter chatting with the bar staff. The bartender had made and set up special *reserved* signs with the twins' names and the words 'Birthday Girl' written on them. Redmond had called ahead to let them know we were celebrating the twins' birthdays today and that we'd be here around noon. It was *Taco Tuesday*, but with it being off-season on the island we had the bar area to ourselves.

Once all the drink orders went in, we deliberated on which tacos we wanted this time. Then, just before fulfilling the beer orders, our friendly favorite bartender first returned with the twins' drinks. But this time, instead of bringing them their drinks in the usual plastic cups, he'd filled two Tulip Glasses with the lemonade. These glasses with bulbous body and flared lip which were normally used for the Belgian dark ales they served.

"Just for the birthday girls!" he announced, setting a fancy glass of lemonade in front of each of them.

"Oooh, thank you!" Hayley squealed, wrapping her hands around the glass.

Ryley leaned forward on the counter. "Muuum—Daaa!" she called down to us, pointing a finger at her special drink. "Thank you." She beamed up at the bartender.

"Very fancy-shmancy," I said back, making a wow face and raising my eyebrows.

"You are both very welcome. Now let's get your birthday taco orders in," he said, tapping a drumroll with his hands on the edge of the bar.

They both giggled and took small sips of their drinks.

Taco orders were simple with the twins. They always went with the traditional taco with the ground beef and fixings like their father. I preferred either the shrimp or pork taco, but today I was going with one of each. While we waited, a server brought out chips and salsa, and some extra queso that they knew the twins liked to dip their chips in.

"Happy Birthday!" came a familiar voice from behind us, just as our taco trays were being cleared away. Den stood with the restaurant's door open wide, the handles of two large white paper bags hooked over each of his forearms. Seeing Den with gifts for the twins was not a surprise, but the person who trailed in with Den was.

Gavin McCray, the twins' teacher, waved his arms over his head in greeting as he followed in behind our much larger friend. "Hey there," he said as he passed behind my and Redmond's stools. He gave Redmond a pat on the shoulder.

"Did you know he was friends with Den?" I asked Redmond.

"No, but they might be more than friends," he said next to my ear, before subtlety motioning for me to peek.

Gavin had a hand resting just above Den's lower back. "Happy Birthday, ladies," he said then to the twins, moving his hand away to shake theirs with the birthday greeting.

"Hmmm, come to think of it, Gavin has never mentioned a girlfriend, nor a boyfriend for that matter," I said to Redmond in a muffled voice. Redmond and he had spent a lot of time surfing together, and they'd taught the twins to surf too, but he never had anyone with him on the outings. Back on Valentine's day I recalled Den saying that he didn't know what was worse — *the loneliness or losing someone*, and I considered if his statement applied here.

Den raised the big white bags in front of the girls. "I've got something special for you both," Den announced, handing each of them a bag. "I had Marq create these for you — he's very creative, as you both know."

I observed the subtle interactions between Den and Gavin, as Marq's words from that same day rang through my memory. He'd said something along the lines that they rarely had someone in their lives, mainly because of *the pain of loss and the difficulty with commitment*. My heart ached as the reality surfaced. I was still intrigued by this new development while also excited to see what the amazing Marq had created. He had spent time with the girls while he was here the last time he had visited from monitoring the Rome facility, and they had done everything from drawing with pencil and charcoal to painting watercolours. They had even done a fun project where they put on their bathing suits and did a painting on a floor canvas using their bodies, rolling around and using hand and footprints to create the work of art. Shifting my thoughts back to the girls, I said, "Let's see — let's see."

To assist with the gift reveal their Poppy and Nana, each held the respective parcel steady as Ryley and Hayley reached into the deep paper bags.

I leaned to the side watching as something white surfaced from within the nearest bag.

"Wow," Darius said, standing then, blocking my view of the emerging gifts.

I got off my stool and moved up the row to get a better look. Redmond had moved too, coming to stand at my back. I tilted my head back to grin at him. "Wow—is right!" I agreed.

The girls each held wings, white feather covered wings with silver tipped feathers along the edges, and these creations had soft silver fabric harnesses made to fit the girls specifically.

"Can we try them on?" Ryley asked, hopping down off the stool, wings out in front of her.

Hayley followed her sister by hopping down from her stool with some assistance from her Nana. "Please, can we?" Hayley pleaded, bouncing on the spot.

"I can't see why not," Den said, turning to check with us.

I nodded. "Sure, but maybe do it outside—where you have more room."

"Here, I'll help you," Lily offered, steering the girls to the front entrance.

"I'll help, too," Gavin said, scooting by me to catch up.

Darius followed behind them like a big—little excited kid, and Redmond and his parents continued along after all of them

"Those are beautiful, Den—please pass on a huge *thank-you* to Marq when you speak to him next." I gave him a hug, but I think it had more to do with seeing him with our—his new friend.

"You know how much we love the girls," Den said. *"They are a bright spot in our sometimes dark days."* The last part he said low for only me to hear.

"We appreciate you all so much." I rubbed his arm in hopes of comforting him. "Let's go check out our little… *angels*, shall we?"

He gave me a playful grin.

After several pretend flights around the grounds of the park across from the restaurant, we convinced the girls they could play with their wings at home in the backyard, as long as they were careful with their gifts. Marq had made them quite solid though. He must have anticipated they would need to be durable to keep up with the high energy of the girls.

The twins had thanked both Den and Gavin for coming, but we'd left the couple at the taco place. When the twins protested, they'd given them the excuse that they still hadn't eaten yet. Den promised to come see them later in the week, and Gavin reminded them he would see them at school tomorrow.

"Happy—Happy Birthday," Gabriel called from the upper deck at the front entrance as our two cars pulled into the drive.

The twins got out, wings on, and before running up the stairs to greet him, they exchanged hugs with Lily and Darius.

Redmond and I too said our goodbyes to Darius and Lily, then climbed the steps after the girls.

Gabriel waved as Darius's car pulled back out of the driveway, then he knelt and hug the girls. "My—what lovely wings you have there," he said, slyly, admiring the beautiful creations.

"All the better to fly with you, my dear," Hayley said, cleverly responding as the big bad wolf to Gabriel's mock of Little Red Riding Hood.

"Nainseadh, Enzo, wonderful to see you both again," he said, straightening, as Redmond's parents hit the top of the stairs.

"You missed a great time at the aquarium," Nainseadh said, reaching for a hug.

"And a delicious lunch, too," Enzo added, shaking Gabriel's hand.

"Big-time," I said, in acknowledgment of the taco feast we'd just had.

"Hey, Gabriel," Redmond said, rubbing his full stomach and opening the front door. "You missed out."

Gabriel glanced down at the girls. "Yes, well—I know, but I had a special project I was working on." He winked at the girls. "Go see what I brought. It's in the hall outside your bedrooms," he added as they hurried inside.

At the end of the hall was a long flat rectangular shaped package wrapped in multi-coloured paper, leaning against the wall that separated their bedrooms.

"Go ahead—open it!" Gabriel said when the girls just stood there staring at it.

The girls tore into the wrapping, resembling two butterflies engulfing a colourful flower, each pull creating leaf-like paper streams. On the last pull, the paper gave way to reveal a white framed full-length mirror.

"It's like Mum's," Hayley said, turning and sharing an enthusiastic smile with her grandparents.

"My goodness," Nainseadh said in surprise, bringing the palms of her hands to her cheeks. "How gorgeous."

"See here," Gabriel said, running a hand down one side.

Ryley gasped. "Shells!"

The mirror frame was covered in white seashells of various formations and sizes. "That's why you made all those trips to the beach?" Hayley asked. "For shells?"

"Yup!" Gabriel responded. "See, I put the ones we found together in the corners. The rest I found on my own—so I could keep it a surprise."

"Well done, Gabriel," Enzo said, examining the workmanship.

"Didn't know you were good with your hands," I said, giving Gabriel a quick pat on his back.

"I've been around," he said. "Learned a few things over the centuries, and I've spent time with a few talented carpenters." He smirked at me.

"Centuries?" Enzo questioned.

"It's a joke, Pop," Redmond said, addressing Gabriel's slip-up. "If I had known, I would have put you to work on the renovations at South Haven," he added.

"Shame no one taught you to drive," I kidded.

"Thank you, Gup!" Hayley said, reaching up for a hug.

Gabriel scooped her up as though she were as light as a feather.

"Can we put it in our bathroom—so we can share?" Ryley asked, extending her arms to be scooped up as well.

"Of course, as long as your parents agree," he said, effortlessly lifting Ryley up into his other arm.

After Redmond set up the large mirror in the twins' bathroom, we spent the rest of the afternoon watching the girls from the back deck as they played a variety of made up flying games with Gabriel.

Birthday dinner for the girls was homemade spaghetti made by their Poppy, followed by a chocolate quadruple layer cake made by their father with the help of their Nana.

When the twins' bedtime approached, Gabriel asked, "May I have the privilege of tucking the birthday girls in for the night?"

"Yaaa," Hayley said, sleepily.

Ryley yawned. "I'm ready," she said, eyes half closed.

They exchanged hugs and kisses with their grandparents, then shuffled off down the hall to their respective rooms.

"We'll be in after to say goodnight," I called after them from the kitchen as I sealed the last of the birthday cake in a plastic container.

"Think we are going to call it a night—it was a long day for us," Enzo said, helping his tired wife to her feet.

"See you in the morning," Nainseadh added in an exhausted voice, before the two descended the stairs to their bedroom-away-from-home on the lower level.

"Hey, I thought Gup tucked you in already?" I questioned Hayley, catching her out of bed and in the bathroom staring at herself in their new mirror. I checked her room, but I had already *felt* Gabriel leave.

"He did." She rubbed her eyes as she continued to stare into the mirror.

Redmond stuck his head through the bathroom doorway leading to Ryley's bedroom. "Where's your sister?"

"In your room." She yawned, leaning in closer to her reflection.

"Okay—back in bed," Redmond said then, guiding her away from the mirror and into her bedroom.

As Redmond re-tucked birthday girl number one, I ducked out of the bathroom on the hunt for my other delinquent child. When I entered my bedroom, Ryley was doing the same thing as her sister, staring at her reflection in the mirror. "What are you doing?"

"Nothing," she said, embarrassment flashing across her face as she glanced my way.

"Right. It's past your bedtime. And you have your own long mirror now," I said, shooing her out of the room. "Birthday girl, number two heading your way," I called to Redmond.

A few minutes later, Redmond came through our bedroom doorway. "Double-tucked," he announced, fatigue finally hitting him, too.

"Great—thank you," I said, standing in front of my mirror, staring at my reflection, wondering what our two little angels had been up to. The light over the mirror flickered. "Did you see that?" I asked, turning to Redmond.

"See what?" he asked, looking over his shoulder at me.

I turned back and… it was just the regular mirror. It had only been a split second, but I could have sworn I saw an image of the twins in front of their new mirror in their bathroom. I reached a hand out and touched the mirror. "Nothing." *Something*.

Chapter 19 

Nordik Spa-Nature, Saturday May 14th, Chelsea, Quebec

Redmond hadn't been happy with the idea of the twins and me going to Ottawa, but my friends had been organizing it for weeks. Unfortunately for the twins, Olivia had found out during the planning that they were too young to go to the spa. Since the spa visit was a big part of what we were doing over the weekend, we made the decision that it would be just me this time. Besides, the trip to Ottawa would be my first birthday celebration with my girlfriends, just us, in an awfully long time. The twins hadn't been heartbroken. The spa idea hadn't really interested them in the first place, nor the idea of being bored with their old mum and her friends at some salty pool. What they had really wanted was just a fun time. So, to curb any disappointment, Redmond said that the three of them would plan their own fun weekend. He still didn't like me going.

I reminded him that no one had called looking for me in months, not since that call to Olivia. I assured him that Gabriel would be around and so would Leo and Nic. He couldn't understand why Gabriel could be with me on this trip, but not the one to Norway. I'd told him it was tricky business, his involvement. Gabriel had said to me he ran a fine line with what he could do or not do, and the last thing he wanted was to have his access to us cut off. I'd told Redmond it was the last thing any of us wanted and that I'd given up questioning the whole thing. Redmond had said no more after that.

We now assumed that Mac, Olivia, and Alison's houses were being watched. We didn't know for sure, but to be safe I would be staying with Vicki at her house. We figured her place was the safest since she had not been with us on the group home visit. Eric was out of town flying some famous hockey player and his family to Barcelona for vacation, which meant I had to slum it on a regular flight. Lucky for me though, Leo had gotten me a First-Class seat to make the birthday trip a little extra special.

When I had arrived last night, to my surprise, Mac, Alison, and Olivia were all here at Vicki's to greet me, giving us even more time to catch up and talk about the spa treatments. We'd relaxed in Vicki's living room, sharing our family updates. Mac and Alison still had kids living at home, so they were more underfoot than Vicki's and Olivia's grown kids. Alison's son had his 10th birthday at the first of April, and I enjoyed hearing all about the scavenger hunt she and Ken had set for Kevin and his friends. They always did creative things to make the day more fun and memorable.

I had been thrilled about having the extra time last night with my girlfriends, since even though we were going to the spa together, the treatments themselves Olivia told me, I would be doing alone. She had booked us for an early 8 a.m. start and it was just under an hour's drive from Vicki's place to the remote spa. And because Mac no longer had her mom-van, Vicki offered to drive her SUV since it could accommodate all five of us. I'd known what I needed to bring to the spa and had packed my suitcase accordingly. I'd brought my only one-piece swimsuit and flip-flops, since the spa provided towels, bathrobes, and everything else.

"Have you heard anything more from Derek and Marq—and the Iceland thing?" Alison asked from the front seat of the SUV.

Before I could say *no*, Vicki spoke up. "I've been to Iceland, twice," she said. "They have black sand on the beaches—did you know that? And the hot springs there are amazing." She went on for most of the drive, sharing everything she knew about Iceland and the details from her visits there, including the shops with the expensive sweaters, and of course, the spas she had been to. Clearly, she was not interested in anything angel related.

Once at the spa, we parked and headed for the main entrance.

"We're all booked for massages and body treatments," Olivia said. "But afterwards, the four of us…." She pointed at Mac, Alison, and Vicki. "… are doing the thermotherapies. Lynn, you're scheduled to do the saltwater pool, as I mentioned last night."

"We've all done it before," Vicki said, glancing around impatiently.

"You'll love it," Mac assured me, retrieving two hair ties from her purse. Then, with one, she whipped her long hair up in a secure top bun. "It's a must." She handed me the other hair tie.

"Thanks—forgot to bring one." Hadn't thought of it, but hair up is the way to go.

"Nothing beats the treatments I had in Iceland," Vicki said, checking her watch. "It would be almost 1 p.m. in Iceland right now— if we were there. But this place isn't bad," Vicki added smugly. She already had her shoulder length hair secured back away from her face with a hair elastic.

"*Okay Vicki*," I muttered under my breath, twisting my hair up into a tight bun as I followed them through the entrance.

"This is the largest spa in North America," Alison said. "The ultimate relaxation experience."

"I'm so excited—you finally get to do this with us," Olivia squeaked, full of enthusiasm.

Turning in a semicircle, I took in the picturesque nature setting of the peaceful wellness center. "You've been telling me about it for years—now I'm finally here."

"They have ten outdoor baths, nine distinct saunas, an infinity pool, and the saltwater flotation pool that you'll be experiencing," Alison said, rambling off some of the unique offerings. "And they have four restaurants."

I liked hearing they had a variety of food, of course.

"And a bunch of other stuff too, like areas just for resting and relaxing, and yoga and meditation rooms," Olivia added.

"I dig their motto. *Good for the planet, good for the body*," Mac said, hiking up her huge purse, making me wonder why she brought such a big bag if all we needed to bring was a bathing suit. "They're proactive about protecting the nature around the complex. They even recycled and reused the wood, stone, and earth during the construction of the place, and put in energy performance equipment."

"Nice—makes me like the place even more than I already do." I reviewed the area map in the lobby. There were designated areas for *silence, whispering*, and *social* interaction.

"We are doing the massages first, then the facial treatments," Olivia said. "They have treatment rooms and change rooms here in this building, but they booked our appointments in another spot, so let's go over to the change rooms there." She pointed out the way to *Massage Area B* on the map for me before heading to the right.

Through the enclosed walkways, we passed by the Mëzz Café, which had a terrace and looked like a fancy coffee shop.

"After our thermal cycle, we should come back for an Apéritif or maybe before heading home," Alison said, adding a Parisian accent. She pulled one of those claw clips from her purse, then secured her hair on the top of her head.

I gave her a warm smile. Alison was actually fluent in French, but I rarely heard her speak it anymore. However, we were on the Quebec side, so there was a fairly good chance she might.

After the coffee spot was Restö, a fancy looking dining and wine place that didn't seem to be open yet. Past the two restaurants and the Spa Boutique, we went through another adjoining walkway and into another building like the first one, but instead of a front desk, it had an info kiosk.

"We're booked for the Urban Detox Facial," Mac reminded. I was glad for the reminder because I couldn't have recalled the name of the treatment.

Vicki pointed at the display board near the kiosk. "I'm doing the Lumëa special treatment.

"Right," Mac responded, "But we're all doing the Classic Massage first."

"Ms. Quinn," a male attendant said at the entrance to one of the treatment rooms.

Vicki waved at the man. "I'll see you all later," she announced, before turning and going off for her massage and *special* treatment.

I leaned into Mac. "What's so special about her treatment?"

"It's an anti-aging treatment for mature skin—we should all probably be doing it," Mac laughed out. "It's exclusive to this spa." She made an exaggerated kiss shape with her lips in and tipped her head side to side, all snooty-like, then she laughed again. "But the one we are doing is fantastic too. It frees the skin and the mind from the daily effects of stress and pollution. They both take about an hour—but it zooms by."

"Classic?" I questioned, regarding her comment about the massage. Redmond had gotten me massages for Mother's day in the past, but it had been quite a while since I had one.

"Ya, it's supposed to encourage better sleep, work on muscle stiffness and tension," Mac clarified. "A welcome stress reliever."

"Creates an overall sense of well-being," Olivia included. "It's relaxing and meditative."

"Okee-dokee," I said. "Relaxing and stress relieving—I'm all in."

"It's supposed to help you feel well, both physically and emotionally," Alison added in a low voice followed by an eye-roll. "Feels good—that's all I care about."

"Ms. Westlake," an attendant said then in a soft voice.

I raised my hand. "Hi—that's me."

"Wonderful." She smiled. "Right this way," she said, aiming an open palm towards the door to another of the treatment rooms.

I waved goodbye to my remaining friends. "Later gaters."

"Meet us in the Zen garden rest area after," Alison said behind me as I was directed to my treatment room.

I turned and gave her a thumbs up before the treatment room door closed.

"You may change out of your clothes here," the attendant said, pointing to a curtained area next to the door. "Then, please lay face down here under the sheet. Your massage therapist will be with you momentarily." She turned away and left through a door on the opposite side to where we had entered.

I quickly removed my yoga pants, t-shirt, and bra, leaving just my underwear on, and then climbed onto the table and slid under the top sheet. Before resting my face in the padded head circle thing, I surveyed the room. The treatment area was what you would expect, soft lighting and warm soft linens on a firm but comfy massage table. There was only one counter in the room, and it had an assortment of creams, towels, and tools arranged atop it. Gentle nature sounds piped in through hidden speakers. The aroma in the room was floral with a hint of citrus, and I took in a long breath before settling into the padded face rest. Then I heard a soft swoosh of the inner door open.

"Hello, Ms. Westlake. I am Juliette," a smooth yet heavily accented voice said. "I will be doing both of your body treatments today."

"Hi." I lifted a hand briefly from the table in greeting but kept my face down. There was the subtlest whirl of wheels as she adjusted herself on the low stool near my head.

"I am going to touch your shoulder now. Please let me know if the pressure is too much, or too light." A warm hand rested lightly on my upper back.

The lights lowered and then I felt the pressure of two hands pressing down and across to my outer shoulders. I closed my eyes, letting out a slow breath, letting go of all my stress.

The massage therapist performed a traditional, classic massage as Mac had put it, addressing my back and shoulders first, and the back of my legs before having me flip over. She did the front of my legs next, then shifted to my arms and upper chest and neck, finishing with a brief scalp massage. "I will be moving on to your Urban Detox Facial next. Would you like a brief respite and some lemon water before I start?"

I was so relaxed, I didn't want to move. "I'm fine—thank you," I said, sharing a relaxed smile up at her before closing my eyes again.

"Wonderful," she began. "There are four steps to this vegan treatment that will rebalance your skin and clear your mind." She lifted my head to wrap a thin terry towel band around my it at the hairline. "Prepare, recharge, correct, and reset…."

The gentle weight of hands on the front of my shoulders drew me from a tranquil altered state to one of awareness, though I kept my eyes closed. "You should feel recharged, and ready to face your busy days ahead," came the voice of the esthetician again.

It was all over, I realized, and yes, I felt refreshed. "Wow, that was amazing." I opened my eyes and smiled up at her kind, peaceful face.

She smiled back sweetly. "It was my pleasure." She pushed away on the small stool and then stood. "Take your time getting up. Then please change into your bathing suit." She pointed to a plush white robe hanging on a hook near the changing curtain. "There is a fresh robe there for you to use. When I return, I will take you over to the waiting area for your next treatment. The Källa salt pool, yes?"

"Yes," I said, glancing up briefly, then shifted my view to focus back on the hanging robe.

"You'll want to use the Kuuro rain shower as part of the treatment. Before and after," she said, before exiting out the door to allow me privacy again.

As she suggested, I took my time, gently getting up from the table, followed then by getting into my swimsuit. I tucked my clothes into the small bag I'd brought and then donned the luxurious robe.

Upon her return to the room, Juliette then escorted me to the rain shower area and instructed me to wait in the Panorama Lounge after, for guidance with my next treatment. It was much cooler here in the wilderness than it had been in town, and the cozy robe they provided was a welcomed pleasure.

I sat reading the brochure on the Källa floating saltwater pool in the outdoor lounge area. According to the write-up, the pool contained 10 tons of Epsom salt in 1,200 cubic feet of water, with only selected and perfectly dosed magnesium salts used. Based on the photo and its description, it was a huge basin of saltwater dug 5 meters deep into the rock. The pamphlet boasted a slew of benefits; purify the body, improve blood circulation, accelerate wound healing, decrease inflammation, stimulate creativity, promote restful sleep, reduce stress, and even release physical and intellectual tension. They maintained the water temperature at 37°C / 98°F, and I'm guessing that was to match your natural body temp.

"*Don't I feel special,*" I muttered to myself, glancing up to look around, noticing a twenty-something female attendant approached where I sat.

"Is this your first experience?" she asked, coming to stand next to me where I sat, a French accent shining through.

"Yes," I said, "Just reviewing the benefits and the do's and don'ts. I like to be prepared." I set down the pamphlet on the table next to me.

"My name is Eléa. Please follow me. I will show you where you can store your belongings." She extended a youthful arm to the left and motioned for me to follow her. "You'll need to shower before and after the treatment."

I had read that in the 'what to expect' part of the brochure, but I'd already showered. "Juliette—my massage therapist, took me to the Kuuro rain shower already. She recommended it—and that I use it after," I explained. I wasn't interested in another shower.

"Wonderful," she said, stepping forward to lead me to the right this time.

Wonderful. That was the third time a staff member had said that. It must be a catchphrase they're taught to use, or maybe everyone here is just *high,* and everything *is* wonderful. I tightened my lips and held back a laugh. The young woman glanced over at me, and I grinned.

She grinned back. "As soon as you enter the Källa basin, please maintain complete silence. It is forbidden to swim in the pool. When treating, avoid rubbing your eyes, and move carefully to avoid saltwater splashes. We recommend you stay a minimum of thirty minutes, but no longer than an hour."

I nodded. I'd read all of this in the brochure.

"To ensure an optimal experience, we limit access to the pool to twenty people at a time."

I'd read that too.

"You look nervous." Her face displayed calm, but her words spoke doubt.

"I do?" I hadn't felt nervous, not until she just asked me.

"Have no fear. An audio guide is available to help you understand the instructions and the steps to follow."

Was she kidding? I wanted to roll my eyes, but she was looking right at me. "How hard could it be to float in a pool?" I said, jokingly.

Her smile returned. She was definitely *high*.

We moved on to where she led me to an area to leave my bag and hang my robe. There was an attendant watching the vicinity, so there was no need for locks, apparently.

"Enjoy," she said before leaving.

Like the treatment room, the light here was also low, and the atmosphere was peaceful. I stowed my bag and hung my robe, then watched as a woman ahead of me stepped in to the saltwater basin. I followed her into the floating pool, observing as she sat down and slowly lean back, arms floating on either side of her body. I moved to the other side and repeated her actions.

It was then I heard a soft male voice coming through more hidden speakers, saying, "Relax your neck muscles, allowing your head to float and your ears to submerge underwater. Clear your mind. Let Källa pass on its benefits to you."

To hustle my relaxing along, I recited in my head the bits and pieces I'd read in the brochure about the treatment. *Weightlessness in the absolute calm... no resistance... physical and mental abandonment... surrender completely... all the muscles in your body relax... embrace the special gravity for flotation therapy... relaxing the nervous system... giving relief to your muscles... reaching the peak of relaxation....*

There's a man... face down in the water... frigid water... like ice... snow is everywhere, all around the water... the sound of footsteps crunching on snow... flashes of the same man slumped next to a pile of old blankets... there's a sweet dark woody scent of hay... and.... I shivered back to consciousness, splashing once before I realized I was still in the saltwater and near the edge of the pool. I was sweating, but I was cold despite the hot temperature of the water.

"Miss—are you okay?" a male attendant asked. I looked over to see him standing above me near the edge of the pool. "It is not uncommon to go so far as to fall asleep in the pool."

"Yes—sorry, I'm fine." I was fine, except for the messed up images I'd just suffered. And I was freezing. *Had I been dreaming?* I'd read that too in the brochure about the relaxing into sleep, but hadn't considered

I could do that, fall asleep in a public place, let alone in a pool. I checked the clock on the wall, noting I'd been floating for almost an hour. Then I made my way to the steps and out to the area where I'd hung my robe. Instead of finding my way back to the Kuuro rain shower, I rinsed off in the shower here under hot water to warm myself. I wasn't exactly in a *rain-shower* mood, not with these grim images flashing through my memory. After, I donned my robe again and set out to locate my friends in the rest area.

"Your skin looks amazing," I heard Olivia say to Vicki as I rounded into the Zen garden.

"The lifting effect of the treatment tones your face and restores your natural glow. It's recommended for all skin types," Vicki said. "They say the results are striking and instant." She turned her face side to side to show them.

"Tu es magnifique!" Alison praised, using her French skills.

"Hey all," I said, breathless, though I wasn't actually out of breath.

"Hey, Lynnie—how were your treatments?" Olivia asked.

"*Wonderful*," I said, mocking the attendants, though the treatments had been excellent, *mostly*. I took the lounge chair next to Mac. "Tell me about the thermal cycle treatment you all did."

"You okay, Lynn?" Mac asked, eyebrows pinching.

"Sure," I said, giving her a flat smile, adjusting my robe around me tighter. I still hadn't warmed up.

"If you say so." Mac gave me a disbelieving look, before delving into a play-by-play of their Thermotherapy treatment. "It's all about alternating between hot and cold temperatures, followed by a rest period. The relaxation ritual is based on a 2000-year-old tradition that originated throughout the Nordic countries. There's a long list of benefits too, of course. The first step is *heat*, exposing your body to intense heat for 5 to 15 minutes. We did it in the Finlandia sauna. This eliminates toxins and the light fever like condition causes your body to react and strengthen your immune system."

"There's a Nordik tradition for this part too—it's the Aufguss ritual, they call it," Olivia added. "Supposed to maximize the benefits of the treatment. It's basically choreographed movements with a towel that creates a breeze with the puffs of steam released when water is poured over the hot rocks. It's kind of fun."

"Then what?" I asked, wishing I had done this treatment with them instead of the salt bath thing.

"We did the Ice Waterfall," Alison said, taking on the next piece. "You have to cool your body after the intense heat of the sauna. Going from hot to cold produces a thermal shock, which closes your pores and releases adrenaline. It's super energizing, but you only do it for like ten to fifteen *seconds*.

"Last is the rest part—you can go through the cycle again, if you want," Olivia said. "But this part is my favorite. You're supposed to rest for at least twenty minutes to restore your body temperature and your heart rate. Balance out your respiratory and circulatory systems— good for the chakras."

"That's why we're here—this is a rest area," Vicki said, as though annoyed by all the talking.

Whatever. The map had shown that this resting spot was a *social* area as well, so talking was welcome here.

"The rest slows adrenaline secretion to make way for endorphins—those are the happiness hormones." Olivia grinned.

"Oh, I like that—I should have done that one with you guys."

With a huff, Vicki pushed up from her lounge chair. "I'm going to go check the gift shop." She glanced at her watch. "It's 11:30, that's half past four in Iceland. They have over 18 hours of daylight at this time of year." She tapped the face of her watch. "And I'd like to get something to eat at the *Biërgarden* after." She tightened the sash of her robe and strolled off.

I glowered at her as she walked away. "Did she just say *beer* garden?" I asked with a sarcastic grin.

"Are you sure you're okay?" Mac asked again, echoing my glower. "And yes, the word means beer-garden." She mirroring my sarcastic grin.

"Nope," I said this time, dropping my grin. The salt water had chapped my lips, and I picked at my lower one.

Mac began rifling through her bag. "Lip balm? Made it myself— it's all natural." She held out a small jar in front of me, but I shook my head. She rummaged again in the huge bag, then produced a plastic container. "Lozenge? The saltwater can make your mouth dry—make your throat feel a bit raw. These are homemade too."

I chuckled at her efforts despite how I was feeling. "I'm not sure you have what I need in that big purse of yours."

"You didn't enjoy the floating pool treatment?" Olivia questioned, worry spreading across her happy face.

"The whole floating thing was cool—but… something happened to me in the pool. I had some kind of weird vision."

Alison pulled a pencil and a tiny notebook from her bag. "What did you see?" she asked, flipping to an empty page.

"It's a weird one," I said, pulling in a long breath. I stared down at my hands in my lap as I gripped the robe tie and let out the breath. "I was working my relaxation—reciting in my head things like *absolute calm* and *weightlessness*, you know. And it was going well—I mean, I completely surrendered to the sensation of it." I glanced up, surveying their faces, seeing them all wide-eyed and concerned. "Next thing I'm witnessing—in my head, some guy in a dark suit face down in ice-cold water. I think it was nighttime, and there was snow all around."

"Were you in the water with him?" Alison asked, leaning in.

"No—but I could feel the cold… and I could hear that sound footsteps make on snow—that crunching noise."

They all nodded.

"Then it smelled like hay, you know—woody, sweet smelling, a little like maple syrup, dark, and rich—like walking into an old barn… then he's there, slumped next to a pile of blankets." I glanced back down at my hands tightening and loosening the tie.

"Horse blankets," Olivia said. "They used them at the barn where the girls used to ride—during winter."

"Did you see or smell anything else?" Alison asked.

"There was someone else there… a woman I think, and… then the smell changed…." I closed my eyes to pull it from my memory. "It was the aroma of… freshly baked bread." I shook my head once and opened my eyes.

"Lynn, are you sharing your floating salt pool adventure?" Vicki asked then, back from her little shopping venture. "It's something, isn't it?"

My back was to her. *"Remind me to tell you about the twins and the mirrors,"* I said slyly to Mac, before turning to face Vicki. "It's something alright—quite the experience," I said in agreement, forcing an ingratiating smile, though I'm sure it came across more melancholy. It saddened me that I couldn't share these things with Vicki anymore. The unusual vision I had in the pool certainly gave me, and now the others, food for thought, but Vicki had made it clear several times now, that this type of cuisine was no longer welcome on her plate. I smiled wearily at the others, then asked, "Anyone else hungry?"

Chapter 20 

Myvatn Nature Baths, Saturday May 14th, Jarðbaðshólar, Iceland

The trepidation Jana felt over Kisur's health had soared to a new high with this fainting spell of his she had witnessed. He'd said it hadn't been the first time and that he'd hoped that taking more of the memory supplements would help. When she'd asked if she could call the doctor again, he had agreed. Doc Jonsson had done a full exam and had found nothing, just like he had the first time. He had suggested a second visit to the hospital for additional bloodwork and scans, but Kisur had *not* agreed to that. He had opted instead for giving the supplements a little more time and she had grudgingly given in to his request.

Jana felt responsible for his care, yet helpless to do anything to prevent these blackout episodes. He may not have his memories, but he was still a man, and often a man's nature tended towards that of the protector. She knew he appreciated everything she had done for him, continued to do for him, but you could only protect a man so much before he felt emasculated. He was always exceedingly kind to her, and extremely helpful and resourceful in the bakery, and she appreciated him for all he did. She cared about him, and she hadn't hidden that fact from him. What she had hidden was how deeply she cared and that her attraction to him had grown over the past months. She had always found him attractive, but the desire she felt now for him, let's just say it distracted her during the day and kept her up at night. She considered them friends, close even, but she found herself yearning for more. But how could she act on her feelings for him? She couldn't. At least not until he remembered who he was, and she knew he wasn't already in a relationship. Her challenge right now was to keep an eye on his health without causing him to feel undermined by her worry.

When she had told Geir about her concerns around Kisur's health, he had tossed out the idea of, *"a day at the spa"*. She had been a few times to the hot springs with Geir in the past and figured it couldn't hurt to share the beneficial experience with Kisur. Besides, a day of relaxing and detoxifying might just be what she needed to aid her anxiety concerning his health. For both their comforts, she'd picked a spa that she'd been to before and one she believed he would enjoy the most. This hot spring was a 2.5 hour drive from town, though she was hopeful it would be worth it.

"The best time to be there is 4 p.m., after the early-bird tourists. And we have about thirty minutes left of the drive," Jana said, gleefully.

"This is outside, right?" Kisur asked with concern in his voice.

She noticed him shudder. "Yes—are you worried it will be cold?" He had never, not once, complained about the cold here, and he always seemed to be comfortable with the weather. "May averages between a high of 8 degrees Celsius and just above 0 on the low, but it is warmer than January when we found—when you and I first met. And the daylight hours are much longer now, more than 18 hours with sunrise at 3:30 a.m. and sunset around 10:15 p.m."

"I know—I've needed to use a sleep mask as the days got longer." He waggled his sunglasses up and down over his eyes. "With the temperate climate and the long days, I find it is surprisingly warm."

Those sunglasses were one of the various things Jana had gotten for him. "And the water temperature in the hot spring will be between 36 and 40 degrees. Certainly not cold." Jana turned a quick glance Kisur's way. "Summer is lovely here but wait until you see what it's like in autumn." She surveyed the current green scenery through the truck's window. "The landscape becomes a panoramic patchwork with shades of gold and brown, while winter brings frequent opportunities to enjoy the Northern Lights—as you already know." She gave him a heartfelt smile, but he was looking out his side window. They had spent many early evenings enjoying the night's sky together.

"You told me there were over forty-five natural hot springs. How did you pick this one?"

She noted him turning to face forward. "I picked one I thought you would like." She pulled her cellphone from the center console and handed it to him, returning her attention back on the road. "Here—look up Myvatn Nature Baths."

When all she heard was, "Hmmm," she turned to look at him. Then, as he raised his sunglasses, resting them on his forehead, he said, "Under the *about*, it says, *Located in the heart of Northeast Iceland, Lake Mývatn is a designated and stunning nature reserve....*" He gave her a knowing grin.

She focused back on the road. "Keep going." She knew nothing about his past, but she did know he had a love for nature.

He went on. "*... Drawing on a centuries-old tradition, the tastefully designed facility offers bathers a completely natural experience beginning with a relaxing dip amidst clouds of steam rising from a fissure deep within the Earth's surface, ending with a luxurious swim in a pool of geothermal water drawn from depths of up to 2.500 meters.* Sounds amazing—I think. If you like that kind of thing. I don't know if I do." He laughed. "Why are there so many hot springs here?"

"It has something to do with geothermal activity and diverging tectonic plates—the *Mid-Atlantic Ridge*, I think it's called. Iceland is located half on the North American plate and half on the Eurasian plate. Volcanic activity is common along these rifts and the water is often heated under the ground—that's the geothermal activity part, and hot springs are the end result."

"Is that something they teach all Icelandic children in school?"

"Ha—no. I didn't know until Geir told me when I mentioned we were going." She laughed, tapping her hand twice on the steering wheel.

Kisur put her cellphone back in the open compartment of the console between their seats. "Geir said I'll have to get naked."

"What?" Her body warmed suddenly. She didn't dare look at him, knowing her face had heated to a blush.

"He said most people don't know until they get there—that you have to take off all your clothes and shower naked with the other visitors before getting into the pools. Is that true, or was he just joking with me?"

"No, that's true." Jana still didn't have the nerve to look at him. "It's actually quite liberating once you get over the nakedness. And don't worry, no one looks—and no one cares." She hadn't thought about this part of the practice, she'd been focused on the beneficial aspects. Not that Kisur, *naked,* hadn't crossed her mind on several hundred occasions during his time staying with her. She had seen him come and go from the bathroom to his room in just a towel. But like the other bathers, she wouldn't look at him. But *Helvíti,* that didn't mean he wouldn't steal a peek at her, she realized.

"How did you and Geir meet?" Kisur asked then.

"We met through my father. I told you that, right?" She stole a glance at him and observed he'd bowed his head.

"Of course," he said, staring down at his hands. "I forgot."

She frowned, shifting her eyes forward, concerned this was a new memory issue. "I think my father thought we'd like each other—and we did, just not in the way my father would have hoped."

"So, you never dated?"

She shot him a confused look. "Geir and I—No—I'm not his type," she said with a snicker.

"Type?"

"Ya—I'm not male." She looked at him again to see him staring at her, blank faced. "He only dates men." She understood that like the range of colours in the rainbow, with choosing a partner or who you loved, people's preferences often varied. She also knew there were sometimes grey areas too.

Kisur nodded before Jana turned her attention back on driving. "Right," he said.

Was she getting a *jealousy* vibe off him she mused? "He's been a great friend over the years. And he helped a lot when my father passed. He took over most of his patients—animal patients. The patients are *easy*, Geir says, it's dealing with the owners and farmers he finds difficult." Jana chuckled a little, remembering the stories Geir had shared with her.

"So… what's the big deal about these hot springs?"

A swift change in subject, she noted. "Well, soaking in the mineral-rich water has many benefits for several systems of the body, plus you can admire the wonderful landscape." She grinned at him. This time he was watching her and not turned looking out the window. "It might help you feel better. Give us both a little relaxation and rejuvenation. It's good for blood pressure and improves circulation. Especially to the brain." She tapped a finger on the side of her head. "Muscle pain relief—I could use that. And it's soothing for your skin, too."

"What are the different minerals—do you know?" he asked, continuing the hot spring topic.

Was that all he got from her explanation, *minerals*? "You can look all this up, you know."

"I know. But I enjoy listening to your voice."

That was sweet, she thought. Lazy but sweet. "Many people feel that the hot springs in Iceland are magical."

He guffawed. "Okay—sure."

"What—are you saying you don't believe in magic?" She glanced at him, then at the highway sign. "Have any of the people in town told you about the Huldufolk?"

"Hidden people?" he translated, his voice skeptical.

"Elves!" Jana stated. "East Iceland houses hundreds of them. Elves are a big part of the cultural landscape here." When she looked at him, he smirked at her. "You don't believe me? I'll have you know that the claimed existence of elves sparks environmental protests to this day. From laying a public road or building a new house. If the future construction has the possibility to disturb the lives of elves thought to be living in its path, it is likely to spark a public uproar."

He laughed, undoubtedly entertained. "Maybe the hidden people of Iceland had something to do with my… circumstance."

He gave her a mischievous look, and she gave him a dubious one back.

"What were you saying the minerals were?" he asked, changing the subject back.

"Are you testing me now?" Jana asked, checking her rearview mirror before turning onto the road leading to the property for the hot spring.

"Nooo," he said in a serious tone. "Just curious. I want to see if I recognize any."

"Calcium…," she said, then paused, letting him register the word. "Potassium... magnesium... sodium... and sulfur—it's good for respiratory problems, and… we're here," she announced. "… in this particular location the strength of the elements is greater than others. But if you don't want to do the pools, you can do the steam bath."

"Steam bath?" He frowned.

"I prefer the pools," she said. "But in the other, the steam rises directly through the floor—it's completely controlled by weather. Typically, the temperature is around 45 degrees, and the humidity is close to 100%. A few years ago, they put windows in the steam baths so everyone can enjoy the beautiful view now." She pulled into the parking area and then into the first available spot closest to the entrance. There were plenty of parking spots having missed the tourist rush. The place could hold over 400 people, but it would be even more tranquil with half the people gone already.

She spied him glancing down at the bag at his feet. "You packed towels for us."

"And swimsuits. I bought you one." It was another item she'd gotten him when she'd picked out those sunglasses.

He grabbed up the bag. "Where do we keep our clothes?"

"You'll get a locker." She shut off the truck and then put her keys in her coat pocket, zipping it closed. "Let's go!"

At the front desk, Jana asked, "How long can we stay?"

"You can stay as long as you want, within opening hours," the concierge said. "Most people spend around 90 minutes." He placed plastic beverage bracelets on Kisur's wrist and then Jana's.

"How does the drink bracelet work?" Jana inquired, sliding the band up and down her wrist. They hadn't had this option the last time she was here.

"Any staff member who is working outside can bring you drinks, and there is a swim-up bar, with both alcoholic and non-alcoholic beverages. And Café Kvika is over there." He pointed to the left. "We offer both indoor and outdoor seating areas—I recommend the outdoor area since it's such a sunny day." He handed Jana a menu card. "The showers are located inside the changing rooms, and there you will find organic soap, shampoo, and a conditioner." He handed Jana another card with a map of the facility on it, but she already knew where to go.

"Takk," Jana said, signifying a *thank you* in Icelandic, before turning her attention to Kisur. "You're quiet," she said, addressing him then.

His eyes were downcast, his expression wary. "I'm feeling a bit… unwell."

"Is it because you have to shower naked with a bunch of strangers?" She gave him a little playful poke in the ribs.

"No… I wish that were the case." He drew a hand across his forehead, then across his cheek and down over his mouth and jaw. "I just feel weak."

"Maybe you could use something to eat." She looked at the menu the concierge had given her. "They have soup and freshly made sandwiches, and fresh salads. Or maybe a muffin?"

"I had plenty before we left. I'll be fine. Perhaps after."

"Are you sure?" Jana asked. They had eaten a late breakfast in anticipation of a later lunch here, and even later dinner once they returned home, but he always ate twice as much as she did.

"The shower will perk me up—and I'm sure I'll feel much better after our time in the pool." He gave her an unreadable smile.

"Okay—but you'll tell me if you feel faint, right?" She ran a hand down his arm.

"Yes—Jana, please don't worry," he said, shaking his head.

In the changing room, Jana took her swimsuit and a towel from the bag, leaving Kisur's swim trunks and the remaining towel with him. He assured her again he was fine, so she maneuvered her way through the crowd of guests to the other side of the shower area. There, she selected an available locker where she placed her swimsuit on an inner side hook. She draped her towel over the door and then proceeded to remove her clothing, placing each piece on the other hooks in the locker. She wrapped the towel around herself quickly and kicked off her shoes to the floor of the locker. Then she went to the nearest shower, turning it on and adjusting the temperature before tossing her towel over the nearby towel rack. What was normally a liberating act, as she had told Kisur, was now a bashful endeavor, considering he was only a dozen people away from her and under his own shower, she surmised.

Showered and toweled, Jana swiftly put on her swimsuit, and secured her locker. Traversing back across the rear of the shower area, Jana found Kisur sitting on a bench in his swimsuit, slouched forward with his towel draped over his broad shoulders.

"Are you still feeling weak?" she asked. His skin was wet, so she knew he'd managed to shower.

He tilted his head up. "Just waiting on you, lovely girl." He smiled at her, but she could tell it was forced. "Let's do this," he said, standing before she could offer another option.

She had the urge to take Kisur's hand as they walked through to the lagoon area for her comfort and his, but it felt too presumptuous, especially in this public place, but to her amazement, *he* reached for her hand. Her heart pounded as she looked down at their intermingling fingers. "This is going to be wonderful," she said then, giving his hand a gentle squeeze.

He squeezed back.

At the stairs into the swimming lagoon, she reluctantly let go of his hand to hold the rail that accompanied the steps down. When she reached the bottom, she turned to face him and then pushed off. Floating away a few yards from the steps, she watched as Kisur took his turn to use the stairs. She smiled approvingly at how well his swim trunks fit, considering she'd had to guess on the size. He was simply spectacular to look at and she noticed a few of the women admiring his muscular physique. Jana beckoned rapidly with both hands for Kisur to join her in the water.

In response, Kisur gripped the railing, then submerged his foot into the water and onto the first step.

And time stood still.

At that first contact, Jana witnessed Kisur's stoic expression turn agonized. She stared ahead helplessly as though held in place as he took another tentative step. When the agony in his face turned to dread, those beautiful eyes of his bulging, Jana forced her way forward through the water. Kisur's body shuddered, and his face sagged, his terrified eyes rolling back into his head. "Noooooo!" Jana screamed as Kisur lost his grip, his body swaying and sagging limply forward and to the side. She reached him just before his face went under.

It took several of the onlookers to help Jana pull Kisur from the water, since this facility had no emergency lifeguard personnel. One of them said it looked as though he'd had a seizure. Jana prayed it was just one of his fainting spells, although that shudder of his body and sag of his face resembled a stroke. Jana's father had insisted she take some basic lifesaving skills as a teen, so she knew enough to check his heart and airways. His heart sounded strong, and his breathing was steady, but he remained unresponsive. To make things even harsher, the nearest hospital was over an hour away, which meant Jana would have to take him there herself.

With more help from a few of the men, Jana got Kisur dressed and into her truck, where they rested him back in a reclined position in the passenger seat. Jana placed one of the towels over his upper body and the other she folded and arranged across the driver's seat for her to sit on. She'd pulled her clothes on over her still wet swimsuit, but she didn't care about her clothes being damp. She only cared about getting him to the hospital as soon as humanly possible. "Thank you for your help," Jana said, quickly climbing into the driver's seat. "*Get it together, Jana,*" she said to herself, as she started the truck.

At the end of the road that had let to the spa, Jana turned onto National Road 1. It was not a straight route, but at least it would take her where she needed to go and without having to read a map.

"You just hang on—you hear me!" she said, reaching over and adjusting the towel at Kisur's neck. "You're going to laugh when you find out I drove you to the hospital in pants that looked like I peed myself," she said, faking a hopeful tone. "Did I ever tell you about my first visit to the hospital for stitches?" she asked then, not expecting a response. For the next hour, she shared the comical story of how she had fallen while ice skating with her father, and he had to take her to the hospital. The story telling hadn't really been for him. It had been more for her sake, to keep her from freaking out as she drove. Finishing the story, she finally spotted the sign for Akureyri Hospital. She followed the direction arrows that led her to the emergency room entrance and adjoining parking spots. She parked and immediately waved over one of the medical staff near the entry's sliding doors.

When the guy saw Kisur passed out in the passenger seat, he called out, "We need a gurney over here!" Two seconds later, another medical staff member with a rolling stretcher was at the passenger door helping the first guy maneuverer Kisur onto it.

In the emergency, a female doctor asked Jana a series of questions of which she could not answer, other than explaining about Kisur's memory loss and that he'd had several fainting spells. And though she had witnessed only the one, this event had been worse. Until the doctors were sure of what had happened to Kisur, they asked that Jana wait outside the exam space while they continued their evaluation.

Jana sat in a waiting chair, staring at the medical staff through the window in the door as they tended to Kisur. Minutes later, though it had felt like hours, the same doctor who had asked her all the questions, approached her again.

"We think he may have suffered a seizure," the doctor said. "There are several types, but we can't know for sure which he had—just yet. Did you notice any behaviors that presented like daydreaming or inattentiveness prior to this occurrence?"

Jana shook her head. "Not that I recall."

"A seizure can start suddenly, with the person stopping their activity. You said this happened at a hot spring. Did you notice him staring off? Loss of facial expression or unresponsiveness, perhaps?

"Yes. His face seemed to droop just before."

"Did you witness any blinking or upward eye movements?"

"Yes," Jana said again. "His eyes rolled back in his head. They did that before—the other time when I saw him faint."

"A seizure can last up to 20 seconds and end abruptly—you stated he passed out, but did he ever come to?"

Jana's panic soared. "No. And it was over an hour's drive here—he never regained consciousness."

"That is a major concern. A person usually recovers immediately, even resuming their previous activity after a seizure. However, if it *was* a seizure, most people generally respond well to medication. We have him on medicine now and we're going to move him to the Intensive Care Unit. All we can do now is wait and see," the doctor said, turning back to the exam room.

Jana stood when the door to the exam room opened and Kisur's unconscious body rolled out.

"I'll keep you posted," the doctor said. She patted Jana's shoulder, then followed behind Kisur's gurney as it was rolled off in the direction of the ICU.

Jana's phone chimed in her hand. She'd been holding on to it since they took Kisur into the emergency room.

The chime was a text from Geir,

How did it go? I'm guessing you are on your way back soon.

Jana didn't text back, she hit dial instead. "Where are you?" she asked before he could even say hello.

"At home—why? Is everything okay?"

"No—I need you to come to the hospital."

"What—which hospital—are you hurt?"

"I'm fine—it's Kisur. The doctors think he had a seizure." Her grip tightened on the phone.

"The Egilsstadir medical center is only 30 minutes away—I'll be right there."

"I'm not in Egilsstadir—I'm at the hospital in Akureyri."

"Akureyri? Why are you there—that's almost 4 hours away?"

"We were at the spa when it happened—this was the closest hospital." Jana blew out a weighted breath. "I know it's far—but I need you here."

"Jana…."

"Please tell me it's not too far—I can't be here… in this hospital, on my own."

"It's not that—I'm coming... it's just... I think I may know someone... who... might know Kisur."

"What do you mean?"

"I met this guy, Hayden—at a bar when I was in college in Belgium. It was just a fling. Anyway—he had the same markings—said his brothers all had the same tattoos. At the end of the semester, he told me he was being recruited by some special ops team."

"All this time, Geir—how could you not tell us—tell me?"

"You seemed happy—so did he. Jana, it's been *years* since I've seen him and well—they don't look alike. Hayden had said *brothers*, so... I let it go."

"Please, Geir—maybe this Hayden guy can help. If something happens to Kisur—I... I don't know—please, just try," she begged.

"I'll find some way to contact Hayden."

Hayden had crossed Geir's mind occasionally over the years, mainly wondering what had become of him. They had both been attending the University of Liège in the French-speaking part of Belgium, he in Veterinary school and Hayden in Criminology. None of their classes had overlapped, but they had connected a few times at the Temple Bar Liege off campus. The last time they had met up, Hayden had even given him his number, but he had never called it. Geir knew their brief time together had been just one of those things, two people sharing some time.

Geir had gotten rid of a lot of stuff from his university days, but he had kept a few mementos, he recalled. Where they were now, he wasn't quite sure, though he had stored items in the closet of the second bedroom. That part of his home he had converted for his veterinary practice, and now that room functioned as his office. Having already locked up for the day when he'd texted Jana, he unlocked the door to the clinic again on the hunt for the boxes he knew should still be at the back of that closet.

Retrieving the smaller of the two boxes from the back of the closet, Geir placed it on his desk. Inside, he found bits and pieces of school memorabilia, photos from his time in Belgium, and a short stack of various pub coasters. The last one in the stack had the logo for *The*

Temple Bar Liege with its white and gold lettering, two green shamrocks in the upper corners, and the gold stylized face of a Viking in the center. He flipped it over and saw numbers scribbled across the back. Hayden's handwriting. The numbers had faded with age and the last number was smudged. It was either a 3 or an 8 it looked like.

Grabbing his phone from his pocket, he called the number using the first option. A recording came on right away saying the number was not in service and he hung up. Then he tried the number again, this time with the 8. It rang but did not go through to where Geir had expected or had hoped it would go. Instead, it was another automatic message, this one directing the caller to use a *new* number. Geir wrote out the new number on the flap of the cardboard box. When he tried this number, the call took him to what appeared to be a central line, asking the caller to leave a message with the name of the person they was trying to reach. When the message beeped for Geir to speak, he said, "Hello—this is an urgent message for Hayden Polar. My name is Geir Sigurdsson. I believe a friend of yours is in serious trouble. Call me as soon as you get this message." He left his cell number and ended the call. Then he saved the number in his contacts, just in case.

His phone rang. But it was Jana. "Hi. I called…."

"He's in a coma," she said before he could finish.

"I'm on my way," he replied, but then the call-waiting on his phone beeped with another call coming through. It wasn't the number he had just called, it showed as *an unknown caller*. "Let me call you back from my truck."

"Okay," Jana said, allowing for him to hang up and answer the other call.

"Hello?" he said, picking up the call-waiting. Geir held his breath.

"*Geir?*" the deep male voice on the other end inquired.

"Yes. Hayden, is that you?" Geir asked, still holding his breath.

"It is—you left a message for me?"

Geir blew out the breath in relief. "I don't know if you remember me, but I believe we've found a friend of yours—and I'm sorry to tell you this, but he's in the hospital and severely ill…."

Chapter 21 

The Home of Vicki & Eric, Saturday May 14th, Ottawa, Canada

We had a delicious lunch in the Beirgarden restaurant at the spa complex, before heading back to Ottawa. Even Vicki had enjoyed her meal, though she had shared with us during the meal and on the drive home, the various restaurants and food she'd had while on her trips to Iceland, noting the famous hot spring's *Geyser* bread with smoked char, which she said was like salmon. It had sounded good, but I had thoroughly enjoyed my meal of Smoked Gouda & Aged Cheddar Grilled Cheese Sandwich, which had come with creamy tomato soup, roasted garlic butter, and kettle chips. And I didn't have to go to Iceland to get it.

"Maybe we should plan a couples' trip to Iceland," Vicki suggested, as she pulled into her driveway. "Eric enjoyed it, so I'm sure your husbands would, too."

"A couple's trip would be fun," Alison said, following the rest of us into the house. "But I can't imagine soaking in a hot spring that smells like rotten eggs." She removed her shoes in the front hall.

Mac only had flip-flops on, so she just flipped them off and they flopped next to Alison's shoes. "I agree on the trip thing, but what do ya mean about the smell? Mac asked, lugging her big bag with her through to the living room.

"Don't you remember Derek talking about Iceland and the hot springs and the sulfur? I reminded, plopping down at one end of the couch.

"Okay—ya, but what does that have to do with rotten eggs?" Mac questioned again, settling in beside me.

"It's the sulfur," Olivia said, taking the armchair next to the couch.

Alison took the space next to Mac at the other end of the couch, while Vicki sat in the other armchair, completing a sort of circle.

"The hot springs in Iceland heat up thanks to geothermal energy," Vicki explained. "That means they can smell like sulfur—which is commonly associated with rotten eggs."

"And gas-fart smells," Mac added, with a cackle.

"You would know," I said, addressing Mac. She had a reputation of being burpy *and* farty.

"Someone's cellphone is ringing," Vicki said as though annoyed again.

I jumped up, recognizing the ring. "That's mine," I said. "Sorry— I left it in my bag at the front door."

In the front hall, I yanked my cellphone from the pocket of my bag. It was Den. "Hey—what's up?" Leo was the only one who ever called me directly.

"Think we've located Kris," he said.

I rushed back to the living room. "How—where?" I asked.

"Hiiii, Redmond," Mac yelled from the couch.

"It's Den." I held up a hand. "Sorry—say that again."

"Leo retrieved a message from the main line," Den said again for me. That was the line they'd set up when they'd all updated their cellphone some time ago. "It was for me—from Geir Jonsson. He's someone I knew from my time in Belgium."

"Kris is in Belgium?" I questioned, rubbing the back of my neck as my stress-free body grew again with tension.

"They found him!" Olivia squealed.

I put my phone on speaker, setting it on the coffee table.

Everyone stared at the cellphone.

"No—Iceland," Den stated clearly through the speaker.

"He's in Iceland? Is he alright?" I shot Mac an anxious glance, then stared back at the phone.

"When I spoke with Geir, he told me the doctors believe Kris had a severe allergic reaction to something environmental."

Mac slapped her thigh. "Derek was right—about his possible location," she said, reaching a hand up over the coffee table for me to give her a high-five.

"Did you speak to Kris?" I asked, smacking my hand against Mac's elevated one.

"No—he's in a coma."

"Holy shit!" Mac shouted, dropping her hand as she gaped at the phone.

I rested my butt down on the arm of Olivia's chair. "How did this guy know to call you?"

"He saw the tattoos on Kris's back—the ones we all have—and took a chance with trying to reach me. Good thing he did. "

"What the hell happened?" Mac asked.

"Apparently Kris and a friend of Geir's were at one of those hot springs when Kris had a seizure."

We all directed our focus on Vicki, though she continued to stare at the cellphone.

"The friend got him to the hospital—it was an hour away. Kris was still unconscious when they got there."

"Where has Kris been all this time?" Alison asked. "Why didn't he contact any of you?"

"Geir said when they found him—he had no memory of who he was or how he had gotten there. Leo and Nic are preparing to go—getting a medivac set up to bring Kris back here."

"Wait," I said, standing. "Sulfur—Derek said most of the experiments involved sulfur—that Iceland was full of it. The doctor said environmental allergen—the sulfur must be what caused Kris's coma. None of you can risk going there for that same reason—sulfur exposure."

Den's voice came through the cellphone as a frustrated roar.

"I can go," I offered. "It's limited, but I have *some* medical experience."

"I'll call you back," Den said, cutting the call short.

When I sat back on the arm of Olivia's chair, she said, "Me too—I can go with you." She got up from the chair. "Let me call Rachel—see if she's available. She is a nurse, after all—would be helpful to have her along."

Mac lifted her huge purse up from the floor and onto the couch. "How can I help? she asked.

"Mac, if I'm going with Lynn, I'll need you to watch over things," Olivia said, returning to the living room with her own cellphone.

"I'd go too. Unfortunately, I have too many dyer commitments with work," Alison said. "But I can be available should Mac need any assistance." She pulled a pen and her small notebook from her purse and perused a few pages. "You know, Mac… I think your locator spell may have actually worked."

"How so?" Mac asked, rummaging in her own bag.

Alison tapped the page she'd stopped at with her pen. "You said you used it on Nic, found him every time. But when you used it to track Kris, the potion gave off a stink like rotten eggs. Den just said Kris was at the hot springs."

"It worked—sort of," Mac recognized. "How about that?" She pinched her nostrils closed.

We spent the next several minutes making a list of what Olivia and I should bring with us. Vicki hadn't said much, other than it sounded like good news that Kris had been located *and* that I'd be needing warmer clothes for the trip than what I'd probably brought with me. We had all figured Vicki would have been more interested in going since she already knew so much about Iceland, but she hadn't offered and none of us had asked.

Before Den called us back, I reached out to Redmond to let him know what had happened. He'd already gotten the news and that Leo and Nic were getting a medivac ready, but he hadn't known what I'd offered in the way of help. "The others can't go get Kris," I explained, recapping the current constraints due to the sulfur.

"I don't like it—it's too dangerous without Leo or one of the others with you," Redmond said. "Let me go."

"There's no threat. According to what Derek found in those experiment notes, none of the Earthbound can be near that much sulfur—not even Thaddeus's guys," I said. "Besides, the medivac unit is here, I'm here, and Olivia and Rachel are here. It wouldn't make sense for them to try to have one set up where you are."

"Why do you have to go?" he pleaded. "Darius is going to freak out when he finds out and can't go with you—you know that."

"I know—but you'll be there to help him keep calm." I didn't really want to explain my feelings about why I needed to go because I didn't have to, it was more that I *wanted* to. "I'll ask Gabriel to meet us there," I said, in place of an explanation. "Once we have Kris safely back here, I'm coming home."

"Promise? I love you more than life, Lynn. I need you home safe and sound—we need you home."

My heart swelled at the devotion in his words, and I smiled knowing he'd finally conceded. "Of course—I promise. I love you too."

Den's callback came immediately following my call to Redmond. "The others accept your offer to help," he said, when I picked up. I put my cellphone on speaker again.

"Both Olivia and Rachel have offered to go as well, and they both have medical experience," I informed him. "Olivia's with the administrative part and Rachel with the actual medical part."

"This extra support gives me even more confidence with your original offer, Lynn," Den replied. "It makes for a much better and more believable execution of the plan. Just so you know—the best flight option Leo could do on such short notice was a 6 a.m. charter flight tomorrow. Can you be ready?"

"Not a problem," I said, looking at Olivia for her confirmation, too.

She nodded. "Rachel doesn't have a shift until later in the week— both she and I will be ready to go."

"Nic and Leo will have everything ready, and the plane decked out for you with the latest medical gear like a regular medivac. I'll have Marq prepare two more fake IDs for Rachel and Olivia, to go with yours, Lynn, and the documentation that will aid you with transferring

Kris to the airport, onto the plane, and out of the country. Good luck to you all," Den said. "Bring our brother home."

"I'm grateful we can help," I said before ending the call. Then I sent Derek a text,

> *Shortcut, you were right! Kris is in Iceland.*

He enjoyed being right, and I promptly got a text back from him. It read,

> *Kris must have crossed from Norway over Iceland on his way to meet the others up north. Got caught up in a sulfur dioxide cloud and tumbled to the ground into one of the pools.*

I passed Derek's message along to Leo, and he confirmed that it really was best none of them were going. Considering the sulfur had varying effects on the Earthbound, who knew what the exposure might do to them.

Before bed, I called Redmond again. "I reached out to Gabriel, to give him the what's-what and inform him I needed him to meet us at the other end when we arrived in Iceland."

"Good—that's something," Redmond said. "I love you, Lynn."

I sighed into the phone. "I love you more. Please don't worry."

"I'll do my best. Sweet dreams," Redmond said, ending the call.

Chapter 22 

The Group Home, Sunday May 15th, 4:30 a.m., Ottawa

Lyndon normally wasn't up this early, but these last few nights he hadn't slept much. Actually, he hadn't slept very much in the past few months if he were being honest.

He had been curious about Lane since that first time he'd seen her, and after that brief visit they had spent together he had found himself distracted and even consumed by thoughts of her. It had been two months since they had last spoken and she'd been kind to him even after he'd confronted her at the university, but he'd been too ashamed to show his face on the days she volunteered at the group home. On that morning they'd spent together with Taylor, she had asked to see his home in the basement. He'd never shown his apartment to anyone other than Taylor, and that had only been during a storm when the power had been knocked out on their street and several other blocks in this part of the city. Taylor hated being in the dark, so did he, but what he hated more was when Taylor was scared. Lyndon was certainly no coward, although he'd been too scared to talk with Lane again. She was scheduled to work tomorrow, and he'd made a vow that the next time he saw her he would make a valiant effort to speak to her. Until then, he would try to focus on Thaddeus's biddings.

As Lyndon did every morning, he checked the location software on his laptop to see that the humans he had hired were where they should be. In the past, he had employed the same shady, basically useless, humans to do some of the more unsavory tasks Thaddeus had asked of him, though they were only as loyal as the cash he continued to pay them.

Thaddeus had asked that he keep watch on the homes and workplaces of the women who had been at the group home, as Thaddeus was hoping to catch this Westlake woman with one of them. He'd also asked him to keep eyes on the third woman, the brunette who had been on the tour of the Ottawa facility. The other who had been with the brunette on the tour, the one with the short blonde hair, had been at both locations, so extra attention had been put on her home. Lyndon had stationed one of his lookouts at her place of work since both she and the brunette worked at the same location. Since the women all lived so close to one another, he had three men alternating with watching their homes. He had two others monitoring their workplaces, but those locations were at opposite ends of the city. He'd given them all basic burner phones for communication, and he had put tracking software on all five of them, to make sure they were where they said they were when they checked in. They had been instructed to text their counterparts at the other houses when any of the women showed up at the home they were monitoring. They were also to text the other's at the workplaces when they left for work and vice versa when they arrived and left for the day. Thus, having eyes on all the locations at all times.

The burner phone Lyndon used for interacting with these henchmen vibrated on the desk next to his laptop. The number 3 showed on the display of the phone. Lyndon couldn't care less what the names of these guys were, and he'd entered the digits of the other burner phones under the contact list using numbers 1 through 5 in place of names to identify them. The guy calling was currently located at the home of the woman who had been at both locations.

"Speak," Lyndon demanded, answering the unusually early call.

"Hey boss," minion #3 said, even though Lyndon had told him many times not to call him that. "One of the young women is here again. This time she's got a suitcase with her.

"And?" Lyndon had provided the minions with photos of each of the prime targets they were to watch. They had spotted two 20-something women coming and going occasionally at this location and had presumed they were the woman's daughters.

"She's unlocking the door."

"What is she doing now?" Lyndon asked.

"Going inside."

Lyndon closed his eyes. "And?"

"No idea."

Lyndon blew out an exasperated breath. He had no patience for these brilliant insights he was being given.

"A car just arrived."

"Who's car?" Lyndon questioned, rubbing his forehead.

"Sending photos now."

Two photos came through on Lyndon's burner, one of the car and the other taken of the driver's side window with the profile of a woman wearing a baseball cap.

"Hard to tell who it is—she's wearing a hat," minion #3 said, stating the obvious.

"What is she doing?" The woman's profile looked familiar to Lyndon, but he couldn't be sure. There was a pretty good chance this was the same woman from the group home, the woman Thaddeus had been searching for.

"Cars running—she's waiting, I guess."

"For what?" Lyndon asked, ready to hang up the call.

"They're coming out. Both have luggage—the small rolling kind— they're getting in the car."

"They—who?"

"The one with the short blonde hair—and the young woman who arrived before."

"Follow them," Lyndon instructed, before hanging up.

Thirty minutes later, Lyndon's burner phone was ringing. It was minion #3 again. Lyndon checked the guy's location. It showed him at the airport.

"She went to the airport—why didn't you call sooner?" Lyndon demanded, answering the call. He had instructed these idiots to alert him immediately if any woman matching the description he'd given them showed up at any of the locations.

"I followed them into the airport—but I can't get past the security—they went into the private charter area."

"You lost them?" Lyndon roared into the phone, squeezing it so hard the casing squeaked. He was at his wit's end with this guy.

"Maybe they are here to meet someone—someone arriving?"

Lyndon ran a hand down his face. "You said they had bags with them."

"Right—Okay—maybe they're taking a trip—a short one, small luggage."

"Find out where they are going. Ask at the charter counter for a list of the flights."

"Okay—on it," minion #3 said, ending the connection.

Lyndon waited an agonizing 15 minutes before his burner rang again. "Finally!"

"Ya—not great news, boss."

Lyndon shook his head. "Go on!"

"They can't share the private charter details because—well, they're private," idiot #3 informed him.

"Did you get any useful information?" Lyndon asked, ready to go over there and give this guy a beat-down.

"They did tell me the charters for today are full—and the only one going out this morning is to Iceland."

Iceland? "There must be another flight going out."

"Nope. But they said the one this morning is a medical transport— medical personnel only—no open seating available."

Lyndon hung up, then grabbed up his regular cellphone to call Thaddeus. Before dialing, he did a quick search on airports in Iceland. Then he checked the time. It was still early, however, he knew Thaddeus kept strange hours, so he made the call.

"You're sure it was her?" Thaddeus asked, through the noise of some violent video game Lyndon could hear playing in the background.

Lyndon ground his teeth. "I'm not sure—but the airport person indicated the flight was a medical charter."

The background noise lowered, and Thaddeus asked, "How do we know this is even the right Westlake—didn't you tell me the other woman's husband was a doctor?"

"Would make sense—with her association to the other two who work at the hospital," Lyndon surmised. This had to be the one with the multiple homes, the one he'd spoken to her neighbors about. They had been out of the country for her husband's work with Doctors Without Borders, but maybe they were heading out again, this time to Iceland. Besides, the research he'd done on the other Westlake woman had been a dead end.

"Makes little sense why she would have been in my building—in disguise," Thaddeus remarked then, deconstructing Lyndon's assessment.

Rebuilding his assessment, Lyndon said, "Not unless she was searching for something—maybe your research—on the sick kids. Or maybe she—they, are under the impression you are doing something unethical with them." Lyndon knew he was.

Thaddeus gave an amused laugh. "Those two women who came for that tour of the facility, they were looking to link to our organization. They ran some kind of special care birthing unit, Amahle informed me. The hospital they work at has one of the largest hospital-based obstetrical services in this province—their interests were more than likely about getting funding for their program. I have to admit, linking with them would look good for us. Can always use more good press."

"True," Lyndon replied. He knew Thaddeus didn't care about the kids. It was his reputation and public image in which he was interested. That and keeping his nefarious experiments a secret.

"Keep one of your guys at the airport—I need you to get to Iceland. Investigate what they're doing there," Thaddeus demanded.

"I'm not sure if you know this, but the small cities where the people live are scattered around the country—some places can only be reached by boat."

"So what—you'll be flying," Thaddeus stated, indignant.

"There are 464 authorized airports in Iceland." He'd looked it up before calling Thaddeus. "How could I possibly know where to find them?"

Chapter 23 

Flight to Akureyri Airport, May 15th, Akureyri, Iceland

This morning, before leaving to pick Olivia and Rachel up to go to the airport, I'd informed Vicki that I would be taking my luggage with me just in case we had to stay the night there. Me driving to the airport made more sense too, since I had to drop off my rental car there eventually, anyway. I wouldn't need it again since Kris would need a medical transport vehicle as well once we landed back home. And as Vicki had stated yesterday, I didn't have any warm clothes for Iceland, so Olivia had provided me a cardigan and a winter coat, along with some office clothes, including a pair of loafers that I had changed into on the plane. I needed to represent my position as the person in charge of Kris's estate, and my jeans and t-shirt weren't going to cut it.

When Leo had contacted the hospital in Iceland, he'd set Olivia up in the role as Kris's doctor, and the fake ID she'd been given reflected that position. Rachel didn't have to fake being a nurse, but she was provided fake ID as well, to protect her real identity and career, avoiding any of this getting attached to her actual record. They both knew hospital and medical lingo and that was mainly what we needed from them, to make this plan work. Although it was an added bonus that Rachel could attend to Kris on the plane should the need arise.

The small plane had four passenger seats, two at the front and two at the rear. In the middle, closer to the back seats, was a large hospital bed with various medical equipment set on either side of it.

"What's medical repatriation?" I asked, reviewing the documentation Leo had given me. I'd taken one of the seats at the front with Olivia, while Rachel had taken one at the back in proximity to the medical equipment.

"It's a combination of medical assistance and transportation to enable a citizen to return to their home country from abroad," Olivia informed me. "It happens from time to time in my department. Pregnant women needing emergency transport from another country back to Ottawa. We tell them not to travel past 6 months—but some don't listen."

"Yeesh! I didn't even like driving when I was pregnant. I can't imagine flying—or leaving the country, for that matter." Pregnant at 45 with twins was challenging enough, thank you very much. Shaking my head, I reviewed the legal documents showing my executorship over Kris's estate, which included decisions regarding his health. "Who has the final say if Kris can come home?" I asked, curious if we might have a fight on our hands getting him released.

"We do—Mom does as the *doctor*, she has the final say," Rachel said. "Mom and I represent the medical personnel accompanying Kris, and we are responsible for his safety in the air. The documentation Leo gave us shows us both as having long-standing experience and extensive knowledge to ideally assess his condition." Rachel came off confident that she knew her stuff, and I knew she could pull this off, but I could tell she was nervous, like we all were. We really didn't know what to expect.

"I'll consult with the treating doctor, but we—Rachel and I, decide whether or not Kris is well enough to travel," Olivia added, flipping the pages forward for me, pointing out the verbiage.

"We are about an hour out from our destination," came the voice of the pilot through the intercom.

"One hour," Rachel said, getting up from her seat. "This air ambulance Leo tricked out is fitted with intensive care equipment, to safely transport a patient in a coma, like Kris," she explained, assessing all the medical stuff again. Rachel waved a hand over the equipment like one of those prize models on a TV game show. "This is intensive care equipment here." She pointed at each of the apparatuses. "A central oxygen tank and optional reserve and a multi-parameter intensive care transport monitor. That's a compact defibrillator-monitor system there, and this is an intensive care respirator for complex artificial respiration." Rachel glanced over at us.

Some of the terms were familiar to me, but it had been a while since I had any real contact with medical gear. I chase down wheelchairs at my current hospital gig.

"She means breathing apparatus and monitoring systems," Olivia simplified for me. "With Kris suffering from an allergic reaction—if he has any breathing issues, that stuff will be helpful."

Rachel held up a long black rectangle that resembled an older model cordless house phone with a thick antenna the same length as the phone part. "We've also got a satellite telephone for global communication, and a patient loading system with this larger than normal mobile hospital bed." She patted the bed. "If Kris is anything like Nic in size, we're going to need it." She gave us a simple grin, then turned to the items further back. "These medical devices at the back here, they're used for constant analysis of a patient's vital signs."

"It's much like an ICU," Olivia said. Her knowledge came from supporting many of the doctors who had worked in the NICU at the children's hospital in Ottawa.

"What's in those cabinets, there?" I asked, pointing to a half-wall of metal doors with the big red plus sign on them.

"Those contain ambulance equipped medications and other medical supplies," Rachel said, opening the top cabinet. "Let's see what we got here… *Adrenalin*, used in the treatment of serious shock like a severe allergic reaction or collapse." Rachel looked at me. "You've probably seen it used in movies to restart someone's heart if it has stopped."

"Like in Pulp Fiction," I said, grinning proudly.

"Right," she laughed out, turning back to the cabinet. "*Propofol*—Kris is already unconscious, he won't need that. *Beta-blockers*, those are used to manage abnormal heart rhythms, like with a heart attack. *Anticoagulants*—those are blood thinners, and…."

"Thirty minutes until landing. Please buckle in and prepare to land," the pilot said, cutting in.

"… there's a bunch of other emergency medications," Rachel finished, shutting the cabinet before returning to her seat.

With the 6 a.m. flight out of Ottawa, and 5.5 hours of flying time, we landed on time in Iceland at 11:30 a.m. Ottawa time, 4:30 p.m. local time. If everything went as planned with customs and the exchange of hands of Kris at the hospital, we might have him back home by 9 p.m. today, Ottawa time.

We had only been inside the airport a few minutes, and I hadn't seen Gabriel, but I felt him around. It was possible he was limiting his involvement until and if we needed his help. Both Olivia and Rachel looked anxious, and I guess I should have been too, but I was mostly excited and any uneasiness I was experiencing was more due to going through customs. I'd done the customs dance enough times in my life, but this was my first time using a fake passport. Even with my trip to Norway, I'd used my real passport. The ones Marq had made for us all had our same first names, but different last. The same first names, we were told, would make public communication for us easier when addressing each other. It made sense, fewer slipups with calling each other by the wrong name. I was Lynn *Robertson*, Olivia was Dr. Olivia *Thompson*, and Rachel had the same last name, sticking with them still being mother and daughter. We also had Kris's Canadian passport and other fake medical records that showed extensive notes on his sensitivity to sulfur.

Thankfully, the Akureyri Airport charter area had a swift check-through for medical emergencies. And as luck would have it, nerves aside, meaning luck was actually on our side today, we'd managed to get through customs smoothly and without a hitch with presenting our bogus passports. Before going out to meet the driver Leo had arranged, we put on our winter coats for the obvious change in climate. When we exited the airport, our driver was waiting out front to take us the short 10 minute drive to the hospital of the same name. Leo had also arranged for medical transport to be waiting at the hospital for transferring Kris to the airport.

At the hospital, we were met at the front desk by one of the facility administrators. Then we were escorted to the ICU, where we were introduced to the medical team lead for the unit.

"May I see your credentials and notification of transport documents?" the woman who had introduced herself as Dr. Bakken asked.

At first when she'd said her name, I'd thought she'd said *bacon*, reminding me it was lunchtime back home, and that I was starving. All I'd managed to get at the airport was a coffee and a donut, and no way was that going to sustain me until we got home. Keeping my composure, I said, "We will need copies of the medical notes from the attending doctor before we leave." I handed her my credentials and both the travel and medical documents from the file.

"You are the one in charge of the patient's... estate?" Dr. Bakken asked, reviewing the paperwork.

"Yes, I'm his executor, which means I also have jurisdiction over his person, should he become incapacitated. Which he has—I am told."

"Quite." Dr. Bakken nodded.

Extending a hand out to Olivia in introduction, I said, "This is Dr. Olivia Thompson, Mr. Snow's personal doctor, and this is Rachel, his private nurse."

"I was informed the patient would be returning to Canada, yes?" Dr. Bakken took a very militant stance, hands clasped behind her back.

"Yes, that is correct," I responded, keeping things as formal as possible. The travel docs stated we were here to pick up a Canadian citizen from their hospital and transport him back to Canada for further treatment. My stomach rumbled.

"There is no record of a Canadian with his name entering the country. And he had no identification to prove who he was," Dr. *Bacon* stated, firmly, adding a slight bump in our road.

"I have his Canadian passport, right here," I said, prepared for just such a complication. "Mr. Snow has dual citizenship with the US and had been traveling with his US passport. He must have lost it somewhere." I presented the passport with the photo page open, then put it back in the leather briefcase Leo had kindly provided for me to carry all the paperwork in. "He had been traveling to Norway when we lost contact with him—how he got to Iceland, we still don't know."

"The woman who brought him here said they had found him with no memory of who he was *or* how he got here. Quite the mystery." I think she smiled, but I wasn't sure because her expression was so tight. "Our scan showed no brain injury. But his lungs—the injury to them, presents similar to that of smoke inhalation."

"He has been missing for 5 months," I informed the doctor. "We'd like to get him home as soon as possible, have his treatment continued there." I zipped the leather briefcase closed as though indicating I was done.

"I'm uncertain it is safe for him to fly," the doctor said then, tossing out a potential roadblock.

I glanced at Olivia, stepping back, and giving her an expression that said, *yer up*.

Olivia stepped forward and said, "My patient's well-being and safety are our highest priorities. To ensure optimum medical care during the trip back, we will update your team on his condition, and— if it makes you feel better, we can facilitate pre-flight doctor-to-doctor consultations. Be assured, I would not issue a fit to fly certificate where a patient of mine has a medical condition that might worsen mid-air."

"I guarantee you, he will get the best possible medical treatment during this journey," Rachel added, that confidence I loved about her so much, oozing out. "We'd like to see Mr. Snow now and speak with his attending doctor to review what was done upon his arrival here?"

Dr. Bakken cleared her throat. "I am the doctor who has been treating him."

"Perfect," Olivia said, glancing between Rachel and me.

The doctor turned away from us and called out, "Anna." She waved for a young woman in scrubs to come over. "Please explain to Dr. Thompson what procedures have been performed on the patient since his arrival here," she instructed as the nurse came to stand next to her.

The young woman appeared uneasy with being put on the spot. She glanced down at her feet for a second as if looking for the answer, then at the chart in her hands before placing her focus on both Olivia and Rachel. "We checked his airway and helped maintain his breathing and circulation. He did not appear to need breathing assistance, but we did administer IV medicines and other supportive care."

Interrupting, Dr. Bakken said, "We have still not determined his specific ailment since there are several conditions that have signs and symptoms similar to those of anaphylaxis. We've ruled out most of the fatal conditions." She then turned to nurse Anna for more.

"We did a creatinine test to measure how well his kidneys were performing, and the results show they are doing their job of filtering the creatinine from his blood. It exits the body as a waste product in urine."

"Thank you—I know what creatinine is," Rachel said. "May I see the patient notes?"

"Yes, of course," Anna said, handing the chart to Olivia instead of Rachel.

Olivia pretended to review the patient chart, though I was sure she recognized a lot of the terms. She then handed the chart to Rachel for her professional review. Rachel glared at the other nurse.

"We used epinephrine to reduce the body's allergic response. Oxygen, to help his breathing," the nurse said. "He has had IV administered antihistamines and cortisone to reduce inflammation of his air passages to improve his breathing. And Albuterol to relieve his breathing symptoms."

"It was my understanding that he was not having any breathing issues when he was brought in," Rachel stated.

Speaking up again, the doctor said, "These issues occurred when he went into the coma. Unfortunately, in most other cases there's no way to treat the underlying immune system condition that can lead to anaphylaxis." Dr. Bakken glanced at Rachel and then Olivia. "Perhaps, some immunotherapy once he's home, to reduce his allergic response and prevent a severe reaction in the future."

If I had been a doctor on the receiving end of that last comment, I would have been totally offended and I could tell by Olivia's enraged expression, she was. As if in defense of the suggestion that she did not know how to treat her patient, Olivia said, "Kris would have removed himself from exposure had his memory *not* been impacted."

This doctor knew that Olivia was this patient's personal doctor and Rachel was his nurse. Both would have extensive knowledge of their patient's needs, albeit pretend knowledge, and would not be ignorant of what should be done.

"Would he not normally carry a self-administered epinephrine?" Dr. Bakken asked, smugly.

"No, he knows to avoid triggers," Rachel replied, handing back the chart to Olivia.

"Please explain—so I don't have to read through this, what was done for his coma state," Olivia requested then.

Nurse Anna glanced at Dr. Bakken first, then at Olivia. "We then followed procedures to relieve any pressure on his brain due to brain swelling. Since we had no knowledge of him having any allergies to antibiotics, we gave him only IV glucose while we waited for the blood test results—in case his blood sugar was low and what had caused the collapse."

"Tests show no indication of an underlying disease, so I believe the coma is due to the seizures," Dr. Bakken finished for her.

"Can you please provide us with copies of these patient notes?" Olivia asked, clearly done with the rundown and as eager as I was to get out of here and on the flight home. "And I'd like to see *my* patient now."

Both Dr. Bakken and nurse Anna nodded and then went off together to do whatever was needed to grant Olivia access to Kris.

Rachel gathered her mom and me close. "Sometimes the cause of a coma can be completely reversed, and the affected person regains function. Recovery usually occurs gradually, though." She glanced up the way to where the doctor and the nurse had gone. "The sooner we get him away from the sulfur exposure, the sooner I can better assess his potential recovery."

"The staff here think he's just allergic to sulfur, but we know it's much more than an acute sensitivity," I said, glancing up the hall as Rachel had done. I noted both the doctor and the nurse disappeared into one of the ICU rooms. Outside the room sat a man and a young woman. "That must be Geir—the guy Den told us about, and the woman must be the friend." I pointed down the hall. "I'm going to go talk with them."

"I'll help Mom review the chart," Rachel said in a low voice. "Get her better acquainted with the tests and terms she might not be familiar with."

"Good plan," I whispered back before heading to greet Kris's rescuers.

Coming to a stop outside the ICU room, I asked the man, "Are you Geir?" Then I glanced at the woman. She was hunched over with her face in her hands.

"Yes—hello," he said, standing and extended a hand to shake. "You're a friend of Hayden's, yes?"

I shook his hand. Den had informed Geir that we were coming and that he and I were close friends. "Yes, my name's Lynn." I glanced back towards Olivia and Rachel. "This is Dr. Thompson—his personal doctor, and Rachel, his private nurse," I said, introducing the two as they approached and came to stand next to me.

"Hello," he said, "I'm Geir—pleased to meet you." He put a hand on the woman's shoulder.

"We are grateful you reached out to Hayden," Olivia said. "I'm going to check on my patient now so we can finish the process of getting him out of here." She gave him a reassuring smile, then she and Rachel left to venture into Kris's ICU room.

"Where are you taking Kisur?" the woman asked then, tilting her head up, acknowledging my presence.

Kisur? "Home," I said, puzzled by the name she had called Kris. "I have the authority to bring him home. You must be Jana." Geir had mentioned to Den that she'd been the one with Kris at the spa. "You were with Kris—at the hot spring."

"Kris?" she questioned, frowning. The confusion on her face reflected my own feelings from when she'd said *Kisur*. She let out a soft, almost laugh. "He had called me that, *Kris*." She drew the sleeve of her shirt across her teary eyes.

I gave her a perplexed grin. "I'm not following, sorry."

"I apologize," she said, sniffing in through her nose as though congested. "My proper name is Kristjana—I use *Jana,* but he chose the *Kris* part without realizing." She sniffed gain. "It seems strange now—knowing… his real name. *Kisur* is just a nickname I gave him. Had to call him something since he didn't know who he was." She wiped her eyes again. "Do you know how he got here? I mean, he has no memories. Not clear ones anyway."

"Jana, come with me," I said, offering her my hand. I was starting to believe there was a bit more here than just friendship between her and Kris. She took my hand, and I gave it a gentle squeeze. "Let's go somewhere to talk, shall we?"

She nodded, then stood, still holding my hand.

As nurse Anna passed me on her way into Kris's room, I said, "Please let Dr. Thompson and Rachel know that I'll be back in a few minutes."

She gave a single nod. "There are family waiting rooms just outside the unit doors," she said, as if recognizing the need for Jana and me to have some privacy.

"Thank you," I said with a grateful smile.

She smiled back and gave another single nod before turning to go back into Kris's room.

Just beyond the ICU area, I found an empty family waiting room and had Jana take a seat next to me on one of the sterile-looking couches. "This is better," I said. "Now we can talk freely." I smiled, checking the temperature of her mood. Her expression was weary, and she dabbed at escaping tears with one of the tissues provided in the room. "Jana, please don't worry. We are going to take excellent care of Kris."

Dropping her head, she stared down at the tissues in her hands. "This all seems very… extravagant… a private nurse and a plane to take him home. Who is he? Some lost prince?"

He was a prince to her, it seemed. "He's not a prince, no. But he is a reclusive wealthy restauranter—a chef by trade, you could say."

She let out another almost laugh but didn't look up. "That explains a lot." She sniffed and dabbed at her eyes again. "I own a bakery, and he… well, he helped me out during his time here. Had all kinds of skills, both business, and cooking. Now I know why." She reached for another tissue. "Why was he in Iceland — do you know?"

I pulled the tissue box closer. "He wasn't supposed to be. His journey only included Norway. He was traveling with the plan of ordering items for his restaurant, meeting with different vendors."

She looked at me then. "How did he end up at my father's property? He was just lying there in the snow." She looked away as if remembering it. "I had to move him to the barn."

Barn? I was suddenly pulled back to the weird vision I'd had at the spa, and the smell of hay. "Into a barn?" I questioned. She'd also said *bakery*, which explained the aroma of bread I'd experience then as well.

"Yes — it's the small outbuilding on my father's property. I needed to get him inside, he was soaking wet, and it was the closest building I could get him to on my own. But my father's property is nowhere near the main road or any bodies of water," Jana explained, shaking her head, still baffled.

"Wow. I can't answer that — but know that he's been missing for 5 months now. We were worried he was dead. If it weren't for your friend Geir — reaching out, we may not have gotten to him in time. He has an exceptionally rare condition. Kris's body and brain — the impact to his memory, he must not have realized the effect that being here would have on him. And it's not something most doctors would have known to look for. It's more than just a severe sulfur allergy."

"What? Not sulfur — seriously? The doctor said environmental allergen — they never mentioned it was sulfur," she sobbed out.

"Why — what does it matter?"

"Because I got him memory supplements, MSM — hoping they would help — they contain sulfur. He recently started taking them twice a day, thinking they would help his other symptoms. But I think they may have extended the memory loss — caused his aches and pains, the poor appetite and digestion." She put a hand over her mouth, then dropped it. "Oh god — he'd been having fainting spells. I took him to the spa thinking it might help — it's like a miracle for most people, but I could have killed him." She lowered her head again, putting her hands over her face, sobbing into them.

I pulled more tissue from the box. "Here," I said, tilting her face up and removing her hands. "Jana—we are going to make sure Kris gets better—trust me."

Jana closed her eyes letting her head flop back. Two tears ran down the sides of her face.

I squeezer her hands. "We just need to get him out of here, away from the environment—away from the sulfur."

Just then, Olivia popped her head into the room and said, "We're ready to go when you are."

Chapter 24 

Once on board the plane, I'd texted Redmond to let him know we were in the air and on our way back to Ottawa. When we'd secured Kris, I'd made it known to Olivia and Rachel just how amazing they both were and how I couldn't have done this without them. *"This was so nerve-racking. How did you do this in Norway around the bad guys—pretending and in disguise?"* Olivia had asked once we were in the air. She'd finally taken in a real breath and had let her nervous system relax. Rachel had given me a pleased smile, then she'd performed her nursing duties by hooking Kris up to the multi-parameter intensive care transport monitor to keep constant analysis of his vital signs. An hour into the flight, I'd changed out of the professional clothing Olivia had loaned me and back into my jeans and t-shirt. I'd also made a call to Leo, giving him the details on the state of Kris's health. There'd been no change, unfortunately, but he was no worse either. Then mid-flight, Kris had stirred a bit, though he remained unconscious for the rest of the trip.

The three of us had been quiet most of the flight, the adrenaline we'd experienced now replaced by exhaustion, the silence interrupted by only the usual plane sounds and Kris's monitor blips keeping us company. As for Gabriel, I'd not seen him once, and I had felt nothing of his presence most the time. Maybe his being with me on this trip had been more of a balancing act for him, I'd surmised.

"We'll be on the ground in 20 minutes," the pilot announced, disrupting my mussing. "Please prepare for landing."

The plane landed and came to a stop at the terminal. Then Rachel and I worked together to get Kris ready for transport off the plane. Rachel had explained to me how the patient loading system with the mobile hospital bed worked and we secured him to be lowered and placed into the medical vehicle Leo was providing. Leo said he would use the same van we'd used for the emergency sewer scheme, this time tricked out in medical equipment and not city service worker paraphernalia. And instead of the city service logo and verbiage on the van's panel walls, they were going with just the white nondescript van this time.

"Okay, Kris. Time to go, sleeping beauty," I declared when the door to the plane opened.

Before we could proceed, stairs were rolled up to the open door, and as a courtesy to the medical emergency flight, a customs and immigrations officer boarded our plane and promptly reviewed our passports and documentation.

Outside the plane, post passport check, Leo and Nic had the back doors to the van open, and they swiftly maneuvered Kris from the unloading system into the van. Rachel and Olivia accompanied Nic with our patient in the back, while I hopped into the passenger seat up front with Leo. The van was open between the front seats and the back area, the inside set up for patient transport, much like an ambulance.

"Any changes?" Nic asked, directing his inquiry to Rachel.

"No. Hasn't stirred since the halfway point of our flight," Rachel said, attaching Kris to the monitors in the van.

While we drove out of the airport and onto the parkway road that took us to North Haven, Rachel and Nic continued with the exchange of medical jargon, conferring on the possible circumstances of Kris's condition.

After the lengthy flights to and from Iceland, getting to North Haven had felt like a blink of an eye. The Guards, the remainder of them, were out front waiting for our arrival. I realized that this was the first time in an extremely long time that all of them were in one place together. And it was Kris's second time ever being here. Though it was a shame it had to be under these circumstances. Greeting were given by all, but no other words were exchanged as they worked as a team to get Kris out of the van and into the house, then up to his bedroom. Kris had his own suite, empty as it was, but it had a bed and exactly what Rachel and Nic needed to get him set up and hooked to the monitoring system to watch his vitals.

After Nic and Rachel had Kris settled, I returned to the main living space to find Olivia and the others sitting on the large multi-sectional couch next to the bar. Low murmurs filled the space.

"Lynn," Den said, as I approached the garrison of Earthbound Angels.

Olivia stood and handed me a glass of wine. "Thought you could use a drink, too."

"*Yer an angel,*" I whispered, grateful she knew just what I needed.

"I just finished updating Kris's general manager again, Francesca—Frank," Den added. "She said to say thank you—to you and your friends, for helping bring Kris back."

"We all want to thank you," Leo said, standing. "You courageously brought him back and kept the rest of us away from unknown peril." They all stood then, each extending an arm, holding out glasses of whatever beverage of choice they were each drinking. "To our brave sisters," Leo hailed, directing his glass at Olivia and me. Deep cheers from the others followed his toast.

"Oh, no need to be so dramatic," I responded, unprepared for the praise. "Olivia and Rachel did the hard parts. I'm just grateful I could help, again. I'm sure you can all breathe a sigh of relief now." I gave them a quick smile and took a long sip of my wine, hoping to move past the awkward moment. There had been no mention of it, but I was relieved Thaddeus hadn't taken Kris, and we hadn't found him hanging in some back room. However, who that hanging angel from my dream was, I still had no clue.

Olivia leaned in and said, "I updated Mac, Alison, and Vicki."

"How did they respond?" I swirled my wine.

"Mac and Alison want the details. Vicki didn't seem to care what happened, only that we were safe and back in the country." She took a sip of her wine. "I tried to give them details, but Vicki kept changing the subject to other things, like how Eric only had one more flying job left and that they wanted someone else to do the flying for them. Go to places farther than his plane could take them." She shrugged.

"You can outline the details with the others later." I shook my head and blew out a weary breath. "I'm staying the night. I want to be here if Kris wakes up."

Olivia gave me a nod. "Figured you would."

"I'll text Vicki—let her know my plan before she heads to bed herself." I retrieved my cellphone from my bag.

"Going to go check on Rachel." Olivia rubbed my arm. "Back in a bit."

"I'll be up after," I said, watching as she retreated from the living room towards the interior entrance to Kris's personal suite. Then I took out my cellphone and wrote to Vicki,

> *Hey Lady. I just wanted to let you know that I'm staying the night at the North Haven. Leo will drop me off tomorrow morning for my flight. Olivia told me about yours and Eric's plans to fly to far-off places. Sounds like a brilliant idea. Thank you again for everything.*

I hit send and went to put my cellphone back in my bag when it dinged in my hand. It was a response from Vicki already.

It read,

> *Hi, sorry I couldn't help. Not that I didn't want to see the guy brought home, I just wasn't comfortable. Not how I wanted to visit Iceland again.*

We all knew she wasn't comfortable with the angel talk these days, and it really was fine that she wasn't up for helping us. I'm not sure how she would have contributed, anyway.

I responded back with,

> *I totally understand. Love you.*

Den and the others were deep in discussion, so I tucked my phone away, set my wine on the side table and went off after Olivia.

"I'll stay the night to watch him," Rachel said to Nic as I entered the bedroom part of the upper suite.

"Okay—we can swap in a couple of hours, so you can get some rest," Nic said to Rachel before turning his attention to me. "Hey, Lynn—Olivia says you're staying the night, too."

"Ya—I'd like to be here when he wakes up," I said with a hopeful grin.

"I'm pretty pooped," Olivia said then. "I'm going to head out—tad too much excitement for me." She half giggled, half cringed.

"Thank you Olivia—Rachel. I said it before—but this was a success because of you guys. There was no way I could have played the executor, the doctor, *and* been convincing." I gave a tired laugh. Olivia wasn't the only one exhausted. My adrenaline had burned up all my energy, although I still wanted to stay awake just in case Kris came to before I had to fly out in the morning. "I can sit with him for a bit. Nic— get Rachel some food, would ya?" I added, then lowered myself into the comfy looking chair next to the bed.

"Will do," Nic said, holding the door for Rachel.

"Find something for me, too, please," I said over my shoulder.

"You got it," Nic said, before shutting the door behind them.

Alone now with our slumbering patient, I took a better survey of the room. The temperature was comfortable, like the main areas of the house, and the lighting was soft, though bright enough to see clearly. Light grey, low pile carpet covered the floor. The bed was king-sized for sure and had a tufted grey headboard. The bed itself took up most of the wall it was up against. The door to the room was on the left and a small side table flanked the far side of the bed. Kris lay under grey sheets and rested his head upon a pillow, encased also in grey and of a similar colour to the headboard. There was no dresser or armoire in the room, only a pair of floor-to-ceiling sliding doors on one wall of what I assumed was to a large closet. The opposite wall was bare, and the wall across from the bed had high windows covered by white blinds matching the white of all the walls. The armchair I sat in I noticed now was of the same style, fabric, and shade of the headboard, and it was quite comfortable. I wondered if this was what all their rooms looked like or if someone had designed it specifically for Kris.

I slid the chair closer to the head of the bed. *"The sleeping prince,"* I whispered softly, focusing on Kris, taking his hand in mine. *"Do you know that story?"* There was no response, though the monitors continued to do their blip-blip. "Let me tell you the tale…," I began, using a regular voice, traveling off into the not-so-well-known Greek fairytale. Redmond had told me about it way back when the girls had asked him to read them Sleeping Beauty for the one millionth time. I recalled for Kris the short story the best I could under the circumstances. "It's a bit dark—I admit. But it has a happy ending," I finished, leaning forward to admire his peaceful face. *"Kris,"* I said, noticing his eyes were moving under his lids.

His hand squeezed mine.

"You're safe," I said in a gentle voice.

"Jana," he breathed out weakly.

"Kris," I said in a firmer voice this time.

His eyes opened, and he turned his head to look at me.

"Hey—hi," I said, then realized he would have no clue who the hell I was. "I'm a friend of Leo's… I'm Lynn."

He frowned. "Where's Jana?"

"She's home. You're home," I clarified.

He slowly rotated his head away from me, taking in his surroundings. "How did I get here?"

"Do you know who you are?"

"Yes," he said, letting go of my hand, only to bring his to his head as though in pain.

I stood, swiftly shoving the chair back. Then went and yanked opened the bedroom door. "Nic—Rachel, he's awake."

Numerous footfalls began thundering up the stairs from the lower level of Kris's suite. As Nic and Rachel entered the room, I stepped back, allowing for them to get in closer to Kris for further examination. Following them came Leo, Den, Zach, Ben, and Marq. There wasn't much room to breathe, let alone move, so I strode out of the bedroom, retreating down the stairs.

Deep murmurs from the males could still be heard as I exited the lower level of Kris's suite into the main living space. I strolled to the area with the large sectional couch to find abandoned glasses, several of them still half-full of alcohol. My wineglass waited where I had set it before going to find Olivia. I picked it up and took in a long whiff of the aroma. A connoisseur of wines I was not but based on the delicious sips I had earlier and its lovely fragrance, it had to be an expensive one. I sniffed it again, then took a big gulp and rested down on the arm of the couch. My bag was also where I'd left it next to the end table, so I set my glass down and pulled free my cellphone. The time displayed 11:34 p.m.

Despite the late hour, I sent Redmond a quick text message letting him know Kris was awake. I also sent him my new flight details for tomorrow, and how Leo had switched it to a later time around noon. But it was also a flight that landed closer to home at the exclusive charter airport 30 minutes North of where we lived as opposed to the one hour drive South.

Apparently, he was still awake because he wrote back right away with,

> *Great news. The others must be thrilled. I'm thrilled you're coming home. Get some rest, Babe. Message me in the morning.*
> *Love you xoxo*

I sent him back *I love you too* and added several more X's and O's to the end. Then I slid my cellphone back into the side pouch of my bag. "*We did it*," I muttered to myself, picking up my wineglass in salute to our success. We brought Kris home.

Leo had provided us with the plan we'd needed, but Olivia and Rachel had been the key to executing the plan and getting him out of that hospital. I hadn't really done anything. What exactly had I been there for? There wouldn't have been any Earthbound there for me to detect. I was fairly confident of that, although it didn't mean there couldn't have been human supporters of Thaddeus in the vicinity. I had to believe he and his followers were still unaware of the existence of Leo and The Guards. Kris ending up in Iceland had been a fluke, a wrong place—wrong allergen kind of thing, and not because someone had done this to him. If this had been on purpose, Thaddeus would never have left Kris in the hands of those naïve humans. He would have already had him in a lab being experimented on. It was sheer luck they even found Kris. And if getting him back here hadn't been the priority, I would have made more time to talk with both Geir and Jana about what had happened.

"Lynn," Den called from the doorway of Kris's suite, pulling me from my musings.

"Hey… how's he doing?"

"Good—really good." Den was smiling. A truly triumphant smile, the type I'd not seen on him in the 5 months we'd known each other. "He's asking for you."

I stood, pointing at myself with my free hand. "Me?" I questioned, setting down my wineglass on the side table.

"Rachel told him you spoke to his friend Jana—now he wants to talk to you." Den held open the door as I crossed the room.

"Have you contacted Geir?" I asked, stopping in front of him.

"I did. I let him know Kris was home safe." He smiled again, this one a reassuring one. "I'll update him on Kris's progress tomorrow."

I nodded and gave him a thoughtful grin, patting the big arm he used to hold the door open. Then I passed through and proceeded up the stairs. I made a mental note to ask him later more about Geir, *and* about our friend Gavin.

As I reached the top of the stairs, I found the door to the bedroom was open, with Rachel coming through it. "I updated Mom—she told me she would update the others in the morning," Rachel said, before heading down the stairs.

"Great—thank you." I hadn't thought to update anyone other than Redmond. I knew Olivia would be on top of it, just as she had done earlier.

When I entered the bedroom, the others made room for me, what little there was, to pass and move towards Kris's bed. Leo was sitting on the edge of the bed, and he was actually laughing.

"Here she is," Leo said, leaning away to reveal a grinning Kris. Then Leo shifted up off the bed and stepped back, aligning with the others. "We'll leave you both alone to talk." Before I could step forward to take the chair next to Kris, Leo pulled me in for a quick hug. He let go then and without a word he followed the others, leaving the room and shutting the door.

"Well, hello again," I said, taking a seat in the chair. "Good to see you in such high spirits."

"Yes—Hello," Kris responded, pushing himself up into a sitting position, leaning back against the grey tufted headboard. "And thank you."

"I was just along for the ride," I said, sharing honestly how I felt.

"That's bullshit," he said with a chuckle. He reached for my hand, holding it in his this time. "My brothers were powerless—and you offered to go—no hesitation." He patted my hand. "Zach also told me about Norway—so don't try to brush it off."

"Well, that was different," I tossed out. "Rachel and Olivia are the true heroes here."

"A joint venture and joint success, I'll say then," Kris conceded, releasing my hand.

Readjusting myself in the chair, I said, "Den said you wanted to speak to me."

The joyful expression on Kris's face shifted to one of concern. "Jana… I wanted to talk to you about her." He glanced down at his hands in his lap.

"How did you end up in Iceland—do you know?" I asked, before getting into the emotional conversation I suspected was coming.

He gave me a quick glance, then returned to focusing on his hands. "I told the others the last thing I remember was flying over Iceland on my way to meet them all at First Haven." He rubbed the side of his jaw. "It's hazy—the how. But I must have landed in water. I was told my clothes were wet when they discovered me. Somehow I found my way to this old farmhouse, and she…." He paused, continuing to stare down at his hands.

"Jana helped you," I finished for him.

He nodded, but kept his eyes focused down.

"Do you remember what happened to you—at the hot springs?"

"Yes… the pain in my gut, the burning in my lungs. I'd felt similar before—not nearly as intense, but the blackouts were the same." He flexed his fingers as though they were stiff.

"Do you remember your time in Iceland—the last 5 months?" I asked, uncertain where exactly the conversation was leading.

"I'm starting to…." He gazed up at me. Pain filled his expression. And it wasn't from anything physical, it was pure heartache. "Does she know?"

"Jana? That you're basically one of seven angelic superheroes living on Earth—*No*."

Air escaped his lungs, and then he took my hand again.

"All she knows is you're a wealthy, reclusive restaurateur living in NYC. I explained to her you have a serious allergy to sulfur in all forms and that was why we had to get you out of there. But… she's not just a friend, is she?"

He shook his head and squeezed my hand.

Chapter 25 

Home of Olivia White, Sunday May 15th, 11:45 p.m., Ottawa

After his call with Thaddeus, Lyndon had taken it upon himself to keep watch outside the home where imbecile #3 had originally been stationed, and had the guy stay at the airport to watch instead.

Lyndon checked the location tracker app on his phone to see if all his minions were at their appointed locations. Just then, a grey sedan pulled into the driveway of the house. The vehicle had one of those transportation company decals in the window. The door to the car opened, and a woman got out. "What the fuuuu…?" he questioned, dumbfounded, watching as the woman proceeded up the walkway, rolling her luggage bag to the front door. Then she unlocked the door and went inside. He could not believe what he had just seen.

Furious, Lyndon hit the speed dial for imbecile #3, who was showing on the locator app as at the airport, where he should be. "The woman with the short blonde hair just arrived back at her house!" he hollered into the phone.

There was a pause and then minion #3 said, "Weird. Maybe she didn't get on the plane."

"How did you not see her leave?" Lyndon spat out. He had spent the morning at the group home, then took over watching the house while minion #3 waited at the airport. He should have been watching the airport, and not this fool, he realized.

"I'm sitting at the arrivals area—she never came through. That would have been a quick trip."

Quick trip or not, this worthless human should have been watching for them. "What about the other two—the young one and the one wearing the ball cap?" he asked, infuriated.

"No idea."

Lyndon closed his eyes, pinching the bridge of his nose.

"Maybe they're still here at the airport—didn't get on the flight. Or they stayed in Iceland—I don't know," the idiot said as though Lyndon and he were brainstorming ideas.

Trying to calm himself, Lyndon asked, "Did you see any vehicles leave the charter area?"

"Only vehicle I saw leaving was a plain white van."

"Did you see who was driving?" Lyndon demanded, losing his calm.

"Wasn't paying it much attention. Should I stay here?"

"No—get back here to the house," Lyndon said, hanging up. Then he looked up the number for the airport charter area and dialed.

"Ottawa International Airport Charters—how may I help you?" the charter person asked in greeting.

"This is… Dr. Lyndon from the Queensway Carleton Hospital," Lyndon replied. "I was hoping you could confirm for me that the medivac arrived. Three of my staff were to be on that flight."

"Yes. The medivac flight left early this morning and arrived back just after 9 p.m. The patient was onboard," the charter person said, validating his request.

"Thank you." Lyndon hung up. He cared little who the patient was and had only needed this verification that they had landed. His only concern now was where had the other two gone. Where had that woman gone, the one driving the car? Maybe she was just that, the driver, someone who had offered to take the others to the airport. What did it matter? He wasn't even sure she was this Westlake woman Thaddeus was searching for. "What a waste of time," he breathed out, hitting the speed dial for Thaddeus.

"An update so soon?" Thaddeus drawled out.

"It appears as though the flight has returned already. Though only the one woman returned with the patient." It wasn't exactly the truth, but Lyndon wasn't interested in explaining how his lookout had missed all of them at the airport.

"How do you know this?" Thaddeus questioned.

"I saw her. She arrived home alone, dropped off by one of those Uber drivers." Lyndon waited for a reaction. When none came, he said, "Looks like nothing—just part of the woman's job. Probably some pregnant lady needing emergency transport home. The woman runs a special birthing unit, you said."

"What of the other two? The driver—the one you thought might be the target?" Thaddeus asked, impatiently.

"I said I wasn't sure it was her. Whomever she was, she and the young one are probably attending to the patient," Lyndon said, discounting the events with more lies. "Waste of time." He'd gotten more comfortable keeping certain details from Thaddeus and lying to him these days.

"Next time be sure you're tracking the right person," Thaddeus ordered before hanging up.

Lyndon pocketed his cellphone. "Right you are, boss-man," he said mockingly to no one. The egotistical angel wasn't his boss, regardless of the fact Thaddeus acted like he owned him. "About time," he murmured, spotting loser #3's car roll to a stop up the street. Lyndon started his car, put it in gear, and then drove off back to the group home.

On the way, he reminded himself that Lane was scheduled to be in on Monday, tomorrow. The thought of seeing her lovely face again filled his heart as he drove. He still hadn't mentioned a word to Thaddeus about seeing Juliette. And Lane, it seemed, hadn't been lying. He'd followed her on several occasions when she'd left the group home, and she'd gone to the university each time. Juliette *was* her professor, though Lane hadn't gone just to see her. There were other professors she had met with, following suit with her explanation of doing her master's degree. Lane, knowing Juliette, had just been a coincidence he hadn't seen coming. He didn't like being caught off guard, and he was very protective of Taylor. Especially after what Thaddeus had done to him.

It had been Lyndon's idea to be stationed at this group home. Thaddeus had treated it like a favor to him, but he didn't care what he thought. He had wanted to make sure Taylor was safe and that no one ever hurt him again, not even Thaddeus. And it provided him with the solitude and privacy he preferred.

Before he and the others had been trapped here on Earth, he'd had bigger responsibilities than watching over Taylor or chasing down some mysterious woman. In fact, it had been his talents matched with Thaddeus's that had allowed them the time to discuss the grievances concerning their roles. Thaddeus's complaints had been monumental, while Lyndon's had been more about a lack of recognition for his contributions. It was a concern he understood now, Thaddeus had cultivated in his head over time, disrupting his serenity in Pleiades. Thaddeus had been the Seraph who oversaw the microorganisms that existed as unicellular, multicellular, or cell clusters. Lyndon's direction had been on the biology of regeneration, the morphogenic processes relating to the changes in an organism's behavior, morphology, and physiology in response to unique environments. Originally, Thaddeus had thought it useful for his end-game of populating the Earth with pureblood Seraphim, being that regeneration was basically regulated by asexual cellular processes. When Lyndon had told him every species was capable of regeneration, from bacteria to humans, Thaddeus hadn't grasped it was more about tissue loss, like when a starfish grows back an arm, and not the independent creation of a complete organism. After discovering that, Thaddeus had considered Lyndon mostly useless and had then set his focus on learning what he could about *creation* by testing on the halflings that were being born.

Lyndon pulled into his parking spot at the group home. Getting out of the car, he checked the locator app on his cellphone once more to see that his lackeys were still in place. They were. Inside, before taking the elevator down to his private space, he went to check in on Taylor.

When Lyndon opened Taylor's bedroom door, he could hear the soft lullaby emanating from the nightlight he'd gotten for him, the one that projected tiny butterflies on the walls. The only time Taylor normally used it was when his nightmares woke him. The frequency of them had lessened since Lane had started volunteering her time here Lyndon had observed. He too, had experienced fewer nightmares since she'd been in his life.

Chapter 26 

North Haven, Monday AM, May 16ᵗʰ, Ottawa, Canada

The term *slept like a rock* was now a tad more relatable after my restful sleep in the North Haven guest room. It was furnished in a similar manor to Kris's room, which answered the question as to if they had decorated it specifically for him or not. Based on the neutral yet luxurious décor of the guest room, much like one of those posh hotel rooms, both Kris's and this room had been set up by Julian and Max as part of a complete esthetic for the home. They may have set up all the suites and bedrooms with a standard look allowing the occupant to customize and make it their own, I figured. Which also confirmed that Kris had spent no thought on making his designated space here more personal.

Dressed and packed, I padded up the hall to the kitchen, where I found a much smaller host of angels to last night's garrison set up at the island. Julian was on the cooking side of the large island while Nic, Leo, and Rachel sat on the eating side.

"Well, look who's up," Julian said when he spied me coming up the hall. "Hungry?"

"Is that a trick question?" I laughed out. "Good morning, all!" The barstool between Leo and Rachel was open, and I took it.

"Good morning," Leo said as I slid into the spot next to him.

"Best coffee ever," Rachel said as a good morning, passing a cup of coffee over my way. "Kris wants to want to see you before you leave."

Nic leaned around Rachel and only nodded, having a mouth full of food, then he swallowed and said, "Hey, Lynn—morning!"

Julian set a dish down in front of me with a beautifully plated hollandaise dressed eggs benedict. "It's a favorite around here." He slid a napkin and cutlery next to the plate.

I stared lovingly down at the exquisite plate of food, then glanced up at Julian. "Will you marry me?" I asked, gazing at him adoringly.

"Hmmm, I'm tempted… but I'm in love with someone else," Julian said with a wink.

"I'd say your loss, but clearly the loss is mine." I picked up the knife and fork and cut a slice down the middle of the egg stack, then made a triangle cut and secured the piece on my fork. "Max is a lucky man," I praised, stuffing the probably too big piece into my mouth. "Yup—my loss," I added around the mouthful of deliciousness.

A chorus of laughter and praise for Julian's cooking prowess accompanied my chewing.

Nic nodded at me again, shoving an equally large triangle of eggs into his mouth. "The best," he said, mouth full, pointing his empty fork at me.

For the next 15 minutes, I devoured my decadent breakfast and two cups of scrumptious coffee, alongside the other likewise happy eaters. Over the rim of my last sip of coffee, I noticed a young, dark-haired woman appear in the entrance from the hallway to the kitchen. *Lane.* "Finally—we meet," I said, setting down my empty coffee cup to turn in my seat.

Without hesitation, arms open, Lane jogged the last few feet of the distance between us. "Lyyynn," she squealed, embracing me. "Thank you for bringing Uncle Kris home."

I hugged her back *hard*, like she was a long-lost member of my family. She kind of was, in a way. Julian and Max I considered new family, so it only seemed fitting she was part of that. "It was a joint effort," I said, grinning up at her as she released me and took a step back.

"I've heard all about you, and your friends—the gathering," Lane said, beaming with appreciation. "Uncle Leo told me all about your trip to Norway too—and the spy job you did with him at the Celaeno building. You're a regular Emma Peel."

"Ha! How do you know who Emma Peel is?" I asked, surprised at her reference. Most people her age were usually more familiar with The Avengers team that comprised Iron Man, Captain America, Hulk, Thor, Black Widow and Hawkeye, and not the original British TV show with Emma Peel and John Steed.

"We watch a lot of old TV shows and movies around here. Anywhere from Get Smart to the newer Mission Impossible."

"Oh, I love spy movies," Rachel said. "Have you seen The Kingsman movies?"

"Of course," Leo said in response. "Don't forget about the oldie-but-a-goodie, *The Man from U.N.C.L.E.*." He grinned at Rachel, then over at me.

Nic placed his knife and fork on his plate. "And all the spy movies directed by Alfred Hitchcock," he added, circling the island with his dishes.

"Wow, that makes sooooooo much sense now," I said, nodding and smiling at Nic and Leo, the TV show theme song *Secret Agent Man* running through the back of my memory. The Guards would have had to learn all that stealthy secret agent stuff somewhere, I supposed. Not like they taught it in college. Or maybe they did. What did I know?

"We'll leave for the airport in about an hour," Leo said, getting up from his seat and taking his empty plate to the sink. "Anything you need to do before we go?"

"Kris wanted to see me—and I'd like to talk with you, Lane," I said, turning my attention back to her. "If you have the time."

"Sure—I have time," Lane said. "And I don't have to leave for the group home until later."

"Going to bring him some breakfast now," Rachel said, taking with her the tray of food Julian had just arranged for him. "Lane, send me the name of that bar-restaurant you told me about."

Evidently, the two of them had made a Gen Z friend connection over the last 12 hours.

"*Drip House on Somerset*—Sent," Lane said as Rachel turned to leave with the plate of food. Then, she slid her cellphone back into her jean's pocket and took Leo's empty barstool next to me. "Did you have some?" she asked as Julian set down a fresh plate of eggs benedict in front of her.

"Oh ya!" I said, full of enthusiasm. "I asked Julian to marry me, but he said *no*." I gave her a deadpan expression, then burst into laughter.

She tried to stifle a giggle with a fisted hand to her mouth, but the absurdity of my statement escaped her in a fit of laughter.

"Eat!" Julian said in a chuckling demand.

"Yes, Dad," Lane responded, giving him an innocent smile.

Leo checked his watch, then said. "Lynn, I need to finish up a few things—but let's meet back here in 45 minutes."

Hopping off the barstool, I said, "You enjoy your meal, Lane. I'll be back down after seeing Kris. We'll talk then—deal?"

"Deal," Lane agreed around a mouthful of her breakfast.

Nic and Rachel were already headed for the door to Kris's suite, and I hurried to catch up with them.

"Good, you're up," Rachel said, entering the open door to Kris's room. "I'm hoping you're hungry."

"If you're not—I'll eat it," I said, although I was pleasantly full.

Kris was sitting up in his bed and looking much better than he had the night before. "Good morning," Kris said, giving the three of us an appreciative smile.

Rachel set the tray of food on Kris's lap before going around the other side of the bed. "Your vitals are good—improved overnight," she stated, reviewing the readings on the screen.

Nic checked a plastic bag that hung off the side of the bed. "Urine output is good—clear," he added. "We'll get rid of the catheter after you get some food down, then I can help you get to the bathroom if you need."

Kris gave Nic a weak grin, though I'm sure he was appreciative of his personal medical staff.

Changing the topic, I said, "I'll be leaving soon to catch my flight back home, but I wanted to see you before I left."

"I'm grateful," Kris said, picking up his utensils from atop the cloth napkin. "Do you two mind if I have some time alone with Lynn—before she has to leave?"

"Not a problem," Rachel said, finishing what I assumed was a patient note on a chart set next to the monitors. "I need to go get a shower and a change of clothes—but I'll be back later to relieve you, Nic." She circled back around the bed to where I stood and opened her arms for a hug. "Safe flight," she said, then whispered, *"I think he's going to be okay."*

"You are amazing. I love you so much," I whispered back, tightening my grip on her a bit more.

"I love you, too," she said, releasing me. "Later, boys."

"Thank you, again, Rachel," Kris said.

"Later," Nic tossed at Rachel as she left the room. "As for you...." He pointed at Kris. "... Don't even think about getting out of bed until I come back." He jabbed his finger at Kris again and then scowled. Then he turned and grinned at me. "Hope to see you again soon—but under better circumstances," he said, wrapping an enormous arm around my shoulders for a side hug and squeeze.

"Me too," I responded, the air returning to my lungs as he let me go.

"I'll come back for the tray later and you can try out your legs," he said to Kris, before turning and leaving the room.

"Okay," Kris called to Nic, waving his fork in the air. Then he whispered, *"I should keep this knife—just in case I need to escape."*

I laughed, sitting down in the chair next to the bed. "If that food is any indication—I think you got it made here." I gave him an exaggerated wink and nodded.

"Ya... you're probably right." He took another bite of the fantastic breakfast and chewed. "You're definitely right."

As Kris devoured his breakfast, I filled the silence. "I'm just going to toss this out there—but did you want me to talk with Jana again?" I watched as Kris paused before consuming his last bite of food, as though considering my offer. "It's totally up to you, but she might need more than just a *'he's doing fine'* from Den to ease her."

Kris chewed his last bite of food, staring down at the empty plate as he set his utensils on it. Then he took his napkin and dabbed at the corners of his mouth, swallowing slowly. "I'm sure the others have told you, but I wasn't a good guy...," he said, pausing again, still focused on his plate. "... for a long time. I know it—I mean, I know it now." He turned his head and looked at me, blowing out a tired breath. "Being with Jana... I realize now how different I was—I wasn't always a jerk, you know, not in the beginning. My... *arrogance* developed over time, and I turned away from the reason for my being here—my being created." He set the tray to the side, away from where I sat, and then focused back on me. "But with Jana, I was just me—the good me, the real me.... When my memories came back, I was reminded of how I used to be before my arrogance took over, the better me, the kinder, more compassionate... *me*." He reached for my hand. Taking it, he placed it in position for a handshake. "Hi, I'm Kris. I've changed."

I shook his hand back. "Hi, Kris. Wonderful to meet you." I gave him an understanding smile.

Still holding my hand, he said, "I am so embarrassed—no disgusted, by my past actions, at the male I was—the bastard that I've been." He glanced down at our clasped hands. "Jana deserves... well, she deserves better than me, that's for sure." He glanced up. "I can't go back... I can't ever see her again... and it is breaking me."

"You know... I had a conversation with Den and Marq around Valentine's Day—about if they had a special someone in their life, and they both mentioned the pain of loss and the loneliness." I held Kris's hand in both of mine. "It hadn't occurred to me until then how difficult something like that would be for all of you—with the slow aging and secrets—and all."

"I need to find a way to explain," Kris said, placing his free hand over mine, sealing the connection. "Maybe I could send her an email. Let her know that I'm doing better, thank her for her kindness and friendship—but... it was so much more than that to me. I can't really explain to her much more, other than what happened to me, and how I'm needed here."

"Kris, you will find the right words. You claim to be a changed… *male*. Use that rediscovered compassion to communicate with Jana. You know her—you'll know what to say."

At 9:30 a.m. Leo loaded my small suitcase into his truck for the drive to the airport.

"I got a chance to talk to Lane about Lyndon," I said as we pulled off the side road from North Haven and onto the main road.

"And?" Leo asked, shooting me an inquisitive look.

"She's scheduled to be at the group home today—like she said. Told me she'd let me know if she sees him this time."

"This whole thing with him catching her with Jules had me on edge," Leo said. "We figure Lyndon mustn't have mentioned it to anyone—bought Lane's explanation about her master's degree." When we stopped at the red light, Leo glanced at me. "I find it interesting that no one has approached Jules, though. I mean, she was in Brazil—now she's teaching in Ottawa. If Thaddeus knew she was here, I believe he would have had someone watching her."

"Does Thaddeus know she has a son?" I asked, realizing the implications now. Leo's concern wasn't about Jules, it was about her son. He was a halfling and one who had come of age.

"I'm going with *no*. Considering how desperate Thaddeus is to find halflings—Mason would be a prize specimen in his eyes. We'll have to keep an eye on both him and Jules for the time being. But like I said, my feeling is that Lyndon has said nothing."

"Why do you think that is?" I asked as we turned onto the long, winding road that led to the airport.

"Lane's theory on Lyndon, is that he's not as bad as we think he is. But my guess is that he's taken a liking to her and if she's around Jules often, he may not want any of Thaddeus's followers near Lane."

For whatever reason, I believed her when she told me about his kindness with Taylor, and that maybe he wasn't the monster we thought him to be. "She did say that he seems very protective of Taylor and who has access to him. So, you could be right about him having the same shielding need for Lane." I shrugged. "Not a bad thing, really."

Leo took the ramp and last stretch up to the departure drop-off area. "I can only hope that's what it is," he said, coming to a stop and putting the truck in park.

Unbuckling my seatbelt, I got out and met Leo at the back of the truck to where he'd stowed my bag. "Now what?" I asked.

"We'll put our attention back on finding Anael's daughter, for the most part," he said, extending the handle on my rolly-bag to hand it off.

"Right—the missing halfling." I gripped the extended handle of my suitcase. "Thank you again for letting me stay the night," I said, rolling the bag over next to me.

"I—we are forever grateful to you, Lynn—to you and your friends," he said, before pulling me in for an unexpected hug. "Helpless is a rare feeling. And one I do not manage well," he exclaimed.

"Ya, well—I'm not a fan of that feeling either. Trust me." I patted his back as if to ease the difficult feeling.

Releasing me from the hug, he said, "Your actions empowered us when we were all helpless."

"Team effort," I said, giving him a compassionate smile.

"Team work," Leo said in response. "Safe flight, Lynn."

"Keep me updated." I turned to go, then paused and said, "Thanks for the flight upgrade, by the way."

Leo smiled. "Anytime," he said, raising a hand in goodbye.

Following the flight security and immigration dance, I took a seat near the departure gate. Checking the time on my cellphone, I noted it was 10:30 a.m. which would be 3:30 p.m. Iceland time, and I took a chance at reaching Geir, hitting dial on the number he had given me.

"Halló," an accented male voice answered.

"Geir? It's Lynn—Den's friend."

"Yes—hi," he said, his voice sounding anxious.

"I'm sure Den has updated you on Kris's condition—but I wanted to talk to you about Jana." I shifted in my seat to look out one of the giant windows that allowed passengers to view the planes pulling up to the gates. "Kris and I spoke… about he and Jana."

"She's been a wreck since you left with him," Geir said. *"I'm here at her place—finally convinced her to get some rest. She's sleeping now."* His last words came out as a whisper.

"Kris said he was going to reach out to Jana, now that his memories are returning." I noticed an elderly couple holding hands in the next row of seats.

"He'll never be able to come back here—will he?"

I tore my gaze from the sweet couple. "No," I said. "Not with his acute environmental sensitivities." I swallowed hard, emotional, understanding the magnitude of the situation. "I can't say what will… or won't happen… but what I can tell you, from my conversation with Kris, is that it was very clear to me that Jana means more to him than either of you could possibly know."

Chapter 27 

When I came through the exit from arrivals, Redmond was there, waiting for me. I rolled my bag over to him and stood there, tilting my head back, gazing up at him. He bent at the knees, wrapped his arms around my torso and lifted me up so that we were face to face, my legs dangling above the ground. He said nothing, but I knew by his imploring expression that I had put him through a lot, too much, and not just with this last trip. It was from this one and the Norway trip, and the accumulation from each time I had put myself at risk. He pressed his lips to mine, tightening his hold on me. The kiss was like it was our first time, like the anticipation of finally pressing our lips together might kill us if we didn't do it. The years with him played like a movie behind my shut eyelids. He had accepted me just the way I was, all of me and the crazy happenings, without skepticism, without argument, and full of love and understanding. He was the love of my life, the father of my children, he was my home.

Redmond ended the kiss and set me down. Hands still holding me, he stared down and deep into my eyes. He shifted his hold, taking up one of my hands in his, grasping it firmly as he snatched up the handle of my rolling suitcase with his other. Then he walked me to the exit in a manner that felt more like we were on a date than the casual routine of being picked up at the airport.

No words were exchanged as we walked the route from inside the airport to the crosswalk outside and to the parking area. At the truck, Redmond held the door for me as I got in the passenger side, then he placed my suitcase in the backseat and proceeded to the driver's side to get in. He paused before starting the car, leaning across the center console my way, sealing his mouth over mine for another loving kiss.

As our lips parted, I stared at him. "You are the love of my life," I said, admiring his handsome yet worrisome face.

"I love you, Lynn," he said, holding my gaze. "Losing you is not something I would survive." We looked into each other's eyes for several heartbeats before he turned away and started the engine.

We held hands on the drive home, still no other words were exchanged. I knew what those few words he'd spoken meant beyond their obvious meaning. Nothing else need be said.

We arrived home to find Darius and Lily standing in the driveway. I was barely out of the truck when Darius scooped me up and over his shoulder and began berating me for putting myself in danger again. "I'm not saying I won't let you go on anymore capers, but you can't do them without me. I'm not getting any younger and you're going to give me a heart attack."

"Wow—yer not my husband—but you sure sound like him." I grinned at Redmond from my position over Darius's shoulder.

"Does he do this to you, too?" I asked Lily as Darius set me on my feet again.

"Don't get me started," Lily said, going in for a quick hug. "We just picked up the girls from school—need to head back to the studio now though."

Darius gave me a gentle shove, then said, "Try to stay out of trouble, would ya?"

"I'll try—and thanks for getting the girls. It was screwy timing with Redmond having to pick me up." Two high-pitched squeals came from the front deck, and I looked up to see Hayley and Ryley on the deck with Gabriel. "Thanks again," I called, turning back as Lily and Darius hopped into his car. I got a wave from Lily and Darius honked the horn as they drove off.

"Muuum!" Hayley yelled, pulling my attention back as she scrambled down the stairs to greet me.

I knelt and embraced her like I hadn't seen her in a year. "I missed you so much," I said, squishing her little body against mine.

"I can't breathe," Hayley said, gulping for breath and giggling as I freed her. She took my hand and led me up the stairs, and Redmond followed behind, carrying my suitcase.

"Hi, Mum!" Ryley called out, waving both her arms back and forth over her head.

"Hiiii," I said, meeting her at the top of the staircase. I knelt again and wrapped my free arm around her for an embrace while still holding Hayley's hand. I glanced up to see an unreadable expression on Gabriel's face. This couldn't have been easy for him either, none of it, especially not being able to assist us.

"Don't you normally volunteer on Mondays?" he asked, as though all was normal.

"Nope. Tuesday, Wednesday, and Fridays," I said, letting go of the twins to stand and give him his own hug. We rarely embraced, and he tensed at first when I wrapped my arms around him. Then he relaxed and encircled me in his arms. *I'm sorry if I scared you,* I whispered against the front of his shirt.

Like a parent, Gabriel kissed the top of my head before releasing me from his hold. "I'll leave you to your homecoming," he said before vanishing.

"Mum, we have a surprise for you," Ryley said, taking up my hand and pulling me through the open door into the house.

Hayley was jumping up and down in front of a large, framed piece of artwork, the image coming into view as I approached it.

"Marq took it—had it enlarged and framed for us," Redmond said, running a finger along the frame's bottom edge. "As a thank you—for bringing Kris back."

The gift was artwork, but not a painting. It was a 2 x 3 foot colour photo of a beautiful moment captured of Hayley and Ryley with Summer and Snow near the opening of the path to the beach. The girls were kneeling in the sand, each face to face with one of the dogs, their noses touching, and their eyes closed. Sun shone through their hair as though a breeze lifted it out behind them. Hovering around the four were several butterflies, a few large white-winged, black-tipped ones, several of the butter-yellow ones, and one lone monarch. I reached out to touch the monarch then pulled my hand back in fear of leaving a smudge print on the glass. "It's amazing—magical, really."

"I'd say," Redmond agreed. "He's got an expert eye for composition. He took several others, but this one was the best."

"I'll be sure to thank him when I see him next," I said, noticing then the girls were smiling, beaming up at me. "What?" I asked, wondering if there was more.

"Show Mum your artwork we put up in our bedroom," Redmond instructed, turning, and rolling my suitcase toward the bedroom.

In our room, on the wall next to my floor-length mirror, was another framed piece of artwork, this one definitely a painting and similar in size to the new photo in the front hall of the twins and their faithful companions.

"Marq helped us," Hayley said, holding up her hand, palms forward.

"But we did most of it ourselves," Ryley added, fluttering her hands at me.

The painting comprised tiny handprints forming the wings of different butterflies like the ones shown in the earlier photo. Finer details had been added to the butterfly shapes with a skilled hand, and more than likely the part Marq had painted, bringing the butterflies to life.

I dropped to my knees again and pulled both of them into a hug. It had felt fantastic to help Leo and the others, but nothing felt as good as being home with my family. "Thank you so much for this beautiful gift—I love you girls so much—and I missed you like crazy."

"They're quite the little artists," Redmond said behind me. From my kneeling position, I turned to look at him. "Marq is considering opening a gallery in Ottawa—with a feature wall for young artists just like our two here. He has a gallery in Italy right now, it's kind of like his cover for him being there near the Electra facility in Rome."

"Rome—now there's a place I'd like to visit—on vacation, I mean," I raced out, making sure he knew it wasn't for any other reason.

"Oh—and I fixed the lights over the mirror," he said then, pointing up at the recessed lighting over our heads. "And the ones in the girls' bedrooms and bathroom, too."

"Was that part of your fun weekend with your father?" I asked the girls, tickling each of them in their armpits and making them giggle. "Let me unpack, and then you can tell me all about it." I stood and crossed the room to where Redmond still held my suitcase. I went up on my toes and kissed him lightly on the mouth, then took the handle of the suitcase from him.

"Com'on girls," Redmond said, waving a hand for them to follow him. "Let's give your mum some time to unpack."

Unpacked and my worn clothes now in the hampers, I left the bedroom to where I found Redmond and the girls at the dining table.

"Mum—we're having a tea party," Ryley said as I approached.

Redmond, who was sitting at the head of the table, handed me a teacup filled with water. "I didn't think you would mind," he said. "The girls helped me tidy up the storage closets downstairs, and we found a box with your mother's teacups there."

"I'd forgotten about these," I said, examining the white fluted teacup decorated with purple pansies and dark green leaves. My mother had saved various teacups given to her from one of my father's aunts. They were all different, not one matching pair in the collection, and it was why I had loved them so much.

"We're being very careful," Hayley said, showing how she was holding the blush pink teacup with both hands. "Da made a special space for them in the cabinet." She set her cup down on the saucer and pointed at the tall open-shelf cabinet behind me, the one that held photos of my mother and my Aunt Kay.

Turning, I noticed that Redmond had rearranged the photos and the few trinkets I had on the open shelves to make room for all the teacups and their matching saucers. "I think it's perfect. Your Grandma Sally would love they are being displayed *and* used. I should have done that years ago." I smiled at Redmond, then mouthed a *"Thank you."* Then I slid into the open seat across the table from the girls. They were kneeling on the bench, which helped them sit up higher. "Tell me about your fun weekend," I requested, taking a sip of the cool water in my teacup.

"We went roller skating," Ryley said. She took a sip from her teacup, making a slurping sound.

"Roller skating—really?" I raised my eyebrows and cut a glance at Redmond.

"Did you know there was a roller rink just north of us?" he asked, bringing his teacup to his lips, pinky finger out.

"You gotta try it, Mum," Hayley exclaimed. "It's really fun."

"I fell a lot, but Da is really good at it," Ryley said, slurping her tea again.

Redmond gave me several eyebrow raises as though confirming Ryley's assessment of his skating talents.

"Oh, I've been roller skating plenty," I said, sipping my tea water with confidence. "Your Aunt Mac and I used to go every weekend when we were in our early teens."

"That sounds like a long time ago," Ryley said with a serious face. "You might need some lessons."

Redmond looked at me, his lips in a tight smile. "I'll show your mum how it's done," he said, gently tapping his teacup against mine.

"It's a date," I said, holding my teacup up higher. "Family skate night."

The girls raised their teacups and cheered.

"Who's hungry?" Redmond asked then, getting up from the table.

"Meeeeeee," Hayley said, before tipping back the last of her tea water.

"Me too," I said in agreement. Both my girls loved to eat, especially when their Da was cooking. So did I. Like mother, like daughters. Hayley and I both detested mushrooms with every fiber of our being, though Ryley and Redmond loved them, but Ryley and I had similar appetites, the fact of the matter being that we were always hungry.

After a fabulous dinner of Redmond's homemade pizza and infamous chocolate cake for dessert, we sat out on the deck as a family until it was time for the girls to get ready for bed.

Summer and Snow followed the twins to their bedrooms, watching as the girls went through their bedtime routines of changing into PJs, brushing their teeth, and washing their faces. Then each dog chose a room, resting down on the floor between the bedroom door and the foot of the bed, as each of the girls slid in under their respective covers.

Redmond and I took turns kissing the girls and wishing them a good night before closing the doors to their bedrooms. "Let's call it an early night," I requested, clasping his hand, and leading him up the hall to our bedroom.

"You just want me to tell you my roller-skating secrets," he teased, shutting the bedroom door behind us.

"You found me out," I said, letting go of his hand to jump up on the bed with enthusiasm that echoed the girls. "Spill." I laid back and plumped a pillow behind my head.

Redmond climbed onto the bed with the energy of a man who had gone roller skating for the first time in decades, every movement calculated as though his legs might give out on him. "If we go roller skating, remind me to stretch after." He groaned as the side of his face hit the pillow next to me. "Who knew roller skating in a circle for two hours could kill a man," he said, mouth partially squished into the pillow.

I rubbed my hand over his back. "I'm sorry I added to the not-so-fun part of your weekend."

"You can pay me back by helping get my jeans off," he chuckled into the pillow, his exposed eye crinkling with his grin. Then he rolled onto his back, grunts and groans accompanying each of his movements.

"Are you really that sore?" I asked, concerned, watching his face contort in pain until he was resting on his back.

"I'll be fine," he said. "But I'm serious, though—I might need help with my jeans."

"Okay," I said, amused, a burst of laughter escaping from me.

"Don't laugh—just wait until you see how *you* feel after."

"This coming from the man who's been training with Super Angels?" I laughed again. "You poor baby."

Redmond reached out a hand and grabbed me, pulling me into him, my cheek pressing against his chest. With each breath he took, his chest rose and fell. I listened to his heartbeat pound and then slow to a resting thump-thump.

"I updated Luc," Redmond said then, his words rumbling through his chest against my ear. "Marq updated Derek, and of course, Darius updated Lily."

"Good." I stretched an arm across Redmond's chest. "Olivia made sure Mac and Alison were given the latest." I lifted my head to look at his face. "Mac actually found Kris—did I tell you that?"

He shifted his head to look at me. "No. What do you mean?"

"Ya, her locator spell worked—well, kind of. Each time she tried it, it gave off that sulfur smell of rotten eggs," I said, resting my head back on his chest. "But she hadn't realized it had anything to do with him."

"Oh—man!" Redmond's laughter rumbled in his chest, causing my head to bounce up and down. "How was he—Kris, when you spoke with him?" Redmond asked.

"Not great. I mean he's memory is back, and he's feeling much better, but…." I blew out a breath and shifted onto my back. "… did I ever tell you what Marq and Den said to me on Valentine's Day—when I asked them if either of them had a special someone in their lives?"

"Nope," he said, groaning again as he turned onto his side to face me.

I stared up at the ceiling. "Marq said they rarely have someone in their lives."

"Why?" Redmond asked, playing with a strand of my hair.

"Mainly because of the pain of loss," I said, my lips pushing out in a pout. "Makes things difficult with commitment—not knowing how long you can stay with someone before… well, before they notice you're not aging like they are."

"How stupid of me—hadn't even thought of that."

"I wished I hadn't mentioned it to them." I turned my head to look at Redmond. "Den said he wasn't sure what was worse, the loneliness or losing someone."

"Horrible to live so long—without a partner by your side." Redmond brushed my hair back from my face, leaning in to kiss me. "I am grateful we can grow old together," he said against my lips.

My cellphone chimed then. I'd plugged it in to charge on my nightstand. The type of chime indicated I had a new email, but I didn't move to check it.

"Email?" Redmond asked.

"Yup." I continued to admire his face.

"Could be an update—you should check it."

"Fine," I sighed, rolling away from him to the other side of the bed, grabbing up my phone. "It's from Vicki."

She'd written,

> Hi, Lynn.
>
> I'm sure you have already come to this conclusion, I'm sure you all have, but I would prefer not to be involved with anything relating to celestials of any kind. I'm in my 60s now, and I'm focusing on enjoying my retirement and traveling with Eric.
>
> What it comes down to is that I don't want to have to watch my back or be fearful of some psycho—child abuser. My role in this is done and has been done since the gathering. Frankly, I was relieved when it was all over. Then you brought things back around again with the helping of these Earthbound on their search. I understand your need to help, and your involvement, I really do, though I hope you can understand why I don't want to do this anymore. It has all become too much. I will always provide translations if you need me, but I'm done. This was my last mission.
>
> Secret Agent Quinn is out.

I sighed again. "Well, it looks like Vicki is out—for good."

"What?" Redmond rolled with a groan to my side of the bed.

I read the email aloud for him, then said, "Let me send her a quick message."

I wrote back,

> I'm so sorry I never realized how all this might impact you. Honestly, I thought you wanted to be a part of it too, like the others. It was selfish of me. I understand that now. I just wanted you with me, with us, and I wanted all of us together again.
>
> It's different for me in that it will never not be a part of my life. Gabriel is a part of my life, my family's lives. He is family and the others have become part of our family now.

> *I'm excited for you and the plans that you have made, and I look forward to hearing about your and Eric's adventures.*
> *Take lots of photos!*
> *Love Lynn*

I placed my cellphone back on the nightstand and then rested back on my pillow.

"Vicki may be out, but it's a good thing you stayed at her place. Since she's not been involved in any of this, I mean," Redmond stated, still on his side.

"Ya, yer probably right." I glanced at him, then turned back to staring up at the ceiling. "It was an interesting birthday, I have to say." Shifting the mood, I blew out a breath and rolled to face him, smiling playfully, then said, "So, what do you wanna do for *your* birthday next month?"

Chapter 28 

SNOW Restaurant, Sunday June 26th, New York City, USA

For more than 6 months, Frank had been running the restaurant all on her own. Not that she hadn't been running it mostly herself before, but now she'd been doing it all, everything from menu planning and ordering the produce, to marketing and social presence, and even mingling with the who's who of the city when they came to dine at the restaurant. She had done whatever had needed doing, all the while saving face and concealing her worry over Kris's absence. The Guards had located him, finally, but Kris had been focused on recovering since then. It had been heavy, both the running of the restaurant and her worry over her missing friend. She was proud of how well she'd handled things and hoped Kris would feel the same once he returned.

This morning, she was completing the last finishing touches for the Pride Event she'd been working on these past few months. Tonight, at the restaurant, she was hosting the city's elite in the LGBTQ+ community for an evening of dining and donating to The Center, and as a closing to the Pride Celebrations that would be happening all day today.

For almost 40 years, *The Center* has been a welcoming environment and resource base for the LGBTQ+ community, both residents and visitors to the city. It's a place to connect and engage, a place to find camaraderie and support. They offer everything from advocacy, health and wellness programs to arts, entertainment, and cultural events. They also provide recovery, parenthood, and family support services, and why it has been her personal favorite organization since its inception in 1983.

"Looks like you have everything under control here," a familiar voice called from the main doors. Frank turned, stunned slightly at the not so familiar appearance of her friend, business partner, and the 2nd Son of Haven, Kristopher Snow.

"It's going great—better than before you left, actually. Nice ball cap, by the way," Frank said as Kris sauntered over. "Where did you get those jeans—the thrift store on East 84th?" She squinted. "And is that a plain white cotton t-shirt you're sporting there?"

Kris gave her a joyful smile. "You look... *different*. Great—but different," Kris said, giving her the once over. "Dare I say, *softer*?"

"This old thing?" She glanced down at her outfit. Frank had changed up some of her usual dark suits and black attire for lighter shades, like the white dress suit she was wearing now. She'd stopped wearing the dark makeup too, opting for a more natural look, since she had no need for mascara with her naturally long dark lashes.

"What's all this?" Kris asked, perusing the wonderful, donated items she'd received. He picked up the case containing an Enzo Ferrari Limited Edition fountain pen.

"These are all for the silent auction tonight. That pen is valued at $4000."

Kris put the pen back on the table. "How much for the ink?" he asked.

"Forty bucks," she said. "But you'll have to get that yourself—the pen doesn't come with it."

Kris laughed, then his face turned serious. "I'm sure you already know this—but the others think the restaurant is being watched," he said.

"They told me. I had a feeling it might be after Marcus was here, grilling me about my working for a *human*."

Kris held her gaze. "How are you?"

"I should be asking you that," Frank said, feeling strangely emotional suddenly.

Kris raised his hand towards her as if offering a handshake. Puzzled, she offered her hand out to him. Instead of shaking it, he wrapped his hand over hers, gripping it firmly, pulling her into a bear hug. "I'm sorry I made you worry," he said, holding her in place, pressing the side of his face against her cheek.

He *had* made her worry, she thought, struggling to escape his hold. But at her size and strength, even after his long recovery, Kris was still stronger than her. "You scared the shit out of me, you bastard," she said, attempting again to free herself. Then she gave in, wrapping her arms around him and collapsing into his hold.

"*Bastard*? I may not have a mother, but that's no way to talk to your favorite person," Kris said as they embraced.

"Second favorite," she said back, giving his ribcage a healthy squeeze.

"How… is Ina?" Kris asked on the exhale to her squeeze.

"Besides being my everything?" Frank said, releasing her hold on his torso and stepping back. "Pissed at me for all the time I've had to put into this event. I've had to work long hours without you here."

"Yikes—the wrath of Ina," Kris joked, brushing a hand down the front of his t-shirt.

Ina was the kindest of them all, and Kris knew it. Especially having to put up with her desire to run this business with him. "Are you taking part in the Pride Parade this year? You know the deal—it kicks off at noon on 25th Street and 5th Avenue—ends at 16th Street and 7th Avenue, before passing by the Stonewall National Monument and the AIDS Memorial."

"I'd love to—but…," he said, then dashed off to the kitchen. Returning he handed her the ornate wooden box that held the expensive cigars. "Here—add these to your auction table." He headed her the box, then turned slowly, as though giving the restaurant a thorough review. "I'm not staying, Frank," he said then.

"What do you mean you're not staying—for the event—in the city, New York? What?" Her hands fisted at her sides.

He stepped in closer and put his hands on her shoulders. "You are my best friend, Francesca."

"Don't you start with that best-friend-Francesca bullshit." She gripped his forearms with the intention of pulling a combat move on him, but then she dropped her head instead, closing her eyes in surrender. She felt his forehead touch hers.

"Frank, you love this place. You were always better at running it than I ever was." He squeezed her shoulders gently. "I've been an asshole."

"Ya, you have." She sniffled, head still down.

Kris chuckled. "I'm sorry for everything—all the BS, for not being a nicer male, for not being a better friend."

She lifted her head, dropping her hold, and glared at him. "Not sure what it is," she said. "Something… in the eyes… your demeanor— maybe… *something*." She shook her head. "You look different, too— and I don't mean the ball cap."

He squeezed her shoulders once more before letting his hands drop. "I *am* different."

"What happened to you? I mean, I know what happened—how you ended up in Iceland and all, but something else must have happened—while you were there—to change your attitude."

"I met someone. She showed me—somehow reminded me of how I used to be before I became such a jerk…."

"Asshole," Frank reminded.

"… Asshole," he repeated.

"I know you can't be thinking of going back there—the sulfur will kill you." Frank put her hands on her hips, ready to dish out a lecture if he needed it.

Kris sighed, then said, "No, I'm not going back."

Frank threw her hands in the air. "Then where—where are you headed?" she asked, shaking her hands at him.

"Well, I'm going to open another restaurant. I found a great location in Ottawa, for a more casual style restaurant/bar… and I'm leaving at the end of the week. This way I can be part of The Guards again—be where I'm needed." He took a quick glance around at the restaurant again. "This place… our restaurant…," Kris said, extending his arms out to the side. "… is all yours—if you want it."

* * *

Frank glanced at the date on the calendar next to the swinging door of the kitchen, July 31st. It had been 5 weeks since Kris had handed off full ownership of the restaurant to her. And like she had done during his absence before taking ownership, she was doing her usual early morning review of the inventory orders when the front door melody chime sounded, notifying her someone had come in. "Hello?" called an unfamiliar female voice, following the chime.

Frank pushed through the swinging door into the main restaurant area. "Hi—how can I help you? We're not actually open for service yet."

Just inside the restaurant's main doors, stood an attractive blonde Nordic looking woman. "I'm sorry to bother you, but I'm looking for Kisur—I mean *Kris*," she said, adjusting her purse strap.

"Kris… isn't here right now," Frank informed her. It had been a long while since any woman had come looking for Kris, she mused.

The woman leisurely scanned the restaurant. "Do you know when he will be back?"

"I'm not sure, actually—he's out-of-town working on something—a new venture." Frank strolled closer. "I'm Frank—the owner. Is there something I can assist you with?" Frank looked back as Ina came out from the back office.

"Hello," Ina said, obviously curious about the visitor.

Frank extended a hand Ina's way. "This is my mate—wife, Ina," she said, fumbling out the words.

"Lovely to meet you both," the woman said, pausing. She nodded. The expression she gave them was one of surprise that quickly shifted into what Frank could only read as understanding. "I knew I was taking a big chance by coming here…." she began again.

"Wait," Frank interjected. "Are you Kris's *somebody* from Iceland?" Frank glanced over at Ina and then back at the woman.

"What?" she questioned, her expression anxious.

Frank stepped forward. "Kris said he met somebody when he was there." This had to be her, Frank grasped.

"I guess I am," she said, tentatively, giving Frank a pleased smile.

"Jana, right?" Frank grinned.

The woman's smile widened. "Yes—Jana—correct."

Frank crossed her arms over her chest. "I don't know what you did—but Kris came back a changed male—man." She needed to work on getting those labels right when speaking with humans.

"Well, I got the same impression from the email he sent," Jana said, appearing more relaxed now. "He wrote that he was doing some changing—working on becoming a better person, a better *brother*. Said he had a lot to make up for." Jana fiddled with the strap of her purse again.

"Ya, he does," Frank said, glancing at Ina again.

Ina gave a small laugh. "I'll leave the two of you to talk," she said then. "I have an errand to run." She gave Frank a peck on the cheek.

Frank watched as the love of her life left out through the front door of the restaurant. The door chime melody sounding again as she did. "Don't get me wrong—he wasn't always an asshole," Frank said, focusing back on Jana.

"I never saw that side of him. Lucky, I guess. Thank you—sorry to bother you," Jana said, turning to leave as though there wasn't more for her here.

"I take it Kris didn't know you were coming?" Frank asked then, stopping her from leaving.

Turning back around, Jana said, "No." She stared down at the floor. "My guess is he would have told me not to, had I given him a heads up." She glanced up but didn't look directly at Frank. "After the way he had looked the last time I saw him—at the hospital, I just needed to know—see for myself that he was truly okay." Her eyes met Frank's.

"Wait here," Frank said, dashing off to the back office. Returning, she said, "I'm sure I'll get an earful from Kris—but here." Frank handed her a square coaster. She waited as Jana reviewed the words on it.

Jana frowned at Frank. "Après SNOW. *After*—SNOW?" she questioned, shaking her head. Then she flipped the coaster over displaying a stylized maple leaf on the backside along with an address.

Shrugging, Frank said, "That's the *something* Kris is working on right now." Frank grinned at her. "It was really nice to meet you, Jana," she said, before turning and heading off back to the kitchen.

As 11 a.m. rolled around, all meaning of staff were in the kitchen in full action preparing for the Sunday afternoon lunch seating. Frank patted the new General Manager on the back as she exited the kitchen. Heading to the back office, Frank halted as a shiver ran the length of her spine. She cut a glance over her shoulder to see… *Thaddeus*. The bastard smiled and waved at her as if they were old friends. Frank's back muscles tensed as she turned and took several calculated strides in his direction. "Sorry, we're all booked for this afternoon's lunch service. Try back next year—or never." Frank crossed her huge arms over her chest, puffing it out like she had done in her bouncer days, back when she had to deal with the riffraff.

"I have no interest in eating here," Thaddeus said, turning his nose up as though unimpressed. "Marcus told me you were working here, for a human—and I just had to see it for myself."

"This is my place. The person Marcus is referring to was just a chef when I found him—I made him famous. Now I just use the name."

"Where is this chef?" Thaddeus looked past Frank in the direction of the kitchen door.

"He's off on an adventure somewhere. I don't really need him now—he's trained up all my other chefs, so no need." Frank stepped to the side blocking his view of the way to the kitchen. "What are you doing here—shouldn't you be running that bogus research facility in Canada?"

"I have seven locations around the world. One of them is here—if you must know." Thaddeus panned the big open space of the main dining area. "Needed to make a stop at my favorite bakery."

Frank knew all about Thaddeus's facilities around the world but didn't let on that she knew. She also knew from Kris that the sadist had an addiction for the Magnolia Bakery just around the corner.

"I'm looking at some new ventures, actually—but it's nothing you would understand."

"Bully for you," Frank said, pushing past him to grab the handle to the main door. "Please don't come again," she added, holding the door open for him.

Chapter 29 

Since returning from my belated birthday weekend with my girlfriends, the one that had started with a day at the spa and ended with rescuing a missing angel and one of The Guards, I'd made spending time with family my #1 priority.

Saturday was now dinner out and a movie, Sunday was cooking together as a family and game night, and after celebrating Redmond's birthday at the roller-rink in June, we'd established a weekly family roller skate night on Thursdays. The girls were fearless as usual, Redmond was a better skater than I had imagined, and my technique, which was not that bad, continued to improve each time we went. Redmond and I had a standing lunch-date every Friday after my morning volunteering, and we made a point of having a real date night once a week, with the assistance from friends taking turns babysitting the girls, which included Den and even Marq when he was here visiting from Rome, turning out to be a win-win all around. My hospital gig had been blissfully uneventful, and I'd not felt or seen any sign of Archangel Diniel. And, with Redmond's support, I had also dedicated more time to my self-defense training at the South Haven.

I'd been back at it several days a week and in the afternoons after my volunteer time at the hospital. Working my body this hard had reminded me that I wasn't in my 20s, or my 30s, hell not even in my 40s anymore. But I was getting stronger and more agile with each session. I had even impressed Den with my reverse weight influence, and touch and pressure point combat skills. Ben had me concentrating on techniques that required no strenuous force while Den had me focusing on techniques that generated maximum force like takedowns, chokeholds, joint locks, sweeps and grappling, steering clear of any weapons training for now. Both methods they were teaching me were about defending and aiding me in escape should I ever find myself at the mercy of a predator.

They'd also advised me on some hard facts. Like depending on the blow, that size/mass/strength does matter, keeping in mind that a woman's bone structure—my bone structure, is naturally less dense, and if a man punches a woman square and hard in the face, he can break her bones. Conversely, if I were to punch a man in the face, I'm likely to break my fingers. Both Den and Ben had agreed that the most useful martial art for a woman to study for self-protection was Ju Jitsu, because it teaches you how to use leverage to your advantage. The techniques show a woman how to use a man's heft against him. But today's lesson was on sneaky moves a woman can pull on a man should he surprise her with an attack.

"You don't have to be a warrior to fight. You're a strong woman with a strong self-preservation sense," Den said, when I groaned about not being big enough.

"Got it!" I said, though I wished I were a warrior and built like our friendly Steward, Purah.

"Moves better suited for you are chops or punches to the Adam's apple and palm strikes to the nose, thumb gouges to the eyes, boxing the ears… and knees or kicks to the groin," Den explained. "Generally, the soft areas of a man's face and groin are all excellent targets. Kicks to the knees could take a guy down as well."

"I'm a fan of elbow strikes, at least for in-close fighting," I tossed out. "I can hit harder with my elbow than my hand."

"And your elbow can take more of an impact," Den said in agreement.

"Plus, you told me that a quick shot to the gut or chin can stun a person just long enough to get away."

"Or at least put enough distance between you and them so you can use your legs, which are your stronger weapons," Den reminded, crossing his big arms over his massive chest.

"What if they have a knife against your throat? What should you do?" I knew that today's lesson didn't involve weapons, but what if the bad guy had one, I'd wondered? "I mean, if they want you to go somewhere, should you obey, if the alternative is to get knifed right there?"

"How likely do you think an attacker would actually knife you?" Den asked, uncrossing his arms.

That was a tricky question and not exactly a rhetorical one, but considering how eager Den appeared, I probably should know the answer.

When I shrugged, he said, "We taught you to fight no matter what. If an attacker is willing to knife you in a public place, he'd do far crueler in a secluded location. Remember, 90 percent of women taken to a secondary location, do… not… survive." He drew out the last words clearly for emphasis to drive the fact home.

"I suppose if his goal is murder, he'd just slit my throat and be done with it."

"His intentions might still be murder, but after your compliance. Either way, you need to fight. Never…."

"I know, never—never—never let him take you to a second location," I said, reflecting to him that I *was* listening.

"Right! Take your chances where you are."

After an hour of practicing different methods to fight off an attacker and several turns on escaping someone who has you pinned on the ground, Den proposed a break. "I refilled your water bottle for you, here," he said, handing it to me. "You need to stay hydrated."

"Thanks." Thirst was a constant during these sessions, so I seized the water bottle and took a long draw from it. Then, before Den could tell me to, I flopped down on the corner of the padded training mat to do some stretches.

"That's my girl—stretching makes recovery that much faster," Den praised, grabbing up his cellphone.

It sure did. I gave him a thumbs-up.

He returned my gesture with his own thumbs-up, then he walked to the far side of the room to make a call. He sat down on the end of the seat at the bench press rack, chatting.

I was out of earshot, but I could see him smiling and laughing as part of the conversation. Despite my having made a mental note to ask Den more about Geir, and about Gavin, after what I'd witnessed with Kris and the pain he'd shown me over never seeing Jana again, I'd thought it best to keep my curiosity to myself. Den's past was none of my business and if there was something between him and the girls' teacher, it would show itself. I secretly hoped there was something there, but I also didn't want either of them to get hurt. Movement near the door to the training area pulled my attention away from my observing Den.

"A little birdie told me you wanted to learn to shoot," Kris said, strolling in and over to the training matts. He was in training gear, similar to what I wore, black nylon tactical pants, a grey close-fitting t-shirt and black combat boots, though I was wearing my ox-blood doc martins since combat boots like the ones The Guards wore didn't come in my small size.

"That wouldn't be a tall auburn-haired bird named Redmond, would it?" I asked, getting up from the floor and rushing over to greet him.

He nodded, then said, "I'll never tell."

"I'd hug you—but I'm all sweaty."

"Ya gross," he said, then swiftly yanked me in for a hug. "I'm told you're getting good—getting stronger."

"She is," Den said, coming up next to us. "Lynn, I need to cut our session short—I have an errand to run."

Kris released the hug. "I'll babysit her," he said before Den turned to leave.

"No worries," I called after him, then I swatted Kris's arm for the babysitting comment.

"Ouch." Kris rubbed his arm mockingly. "Show me some guns."

"Be afraid," I said, giving him a double bicep pose.

"Wow—check you out." He squeezed my biceps. "Speaking of guns, I brought you a little surprise—as a thank you—you know for rescuing me," he said, scrunching up his face and shrugging, pretending as though he considered the event as nothing.

"Oh that—ya, no biggy. You coming to visit is thanks enough." I rolled my eyes, but I really was thrilled he was here.

Then, from behind his back, in his left hand, he presented me with a black pouch.

"Whaa…?" I questioned, glancing back and forth at each of his hands. The item I recognized as a pocket holster only because Redmond had one, and in his left hand he displayed a small black handgun.

"It's yours," Kris said, extending his hands out to me, bringing them side by side so the sides of his hands touched.

"Mine?" I stepped back, suddenly anxious about being near the gun.

"You said you wanted to learn to shoot—better to have your own to practice with." He slid the gun into the holster pouch.

My mouth gaping, I stared down at the holstered gun then back up at his face.

"It can be intimidating at first—even scary, I understand that. But don't worry, we'll take it slow." He clasped my elbow, steering me back to the corner of the mat where I'd been stretching. Then he guided me down, lowering himself to the mat. "Let's go over the gun's anatomy first—it's not loaded by the way."

I sat next to him, watching this time as he *removed* the gun from the holster.

Waving the holster, he said, "This is a soft pocket pistol holster, and it works great inside your waistband, pocket, or purse. They call it the comfort holster and it's the thinnest one available, and it conceals very well." He handed it to me.

It was lightweight, soft, and pliable.

"Redmond told me he has an M&P9, this is similar, but the Shield is smaller," he said then, holding the pistol out. "They took the features and power of the full size M&P and put them into a smaller, slimmer, lighter weight pistol. The laser sighting is nice, lets you use it day or night." He flicked on the red laser. "Wherever the red dot is, a bullet will follow. Makes aiming easier, but it can also give away your position before you shoot." He shut off the laser, then took up my empty hand, placing the gun on the palm. "Feel that?" he said, running a finger over the surface. "Textured grip for enhanced control."

I dropped the holster to use both hands to hold the gun. Then I ran a thumb over the surface. The gun was supposed to be lightweight, but it was much heavier than I thought it would be.

Kris took the gun back and removed a silver piece from the inside. Then he took a similar-looking piece from the thigh pocket of his pants. "This is the magazine, these are cartridges—the front copper part is the actual bullet." He handed me the empty magazine from my gun first, then the one he'd taken from his pocket.

Clearly, the magazine with the bullets was heavier and must add to the weight of the gun. I said nothing and handed both magazines back to him. Then Kris ran down the different parts of the pistol, from the magazine well at the bottom of the grip, to the trigger, trigger guard, muzzle, barrel, chamber, pointing out both front and rear sights, the hammer and slide release and lastly the safety.

He ran through them all several more times, explaining their purpose and until I could recite them by heart as he pointed to the various parts. "Nicely done," he said, sliding the magazine with the bullets back into his pocket. "Now let's go to the range." He pushed up from the floor and extended a hand to help me up.

I took it. I was feeling majorly wobbly, not from the training session with Den but from the info dump Kris had just laid on me and the thought of actually shooting a gun. Still, I followed Kris to the enclosed shooting range on the opposite side of the parking area from the training room. We came to stand in front of what Redmond had referred to as the *bullet trap*, the lane area of the gun range. This range had seven lanes.

"If we were actually shooting, I'd get you to put on ear and eye protection when in here." He pointed to a set of both on the shooting bench. "Just to be on the safe side, treat every firearm as if it is loaded—even if you know it's not, and keep it pointed down range. The full length of these lanes is 25 yards, but there's a mechanism that can bring the target closer if needed." Kris took a shooting stance, legs parted at shoulder width, arms extended, holding the gun out. "Always keep your finger outside of the trigger guard until you're ready to fire." Kris set the gun down on the shooting bench. "If you're not ready, please don't feel pressured to do so," he said, his dark navy-blue eyes fixed on me, his expression one of concern.

He was an expert in all things regarding weaponry and he had been skillful in his instructions to me. I understood everything, all of it, but honestly, I still felt uneasy, queasy actually, as I still wasn't sure I was ready to pull the trigger, bullets or not. "This… this gift, I really do appreciate it and I'm so glad to see you—doing so much better, by the way. But you're right—I'm not ready, sorry." I turned and stared down range at the target. It displayed the torso of a cartoon version of a classic zombie frayed clothing, and all. Normally, something like that would have totally amused me, but I was too nauseous to laugh. "It was so generous of you to come here. Sorry if I wasted your time."

I watched from the corner of my eye as Kris placed my new gun back in my new holster. Then he turned me to face him. "Lynn—don't worry about it—enough with the apologies, please," he said, sympathetic and full of understanding. "Shooting a gun is not something one does lightly." He paused and handed me the holstered gun. "You take as much time as you need—seriously."

"I want to—I want to be brave enough… I feel the need to know how to shoot."

"But you're just not ready, like you said."

I nodded and forced a grin.

"And brave—has nothing to do with it. You're one of the bravest people I know."

We spent the next half hour catching up, me sharing the uneventful last 2 months of my life, and him with the details of what he'd been through with his recovery. He didn't bring up Jana, so neither did I.

"You should drop over later, meet Redmond and the girls in person," I said to Kris as I wheeled my bike back through the garage and out the security door. "I'm really proud of you," I said to him, before pushing off and peddling up the road.

"I'm proud of you, too," I heard Kris yell out to me.

I waved back at him and then continued my ride home.

When I rode up the driveway, a cellphone text chime sounded from within my knapsack. I stowed my bike first, then checked my phone.

Olivia had messaged me with,

> *Hi Lynnie. Mac said she found something witchy regarding the mirrors, about an obsidian 'spirit mirror' used by John Dee, involving divination, and talking to angels. There's more obviously, and Alison recorded most of it in her notes, but I just wanted to give you a quick follow-up regarding what you shared with us about the twins and the mirrors.*

I wrote back,

> *Hey, just got home from my training, need to shower, eat, you know. If you guys feel up to it, let's circle back and have a video chat tomorrow on the topic.*

Years ago, I had read about John Dee as part of my research into Enoch when all this angel stuff had first started. Dee was a mathematician and an occultist, among other things, who studied the supernatural, and claimed to have received the Enochian language from angels in the late 16th-century. They used the language in Enochian magic, which Mac had explained to me was a system of ceremonial magic. I hadn't thought about it in a very long time, but I was definitely curious now to hear more about what Mac had found. I had said nothing to Redmond about the mirror incident, mainly because I didn't want to worry him. But, if I found out something useful from Mac, I would for sure share it then.

I noticed that the girls were outback with Summer and Snow, but I needed a shower, and I quickly went into the house and up the inner stairs. Then I crossed the living room to my bedroom where I found Redmond sitting on the bed, plugging his phone into the charger. "Come see what Kris brought me," I said, darting towards the ensuite bathroom and into the walk-in closet.

"You saw Kris?" Redmond asked, entering the closet behind me.

I turned to him and held out the holstered gun. "He dropped in at South Haven to show me how to shoot—gave me my own gun."

"Kris taught you how to shoot?" he asked, taking the gun for his inspection.

"Yup," was all I said. He had taught me, that wasn't a lie, but I didn't want to explain how I hadn't actually shot the gun yet. "Can you get the gun safe down for me?"

Redmond reached over my head to the tippy-top shelf where he kept it now and extracted the metal safe from its confines behind a stack of old photo albums. A ringing sounded then from back in the bedroom. "That's my phone," he said, handing me the locked box.

The key for it was on a hook next to Redmond's belts, and I grabbed it up to unlock it. Then I placed the gun into it next to Redmond's, I shut the lid, locked it up again, before hanging the key back on the hook. Redmond still needed to put the safe back up on the top shelf for me, so I called out for him. "Hey—need your help, again."

He appeared in the opening to the closet, a mournful expression on his face. "That was your brother," he said.

"Why did James call you and not me?" I handed him the safe.

"He didn't want to upset you, but something spooked the dogs...," he said, taking the metal box, hiding it away again behind the photos. "He took them out for a walk, hoping to get rid of their nervous energy... and Skye collapsed."

"What—oh my god!"

"He took her to the vet, said they made her more comfortable... *but*... her heart gave out."

"Oh no—he must be devastated." My heart ached. James didn't have kids, but the dogs were like his children.

"He said it was really hard, but that she was 15 years old—Radar is 12 and showing his age too. He said he'd call you tomorrow."

Tears pooled in my eyes. "I'm gonna take a shower… but I think I might need a little walk on the beach after by myself," I breathed out with a heavy sigh.

He nodded. "Take your phone with you, please," Redmond said as I left the closet.

I took my time in the shower having had a good cry, then I got dressed and went down the back deck stairs for my walk.

"I'll be back soon," I said to the girls, leaving them to continue playing in the yard with the dogs.

No less than 5 minutes into my walk, my phone bussed in my waist pouch.

It was a text from Lane, though all she'd written was,

Call me when you can. :)

Lane had been scheduled to volunteer the Monday after we'd retrieved Kris from Iceland, and I had asked her at the time to contact me should she see Lyndon again. She had, several times after, in fact. And each visit, they'd had a marvelous time, she'd informed, and that she felt he was becoming more comfortable with her and the idea of showing her his living space in the basement of the group home. Taylor had drawn the space, but for what reason, we still weren't sure. Lane had ensured Leo that she felt safe with Lyndon, and I trusted that she did. But could we trust Lyndon? That had yet to be determined.

I texted back, saying,

I'm out at the moment. Will call tomorrow. xo

I wasn't in the mood to talk about the Earthbound right now, having had a full morning with two of them. What I wanted was to talk with my brother, but I knew he preferred to deal with his grief alone. Instead of calling, I texted him a heart emoji, accepting that I would have to wait until tomorrow for a conversation, and continued with my walk.

Near the turnaround point for my usual beach walk, I spotted someone sitting on one of the sand dunes next to the path that led to a delightful little beach cottage. As I got closer, I saw it was a woman with long red hair pulled back in a ponytail. She seemed so familiar.

"Lynn?" the woman called out in question. "Dr. Stone—remember?" she said, pointing at herself, flattening her palm over her breastbone.

"Dr. Stooone—yessss, hi!" I said, recollecting our meeting at the hospital.

"Call me Grier," she said, standing and brushing the sand off the back of her pants.

"Grier—nice to see you again. What brings you out here, besides the lovely beach? Thought you weren't starting at the hospital until September?"

"I'm not. I just bought the little cottage up the way." She waved a hand indicating the path to the cottage. "I'll be moving in permanently at the end of August. But the place still needs a few minor renos, for my home office. I was just taking in the scenery before I had to leave." She pushed her lip out in a pout.

"Oh my gosh—I love that little cottage. I was tempted to buy it myself, but we found a great place further up the beach—we needed more room, anyway."

"We?" she asked, giving me a sunny smile.

"My husband and me—and our two girls, and two huge dogs," I laughed out. "Speaking of which—I should be heading back—just needed a little stroll on the beach."

"It's such a wonderful surprise to catch you out for a walk. I don't know anyone here—so it's great to see a familiar face."

"Well, I'm not far, really—kind of makes us neighbors now. And I guess I'll be seeing you at the hospital, too." I grinned, pleased to see her, pleased at knowing she'd be close by. Other than Lily, I had no other girlfriends here and the prospect of a potential new one gave a little lift to my otherwise blue mood.

"I'm only on call there, so unless there is an emergency, probably not." She checked her watch. "You're not the only one who has to go—I need to head back down to Miami."

"Neighborly visits and walks on the beach, it is then," I said, "And a more enjoyable option than the hospital."

We exchanged phone numbers and then we each set off in our respective directions.

As I hit the edge of the path that led from the beach down to the backyard, I sensed we had a visitor.

"Mum—it's the fairy warrior," Hayley called to me as I pushed past the low hanging palm leaves.

Purah was kneeling on one knee, talking to the girls as well as Summer and Snow. As I approached her, she turned to look my way and then removed her helmet. Placing it under her one arm, she stood and greeted me as she had that first time, bending at the waist in a low bow, stomping the staff she held in her other hand. Her long white braid swung forward on the bow, then slid back over her shoulder as she straightened.

"Girls, take the dogs into the house, please," I said, with a tight smile.

"But Mum," Ryley began in protest.

"Now, please." I said, more firmly, though still smiling.

The girls each took a turn shaking Purah's hand and saying goodbye, then they gathered up the dogs and retreated inside.

"Are you here to tell me someone has been watching my friends?" I asked, coming to stand in front of her. I'd forgotten how tall she was, towering over even the height of Den who was the biggest and tallest of The Guards. But those crystal blue eyes of hers, those I'd never forget. "We already figured Thaddeus would have someone keeping tabs on them, their homes and workplaces."

"So, you know already," Purah acknowledged, relaxing her stance. "And I know about your trip to Iceland," she added with a little smugness.

"I'm sure you are aware of the sulfur issue and the experiments, too." I put my hands on my hips.

"Yes." She nodded, shifting her feet as though uncomfortable with the comment.

"Derek says he's been working with Nic and Leo on the details he found about the experiments—might help with the future safety of the other Earthbound," I said to reassure her.

She gave me a bright smile that washed away any discomfort I thought she might have been feeling. Then she looked past me to who I had already sensed was standing behind me. *Leo.*

"Hello," I heard him say as I turned around. The greeting wasn't meant for me, as he was clearly staring in awe at Purah.

I couldn't blame him. It was hard not to be enamored by her. "Leo—Purah. Purah—Leo," I said in introduction, but apparently they were already having a moment I realized, feeling invisible. It's a shame I couldn't do the invisibility thing at will, I mused.

"Is it safe for you to be here?" Leo asked. "I mean, will you be reprimanded?"

"So far, there has been no scolding for my actions," Purah assured him, her smile radiant. "Though I grow lonelier each day. My sisters—the other Stewards, are the only Seraphim I see now." Her expression saddened.

Leo strode forward as though compelled to comfort her. "How do you spend your days?" he asked, coming to stand within arm's reach.

"Well... I try to visit with the other Stewards, but they are very busy tending to the Seraphim on their stars. Sometimes I travel back and forth to Earth with the use of my staff, though I prefer to come and go to locations where I am safe—like this one, where I can show myself. I also frequent the lab locations—there I can veil myself and observe. However, I have not seen Thaddeus at the Ottawa facility for some time."

"Maybe he's at one of the other locations," I interjected.

Leo glanced my way, his expression tense. "The others are watching those locations. Den is back and forth between the Alcyone center in the Netherlands—Amsterdam, and here," he stated. "There has been no sign of Thaddeus at any of those locations."

"He is rarely—if ever at the Norway facility, nor the ones in Rome, Japan or Amsterdam," Purah said, pulling the focus back to her.

"No one is watching New York," I reminded.

Leo's tense expression softened as he gazed at Purah. "He doesn't venture out much, but he does have his favorite stops in each city."

She nodded. "But... you have no one in Brazil."

"Those who were watching the Taygeta facility in Manaus City, are all in Ottawa now. Nothing new has happened at that location in years and no other Earthbound are in that region of the world, including any of Thaddeus's followers. It's just a facility run by humans now."

"I overheard Marcus speaking to Thaddeus about some new venture, something to do with cellular regeneration." Purah turned her beautiful face my way, her eyes filled with anguish. "Thaddeus, I believe… is heading to Brazil."

Chapter 30 

Kris leaned over the construction plans spread out on the table in front of the bar, reviewing the different construction teams that would be coming and going this week to get the place up and running, while Leo sat behind the bar clacking away on his laptop.

"I need to find a rock-star general manager for this place," Kris said, stepping back from the plans. "Going to be hard to find someone like Frank."

"Jules said you offered her son Mason to come help work on the menu with you, as part of his Food and Nutrition Sciences program at the university," Leo said, looking up from the laptop screen.

"I did," Kris said. "He told me you found him and his mom a spacious condo in a high-rise just off campus with tons of security."

"The place is really great," Leo said. "I would have offered for them to stay at the North Haven, but we've only got the one extra room."

"Heard back from Shayne—says he's in," Kris said. He'd called on a fellow Earthbound and old friend of theirs, Shayne, who lived less than 30 minutes from the downtown area.

Shayne had a log home on the Quebec side near the Camp Fortune ski hill. He'd been one of the first males Kris had been introduced to and was an expert in hide and find covert style operations. He'd been in three wars, the First World War, Second World War, and the Gulf War, *three wars too many*, as he says. He had managed to evade the draft for the Vietnam War, saying something about hanging out with the Beatles during their anti-war movement. Over the years he has developed a mastery in concealing identities, and they had learned much from him. And he just so happened to be an exceptionally talented bartender too.

Back in 1975, Shayne worked at the famous Chateau Lafayette, or 'the Laff' as it's commonly known, and Ottawa's oldest tavern in the heart of the Byward Market, just down the way and probably the original Canadian dive bar. Shayne worked there for 5 years before stepping back from society in 1980. He stepped back in again for his time in the Gulf War in 1990, then chose to disappear again until 2016, when he came looking for a job at the Laff again, claiming to be the son of their long standing bartender, Shayne senior, who Shayne junior woefully shared had passed away at 70 the year prior. Based on the photos the owners had of Shayne *senior*, the family who had been running the business for the past 56 years, they couldn't deny the uncanny resemblance. They were saddened to hear the news about Shayne senior, but they had offered him a job on the spot, hoping he was as good as his notorious bartender father. Shayne worked there again for another 5 years, until last year, stretching his time there best he could considering his slow aging.

Kris tapped the bar with his knuckles to get Leo's attention. "Shayne said to let him know when we had bar staff and he'd come in and train them up."

"Okay, good," Leo said, still focused on his laptop.

Kris fluttered a large piece of cardboard at Leo, causing airflow to lift Leo's bangs off his forehead. "Going to put this sign in the window," Kris chuckled out. He'd written on it, *Hiring For All Restaurant Staff* with the contact number, and *For General Manager Position - Inquire Within*.

The bell over the door jingled as Lane walked in. "I'll come work for you, Uncle Kris," she said. "Love the bell, by the way."

Kris had kept the bell there from the previous establishment because it reminded him of Jana's bakery. Not quite his style but then Après Snow wasn't like his previous restaurant style either. Kris had wanted to reach out to Jana several times after he'd written his goodbye email, wondering what spending time with her would be like now that he had his full memories back. He'd never been close to any female, nor had he ever experienced the strong feelings and attraction he had for Jana, but the reality was, he could never return to Iceland again.

"Got any bar or restaurant experience?" Kris asked as he went to stand behind the bar.

"Nope, but I've been to all the good ones in the downtown market area," she said with a cheeky grin, typing something on her cell phone. "I researched this location—apparently some riot occurred on the site back in 1849—The Stony Monday Riot." Lane held up her phone to show him the article. "And it was also once the location for a popular bar back in the 80s called Stoney Monday's."

"Marvelous." Kris chuckled. "Don't you have class today?"

"Civic Holiday long weekend—remember?" Leo said, leaning over for a cheek kiss. "Hi Lane."

"Right. Why is that again?" Kris asked, bending down for his own cheek kiss. He'd grown to love having Lane around. She was funny, kind, and intelligent, and he appreciated people now with those qualities.

"You've been in New York too long," Leo stated. "The first Monday of August is always a public holiday in most provinces and territories."

Lane hopped up and sat on the bar. "It's also Emancipation Day—British Parliament abolished slavery in the British Empire as of 1 August 1834," she informed him. "But that's always on August 1st so the two don't normally coincide."

"You're just so smart," Kris praised. "So then, what are you doing today?"

She let out a heavy breath. "I was supposed to see Lyndon today at the group home, then go to the Drip House," she said. "Was going to be our first time doing something away from the group home." She hopped off the bar and went over to the table with the construction plans on it. "Maybe when I see him next, I could suggest we come here—when you're open. That way you could observe him yourselves. See how he behaves." She turned and strode back to the bar.

"That would make for an interesting date," Kris said, opening the first of many boxes containing the numerous variations of bar glassware. He began sorting through, indicating on the tops of the boxes with a marker of what was what for later.

"It wouldn't be a date," Lane said, rolling her eyes. "Uncle Leo, what are you working on?" She took a seat across from Leo at the bar this time.

"Been searching through different databases and records—looking for Anael's daughter." He glanced up quickly and gave her a grin. "The adoption records were sealed, and Anael didn't know who the new parents were—hadn't wanted to. But now the Access to Adoption Records Act, allows parents of a child placed for adoption to apply for identifying information from birth and adoption records, as long as the child is over 19—which she is." Leo typed something on the keyboard. "Here we go," Leo said. "The Adoption Disclosure records show the adoptive parents as deceased—which makes their names public record now."

"Any mention of where the daughter was placed?" Kris asked, stacking another box.

"No, but here—I found the adoptive mother on this family lineage website, shows the mother had a sister." Leo typed some more. "No living relatives noted on the father's side."

"She must have gone to live with the aunt," Lane suggested.

"And she would have been—what, 10 years old at the time based on her date of birth," Kris proposed, reading the screen over Leo's shoulder.

"The timeline fits," Leo said. "I'll keep working to track her down."

Lane spun on the barstool. "Someone's outside reading your employment sign," she noted.

Kris continued marking the boxes, but observed Leo glance up from his laptop as though to see who was outside reading the sign. Kris shifted his view catching something on the screen of Leo's laptop. "What's this?" he asked, pointing to a name on display.

"The names of the biological parents," Leo said, focusing back on the screen. "Anael used the birthfather's last name as hers—like they were married—told the adoption people he died."

"This is the name of her biological father?" Kris questioned, bewilderment setting in.

"According to Anael, yes." Leo turned, looking Kris's way.

Kris held Leo's stare. "That can't be right," he said, shaking his head.

Leo frowned. "Why?"

"Because I know that name," Kris said, glancing back at the laptop. "*Reider Stephansson* is Jana's—it's her father's name."

The old-fashioned bell over the door jingled again and Leo glanced to the door, though Kris stayed fixated on the screen.

"Hello," Kris heard Leo say. "You were the one reading the job posting sign in the window earlier."

Kris glanced up then and his mouth gaped. "Jana?" he said in disbelief.

"Hi," Jana said, giving a little wave, her beautiful smile beaming back at him. "I'd like to apply for the general manager job."

Chapter 31 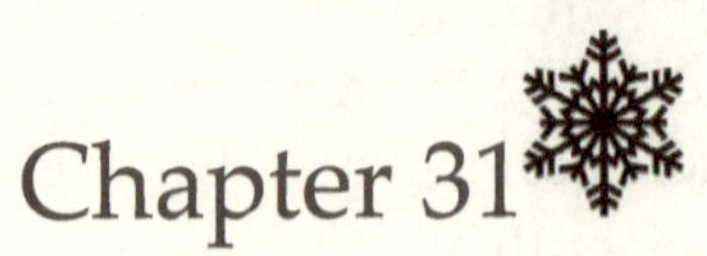

The Merope Building, August 1ˢᵗ, New York City

Lyndon remained stoic as Thaddeus glared at him and then examined his attire once again. Why Thaddeus had the need for him to come here in person instead of just calling, Lyndon did not know, but he was not impressed.

"You've really cleaned yourself up," Thaddeus stated, circling Lyndon a second time. "Got yourself a female, perhaps, one who can stand to look at you—or is she blind?" Thaddeus laughed out.

Lyndon held steady as Thaddeus guffawed at his distasteful joke.

Moving on from criticizing Lyndon's appearance, Thaddeus said, "As you know, several months ago I had Amahle follow up with those women—the ones from the hospital—who did the tour. But nothing has come of it."

"Maybe it was what it was—just a tour," Lyndon suggested. "Like the Iceland thing, just par for the course with their childbirth program."

"I don't wish to waste any more time on those two," Thaddeus said, ignoring Lyndon's comments.

Lyndon couldn't care less about what those women were up to. Though, Thaddeus it seemed, was becoming more desperate since nothing had developed from that Iceland incident either. Lyndon had searched for record of any medical personnel with the name Westlake. All he'd found was the husband of that other woman, and another dead end.

"What did you find at the brother's home?" Thaddeus demanded.

Thaddeus had asked Lyndon to check out the brother's place again, the one related to the other Westlake woman. Insisting he dig deeper. "There was no sign that anyone other than the guy, lives there," Lyndon said. He'd searched the home when the guy was out walking his dogs. "Though there was a photo of him and that woman—the one I saw at the group home. She was in a wedding dress," he added.

"She's married?" Thaddeus questioned, like somehow it was impossible.

"Maybe she has changed her name," Lyndon suggested, though he couldn't understand Thaddeus's obsession with this woman. "Originally, when I researched her, the last records were as of 2006, but after I discovered the photos, I did another search."

"And?" Thaddeus questioned impatiently.

Lyndon so badly wanted to roll his eyes, but that would not serve him. The sooner he got out of here and back to Ottawa, the better. "I found a 2007 marriage license."

"What!?" Thaddeus spat.

One nerve, Lyndon had one nerve left and Thaddeus was on it. "The husband's name shows as William Lockridge—no other records found for her after that—and no records for him either, not since 1983," Lyndon said, rushing out the words.

"Check out this Lockridge person," Thaddeus commanded, his wrathful expression giving Lyndon the impression Thaddeus's head might explode at any minute. "See if he or any of his relatives still live in Ottawa."

"On it," Lyndon said, turning and heading for the door, eager to get out of there.

"One more thing," Thaddeus said then.

Lyndon ground his teeth, then swiftly turning back around.

"I'll be leaving today—won't be back for some time, and don't ask where I'm going," Thaddeus said covertly, as if Lyndon gave a damn.

"Understood," Lyndon said, taking his leave, finally.

He had expected to see Lane again today at the group home, but he'd been summoned to do more of Thaddeus's bidding. He and Lane had spent every Monday together with Taylor since mid-May. Today they were supposed to venture out of the group home, just the two of them, to a coffee shop called the Hintonburg Drip House.

Braving a meetup with her in public was a huge step for him, but he hadn't wanted to give up any chance to spend time with her. They had talked for hours about everything from literature and music they enjoyed, to foods they like and disliked. They liked a lot of the same things, but both hated Brussel sprouts. She also seemed to like the way he'd changed his look, with the new clothing and tidier appearance, and she complemented him when he wore something new. On occasion, she'd even reached out and touched him, feeling the fabric of his sweater or to straighten the collar of his shirt. He had felt self-conscious at first, but each time he was with her, he grew braver, believing his disfigured face did not bother her. In fact, she often brushed his hair back away from his face when he tried to hide the scars from her. He'd made sure to keep it clean, had even purchased some expensive shampoo and conditioner he'd seen online, since he enjoyed the caress of her touch as her fingers smoothed his hair back. But now he'd have to miss their time at the group home and their coffee date. It wasn't a date really, he knew that, but he had wanted it to be special, and it was why he had dressed in the new clothes he'd gotten, the dark blue jeans and white button down short-sleeved shirt. He'd even gotten a new pair of shoes, loafers instead of his regular combat boots. And his new casual outfit had been the reason Thaddeus had teased him so.

Lyndon, like the other followers, had felt beholden to Thaddeus because he had been the only one of them who had been prepared to be on Earth, and therefore they had all had to rely on him for the protection and shelter they'd needed in the beginning. Thaddeus had made plans for certain followers to run his facilities. The others, like him, Thaddeus treated like his personal messengers or trackers. Ariadne had hated the role, and she had taken off the first chance she'd gotten. Thaddeus had made sure they all had money, enough to survive. He'd constructed an identity and history for himself, but Lyndon and the others had no records to show who they were, so getting legitimate jobs was out of the question, and now they were stuck serving Thaddeus.

Lyndon had created a personal space for himself in the basement of the group home. He had become proficient at taking care of himself, his existence, teaching himself how to use a computer and obtaining helpful software for the tracking tasks Thaddeus demanded of him. And he had become an excellent cook. He adored spending time with Taylor and hadn't been upset with his assignment at the group home. On the contrary, he'd been grateful not to be under Thaddeus's thumb anymore.

For a long time, before coming to Earth, Thaddeus and he had been partnered on the Celaeno star, but he realized too late, Thaddeus had not shared all his plans with him, not with any of them. It could have been worse, Lyndon supposed, had Thaddeus not made any future plans. All of them would have had to go through what the other Earthbound had, when Thaddeus had tricked them, stranding them on earth 120 years ago. From what little he knew of the others, some had found ways to survive and make a living among and sometimes with humans. Unfortunately for their rare offspring, Thaddeus had already found a way to use them. Lyndon vowed to never let Thaddeus use Taylor again.

Before returning to Ottawa, Lyndon used the computer in Marcus's office to do a deep dive on this Lockridge guy, searching for any records of family still in the Ottawa area. The records showed only one name listed, *David Lockridge*, and one address associated. Lyndon added the address to his cellphone's GPS and then went to the building's roof to take off and head back to Ottawa.

Lyndon set down behind a cluster of tall bushes near a house one property over from the location he'd entered in the GPS. The address he sought had a real estate sign on the front lawn. Through the large front window he could see the place appeared empty of furniture, although, there was a man out front mowing the lawn. "Good-day!" Lyndon hollered over the sound of the lawnmower, waving at the man as he approached. "Is this still the Lockridge residence?"

The man shut off the mower. "Hello, yes—well, it used to be," he said.

"Used to be?" Lyndon asked, frowning.

"David moved," the man said. "I just keep the yard trimmed and tidy for the realtor."

"Oh, I see." Lyndon rubbed his jaw. "I don't suppose you know where he and the family moved to?"

"The family...," the man began. "... Joan, his wife passed away over 20 years ago, and the kids are all grown and gone, so David was the only one still living here."

Lyndon scrambled for an explanation for his inquiry. "I've been out of the country for quite some time—it was silly of me to expect them all to still be living here," he lied, giving the impression he was familiar with the family. "Was hoping for a quick visit before I had to leave again." The name on the marriage license Lyndon had found, had been *William* Lockridge not David, but more than likely one of the *kids* this man had just mentioned. "Is... David still living here in the city?"

"Yes, but he moved into a long-term senior care facility early last year," the neighbor informed him.

"Do you recall which one?" Lyndon asked, giving the man his best kind smile, hoping for a bit more detail.

Thankfully, the man smiled back. "St. Patrick's, I believe."

"You have been most helpful," Lyndon said. "Thank you—have a wonderful day."

"Glad I could help," the man called as Lyndon strode back up the street.

Lyndon did a quick search on his cellphone for the senior facility. Finding the address, he took off in the pursuit of more answers.

At St. Patrick's long-term care facility, Lyndon introduced himself to the front desk nurse as an old friend of the family. "I'm leaving today—military deployment, and I was hoping to see David before heading out. I won't be back for quite some time you see."

The nurse scrutinized Lyndon's long hair, which was clearly not military style, he realized. "I always let it grow out between deployments," he said, pushing his hair back, revealing his facial scar, hoping the nurse would identify them as a war injury.

The nurse gave him a weary smile then. "Yes, I can understand that," she said, handing him a clipboard and pen. "You'll need to sign in, and I'll need to see some form of ID."

Lyndon produced his fake driver's license and signed in.

"Mr. Lockridge is in the library, down the hall," the nurse said, pointing to the right of the entrance.

"Thank you," Lyndon said, smiling, turning the handsome side of his face to the nurse.

The nurse nodded, and Lyndon could have sworn she blushed.

Lyndon didn't know what the old guy looked like, but luckily for him there was only one man in the library. He was sitting in a chair facing out the window like Taylor often did in the group home's playroom. Lyndon approached the man. "Mr. Lockridge," he said, circling around in front of the window to face him. "I'm an old friend of your son."

The man slowly looked up at him. "Is it supper-time already?" he asked, squinting to read his wristwatch.

Lyndon sighed and then knelt in front of the old man.

David tapped his watch. "I heard we're having cherry pie for dessert."

"That sounds delicious," Lyndon said softly, recognizing the man suffered from one of those age related human illnesses like dementia. "Sir, I'm looking for your son, William," Lyndon stated, even though there was a slim chance he'd get anything valuable out of the old guy.

"William," the old man said, pausing. "He lives in Florida."

It was something, not the details he'd been looking for, but still something, and quite unexpected, Lyndon mused. "Thank you, Sir. Enjoy your cherry pie," Lyndon said, before standing and going on his way.

At the group home, in his private space, Lyndon brought up a software program on his computer to perform the search necessary in locating this *William Lockridge* now living in Florida. Lyndon typed the name into the software, selecting Florida as the search radius and hit enter. Then he grabbed up his cellphone and dialed Kendrick in Norway.

The phone rang five times. "Lyndon—do you have any idea what time it is here?" Kendrick questioned sleepily.

Lyndon checked the time on his cellphone. It showed 6:15 p.m. which meant it was just after midnight there, but he didn't care.

A breathy yawn came from Kendrick. "If you are calling about that woman and her twin sons, tell Thaddeus we've not heard anything from her."

He wasn't calling about that, but he said, "You must have done something to scare her off." Thaddeus had been enraged over Kendrick not sealing the deal on those twins. Lyndon hadn't wanted Thaddeus to have access to them, but he enjoyed tearing a strip off Kendrick whenever he got the chance.

"You're the scary one—with that face of yours," Kendrick taunted childishly, like a schoolyard bully.

Lyndon rolled his eyes. Ignoring the taunt, he said, "Send Addison to New York City, I need another tracker there to replace Zuriel." Marcus had Zuriel staking out some fancy restaurant there, but Lyndon wanted him. He would normally take care of things himself, but he wanted to remain here in Ottawa close to Lane.

"Why—where's Z?" Kendrick asked.

Lyndon glanced at the computer screen as the search results loaded. "I have another job for him."

The Guard Trilogy Extended Series

Book 5 – Haven Lost
Much more to come…

Learn more about author N. L. Westaway at
www.NLWestaway.com